April-May June

Message in a Bubble

PATRICIASRIGLEY.COM

April-May June Series

Book One - A World Apart
Book Two - Mad About Magic
Book Three - Message in a Bubble

April-May June
Message in a Bubble

ଢ଼

By Patricia Srigley

Wingate Press
Toronto, ON

Library and Archives Canada Cataloguing in Publication:
Please contact the publisher for this information

ISBN 978-0-9780758-2-8

Layout design by Wingate Press
Cover Design by Stacey Lynn Newman
Illustrations and cover artwork by Patricia Srigley

Published by:

Wingate Press
Toronto, ON

Printed in Canada

April-May June

Message in a Bubble

1 – Message in a Bubble

The noise that disturbed April's deep sleep wasn't loud but it was familiar, and not in a good way. The soft pop was followed by a sharper clatter. It was the soft pop that was most alarming.

April jerked up in a cold sweat, her heart fluttering like a trapped bird, stopping the breath in her throat. Something had woken her up. A noise? No, two different noises – a soft pop and a sharp clatter.

"Who's there?" April called. "Raina?" Her best friend's lack of response was not reassuring. "Salm? DewDrop?" She whispered her adopted sibling's names before she thought to concentrate her magical senses on her tower room. It was empty, save for herself.

April flopped back on her pillow, weak with relief. There was something about being jarred from a sound sleep that made her feel sickish. It likely came from growing up in a world that was so dangerous, you half-expected to get eaten before the sun rose on each new day.

"You're alone, now go back to sleep. You dreamed the noise, both noises," April muttered to herself. And she needed a proper rest since school resumed the next day, the month of hibernation holidays had passed much too quickly.

1

She might have drifted back into slumber, except for a niggling doubt. There had been a noise, hadn't there? Two noises. Maybe she wasn't alone. In the past, she hadn't been able to sense the dangerous Drake Pitt or the imp Brag. She hadn't been able to sense the two most threatening creatures that she had encountered in her new home, the magical elvan realm of New Haven. Maybe she wasn't alone after all.

Once that thought slipped into her head, it was stuck there.

"Cat's claws," April cursed and swung her legs over the edge of the bed, at the same time concentrating to light all four of her candles. They flared brilliantly, proving that the room was as empty as it should be.

"Good!"

Intending to have a drink of water and go right back to sleep, April stepped toward the ever-flowing basin of water in the corner of her room and that's when her foot discovered the object that had made at least one of the noises that had woken her up.

She trod on something cold and hard and sharp.

"Ouch!" April jerked her foot back to reveal a golden chain coiled on the floor; attached to the chain was an all-too-familiar crystal vial. The imp Brag had taken the vial with him when he left New Haven more than one month ago, so what was it doing on her floor? A soft pop, followed by a sharp clatter. A soft pop like a bubble bursting? Brag did specialize in magical bubbles. He could have floated the precious object into her room. But was he back in New Haven or had he accomplished the feat from a distance? His bubbles had tremendous range, as she knew from firsthand experience.

"Brag." Suddenly chilled, April wrapped her arms around her body and tiptoed over to her window, afraid of what she would see below the tower. The scene was reassuring - nothing except a deserted shore and the gentle surface of the lake sparkling in the weak moonlight. No smelly imp was climbing up the side of her tower. "No Brag," April breathed in relief.

She returned to her bed and examined the crystal vial more closely. It was definitely the same one that Brag had taken because the name August (or maybe the month) was engraved on the golden stopper. It was written in the script from April's former world, and she was the only elf who could read that ancient text. The vial was no longer empty as it had been the last time she had worn it around her neck. Now, a curdled brownish-red liquid filled the tiny container. It looked gross.

"Hmm," April murmured, curious but not foolish enough to unstop the vial. Knowing Brag, the contents could be truly hazardous.

If Brag was trying to send her a message, she wasn't sure what it was. Since Brag was not very smart, he probably wasn't good at sending clues. Neither could he read or write, so he certainly couldn't script a note. If he was trying to tell her something, April would have to guess what it was - unless ...? Maybe Brag had found the other lost elf in the Outer-world, the one he had told her about before he left. Had he found the owner of this necklace? Is that why he had sent it? But if he had found the elf, surely the elf could have written an accompanying note. Or Brag could have simply pointed the elf towards New Haven. He knew how to find the world blindfolded.

April groaned and rolled under her blanket. She could spend the whole night guessing and probably come up with a hundred possibilities to explain why Brag had sent her the chain. Or two hundred. Or maybe Brag would show up and tell her. At this point, April might be happy to see him, well – not happy, but certainly willing to listen to his words before she sent him on his way.

Her churning thoughts chased each other around her head in an endless circle. Too restless to sleep, April got up again and paced. It felt like her head was a hive, filled with buzzing bees. Bees with insomnia. She was still pacing when Raina slipped into the room, nearly scaring her to death.

"Ah!" April jumped an inch at her friend's sudden appearance.

"I saw your light from my tower window when I got up for water," Raina said, sagging down on the end of the bed. "I bet you can't sleep because we have school tomorrow."

"No, school never keeps me awake. It's this." April handed over the chain. As soon as Raina recognized the object, she tossed it back. She wasn't half asleep anymore.

April abandoned her pacing and slumped down beside the elf. Raina's face had paled, making her freckles stand out like muddy splatters. "Sorry Raina, I should have waited until morning to show you."

"But where did you get it? Is ... is Brag back? Is he here?" Raina flashed a terrified glance at the window, her dark eyes too wide.

"I don't know. The chain must have floated into my room in a bubble. I heard a pop."

"A pop? Yes, it probably was a bubble," Raina agreed. "April, what do you think it means?"

"I don't know, it could mean anything. Brag sent it." That said it all.

"True." Raina squinted and peered closer. "Yuck! What is that brown lumpy stuff inside the vial?"

"I don't know what it is, but I'm not about to open it," April said.

Raina tugged on her pointed ear nervously. "What are you going to do with it?"

"I don't know." It was the only answer April had this night. She slipped the chain over her head, it seemed the best place to keep it. "Actually, I feel like a walk. I'm going to go look around outside, see if there is any sign of Brag." April gave in to an edgy urge to stretch her legs and strode out of her room.

Raina trailed after, down the long spiraling stairs on tiptoe. "But ... you shouldn't walk around alone in the middle of the night, especially after finding the vial. It's not a good idea."

"I'll stay in the front garden," April promised and grabbed a torch from the sconce by the door. She slipped silently into the dark night but she wasn't alone. Raina had come along and she definitely wasn't pleased about this midnight stroll.

"April, let's go back to bed. We have school tomorrow. And see, Brag isn't here." Raina swung an irate arm around the garden, sticking close to April's side.

"No, he isn't. You should go back inside, Raina. I'll follow in a minute." Perhaps it wasn't the wisest course of action to go exploring after the vial had appeared in her room, but April was feeling restless and fidgety. However, the exploring was better done alone. Brag was unpredictable and possessed the most powerful magic April had ever seen, she never wanted her friends anywhere near the imp. *She* never wanted to be near him, but at least she had some magical defense, not that it had ever helped in the past but it was better than nothing.

"I'll come inside soon," April repeated and crossed the front garden to skirt the shore of the lake. Nothing moved, save herself - and Raina. Raina had stayed with April like a shadow, but not a quiet shadow.

"April, come back to the house. Now!" she hissed.

"I will in a minute, I promise," April pacified her and headed east, since all trouble seemed to come from the east. Even April had come from the east, not that she was trouble. Not really. She had saved the forcefield that guarded New Haven from all the large and dangerous creatures that would enter it, and all the extreme weather that could harm a small elf. But still, saving the forcefield had not gone as smoothly as she would have liked. Neither had confronting Brag. That had not gone well at all. It had taken three months to get rid of the imp - three months of trouble.

"April, this is not the way back to the house," Raina pointed out, more forcefully.

"I'm only going a little further." April magically lit the torch and followed her feet east, simply pacing straight, rather than being confined by the walls of her room.

"April? What are you doing? I want to go home." For some reason, Raina was becoming distraught.

"I'll turn around in a minute."

"But you've said the same thing ten times and you're still walking," Raina cried.

"I don't think I've said it ten times, only once or twice."

"At least ten. More than ten." Raina stomped her feet in frustration.

She was exaggerating. April kept walking, wholly unconcerned. As long as she was home before sunrise, there would be plenty of time to get ready for school.

It was a lovely night for a stroll and they didn't encounter so much as a bug, although Raina's increasingly strident voice was probably scaring every living thing away. Raina was getting very upset with April and all April was doing was walking.

At some point, Raina stopped talking to April.

A short time later, she dashed in front of April and ordered her to stop. April tried to halt then, she really did, but it was as if her feet belonged to someone else, someone determined to walk east. April slammed into Raina and knocked her down, hard. She couldn't even stop and help her friend up, she just kept on going.

Raina didn't follow, April was suddenly alone. She yelled for Raina to come back, she shouted that her feet weren't working, but Raina had already gone.

Now that April realized something was very wrong, she tried to turn around. She couldn't do that any better than she could stop. Her feet had developed a mind of their own, and they were taking her east, whether she wanted to go with them or not.

She might have walked all night if her torch hadn't sputtered and gone out. Her feet kept going. April tripped over a root, banged into a tree and fell down. As if waking from a dream, she lay on the ground staring up at the starry sky in a daze. It felt like she had been sleepwalking. She must have been sleepwalking.

"Weasel whiskers!" April stood up, dusted off and stepped on something cold and hard and sharp. "Ouch!" she picked up the vial and felt it with careful fingers. The glass hadn't broken in the collision with the tree, but the chain had. April stuck the thing in her pocket, broke a branch off the tree that had knocked her down, lit it and started walking – west.

When the sun began to rise, April still wasn't home. She blinked at the orange horizon, bewildered. How could it be morning? She hadn't hiked all night, had she? But there was no denying the sun, it kept to a very regular schedule. April must have walked much longer than she'd realized. No wonder Raina had gotten so mad and abandoned her.

As tired as she was, April started running; she didn't want to be late on her first day back at school. Even so, the sun was fully up when April slipped through the side door and snuck up to her room without being seen. Sleepwalking or not, she didn't want to get in trouble for wandering the woodland in the middle of the night. That had already happened too many times when Brag was in New Haven.

Her adopted mother's voice brought her back to the present with a bump. "Girls, you're late for school. Get downstairs, now! I'm leaving for work," Mrs. Poole hollered from below. She sounded mad. Raina must have slept in too, or else she hadn't made it home through the dark forest. Maybe she had met up with Brag! In a panic, April tossed her earthy nightshirt into the corner and yanked on a dress. It was almost as stained and wrinkled as the nightshirt, but it was clothes.

April spun downstairs, then up to Raina's room to check on her friend. It was a great relief to find Raina unharmed. She was awake, completely dressed and fussing over her perfectly neat shoulder-length brown hair in front of the mirror.

"You made it home okay, Raina? I'm so sorry about last night, I think I was sleepwalking," April said in a rush and tried to explain about her feet.

Raina cut her off. "We're late for school, we can talk about this later." She took a good look at April and sighed with gusto. "I'll make lunches. Go find your books and ... and fix yourself up a bit. Okay?"

"Oh. Okay." Deflated, April returned to her room, looped her long hair in a knot, searched fruitlessly her pack and joined Raina in the kitchen. Everyone had already left. Raina didn't comment on April's feeble attempt to make herself more presentable, but her rolled eyes and shaken head made her opinion crystal clear. She rushed April out the door and they ran all the way to school.

The first class was half over when they stepped into the room, very late. Even the overly cheerful Ms. Merry-Helen's wide smile lost a bit of tilt at the corner of her lips. April wasn't sure why her entrance generated a lot of snickering, mostly from the girls when they looked April up and down, but it did. Was it because she was so unkempt? She suspected it was.

Cherry Pitt was sitting by the window, surrounded by her usual friends – Marigold Primrose, Lily Waters and Starla Rising. April hadn't seen the nasty elf since before the holidays when they had exchanged private words and threats over Cherry's evil actions. Cherry didn't merely snicker, she primped her smooth golden curls and said, "You better be careful Raina, April's condition might be contagious. We don't need two savage elves in this class, one is certainly more than enough." Her scathing tone was meant to be heard by everyone.

Raina flushed as red as April, ducked her head and hurried to her cushion.

April sat down fast. She never seemed to start school well after holidays. Or after weekends, sometimes. Or even on regular days, all too often.

"Enough of that," Ms. Merry-Helen said and as if to make up for the time off, she assigned extra reading and an essay about why bugs have different numbers of legs.

In the second class, Living in Elf Society (L.I.E.S. for short), the volatile Mr. Parsley ranted and raged at April for at least five minutes because she was missing her books - they were as lost as her pack. Mr. Parsley didn't like April, he hadn't liked her since she first appeared in his classroom less than one year ago. She was his favorite student to yell at and he never missed an opportunity.

April sat silent through his tirade, watching his bushy black moustache. It looked about to launch off his face and attack her, and his shouting nearly deafened her ears. After he finished taking her to task, he assigned a pile of homework about the complicated ruling structure of New

Haven, which included the King, the Elders and the members of Seelie Court. Most of the students must have assumed the homework was April's fault because they shot her dark glances out of the corner of their eyes. April hunched down on her cushion, trying to shrink from sight. Sadly, she did not have that magical ability.

And in Mathematics, Mr. Bladderwrack spent the whole period writing problems on the slate board, to be solved at home. There were twenty-five, and not a single one was easy or short. It was lucky that lunch came after math, April's hand was too cramped to keep writing on the birchbark she had borrowed from Raina.

At the welcome end of that class, Raina whispered, "Didn't you forget your pack at school before the holidays?"

"Oh, I think I did."

April went searching for her pack in Mr. Flynn's room. It wasn't there, but she finally tracked it down at the office. The office elf, Ms. Figwart, had it stashed under her table. April suspected the elf was hiding it since April had been such a nuisance to her in the past.

When April stepped out into the school meadow, Raina was sitting with Airron and Peter, as usual. What was not usual was that Heather and Willowna had joined them. April squeezed in, happy to see the boys. They were good friends.

The lunch period was almost over so April gobbled her food, quite starved after the night of futile walking, no breakfast, and a long morning of overwork. She only slowed down when Raina elbowed her. Heather and Willowna were giggling.

"You're eating like one of those Outer-world pigs," Raina whispered.

"Oh, sorry," April mumbled, her mouth too full, which only earned her another reprimand.

Heather and Willowna packed up and left then. Raina went with them, rather abruptly. The three girls walked gracefully away, all pretty colours and shining hair, heads close in confidential sharing. Watching them, April felt excluded … different … lesser.

"I think she's mad at me," April said quietly to Peter, eyes on Raina.

"Why?" Peter offered April his last muffin. She had been eyeing it covetously, but her appetite was gone now. She shook her head.

"The vial that Brag took with him when he left – it appeared in my room last night. I think he floated it there in a bubble. The vial was full of really gross brown stuff. Anyway, I went out to look for him and walked kind of far." The memory of that part of the night was still as foggy as an earthbound cloud. April couldn't quite remember why she had walked so far and guessed she really must have been sleepwalking, which would explain why she hadn't been able to control her feet. "Raina came too. I kind of ran her over and then I lost her in the forest."

Peter didn't ask about that part, he said, "Could I see the vial?"

"Let's have a look at this gross brown stuff," Airron prompted impatiently.

Both boys leaned closer. Peter's golden-brown curls and Airron's slicker cap of raven's wing black almost knocked together.

"Sure." April reached under her shirt and yanked out the chain. It was the wrong one, this one held the golden tag with her engraved name and magically changing age. She felt for the other one. It was elusive, it was more than elusive – it was gone. Then a hazy memory surfaced. "Oh, it's in my pocket. It's at home."

The gong sounded anyway, there was no time to discuss the vial.

Airron went off to his fairy class with Mr. Flynn, and Raina would be attending her merrow class with Mr. Leech. She had been hoping that Mr. Leech would be replaced since he was less than competent as a teacher, but they had spotted him in the corridor between classes, flashing his white smile and flexing his muscles at any elf that chanced to glance his way. He was still teaching at New Haven Academy, there was no doubt.

April and Peter turned toward their pixie classroom, curious to see who their new teacher would be, since Ms. Larkin-LaBois was not returning.

Ms. Summers greeted them at the door. April was pleased to see her; she was a very good teacher, being young, energetic and enthusiastic.

They claimed their usual table in the center of the room. April glanced around, everyone was already present. Cherry Pitt was seated by the window with her best friend, Marigold Primrose. Cherry curled her lip briefly at April, but at least she kept her mouth shut.

Ms. Summers began the lesson by saying how happy she was to be back from exploring the wild frontier outside New Haven. In fact, the teacher didn't look happy at all, she looked kind of despondent. Neither did she teach a lesson, she merely talked wistfully about her adventures in the Outer-world, frequently consulting April about the names of unusual creatures and weather patterns.

After pixie class, they attended Literature with Mr. Flynn. April was pleased to hear that they would be continuing to write their own stories and myths. It was more fun than reading. April always had a lot to write, although half the time no one had a clue what her stories were about. No animal larger than a mouse lived in New Haven so elves had a hard time comprehending the grandeur of a long-legged moose or the sheer bulk of a furry bear.

The last class of the day was Sports with Mrs. Myrrh. As soon as they walked outside, it was obvious that they were finished playing Basketberry. A new collection of equipment lay in the open meadow.

"What do you think all those rocks are for? And the vines?" April asked, glancing at her friends. They knew a lot more about Sports than she did.

"Don't know. Must be something new." Airron considered the apparatus, trying to determine its purpose. He couldn't and shrugged. They would need further instructions, and probably a demonstration.

Mrs. Myrrh ordered them to stop chattering and sit in a half circle on the ground. "So! Welcome back. I am sure you have all noticed that we will be starting a new sport." The tough, energetic teacher motioned towards the rocks and vines. "Would anyone like to guess what our next activity will be?" She didn't wait for an answer. "No? Well then, this activity is called rockput. It requires many physical skills – strength, accuracy, and coordination, to name a few. It can also be somewhat risky, so you will all have to be extremely cautious and alert while you are rockputting."

"Rockputting?" April whispered to Raina. April had never heard of it.

Raina murmured, "I think Salm did this last year."

"Now, I would like you all to pay attention to the line dividing the meadow in half." Mrs. Myrrh paced over to a clearly marked white line and tapped it with her toe. "Right here, you can't miss it. The first rule of rockput is that no elf will launch their pebble unless every last elf is on the safe side of the line. The safe side is where you are all sitting now, the side nearest the school." Mrs. Myrrh hopped onto that side of the dividing line. "The far side away from the school is where you will aim your pebbles." She jumped over the line to the other side. "Clear?" The class nodded as one. So far so good.

"The second rule is that everyone in the vicinity will wear a protective acorn cap for the entire class. Hydra … or Delta, whoever you are, distribute the caps." Mrs. Myrrh pointed to a nearby basket. Apparently the teacher couldn't tell the twins apart, neither could April.

She plopped the acorn cap onto her head when Hydra or Delta handed it to her. Some of the girls fussed about messing up their hair. April's was already a disaster as usual. The cap would hide the worst of it.

"Right. Next, you will have noticed that each vine has a securely attached seedpod in the middle of the length." Mrs. Myrrh picked up one of the vines, she dangled it from her fingers and pointed. Sure enough, tied into the middle of the vine was a hollow dried seedpod, sliced in half to form a bowl shape. It was the perfect size to hold one of the pebbles. April thought she was starting to figure this sport out.

"Watch closely and stay well back," the teacher warned before she picked up one of the round stones and loaded it into the seedpod, grasped both ends of the vine and started swinging the contraption around and around over her head until it was moving so fast you couldn't see it and it made a whistling noise. When there was sufficient momentum, she released one end of the vine and flicked her wrist. The pebble rocketed across the meadow and landed halfway to the trees, on the dangerous side of the line.

"Not a bad shot." Mrs. Myrrh nodded briskly with satisfaction and turned back to the class. "I'll leave my rock there, bonus marks to anyone who beats it. The technique that I have demonstrated is the simplest method to sling a pebble. After you have all mastered it, we will attempt some of the more complicated spinning techniques. Now, any questions?" No one raised a hand.

"Hop up and get started."

The teacher organized them into four well-spaced lines and blasted her whistle when it was time to begin.

The students at the head of the rows started swinging. April was at the back of her line with Raina. She was in no hurry to sling pebbles, the whole activity looked highly questionable in her opinion. Pebbles were soon soaring in all directions, high and low, straight up into the air, and even backwards toward the school. Stones were flying everywhere. Both sides of the line looked equally hazardous.

"Ready to duck? Do you think they have my Dad on standby for medical emergencies?" Raina grinned, thinking along the same lines.

"I hope so." The little acorn caps only protected so much, and they kept falling off. A lot of students hadn't bothered to put them back on. Mr. Poole, a Healer, might be very busy in the near future.

When they reached the front of their particular line, April went first because Raina shoved her forward. Determined to cause no injuries, April spun her pebble weakly around a couple of times and released it without any momentum. The rock arced sideways and landed on Raina's toes.

"Ouch!" Raina cried, hopping around on one good foot, grimacing in pain.

"Oh, Raina, I'm really sorry," April exclaimed, feeling terrible. "Are you okay?"

"No!" Raina yanked the equipment out of April's hand and took her own turn. She was much more aggressive with her pebble, she swung it enthusiastically over her head every bit as fast as Mrs. Myrrh. But she wasn't as good at aiming, when she released her pebble it flew straight up into the air.

"Head's up," April shouted in warning, expecting the stone to come pelting down on some unsuspecting elf. Instead, there was a cry of pain from above. Everyone looked up and gasped. A flash of red and gold wings signaled the presence of a winged elf overhead - a royal fairy.

Raina cried out louder than anyone. "Oh, no! Skylar, are you okay?"

He landed fast, gripping his shoulder and trying hard to hide his pain.

Mrs. Myrrh reacted with decisive speed. "Enough, stop! No more rockput until we post a warning for fairies to stay clear of this area." She ran around snatching pods out of elves' hands. "Everyone is dismissed," she added, even though the final gong would not sound for many minutes.

Still clutching an armful of trailing vines, the teacher rushed over to Prince Skylar and bowed. "My apologies, my sincerest regrets. I should have thought to post a warning. Oh my, are you injured?" April had never seen Mrs. Myrrh so flustered, not even when Seamore had collided with Cherry before the holidays, knocking her deeply unconscious.

"I am fine. No harm done. Please rise, there really is no cause for concern." Skylar was visibly embarrassed by the fuss. The majority of the class was standing around and gawking at the shy, handsome young prince. Even though they had been dismissed, no one was leaving.

"Shall we depart?" Skylar took Raina's arm to start her moving away from the school. April scooped up both their packs and Airron and Peter invited themselves along. Airron was most insistent about coming. Even Heather and Willowna joined their number, blushing and giggling, their eyes on Prince Skylar.

"Oh, Skylar, I'm really sorry about hitting you with the stone. You're going to have a huge bruise." Raina touched his shoulder in concern. It sounded like Airron growled low in his throat.

"I am fine, please do not upset yourself," Skylar repeated, but he did not remove her hand.

"What were you doing at school?" April asked curiously. He had never met them at school before.

"Oh, yes. April? My father and I would like you to join us for dinner this evening. We apologize for the short notice, but his schedule has been rather hectic lately. He has had an unexpected cancellation and is free tonight."

"Me? For dinner?" April checked.

"Yes."

"Only me?"

"Yes."

"But why?"

"I confess, he did not say. He asked that I escort you back to the Keep, and it would be my great pleasure," Skylar added.

It seemed weird to April, but she couldn't really refuse. The invitation had come from the King, after all. "Okay. Am I supposed to change first? Into something fancy?"

"No, it will be a casual dinner. No need to fuss, you look fine." Skylar smiled gallantly. April knew she did not look fine, but Skylar probably hadn't noticed. He only had eyes for Raina, as always. "We can walk Raina home first, however. There is always time for that."

Airron growled again, a little louder. Prince Skylar must have heard the feral noise, but he ignored it as if he was as deaf as a worm.

Skylar set such a dawdling pace that Salm caught up with them. Salm was the same age as the Prince, both boys were sixteen. Salm laughed heartily when his sister admitted to hitting the Prince with a rockput stone.

"We did that sport last year, but only for two days. I'm surprised Myrrh is doing it again. My class had one broken arm and two students knocked out and that was on the very first day. The second day was worse. She cancelled the activity pretty quick after that," Salm reported.

"We only had bruises, and Skylar's injury, but we only had half a class," Raina said. "I wonder if we'll do rockput again tomorrow."

At the last path before the Pooles' home, Skylar slowed to a stop and offered April his arm. "We should go now, don't want to be late," he murmured.

11

"Are you sure I shouldn't change? It would only take a minute."

Raina answered for Skylar. "April, you can't keep the King waiting. You look ... acceptable." Her opinion had changed since the morning.

"Are you sure."

"I'm sure."

"Okay." April trusted Raina's opinion completely.

"Farewell Raina, I look forward to our next meeting. Salm, Peter, Airron. Girls." Skylar nodded to everyone.

"Bye," April called to her friends. It felt a bit like she was being elfnapped. She tried not to think about the hill of homework that she would face when she got home. Something else niggled, it felt like she was forgetting something ... something important. The vial – that was it! April tugged Skylar to a stop. "Raina!" she called. Luckily her friend was still within hearing range. April hurried back to her.

"What is it?"

"Could you check in my room for the vial? I kind of lost it. Look in my nightshirt pocket, it's on the floor."

"April! That was a dumb thing to leave around. It could be dangerous! What if DewDrop found it and opened it!" She sounded really annoyed. "You have to be more careful."

"I know. Sorry, I didn't mean to forget," April said lamely. She couldn't seem to do anything right these days.

"Oh, I'll find it." Raina waved to Skylar. Airron grabbed her hand and tugged her beside him.

"Vial?" Skylar asked.

While they hiked to the grand Keep, April explained the peculiar series of events that had happened the previous night.

"Goodness. It is fortunate both you and Raina were unharmed. Do you think Brag has returned?" Skylar asked in concern.

April wrinkled her nose and thought hard. "You know, I don't. I have no idea what last night meant, but I don't think Brag is in New Haven. And even if he is, I don't think he would hurt anyone or cause any harm, not now that he knows us and an elf saved his life."

"Well, that is good to know. I do trust your instincts," Skylar assured her. "You are not too tired to join us for dinner, after the sleepless night?"

"No, I have to eat anyway." April could last through dinner.

As soon as they reached the Keep, red and gold uniformed guards bowed them through the outer thorny wall that safeguarded the sanctum. More guards bowed them through a second thick stone wall and into the actual Keep.

Skylar disappeared briefly to get a dinner robe before he took her to meet his father. "Can't eat bare-chested, wouldn't do!" He winked, buttoning up as he walked.

King Skylar was awaiting them in a huge room with a very long table and enough cushions to seat the entire High Court. It looked like there was enough food to feed them, too. If this was casual, April would hate to see a formal meal. By comparison, she felt as grubby as a dung beetle. She really should have taken the time to find a pretty clean dress and untangle her mop of hair. She was surprised that Raina had let her visit the Keep in her present condition.

The King kindly didn't seem to notice. He was being polite. "April-May June, I am so pleased that you could join us. I do apologize for the late invitation. Next time I will inform you much earlier." He motioned her up as soon as she bowed.

"My thanks for ... for inviting me." April wasn't sure what he meant by 'next time' and jumped when an unseen elf slid up to her elbow with a tray of fancy snacks. They looked delicious and April helped herself, she was starving. Prince Skylar grinned and grabbed a handful.

"The appetites on you young elves." The King smiled indulgently at his son. "Although you aren't so young any longer, seventeen on your next birthday, Skylar. The years have passed quickly. And April, you will turn sixteen, an age to start making decisions about your future."

April was surprised the King knew her age. "Yes," she agreed, between bites.

"How did you occupy yourself during Hibernation holidays? Have you been learning to fly now that you have magical wings?" The King seemed sincerely interested.

"Uh ... no. Not yet. I'm a little bit scared of heights," she confessed.

"Really? Well, Skylar could teach you to fly. Yes, marvelous idea. You could start next weekend." It sounded like the King had already made up his mind. April had been hoping to never fly again but hesitated to say so and present herself as a coward.

"Umm ... okay, if Skylar wants to," April said, hoping Skylar would decline.

He agreed easily. "Of course, delighted."

"Perfect. Next Saturday, and you can dine with us after the flying lesson. Perhaps we shall host a small gathering! Yes, of course we will." The King nodded, looking very pleased with himself.

They sat down to eat directly; there was all too much food and the meal dragged on much longer than dinner at the Pooles. By the tenth and last course, April was fighting to stay awake and keep her head out of her dessert. At least the meal was almost over, it must be if they were eating dessert and surely there wouldn't be more than one dessert.

Prince Skylar refused tea and stood up as soon as the last shells were carted away by yet another serving elf. There seemed to be a whole army of them hidden behind the walls. "Father, I will escort April home now. She had little sleep last night and still has homework to do," Skylar explained for her.

"Of course, of course. I'll send for the mice, save you walking home." King Skylar motioned to an elf that had stood silently by the door

13

throughout the long meal. He hurried away at the King's nod. Mice? What was he talking about?

April bowed and stifled another yawn. "My thanks for dinner. It was delicious."

"Only the first of many, I hope. Until Saturday," the King reminded her.

Prince Skylar led the way to a side door and then stood waiting.

"Why was your father talking about mice?" April yawned widely behind her hand now that they were alone.

"You are going to have a ride home. It is quite a treat. Look." He pointed.

April wondered if she was dreaming when an elaborate red and gold, large-wheeled carriage glided smoothly up, pulled by a matching team of six lively white mice. There was even an elf to drive the cart, neatly turned out in matching colours.

April's eyes widened. "I'm going to ride home in that?"

"Unless you would rather fly."

April laughed.

Skylar grinned back and offered a hand to assist her up the three narrow stairs and into the cozy compartment behind the driver's seat. She snuggled onto an oversized cushion with Skylar. "Ready?" he checked.

"Ready!" She couldn't wait.

With a chorus of squeaks, the mice scampered forward. April was suddenly wide awake; the fresh breeze picked up when the mice sped down the hill towards the town square. The view was beautiful, the night sky sparkled with stars above and the earth glowed with torchlight below.

April relaxed back, delighted. "This is a great way to travel!"

"Yes," Skylar agreed. "Not as exciting as flying, but comfortable. I've been told it is very romantic. Perhaps Raina would like to take a spin after I drop you off?"

"Maybe." April couldn't speak for her friend. "So, you're supposed to teach me to fly? You don't have to, you know. I'm not in any rush to learn. One flight was more than enough." Even though her new magical wings had saved her life, she had no desire to test them again.

The cart lurched off the slope and coasted into the town square, elves turned to stare or bow. Skylar nodded around absently. "I look forward to teaching you to fly. You should learn, April. I know you will love flying once you've had a true taste of the excitement of gliding and soaring."

April felt queasy just thinking about it. "I don't know Skylar, it scares me."

"You should at least give it a try. If you don't enjoy the experience, you don't have to fly, but you should know how," Skylar said. "And don't forget to bring something formal to change into afterwards, for the gathering. Do you think Raina will be available to accompany you?" He was back to that.

"You'll have to ask her," April said, "If you want her to go."

"I do want," Prince Skylar breathed longingly. He really was besotted.

The square was left behind and the mice had to strain to pull the cart up the facing hill. They crested it and raced down the next rolling slope. In no time, the mice were stopping in the front garden of the Pooles' house. Their arrival must have made enough noise to alert the household. Raina and Salm rushed out, followed by Mr. and Mrs. Poole, and even little DewDrop in her nightshirt. There was lots of 'ohhing' and 'ahhing'.

"Wow!" Salm admired the cart and swung April down. "Pretty fancy. Fast mice?" he asked Skylar.

"The fastest. Raina, would you like a tour around the woodland?" Skylar asked smoothly. Salm looked so crestfallen that Skylar quickly amended the invitation. "And Salm too, of course."

"Love to." Salm leapt into the carriage, barely touching the stairs. Skylar lifted Raina right onto the first high step. He hadn't done that for April. Raina blushed brilliantly, it was lucky that Airron had already gone home.

"April, are you going to accompany us?" Skylar asked, before he climbed in himself.

"Come on, April," Salm encouraged. "I don't want to be a third wheel."

April didn't understand. The cart already had four wheels. She shook her head. "I have homework so I better not." And if she took another cart ride, she would surely sleep through it.

Raina leaned over the edge and motioned April closer. She slipped something out of her pocket and into April's hand, whispering, "The chain was broken, I fixed it." Raina had located the vial.

"My thanks, Raina." April waved good-bye alongside the Pooles as the cart raced into the darkness.

"I do hope they don't drive too fast," Mrs. Poole said, giving April a one-armed hug. "How was dinner with the King?"

"Good. Lots of food, a bit too much. But it was all really good." April didn't offer details, there had been too many courses. The meal was a blur of food.

"Well, you look exhausted. Didn't you sleep well last night? Best get to bed, maybe you should do your homework in the morning," Mrs. Poole advised.

April knew a good idea when she heard it. "I think I will." She entered the house without bothering to wash her feet in the basin. She had ridden all the way home and her feet were clean, more or less.

As soon as she reached the privacy of her room, April examined the vial. It hadn't been opened, it still contained gross brown scum complete with congealed floating lumps. April really hoped the substance wasn't dangerous since Raina had kept quiet about the vial. As well as not wanting to worry her parents, Raina probably didn't want to admit that they had been sneaking out of the house and wandering the forest in the middle of the night again.

April brushed her teeth, pulled on her nightshirt, and then dropped the vial over her head so she wouldn't lose it again. And she certainly didn't want DewDrop to find it and open it. April had intended to crawl right into bed, but for some reason she didn't feel sleepy anymore.

Giving into the impulse, she tiptoed downstairs and used the side door as an exit. No one heard her leave. She ambled through the front garden and along the shore of the lake. Then, she went a little further, igniting a branch to light her way. She automatically turned east and started walking, it seemed like the most natural thing in the world.

It was a perfect night for a stroll, April kept going and going and going. She might have walked forever, if bright torches hadn't appeared ahead. And it wasn't only torches, huge white mice came barreling towards her – fast!

April gasped and tried to leap out of the way but her feet wouldn't let her change direction. Maybe she was sleepwalking again, but it didn't feel like it.

April screamed as loud as she could and waved her glowing stick wildly when the mice aimed to crush her. The driver spotted her at the last minute and bellowed for her to get out of the way, as if she didn't know better. He hauled hard on the reins and the mice veered sharply right, but they couldn't change direction fast enough. April was still trying to leap aside when the lead mouse brushed by her, knocking her to the ground. Aside from a few trampling paws, April was fine until the cart arrived. It was a lot bigger and harder than a mouse. It came close to missing her, except for one corner. There was a terrific thump and April saw a rain of stars fall down from the sky all around her. And someone was shouting, but it wasn't April.

"I'm okay," April told the sky and stayed where she was on the ground. At least her feet had stopped walking east.

"April! April, are you hurt?" Raina's pale face appeared, blocking out the stars.

April considered the question, trying to regain her senses. "Yes. No. Yes, yes, I'm okay."

"She's okay, sort of," Raina broadcast. "What are you doing in the middle of the forest in your nightshirt? Oh." Raina didn't wait for an answer, she must have guessed that this was a repeat of the previous night.

April needed assistance to stand; Salm supported her to walk but it wasn't far, only into the cart. And her feet didn't try to take her anywhere else. Everything seemed to be happening in disjointed fragments with blank spaces in-between. As soon as she tumbled onto a pillow, April couldn't open her eyelids no matter how hard she tried.

"April, we'll have you back to Mr. Poole in no time," Skylar promised, patting her hand. She couldn't wake up enough to tell him that she was fine and didn't require any healing. The next time she woke up it was

16

because someone was trying to haul her out of the carriage.

"Hang on." Salm scooped her up and carried her towards the house as if she weighed no more than a minnow fish.

"Put me down. I can walk," April protested weakly.

"I don't think you can right now. My Dad will have a look at you, so just relax. Enjoy the ride." It was a nice ride, held close against Salm. They were in her room in what felt like the blink of an eye and Salm put her in exactly the right spot – on her comfy bed.

"My thanks," April murmured.

"My pleasure. Raina is getting my father."

"Don't wake him up. I'm okay."

"If you say that once more, I might believe you." Salm was joking. He moved around the room and returned with a cool, damp cloth for her forehead. "You're getting quite a lump, glad there's no blood." Salm had a strong aversion to blood, it made him faint, one reason he refused to follow in his father's footsteps and apprentice as a Healer. Salm would finish school in a few months and hadn't yet decided what he wanted to do with his future. It had become a strong bone of contention between Salm and his parents.

"Glad there's no blood," April echoed, her room spinning.

"I couldn't figure out why you didn't jump out of the way, Raina said the same sort of thing happened last night. April, are you awake?"

"Yes. Can't control my feet, think I'm sleepwalking," she mumbled.

"Strange. We'll have to tell my parents now. No choice if this is going to happen every night."

On cue, his father rushed into the room with his sack of medical supplies. Mrs. Poole was on his heels, followed by Raina and even Skylar. Only the royal carriage driver was missing.

There was a lot of fussing and April wanted nothing more than to be left alone. Finally Mr. Poole declared that she would recover and everyone left. April got to close her eyes and sleep peacefully for the rest of the night. She didn't sleepwalk anywhere, unless she slept through it.

2 - These Feet Were Made for Walking

Except for a slight headache and some stiff muscles, April felt fine the next morning. She woke early and showered in the waterfall, rinsing off the coating of earth from the previous night's misadventure. At a leisurely pace, she braided her wet streaky hair and examined her injury in the mirror. The bruise on her forehead matched Skylar's shoulder. It looked exactly like she had been hit with a rockput pebble. The mark was easily hidden by combing some bangs down over her forehead. After almost a year of seeing only dark-eyed New Haven elves, her bright blue eyes looked distinctly odd when she gazed in the mirror.

Making an effort to not be her usual mess, April dug out a matching top and skirt that were barely wrinkled. It was when she tugged the top over her head that she noticed something was missing – again. Something important. There was only one gold chain around her neck, not two. The missing chain was the one that held the vial.

"Slug slime," April groaned softly.

It must have been torn off when the mice knocked her down. She would have to try and find it after school, if she could recall the route that she had walked and where she had been run over. April closed her eyes and strained to remember - she couldn't. The evening was a fuzzy blur and the east was a huge area to search for something small enough to hold in her hand. With luck, Raina would remember where it happened, or Salm. Too bad Peter hadn't been in the cart. With his almost magical sense of direction, he probably could have pinpointed the location to within an inch.

Everyone was still sleeping, so April ate breakfast alone in the front garden. As always, it was the most beautiful of mornings in the magical realm. Insects chirped and buzzed happily while the sun rose higher to warm the world and dry the sparkling dew.

When everyone appeared to be sleeping late, April went back inside to do some waking. She roused Raina first. Raina looked surprised to see her. "April? How are you feeling? Are you going to school?"

"Oh, I guess so. I'm up and I feel okay. I even brushed my hair and found clean clothes," April said proudly.

Raina checked her over and nodded. "Nice to see you looking tidy. Now that you're older, you really should fix yourself up more."

For some reason, the words hurt. "I should? Why?"

"You're a girl April, and you're fifteen, almost sixteen. That's why." Raina's voice carried an impatient message. She probably got tired of explaining things to April, she had to do it a lot.

April didn't ask any more questions. "I'll make lunches while you get ready," she said and left Raina to dress.

April detoured to wake up Salm. He was dead to the world. April had to shake him and shout. His eyes were only half opened when he sat up and swept his hair back. It was the same brown colour as his sister's, but not nearly as neat. His hair hadn't been trimmed in months and had grown long and shaggy.

"April? You're feeling okay? You could have taken a day off school, you know. My father might insist."

"I'm fine. But you look tired, Salm. Was everyone up late?" April asked. Maybe that's why Raina seemed out of sorts.

"Ya, pretty late. Raina had to tell my parents about what was going on. They weren't pleased about being kept in the dark about the vial," Salm said.

"Oh. But were they mad?" April asked guiltily.

"Kind of."

At least April had slept through it. "You better hurry, Salm."

She woke DewDrop next and sent the small elf to wake her mother and father. April didn't want to face them.

By the time Raina and Salm made it to the kitchen, lunches were ready and waiting. They all fled the house before the parents came downstairs.

School was in sight when Raina mentioned, "My Dad wants to

examine the vial with Mr. Stone. You'll have to give it to him after school. I forgot to tell you to leave it out this morning. We couldn't find it last night, I didn't know where you had hidden it."

April hadn't had a chance to tell Raina about the missing vial. She did so reluctantly. "Umm, well, I kind of …lost it."

"You lost it? Again?" Raina sounded fed up. "April! Where did you lose it?"

"If she knew where she lost it, it wouldn't be lost, would it?" Salm interjected.

"I think I lost it in the woods," April said quickly, before they started arguing. "I think it came off when the mice ran me over. Do you remember where that was? Exactly?"

"Good grief, no! We drove all over the place, really fast. Salm, do you remember?" Raina asked.

"No. You don't remember, April? You were the one walking," Salm pointed out.

"I know I was the one walking, but it's like I'm sleepwalking. I go into this foggy trance when my feet take over. I don't realize that I shouldn't be walking east. My brain gets all fuzzy. I wonder if I'm under some sort of nightly sleepwalking spell?" she mused.

They had reached the edge of the school meadow. A flow of bodies was already streaming in the front door. They were almost late.

"We'll figure it out after school. Bye." Salm gave April's braid a tug and dashed off.

"We're going to have to search the whole forest." Raina frowned, walking slower. They were the last two elves to straggle into the building.

"I do have some idea where to look. I know I walk east, I just don't know exactly where east," April said, trying not to sound completely useless.

Mrs. Merry-Helen greeted them with her face wreathed in smiles. "Hellooooo, hellooooo. Great to see you on time today! We have a delightful lesson planned!" The large teacher turned toward the slate board with a bounce. "Let's not waste a precious minute! I am overjoyed to announce that I am planning a thrilling series of marvelous field trips!"

April swallowed a groan. Bad things always happened on field trips, it was like she suffered from a field trip curse. Or maybe the whole class did. It probably wasn't a coincidence that as soon as weird stuff started to occur again, Mrs. Merry-Helen scheduled field trips.

"The first planned outing is in two weeks, on Friday. And we will be visiting - " The teacher paused dramatically so that she could smile even wider, if that was possible. It was, but April was afraid the teacher's face would break. "We will be visiting the mysterious southern caverns, only home to the very rare eggstones. We have been granted special permission to descend into the earth and tour the entire mine while it is closed for expansion."

The class buzzed with excitement and Mrs. Merry-Helen let them talk.

"Caverns? Mining eggstones?" April had never heard of either.

"Yes!" Raina couldn't contain her excitement. "This is super. I can't believe we get to tour the caverns. Very few elves are allowed in. The teacher must *know* someone really important," Raina enthused. "And on Friday in two weeks! That's not too far away, is it? Oh, I can't wait."

Every student in the room looked as thrilled as Raina. The only exception was Airron, who didn't like confined places. He had a fear of closed in spaces, rather like April had a fear of heights and Salm had an aversion to blood. But Airron refused to admit that he was scared of anything, he always tried to act as tough and fearless as a stone.

Mrs. Merry-Helen finally waved the class to silence so that she could discuss the details of the cavern trip and outline what learning would be involved. They couldn't just go for fun, that wouldn't be acceptable for school.

April was thoroughly yelled at in the second class, for not doing her homework. Mr. Parsley's deep voice all but shook the walls. In Mathematics, April got a big round zero for not finishing even one of her twenty-five problems. When the rest of the class departed, Mr. Bladderwrack delayed April to discuss her poor marks and by the time she reached the meadow for lunch, Raina was eating in a different spot with a group of girls. They were laughing and chattering, heads so close together that it must have been secrets they shared. When Raina spotted April, she didn't wave her over to join them, she leaned closer to Violet and kept talking.

Not sure that she was welcome, April headed for their usual patch of moss. It was empty; the boys had already eaten and run off somewhere. April sat down alone and hoped Raina would join her. She didn't.

April nibbled self-consciously and watched the pretty cluster of girls out of the corner of her eye. Raina shone amongst them. April wouldn't have fit in at all. After growing up in a very different place, she wouldn't know what to chatter about, and pretty she would never be, with her weird blue eyes and strangely streaky hair which included an unfortunate green hue. And there was no denying her shortness; April was the shortest elf in the whole class.

Lately, it felt like Raina was growing up while April was staying an awkward girl. Maybe that's why Raina wanted new friends, friends that she had more in common with. April could understand that, but it made her feel lonely even while she was surrounded by hundreds of elves.

When lunch ended, April was the first student to reenter the building. That had never happened before.

Ms. Summers had a surprise announcement for the pixie class. She, too, was planning some trips away from the school, to visit sites relevant to pixies. The first outing was to be a forest scavenger hunt. She wrote down a list of plants that she wanted the class to become familiar with. The column was long: mayflower, bloodroot, flax, waterlily, boneset, sneezeweed, touch-me-not, woundwart, ironweed, pokeweed, yarrow, Jimson weed, feverfew, tansy, mullein, pokeroot, fireweed, mint, red clover and rosehip. Some of the plants were dangerous, some were edible and some were used for medical treatments. And this list was only the beginning, the teacher promised more in the days to come.

When the class finished copying down the names, Ms. Summers informed them that they would spend the next week and a half learning all about sixty different plants, including how to handle them, where they were most likely to grow, and how they were used by elves. After the learning was finished, students would pair up and search for the plants. The first students to return to school with a complete set of fresh-picked samples would be the winners of the scavenger hunt.

"Sounds like fun," Peter commented.

"It does," April agreed, since it wasn't like a real field trip. They would simply be walking around in the forest and looking for plants. With Peter as her partner, April was sure to be on the winning team. Peter was really smart and always got high marks, and since he could find his way around the woodland as well as Elder Scarab, they couldn't lose.

Ms. Summers tapped the slate board for attention. "In order to ensure that each of you learn about the plants, partners will be chosen at random immediately before you start the scavenger hunt, and everyone will have to find a different sampling of the sixty plants, so you will need to learn about every last one. Clear?"

It was all too clear. The scavenger hunt was going to be harder than April had thought. And April wasn't the only student who was disappointed about not getting to choose partners, it looked like everyone was.

"I was hoping we could be together," April whispered to Peter.

"We might still get partnered up. There is a good chance, since there are only seventeen students in our class." Peter said. New Haven's pixie population outnumbered both gilled merrows and winged fairies by about two to one. The merrow and fairy classes each had less than ten students.

"Stop chattering and pay attention, Peter." Ms. Summers resumed her instructions, promising the scavenger hunt would be held the very next week, on Friday, if the class worked hard. She put checkmarks beside the hazardous plants that needed special handling. One plant even had three checkmarks, flagging it as highly toxic, possibly life threatening. It was Jimson weed. April made a point of remembering that one. The rest of their time was devoted to doing little sketches of each plant from samples the teacher provided. Since April couldn't draw to save her life, all of her plants looked exactly the same - like hairy sticks.

Peter looked over her shoulder and laughed. "You better hope your partner can draw."

"Can you draw them for me?" April appealed. He would have, but it was time to change classes.

In Sports, they were still doing rockput. The pebbles were flying further and harder than on the previous day. April tried her best, since she didn't want to get zero in yet another class, but she had trouble aiming the stones. They went every which way; she even hit Raina with one, again. It wasn't very hard and didn't do any damage, but Raina reacted with uncharacteristic curtness. "Good grief, April. Do you have to be so uncoordinated? Go shoot over there, away from me."

April walked to the other side of the field, hurt and puzzled. She knew friends got into fights and could still be friends, but this wasn't a fight. Raina was acting like April bugged her. April wanted to talk to Raina about it, but not at school.

There was no chance after school. Airron and Peter walked them home as usual, and Heather and Willowna came along - again. Raina was hanging around with them a lot these days. Too much, in April's opinion.

While they meandered through the undergrowth, Peter talked about the pixie class scavenger hunt. Airron had similar news. Mr. Flynn had planned a flying trip to study the geographical layout of New Haven. His class of fairies would tour around the entire perimeter of the elvan realm, following the circular forcefield and mapping the nine hills that held the nine paired Echoes, ancient and mysterious creatures that generated the magical forcefield that protected New Haven.

Raina was envious. "You're all really lucky. Mr. Leech has us memorizing water plants out of a stupid book. We could have a swimming scavenger hunt, it would be a lot more fun than sitting at a stupid desk staring at a boring book," she griped. "Maybe I'll suggest it to him. He would never think of it on his own, well … he really doesn't think, does he? Except about his muscles." She shared a knowing smile with Heather and Willowna.

"But he does have nice muscles," Heather said.

"Doesn't he?" Willowna gushed.

Raina stayed on topic. "If I organized the scavenger hunt, maybe he would let us leave the classroom." She was very good at organizing.

Salm caught up when they were almost home. "I thought you might be going to search for the vial," he mentioned. "I can help."

"The vial is lost? But Raina found it after school yesterday. We saw it," Peter said.

Raina hadn't mentioned the events of the previous night yet, she had been strangely close-mouthed about the whole episode.

"She found it. I lost it again," April said, embarrassed.

Airron chuckled. "You lost it again?"

"Well, it wasn't my fault. I think I was sleepwalking, and the mice ran me over and Skylar's carriage." They didn't know what she was talking about. Raina made a funny face at April - fierce and intense, almost threatening.

"Why are you making that face?" she asked Raina.

Raina grabbed her arm and yanked her close. "Shush!" she hissed.

"Shush?" April stared at her blankly. "About what? Skylar's carriage?"

"Sometimes I think DewDrop is older than you," Raina snapped disparagingly and shoved her away. April knew an insult when she heard one, Cherry couldn't walk by April without spouting some nasty slur, but Raina had never insulted April before. The words hurt as much as a physical injury, maybe more.

Peter lifted a branch aside and waited for them to pass, looking uncomfortable.

Airron didn't even notice the courtesy, his attention was fixed fully on Raina. "Skylar? Last night? What were you doing with Skylar last night? And why was he running April over?" He looked mad already; he always did when Skylar was involved.

Salm volunteered to tell them about April taking another walk east and getting run over by the royal mice. He went on at length about the fancy carriage and super speedy mice and the long ride Skylar had arranged.

Listening to the events, Airron crossed his arms over his chest and stopped talking at all. He began to look quite thunderous, like a growing storm cloud.

"Well, are we going to search for the vial?" Salm asked, at a bit of a loss when no one seemed interested in hearing about the racy carriage.

Prickly silence answered his question.

Raina and Airron walked along, coldly ignoring each other until they arrived in Raina's front garden. Given the uneasy silence, April didn't chance opening her mouth again, she didn't want to do further damage.

By unspoken agreement, finding the vial was postponed. The boys didn't stay for dinner as they usually did, they both left rather abruptly. Heather and Willowna stayed instead.

Everything seemed to be changing and April didn't like that at all. She ate silently while the three girls chatted nonstop. April hoped Heather and Willowna would leave as soon as dinner was over, so she could talk to Raina and clear the air before bedtime. She didn't have a chance, apparently plans had been made.

"I'm going over to Heather's," Raina said, standing up as soon as dessert was cleared.

April rose too, ready to accompany her friend.

"Umm ... April, don't you have a lot of homework to catch up on?" Raina said. Her eyes were darting around, looking everywhere but at April.

April got it. She sat down, her cheeks hot. "Yes, I better stay here." She pretended an interest in her food, poking at a bit of crab apple skin until Raina and the girls left. A heavy silence lasted overlong, broken by Mr. Poole clearing his throat and Mrs. Poole stacking dishes more quietly than usual.

DewDrop came to stand beside April and placed a hand on her shoulder. "You can play with me instead," she said sweetly.

"My thanks, Dewy, but I really do have a stack of homework, I better get to it." April fled before she cried in front of everyone, and she hardly ever cried.

Convinced that Raina didn't like her anymore, April couldn't concentrate at all and didn't finish any of her work, not one single page. Too sad to stay awake, she wrapped up in her blanket and fell asleep. At least she didn't sleepwalk that night.

Raina sat with the other girls at lunch again the next day, avoiding both April and Airron, it seemed. Airron was still mad about Skylar. But the four friends did walk home together as usual, except Heather and Willowna came along again. April didn't think she liked the two girls anymore, she thought she might hate them but wasn't sure why.

When they all stepped into the front garden, Skylar was waiting. April was happy to see him, but his timing could have been better. He was holding a bouquet of fragrant clover flowers tied with red and gold ribbon.

Airron turned an alarming shade of purple, as if he was going to explode. Raina bit her lip and stared at the moss. The tense situation seemed to be coming to a head between the three elves because both Skylar and Airron liked Raina, a lot.

And it did look like Raina was confused herself. She had known Airron forever and he was one of her best friends, but Skylar was older and exciting, and he was the Prince. Of course, Skylar being the Prince only complicated the situation further. Due to his born position in New Haven, Skylar could only date other fairies. And Airron's mother encouraged the same, even though Airron wasn't a prince. According to New Haven tradition, Raina should date another merrow.

Skylar approached the uneasy group with a smile, then did something unexpected. "April, these are for you." He smiled warmly and handed her the flowers. "I am deeply relieved to see you recovered from the accident."

The tension was diffused in a hummingbird's heartbeat. Heather and Willowna both stood with dropped jaws, and Airron laughed too heartily. "Heard you ran April over," he grinned.

"Actually it was my driver - " Skylar began.

"Right, right," Airron cut him off and thumped him on the back until Skylar told him to 'watch the wings'.

"Um ... my thanks, Skylar. They really are beautiful flowers. They smell great. What do I do with them? Won't they die now that they've been picked?" April had never received a bouquet of flowers before.

"You ... um ... put them in water," Skylar suggested.

"In the house?" April asked. The flowers would float away if she put them in the lake.

"Yes, in the house." Skylar smiled down at her, his eyes filled with laughter as if she had said something funny.

"Do you want to come in for snacks?" Raina interrupted, abruptly.

"Thank-you for the invitation but I have a dinner meeting scheduled with my father and several representatives of the High Court. April, a word?" Skylar took her arm and escorted her away from her friends. April could feel lots of eyes boring into her back. Everyone's.

"What is it?" April asked, as soon as he stopped her out of hearing range.

"I hope you don't mind helping me out. I would like to ask Raina to come to the gathering next Saturday evening, but it doesn't seem like the best idea to mention it in front of Airron. He always seems to be around, and he does seem vexed with me. Well, I guess it is to be expected given the circumstances. I was going to ask Raina the other night, but after your accident it hardly seemed like the appropriate moment. Perhaps you could mention it to her, in private," Skylar appealed.

"Oh. Oh, I guess so." April felt pressured by being placed in the middle of this situation between her good friends, but wasn't sure how to deal with it. There was probably no harm in telling Raina about the invitation, the decision about whether or not to go was Raina's, after all. April was delivering the message, nothing more. She wasn't betraying Airron, even though it kind of felt like it.

"Wonderful. Thank-you, April. And I hope you like the flowers. My father was most concerned to hear about our carriage running you over, he insisted I bring the bouquet over directly." April was the most surprised elf in New Haven when Skylar leaned close and kissed her softly on the forehead. "There, all better," he said affectionately. "See you next Saturday, I'm looking forward to it." With a graceful bound and a swoosh of wings, he disappeared into the canopy of leaves.

When April walked back toward her friends clutching the flowers, Airron was the only one that looked pleased and he looked too pleased. Heather and Willowna looked ... was it impressed?

"So, April – a bit of a change in the wind? You have a date with Skylar? Next Saturday?" Airron winked.

So that's what her friends thought! And that's why the girls looked impressed. About to deny Airron's words, April hesitated. It felt good to have her classmates look at her with awe, especially since Raina's attitude had so hurt her feelings lately. If elves thought she was dating the charming Prince, maybe she would be invited to Heather's house with the other girls. And Raina was dating Airron, not Skylar, so it didn't matter if she thought April was going on a date with the Prince. Maybe she would be impressed, too. Maybe it would even help Raina out, if Airron wasn't mad about Skylar anymore.

April was a terrible liar and flushed when she said, "Uh ... yes, a date. Skylar is going to teach me to fly, and I'm invited to stay for dinner ... after ..." She trailed off, preferring someone else to speak now. She felt awful for spouting lies, and her cheeks grew hotter.

"No need to blush. Flying, eh? About time you learned, good for you.

The Prince will be a fine teacher, sounds like an exciting date," Airron enthused.

"Oh. Oh, well I hope you have a good time," Raina said, but it didn't sound like she meant it. She didn't look impressed, she looked hurt and angry. With a huff, Raina turned and marched stiffly away. Heather and Willowna went with her, one on each side as if emotionally supporting her.

April watched Raina leave with a sinking heart. It had taken less than an impetuous minute to lie, and a fraction of that time to know she had made a big mistake. Lying had just made matters worse with Raina, not better. April wasn't going to let that happen. She was going to confess her crime and fix things, but not until Heather and Willowna left.

"Can't say I'm surprised at this sudden interest on Skylar's part, now that you have wings," Airron said leadingly. "Not to mention gills, and the magic of course. Quite a lot to offer the royal line. Nope, not surprised at all. So, are we going to go and search for that missing vial?"

April had forgotten all about the vial. "We should, before someone else finds it. I'll go ask Raina if she's coming." April dashed for the house.

She spiraled upstairs but Raina's room was deserted. April couldn't find the girls anywhere else in the house. They must have gone straight out the backdoor. And April had definitely not been invited, she had been ditched. That was as clear as the noonday sun. "Owl pellets." April retraced her steps to the kitchen. She walked in and got pelted with a pea. Food was flying around the room as if it had wings.

"Is this how you make snacks?" she asked Airron, the only one in the room.

"A little tossing doesn't hurt food." Airron proceeded to juggle three peas perfectly. He was in a jubilant mood. "Where's Raina?"

"Gone. She left with those girls." April caught a pea when Airron tossed another one her way in the middle of juggling.

"Maybe they went to look for the vial. Let's see if we can find her." Airron moved for the door. They could search for Raina and the vial at the same time.

"But where's Peter?" He seemed to be missing, too.

"He had to leave, suddenly remembered that he had to meet someone," Airron said.

April had been counting on Peter's uncanny sense of direction, and his magical ability to sense gold. With his help, they could have found the vial in no time. He hadn't said anything earlier about having to meet someone, it seemed strange.

Only two of them were left to search. They walked east and April tried really hard to remember exactly where she had traveled, but the memory was elusive. They hiked silently, munching on the peas they had brought along.

Searching for the vial was a lot like looking for one particular pine needle in an entire forest of pine trees – next to impossible. Neither did they find a sign of Raina.

Airron was the one that called a halt when the sun touched the horizon and the light began to wane. The forest floor was deeply shadowed at that point, they wouldn't have been able to find the vial unless they stepped on the thing.

"Beetle dung," Airron swore. "My mother's going to be really mad if I'm late for dinner. I better fly from here. You know the way home?" Airron asked, tugging off his robe.

"West," April replied smartly.

"Right you are." Airron draped his robe over his pack and took off with a bound. He waved from overhead. He would be home long before April.

She waved until he was out of sight, then slumped unhappily down on a stone to think. Thinking was always best done by yourself. After growing up alone, April didn't always understand the emotions of other elves, but she was pretty sure she had figured out why Raina seemed mad at her for supposedly dating Skylar. Raina liked Skylar, even though she was dating Airron, so she didn't want April to date Skylar either, which didn't seem fair. And Raina had been awfully quick to think the worst of April when she should know that April would never do anything to hurt her best friend, at least not on purpose.

The longer April mulled things over, the more injured she felt. She hadn't done anything wrong (except tell one small lie) and Raina was mad at her, again. April scuffed her toes into the earth and blinked hard. A glint of gold caught her eye. The chain?

April leaned closer. Yes, it was laying right there, glowing at her. Mocking her! She must have walked right past it – the thing was partially covered by a leaf. April wouldn't have even noticed the metal if she hadn't sat down to wallow in her misery on this particular stone.

With a nervous hand, April reached for the chain, hoping that the vial hadn't been broken, perhaps releasing a dangerous magical substance into New Haven. She held her breath until the vial emerged from beneath the leaf; it was intact and still filled with brown scum.

"Bright side," April murmured in relief. "Time to go home and straighten out this mess." She slipped the chain over her head, determined not to lose it again. She took a couple of steps west, then turned east. She felt like stretching her legs a bit before she went home.

April walked until the crescent moon rose and the sky blackened around her. When she passed a couple of fireflies, she communicated with them magically to request that they light her way. The small insects weren't busy, they were perfectly willing to detour east. April walked along humming to herself while her escort blinked their lights in rhythm.

When something swooped down from overhead, it was unexpected. For a split-second April thought it was a bat or an owl, then she remembered that she was still inside New Haven. She hadn't made it through the barrier yet.

Without warning, she was scooped up from behind and lifted into the night sky.

"April, are you all right?"

"Skylar? What are you doing here?"

"I might ask you the same question." He had a point.

"Hey April!"

"O'Wing!" April hadn't spotted him, gliding by Skylar's side.

"Where are you going?" he asked her.

"I … I'm not sure, but I have to go that way." She squirmed to point behind her.

"Stay still," Skylar advised, "And hold onto my neck."

"Skylar, you have to turn around. I have to go that way!" April didn't hang onto his neck, she shoved away from him.

He clung tighter. "No! I'm taking you home, now settle down and hold on!"

April couldn't settle down, she was growing increasingly distraught for no rational reason. Skylar kept soaring west and April began to fight in earnest to be free. Wrestling in mid-air with a fairy who needs his arms to fly was not the smartest thing April had ever done.

"Stop! We're going to crash!" Skylar hollered, plummeting and trying to hang onto her arm when she wriggled out of his grip. April yanked one last time and then she was falling. Before her magical wings could appear, O'Wing dove down and caught her. She was lucky he was there, since her wings would have been uselessly trapped inside her clothes.

She slammed into O'Wing with force, knocking the wind out of both of them. As if waking from a nightmare, April came to her senses and stopped trying to thwart her rescue. She latched onto O'Wing with a pounding heart, newly aware of how high off the ground they were. "My thanks, O'Wing," she panted.

"April, what's going on?" Skylar called, angling so close that he brushed wings with O'Wing.

"I … I don't know." She closed her eyes and gripped O'Wing's neck with shaking arms. "I think it's my feet again," she said. "It must be my feet again. For the third time, they're walking east and I have to go with them." April laid her head wearily against O'Wing's shoulder. "It's nice to stop walking. So, what are you doing out here?"

"Searching for you. The Pooles sounded the alarm that you were missing. We flew east, it wasn't hard to find you."

"The fireflies?" April guessed.

"The fireflies. Will you be able to stay put if we return you home?" O'Wing asked.

"I don't know. I don't know what's happening."

O'Wing was winded by the time he landed in the front garden and released her. The Pooles were awaiting word in the kitchen and they had company. Head-Elder Falcon and Elder Scarab were installed at the table, sipping fragrant flower tea. It looked like a small, cozy gathering except for the concerned expressions. Those cleared as soon as April walked in, flanked closely by Skylar and O'Wing.

"Oh, thank goodness! You found her." Mrs. Poole jumped up and bowed. Skylar motioned her up, keeping a firm grip on April's arm. He wasn't taking any chances on her escaping. Skylar passed her over to Mr. Poole. April was led to the table and sank tiredly onto her cushion.

"How are you feeling?" Mr. Poole didn't seem to know what to do and settled for checking her eyes. He had no experience healing magical afflictions.

"I'm not injured. I'm pretty sure it's a spell of some sort, maybe a sleepwalking spell," April said.

"You certainly seem to be awake, and you look healthy."

"I feel normal now," April agreed.

"Upsetting everyone for no reason, are you? Keeping us up half the night?" Elder Scarab sounded extra grumpy. He must have been worried about her. April smiled at him and he tightened his lips, his version of a smile. He was one of the rare New Haven elves with magic, and always spoke his mind. April enjoyed his crotchety company.

"That will do, Clayton." Head-Elder Falcon tucked his long white beard under the table and smiled properly. He was older than Elder Scarab but lacked the interesting pattern of wrinkles usually found on an aged face. It was probably because he almost always wore a placid expression, even in times of crisis. "April, I am overjoyed that you are returned to us unharmed. We will have to safeguard you, however, if these nightly trips are going to become a habit."

"April, are you having an overwhelming urge to travel east at this moment?" Mr. Poole asked.

April concentrated on her feet. "No, I don't think I am. I think it's stopped." She stood up and circled the table. "Back to normal," she was pleased to report, reclaiming her cushion.

"Good, good," Mr. Poole said, but a deep crease remained between his eyes.

April ate some snacks for a late supper while the adults tried to figure out what was going on. They were guessing, they really didn't know. Skylar and O'Wing snacked too, before they took their own departure.

There was no sign of Raina. As happy as she was to be home, April couldn't help but ache inside that Raina had not waited up to see that she was safe. She would have waited up for Raina, if Raina had been missing.

The night was half over when April dragged up the stairs to her room on sore feet and all of her felt heavy. She couldn't fall asleep for the longest time. She wanted to talk to Raina so badly and confess her lie, but didn't think it would be wise to wake her friend in the dead of the night. Raina was already mad at April, disturbing her sound sleep would probably only make Raina madder.

It was nearly dawn when April drifted into restless dreams and no one roused her for school. She had been given the day off.

The sun was high when April ventured downstairs and showered in the waterfall, and made an upsetting discovery. The vial was gone – again. When had she lost it this time? Maybe it had come off when she was wrestling with Skylar or O'Wing in midair. If that was the case, it was probably lost forever unless she could enlist Peter's help to track the gold, although the task might be too much even for him since the vial could be anywhere in the vast eastern woods.

Too preoccupied to do homework, April basked in the warm sand by the lake, waiting for Raina to arrive home.

Salm was the first elf to turn up. He veered toward April and sat down to join her. "Hey April. Enjoy the day off?"

"It was quiet." April kicked at the sand.

"I'm glad you got home safely last night. I tried to wait up but my parents sent me to bed as if I was DewDrop." Salm pulled a face.

"Raina too?" April asked.

Salm hesitated to answer, an answer in itself. April scowled across the lake, tempted to dive in and never come up again. She could do that – she had magical gills.

"I listened from my room to make sure you were okay. Raina would have done the same," Salm said, transparently trying to make her feel better.

"Would she?"

"Of course. You could have been hurt or worse if you'd made it through the barrier before Skylar stopped you. Who knows what's waiting for you out there, trying to get you to leave New Haven. You might not have been able to come back. I'm just glad Skylar was there to look out for you," he said.

"Raina won't be happy about that." April trickled warm sand through her fingers.

.   "Ah, April." Salm leaned closer, warm against her side. "Why would you say that?" He hadn't been around for yesterday's drama.

"Raina's upset with me, about Skylar, about everything." April felt it was safe to discuss this with Salm since he was not one of the parties directly involved. "I kind of lied … about going on a date with Skylar, because the other girls seemed impressed when they thought he was asking me on a date." April stared at her toes, shamefaced. "I thought they might want me to hang around with them if they believed I was dating Skylar, because they don't want to hang around with me now, not even Raina. But Skylar really only wanted to talk to me about Raina. He wants Raina to come with me on the Saturday, but he didn't want to ask in front of Airron. And the King is the one that keeps inviting me over and sending Skylar to see me, it's not Skylar. He doesn't like me, well he does like me, I hope, but not in a special way. Not the way he likes Raina."

"No, Skylar isn't fickle, he really is stuck on Raina." They all knew it.

"He is," April agreed.

Salm nudged her. "April, you don't need to lie to impress anyone. You're impressive enough, with your magic and saving the forcefield, and taking on Brag."

"But those are different things, and I'm not even supposed to use my strong magic anymore except for emergencies. On normal days, I don't dress right or say the right things and I think I'm failing school. And I've never dated, not really, not like the other girls. Sometimes – a lot of the time, I don't feel like I belong, not with the girls." April buried her toes in the sand. "And lately, Raina seems more like the other girls, and less like ... my friend."

Salm couldn't deny that, it was all too obvious. He simply said, "You need to talk to Raina about this. Tell her the truth about Skylar. Tell her what you just told me."

"I would if she would stand still long enough for me to say the words."

"I'll help you catch her," Salm promised, still trying to cheer her up. "Come on, help me start dinner?"

"Okay."

Raina didn't come home until the meal was ready and the whole family was waiting for her. She barely ate her serving of yucca pods and wouldn't look anywhere but at the food in front of her. April had never seen her so withdrawn.

"Raina," her mother prompted as soon as the shells were cleared. "What's wrong, honey?"

"Not a thing." She sounded downright belligerent.

"Are you sure?"

Raina didn't answer, except to scowl.

Mrs. Poole didn't ask again. She handed out roasted prickly pear for dessert, Raina shoved her serving rudely back. "I don't want it. You know I hate it."

"Would you like something else?"

"No, I don't want any stupid desert," Raina retorted.

Mr. Poole slammed his hand down angrily on the table. "Raina that is enough! If you are going to have a childish tantrum, do it in your room. And you can stay there for the rest of the night if you're going to be rude to your mother!"

"Fine with me." Raina stomped out of the kitchen.

April jumped up to follow her.

Mr. Poole stopped her. "April? There is an important matter we need to discuss before the hour gets any later."

April sat back down. "It's the walking east, isn't it? The sleepwalking?" Even an imp could have figured it out.

"Yes, it's the walking east. Head-Elder Falcon suggested that we take some precautions to ensure your safety," he said gently. "I have considered the matter at length. We need to make sure that you cannot leave here."

"Can someone watch me?"

"We don't want to leave anything to chance. This magical spell that forces you to walk east has proved very strong. Someone will watch you, but we need an additional safeguard, since we've all been short of sleep the last few nights. I picked up a device from Head-Elder Falcon on the way home. We created it to restrain Brag, but it has been thoroughly cleaned, even boiled. Anyway, you will not be able to leave your room with this device restraining you. I know it isn't pleasant, but it is necessary. Better than locking you in the underground chamber where your magic is almost powerless."

April nodded uncertainly, she didn't want to be locked in the horrible chamber deep under Seelie Court. One stay in that place had been more than enough.

"And we'll stay with you all night, we'll take it in shifts." It was obvious that Mr. Poole wasn't comfortable with restraining her.

"I'll take the first shift," Salm offered. "We can play a game or something."

"I'll have Raina take the first shift, Salm," Mr. Poole stated firmly. "April, let me show you how this device works." He lifted something onto the table and snapped it together. The thick metal chain clinked sharply. It looked like a horrible trap.

"Am I supposed to ... to wear that?" April asked in dismay.

"Yes, yes. But it isn't as bad as it looks, I promise. Tried it on myself. It is for your own protection, remember. Now, if you are ready, I'll install it in your room and attach you for the night. I'll send Raina in to sit with you as soon as you're settled. Do you want to bring up your homework?" Mr. Poole rose and fidgeted with the chain.

"No, that's okay." April wanted to talk to Raina, she didn't want to do homework. She moved ahead with a sickish feeling in her stomach at the thought of being chained up.

When they reached her room, Mr. Poole efficiently clamped one end of the metal around the leg of her bed and the other end around her ankle. He fiddled with something to lock both ends closed. It was a simple device and the chain allowed her limited movement around the room.

"There, not so bad, is it?" Mr. Poole stuck something in his pocket and patted her shoulder. "You have access to your basin and bed. Hopefully the restraint won't keep you awake. Now, are you at ease with this?"

"Yes." Maybe.

"Are you sure?" Mr. Poole lifted her chin. It was a very fatherly gesture.

"I'm sure." April worked up a smile because he looked so burdened.

"Good. I'll send Raina to sit with you now. I hope her mood has

34

improved since you will be a captive audience." He winced at the terrible pun. "And in the morning I will release you. Okay?"

"Okay. Good-night." April sat down on the edge of her bed. She couldn't wait to talk to Raina and straighten everything out.

It was a long wait. April changed into her nightshirt, brushed her teeth and paced awkwardly around the room, by which time Raina still hadn't turned up. And April was in no position to go searching for her friend. Maybe Raina wouldn't come at all. Maybe she didn't want to talk to April ever again. April paced a few more times, finally stopping beside her window. On the shadowy ledge, a small package was all but invisible.

Curious, April unwrapped the cloth to find a most unexpected object. The lost vial was back, again. A note from Skylar explained that it had come off in their tussle. He had stuck it in his pocket and forgotten to return it after all the excitement.

April held the container up to the light and made sure there were no cracks. The sludgy brown scum hadn't changed. "Good." She dropped the chain over her head and resumed pacing, except she was tired of walking around her small room. She wanted to go outside.

The longer she resisted the urge, the stronger the feeling grew. April clanked toward the door as far as her metal restraint would allow, then she was stuck. She tugged hard when a claustrophobic feeling threatened to smother her, but short of taking her bed along, she couldn't descend the stairs.

April grew frantic to escape her room. She yanked harder, not able to think clearly. The bed banged against the wall but wouldn't move further. Then April spotted the window, she could reach the window. She could even crawl up on the ledge and jump. That would get her outside! April hauled herself up onto the window ledge. She was poised to leap when Raina appeared in the doorway.

"What's going on?" Raina demanded. "What on earth are you doing?"

April didn't answer, she leaped.

Raina screamed and April fell as far as her chain would allow. It wasn't all that far. April found herself dangling by her ankle, staring at the lake below. Hanging upside-down brought back too many unpleasant memories of her time with Brag.

"April?" Raina called from above, leaning out the window.

"Here." She wiggled like a fish on a line. She needed to get free, she needed to go east!

"Are you jumping out the window because of the spell?" Raina asked.

"I hope so." April didn't know why else she would be jumping out her window. It was a stupid thing to do, especially when she was chained to her bed.

"Stay still. I'll get Salm and my Dad. We'll pull you back up." Raina disappeared from sight.

April didn't want to miss this opportunity to clear the air, before she left to go east. "Wait! Don't go, I have to tell you something first."

But Raina was already gone.

Mr. Poole and Salm were quick to arrive. They hauled April back up by her ankle. As soon as she was returned to her room, April was ready to climb the walls. "I really have to go now. You need to set me free," she begged desperately, wrenching at the chain as if she was strong enough to break it.

"That wouldn't be a good idea. April, calm down. I'm going to give you something to make you relax and sleep. I will be right back. Salm, Raina, watch her."

The words were unnecessary. Both elves had wide eyes fixed on her tug-of-war with the chain. Maybe she was a little out of control but she wasn't going to hurt anyone. However, she did need to get out of the room. There must be a way. Salm was blocking the window. Raina was blocking the door. But the bed – the bed was made of wood. Wood burned!

Before she knew what she was going to do, April closed her eyes and concentrated. Her extreme emotional state made the resulting fire spark like a small explosion. With a loud bang, the leg of the bed flared bright orange and turned to ash, and then she was free, except for the trailing metal attached to her leg. April ignored it and aimed for the window again. Salm lunged for the metal and Raina screamed for her father. The end of the chain was too hot for Salm to hold and Mr. Poole didn't make it upstairs fast enough.

With a flying leap, April dove through the window and fell towards the lake. Her wings appeared, then disappeared when she hit the water. The heavy metal pulled her down to the bottom as if she was a rock. It was lucky she had magical gills or she would have drowned. As it was, she was unable to swim and had to drag herself slowly across the lake bottom while the heavy chain kept getting tangled in the forest of rubbery lakeweed. She made slow progress through the black water, but at least her feet knew exactly where to go.

A welcoming committee was waiting in the shallows on the opposite shore; her eastern route had become predictable. Salm held up a torch as soon as she waded ashore.

"I'm going for a walk. It's a lovely night, isn't it?" she said.

When she passed by Mr. Poole, he reached over to fiddle with the chain, unlocking it. "It seems the restraint was not a wise idea after all," he said.

"Dad, why don't you attach it to a tree?" Raina cried. She sounded worried even though she was mad at April.

"And have it come down on our heads? Or start a major fire? I don't think so. No, we need another solution." And he had one, Mr. Poole had come prepared. He handed April some small black seeds. "Eat them."

"My thanks." She was kind of hungry. April ate the seeds while she walked east and soon started to feel kind of dopey and disoriented, and then very, very sleepy. She didn't remember anything else until she woke up in her room the next morning.

April gazed across the room, trying to recall the previous night. There were clues to help her with that. The bed was crooked because one leg was missing; the corner was propped up on a broken stick. A burnt odor lingered in the air. A wet nightshirt was draped over her window ledge. The clues triggered a vague memory of sleepwalking, which surfaced and became horribly clear.

"Oh no." April buried her face into her pillow, wishing she hadn't remembered her humiliating actions - ever. This spell or curse or whatever was getting to be a real pain.

April struggled to her feet, too many muscles aching. She dressed for school automatically and noticed that her neck was completely bare. She might have screamed in frustration if the household hadn't been sleeping. Both her gold chains were gone this time. April scanned the room in case someone had removed them. Nothing. But her wet nightshirt was looking a bit lumpy. April picked it up and shook. Two gold chains fell out, twisted together.

"Not lost at all," April told herself and untangled them. The tag went back around her neck but she hesitated to wear the vial yet again, since around her neck was clearly not the safest place to keep it.

April dropped the vial into her dresser drawer and slammed it shut, wishing the troublesome object would simply vanish. All her troubles seemed to have started when the item had appeared on her floor. She froze – all her troubles *had* started the night the vial had appeared on her floor. Could it be controlling her feet? She might have considered the possibility sooner, if the trance-like state didn't muddle her thoughts so completely.

She closed her eyes, thinking hard. Last night, it was after she found the vial on her window ledge that she had tried to walk east. And the previous night? It was after she found the chain in the forest that she started walking east. And the time before that, it was after Raina returned the chain that April had hiked east and been run over by the mice - and the night before that? Yes, she had worn the vial that very first night, after she found it on her floor. There was a distinct pattern. Surely it was more than coincidence that every single time she walked east, she had been wearing the chain.

To her knowledge, no one had worn the vial except her. It would be easy to test her theory by trying the chain on another elf. If they wanted to walk east, she would know her nightly wanderings were caused by the vial.

April finished getting ready for school and took the chain downstairs, looking for Mr. Poole. The house was too quiet, both parents were asleep. They had probably been up half the night - again. April wasn't about to wake them up. She took the vial back up to her room, thinking about where to hide it until after school. She turned in a slow circle, studying the space. Nowhere inside seemed safe enough, but what about outside? Outside was an inspired idea!

April climbed cautiously onto her window edge, balanced on tiptoe and reached way up. The conical roof had a slightly raised lip. She felt the area with her hand. It seemed secure and DewDrop couldn't access the hiding spot, she was too short. Pleased with the location, April stashed the vial in the trough and hurried downstairs.

Everyone was still sleeping.

April woke Salm first. He groaned and tried to swat her away like a pesky fly.

"Salm, time to get up for school!"

"No. Can't be."

"Was it another late night?" she guessed.

"Ya." He pulled his pillow off his head. "Don't wake my parents, they said to let them sleep late. I'll get DewDrop up."

"I'll wake Raina." It would give April an opportunity to talk to her and hopefully clear the air. It didn't work out that way. Raina's bed was empty; she had already left for school early, and quietly. Avoiding April? It did seem so.

A surge of anger gripped April. Talking to Raina was turning out to be such a challenging task, maybe April didn't want to talk to her anymore. Maybe if Raina didn't want to talk to April, April didn't want to talk to Raina.

She set off for school alone. She had already missed one whole day and she didn't want to be late, not with the field trip and scavenger hunt coming up. It was already Friday.

3 - Scavenger Hunt

In Mrs. Merry-Helen's class, the teacher was rushing to teach them all about the caverns, the mining process, the new excavations and the eggstones. April couldn't take in half of what was said. It felt like her brain was processing information at a fraction of the normal speed; even her hands were slow and clumsy when she tried to take notes. April suspected her drowsy condition was a lingering reaction to the weird seeds.

In math, Mr. Bladderwrack handed her all the work she had missed. April had twice as much work to do and she was lousy at math, especially when her brain wasn't working properly. Mr. Bladderwrack wouldn't let her leave the classroom until she finished and April missed most of lunch. By the time she got outside, Raina was sitting with the other girls again and didn't seem to notice April.

"Fine, then," April muttered and pretended she didn't notice Raina either. At least the boys were in the usual spot. Airron scooted over to make room on the moss.

"Hey, April. Heard you went for another walk last night. Salm told me, said it was along the bottom of the lake. And you exploded the leg off your bed?" Airron made it sound like a joke.

"Yes." April nibbled on a raisin. "But I think I've figured out what's causing me to walk east, so it shouldn't happen again."

Peter had been looking preoccupied, but apparently he was listening. "What's causing it?"

"The vial, I think. I only get weird when it's around my neck," she explained.

"The vial has magic?"

"I believe so, but I still have to test it on another elf. Although it might only work on a magical elf, that is possible," she said thoughtfully.

"Interesting." Peter looked completely intrigued. "Do you have the vial on you?"

"No, I didn't want to carry it around since I keep losing it. If another elf tried it on and it made them walk east, the barrier would kill them, so I left it at home, very well hidden."

"Makes sense that the vial is behind this mess. Brag sent it," Airron said, his eyes on Raina walking away.

The gong sounded before April could finish half her raisin or answer Peter's question about where she had hidden the vial.

Ms. Summers was continuing to teach them about the vegetation that they would be hunting on the scavenger hunt. April had missed the previous day's notes on twenty new plants. Peter silently handed over his birchbark for her to copy. She tried, but there was too much new information on the board that she had to write down first, and since she couldn't recognize any of the plants based on her inept sketches, it seemed pointless to add to the list. She handed back Peter's notes without copying them down. If she wasn't teamed up with someone capable for the hunt, the contest would be a disaster. She would be nothing but a hindrance to her partner.

On the way to the last class, Sports, Airron told April what she had missed in rockput the previous day. He pointed out several bruises, one on Seamore and another on Woody. Cosmo had a spectacular black eye and was very proud of it, judging by the way he was strutting with his chest out. April didn't see Peter anywhere, which seemed peculiar, and Raina was still hanging around with Heather and Willowna, chattering away as if they were her new best friends. It looked like April had been permanently replaced.

"I'm surprised we're doing this sport again," Airron chuckled, still talking about rockput. April lined up with him, wishing she could feel as cheerful as the meadow looked. It had a brightly festive air due to the big flags that decorated the surrounding treetops, warning off passing fairies.

"April, do you want to go first?" Airron asked when they reached the front of the line.

"No, you go." The students were launching the pebbles using a different technique which they must have learned while April was absent. She hung back and watched Airron. He did a very good job of swinging and launching his rock. His whole body spun around with the stone. When released, it flew in the right direction and went really far. April noticed Raina watching Airron from an adjacent line. She looked impressed. April waved and smiled, Raina didn't respond. She wasn't acting nice at all.

"Come on, April. Give it a try." Airron shoved the equipment into her hand.

April loaded her stone into the seedpod, then energetically swung the vine in circles over her head, venting some of her frustration.

"Stop! Not like that – the way I did it." Airron showed her how to hold the vine and how to swing properly, turning her whole body in circles. He did it with his arms wrapped around her from behind, so they could swing with enough momentum. They both ended up spinning like a whirly-gig in the wind. "Now release," he said. April let go and the pebble sailed quite a distance, landing on the safe side of the line.

"That was a good shot!" April enjoyed a sense of accomplishment that she rarely felt at school.

"Great. Now try it without me." Airron backed off to a safe distance and April caught a glimpse of Raina's face. She looked truly outraged - at April. Was it because Airron had helped her? If that was the reason, it seemed just plain silly.

April had to concentrate on her rockput so she stopped watching Raina and began spinning faster. She released her stone properly and it didn't hit anyone, it plopped into the empty side of the meadow, not nearly as far as the first one but far enough.

"Not bad at all," Airron complimented and they returned to the back of the line.

"I think Raina is mad that you helped me," April whispered, while they waited for another turn. She still couldn't spot Peter anywhere.

"Really?" Airron shot a glance at Raina, who was watching them out of the corner of her eye and frowning ferociously. "You know, I think you're right." Airron grinned wickedly. "Interesting. Very interesting. Maybe it's her turn to see what it's like."

"What what's like? Rockput?" April asked blankly.

"No. Never mind. Come on, we're almost at the front of the line again." Airron took his shot and then insisted on helping April again, wrapping his arms around her and spinning both of them even though April knew how to shoot now. Raina started looking furious enough to explode.

When April intercepted Airron's gloating gaze sliding over to Raina, she realized what he was about. He was using April to make Raina jealous. He was doing it deliberately! None of her friends were being nice.

Already feeling ragged around the edges, April almost lost her temper right in the middle of class. Faint thunder rumbled in the distance before she realized how angry she was inside. Ignoring the skittish glances of her classmates, April took a calming breath and counted to twenty – the last thing she wanted was to create a wild storm over New Haven.

41

When Mrs. Myrrh approached with a nervous expression and quietly suggested that April go home, she was happy to leave. She collected her pack and stormed off without a backwards glance. If Airron wanted to make Raina jealous, April did not want to be involved. And if Prince Skylar was going to ask Raina out, he could do it himself. And if Raina wanted to think the worst of April and have new friends, that was fine with April. Maybe it was time April made some new friends of her own.

She wasn't paying any attention to her surroundings when she almost bumped into Elder Scarab. He was always wandering around the woodland for one reason or another, or no particular reason at all.

"April, you got your own personal black cloud today?" he asked.

"Oh no, do I?" April glanced up, hoping she hadn't created a thunderhead.

"Not a real cloud," Elder Scarab scoffed. "A bad mood cloud. You don't look so happy."

"I'm not so happy. I'm not happy at all," she said frankly.

"I'm heading for my favourite berry patch. Why don't you come along, tell me all about it. You can even have a berry or two." It was a very generous offer, for Elder Scarab.

"Okay." It was better than going home and moping in her room.

"Thought I saw Peter lurking around near your house. Think he's waiting for you?" Elder Scarab arched a scraggily eyebrow in that direction.

"No, he should be in school, although I didn't see him in Sports. But I did leave early … got sent home early," April amended.

"Heard the thunder."

"Is that why you came to meet me? To make sure I don't do any damage?" April asked suspiciously.

"Could be. So, what's troubling you?" he asked.

April followed him through the rough undergrowth and unloaded all her troubles. She talked about the Prince and Raina, and Airron and Raina, and Peter and even Salm. And she remembered to tell him what she suspected about the vial. Elder Scarab was a good listener, he grunted and snorted and nodded in all the right places, and he didn't try to get a word in edgewise.

When she stopped for a much needed breath, all he said was, "Fun to be young. Everything's a big deal."

"Fun? It's not fun at all. Everyone's mad at me or I'm mad at them. Well, not everyone, but enough of my friends, especially Raina," April griped.

Elder Scarab ducked under an enormous rhubarb leaf and they popped out in a lovely raspberry patch.

"Berries'll make you feel better. Watch the thorns." Elder Scarab didn't say another word, he started eating. April followed his lead, maneuvering carefully around the plethora of sharp spikes. Elves had to be extremely careful in raspberry patches, it was easy to get nasty wounds.

April wandered around examining the fruit, finally selecting two perfect juicy berries. If they had been any riper, they would have fallen off by themselves. Both were high above her head. April shimmied cautiously up the strong woody stem, avoiding the thorns. She enjoyed her first berry where she perched, and carried the second one down to eat on the way home.

Elder Scarab was still feasting, reaching up to nab berries off the arched stems, so laden with ripe fruit that the growing ends had been pulled down to brush the ground. "April, you can have more than two. Eat your fill, plenty for both of us," he growled softly.

"Oh, okay. My thanks." April selected a couple more and trailed after Elder Scarab while he ate a pathway through the patch. Then he escorted her all the way home and left her at the door, promising to inform Head-Elder Falcon that the vial might be the cause of her nightly wandering. After unloading her problems on Elder Scarab, April felt almost cheerful when she entered the house.

Everyone was in the kitchen. Dinner was ready and waiting. "April, there you are. We were getting worried," Mr. Poole said, pulling out her cushion. He did look strained.

"I walked home with Elder Scarab. We stopped for berries. I didn't realize it was so late, sorry." She accepted the shell Salm passed her. "I ... left school a bit early. Was Peter here looking for me?"

"Didn't see him." Salm helped himself to a heap of food. He was always hungry.

Raina didn't respond to the question at all, she ate as if eating required all her attention.

Over tea and dessert, Mr. Poole brought up April's sleepwalking problem. "April, I want to talk about what we will do to restrain you tonight. The poppy seeds will put you to sleep again but they are very strong, and there are side effects."

"Oh, I don't need to be restrained. I think I've figured out what's making me walk east and it shouldn't happen tonight," April was happy to say. "I was going to talk to you about it after dinner."

"Really? But ... what is the root cause of your sleepwalking?" Mr. Poole sounded skeptical.

"I think it's the vial. I found it in the forest, then I lost it again, then I found it again."

Mr. Poole was looking confused.

April simplified her explanation. "Every time I've walked east, I've been wearing the vial. So I won't wear it, and I won't walk east." It was a simple solution.

"Do you have the vial now? Or is it lost?" Mr. Poole asked. How could he not?

"I have it," April said with satisfaction. "I hid it upstairs."

"Go get it and we'll test your theory."

April went to fetch the vial. She hopped onto her window edge and felt for it with her hand. She couldn't feel the vial anywhere. She leaned in both directions, tracing the lip of the roof. No vial. Growing frantic, she reached even further and almost fell off the ledge. "Snake scales," she ground out. She would have to climb up and look with her eyes.

Keeping her gaze fixed upward and not on the lake far below, April hauled herself onto the roof, digging her toes into the rough stone wall to help her climb. She made it and sat on the edge, legs dangling. The roof was steep and her perch was precarious, but she could see that the vial was gone. Its disappearance made no sense, unless Brag had floated it away again.

It was time to get off the roof. April flipped onto her stomach and slid down, feeling for the window ledge with her toes, sliding further and further. She would have found the window edge eventually, if the piece of roof that she was clinging to hadn't come loose. April made a wild grab for anything intact. She missed and slipped and suddenly she was falling.

April screamed and plummeted toward the lake. Her magical wings appeared, stuck inside her clothes. She landed with a hard stinging splash and sank. Cursing bubbles, she kicked for the shore. When she waded onto land, she did not arrive unnoticed. The family had come outside to investigate.

Mr. Poole was scratching his head. "April, what's going on?"

"I fell in the lake." It was pretty obvious.

"Uh … why?"

"Please don't ask. And the vial is gone."

"Gone?" Mr. Poole echoed blankly.

"Gone, but I didn't lose it this time. It's not where I left it." April dashed water out of her eyes. "I don't know what happened to it."

Mr. Poole ran a harried hand through his rapidly thinning brown hair and motioned them all back to the house. Mrs. Poole handed April a towel at the door. April dried off on her way to the kitchen, trying not to drip.

"Do you think someone has removed it from your room?" Mr. Poole asked, settling back on his cushion.

April shrugged helplessly. "Maybe Brag floated it away again. I don't know."

"Of course you don't know. DewDrop, did you take anything out of April's room?" Mr. Poole asked gently.

"No, I didn't take anything." She looked up at her father with big eyes. "I wouldn't."

"I know, honey. Salm, you didn't remove the vial for some reason?" his father prompted.

"Of course not."

"Raina, did you move the vial?" Mr. Poole was leaving no stone unturned.

"No," she said shortly, nothing more.

"Well April, I'm afraid this means we will have to take some precautions to make sure that you don't try to leave once the moon rises, since we can't confirm that the vial was the cause of your wandering. That's not why you were jumping in the lake, is it?" he asked as an afterthought.

"Uh... no. That was an accident."

"I see," he said, even though he clearly didn't. "Well, a few seeds won't do any harm, short term," he added, his tone reassuring.

"But I'm pretty sure it was the vial making me walk east," April stressed. She didn't want to take more seeds, they made her feel dumb and slow. She felt dumb enough, after falling in the lake.

"April, this whole episode is mysterious and disturbing. I suspect that we don't know all the factors involved and we don't want to chance losing you. If you did make it through the barrier, none of us could follow to help you. You know that."

"I know."

Raina hopped up and said, "I'm going over to Heather's." She didn't seem to care about April's plight in the slightest.

April didn't suggest going along. She knew she wasn't welcome and neither would the Pooles allow it, since she was at risk of disappearing forever.

Mr. Poole was the one that stopped Raina. "Raina, I would like you to stay home tonight and take the first shift to watch April. Your mother and I had little sleep last night and would like to go to bed early."

"I'm not staying home tonight. It's Friday! Salm can watch her. Or why don't you call Skylar, he wouldn't mind. He jumped at the chance to play the big hero the other night. Or how about Airron, he would fly over in a heartbeat," Raina burst out before she slammed out the front door.

"You haven't had a chance to talk to Raina?" Salm guessed.

April shook her head.

Mrs. Poole asked, "April, is there a problem?"

"Yes, but it's not my problem," she huffed and went to her room. She didn't bother to light a candle. She brushed her teeth in the dark, left her wet clothes in a heap and yanked her covers over her head. She felt like dung. Who would have guessed it could make an elf feel so bad inside to lose their best friend? Even though April was mad, the thought of losing Raina's friendship forever made her feel sick to her stomach. It made her feel as lonely as when she had been lost in the forest.

When April heard footsteps ascending to her room, her heart leapt in hope that Raina had returned. She sat up and magically lit a candle. The light revealed Mr. Poole, entering with more small black seeds.

As soon as she ate them, April fell deeply asleep and didn't waken until the next afternoon. Saturday. Gripped by a heavy lethargy, she spent most of the day in her room, staring numbly at the walls and content to do so. Sunday was the same. Raina didn't come to see her once; she went out again.

After two perfectly safe nights, Mr. Poole decided that they would try a night without the seeds, citing that April had school the next day. It was obvious that she would not be able to function in school if she was eating the seeds at night. She could barely function at home. "But we will watch you, we'll take it in shifts again," Mr. Poole said with resignation.

April felt awful for disrupting their lives.

Monday morning, April woke up ridiculously early, and it felt like a bad mood cloud really did hover above her head. Uncaring, she tossed on the nearest clothes from a wrinkled pile on the floor and walked downstairs. Mr. Poole was asleep on a cushion at the bottom of the steps. He looked so exhausted that April didn't have the heart to wake him up. She tiptoed past and left for school directly.

When she reached the meadow, a few students were already there ahead of her. Peter was one of them, sitting with Cherry of all elves. When Cherry spotted April, she rose with a disdainful sniff and sauntered away.

April walked uncertainly over to Peter. "Hey Peter."

He flushed, there was no denying the guilty redness of his cheeks. "Hi April. You're here early for a change."

"Why were you with Cherry?" Her tone came out accusing.

"No reason. She sat down to ask me some questions about the scavenger hunt plants." He shrugged nonchalantly "No big deal."

April wasn't so sure. Normally Cherry wouldn't be caught dead hanging out with April or any of April's friends.

"Sit down, April."

She sat down and after an uncomfortable silence asked, "Were you looking for me on Friday? At my house?"

"No," Peter denied quickly. "Why would you think that?"

"Elder Scarab said he thought he saw you there." April crossed her legs and leaned on her pack.

"Must have been someone else," Peter mumbled, pulling homework out of his bag.

"I didn't see you in Sports," April recalled, ignoring the obvious hint to get to work.

"I was there. Come on, let's study the plants for the scavenger hunt." Peter placed his birchbark notes between them.

April yawned, she felt too sleepy to study.

"Do you know the sixty plants?" Peter asked, nudging her.

April sighed. "Not even close. I might know nine or ten, the ones I already knew. I really hope you're my partner."

"I think you might need me as your partner." Peter studied his notes and April napped. The gong woke her up. Neither Salm nor Raina were in the meadow, which seemed peculiar. They must have slept in. April probably should have woken them up before she left.

When Ms. Hawthorn came to the classroom door halfway through Ms. Merry-Helen's lesson, Raina still hadn't turned up.

The head-elf motioned April out into the corridor. "April, elves are searching for you," she stated quietly.

46

"But I'm right here."

"Yes, I can see that. My eyes do work," Ms. Hawthorn said dryly. "The Pooles believed that you disappeared during the night again and a large number of elves are searching eastern New Haven for you," she explained. "Perhaps you should come with me to the office."

Her no-nonsense stride moved her briskly down the hall and April followed with a sinking heart. She had caused problems again, it seemed, without even trying.

April said lamely, "But I didn't get lost, I only came to school. I guess I should have left a note."

"A prudent idea, given the present circumstances," Ms. Hawthorn agreed crisply.

The morning went downhill after that. Raina sailed into Mr. Parsley's class late, her face tight and angry. It was lucky that the teacher didn't yell at Raina for being tardy, there was no doubt that she would have yelled right back.

At lunch, Raina joined her new friends, without even saying she was glad April was safe.

Airron laughed so hard over the mix-up that he almost choked on his flat bread. He tossed an arm around April's shoulders to hold himself upright. April could feel Raina glaring at her back and she shoved Airron's arm off. Enough was enough.

"No sign of the missing vial yet?" Peter asked, changing the subject.

"No, and I searched my whole room from top to bottom. The rest of the family searched the house. I don't know what happened to the thing but it hasn't magically reappeared. I just hope no one finds it and tries it on. If any elf except me goes east through the barrier, they'll die." April couldn't think about that without feeling responsible.

Peter nodded his head with a jerk and didn't look so happy himself. April studied his troubled face while she had the chance. He looked as guilty as she felt. But about what? Something was definitely bothering Peter. He hadn't been himself for weeks. And he was hanging out with Cherry.

"Peter? Is everything okay?" April asked.

"Sure," he said, standing up even though the gong hadn't sounded. "Umm ... maybe you should search your room again. Maybe the vial is there somewhere. Wouldn't hurt to look again. See you in class." With a stiff stride, he crossed the meadow.

"What's wrong with Peter?" April asked Airron.

"I honestly don't know." Airron adjusted his wings under his robe and gathered his scraps of lunch together. "Something has been bugging him lately but he won't tell me what it is, and I have asked." He cocked an eyebrow in Peter's direction. "He'll tell us when he's ready. You know Peter, he keeps his own council more than the rest of us."

In pixie class, Peter was no more forthcoming. April tried to memorize a few plants but her drawings were useless. To make matters worse, Ms. Summers started teaching them about even more plants, April hadn't known there were so many plants in the whole world. And her brain still felt as dim and slow as an imp's.

Rockput went as smoothly as it ever did. Several students were injured, but not seriously. Rocks were going further and further as students became more skilled at tossing them. One of Seamore's stones even flew through a classroom window but since it didn't hit anyone, it wasn't considered cause for concern.

When the final gong sounded, April waited to see who was walking home together. Raina disappeared like a shadow in the sunlight, so April joined Peter and Airron.

"Raina really can be stubborn," Airron grimaced. "She's mad at me, too. She won't talk to me at all. Shouldn't have tried to make her jealous, I guess."

"And you shouldn't have used me to do it," April snapped.

"Hey, she was already mad at you. That wasn't my fault. More mad doesn't make a difference! Don't worry, we'll get things straightened out soon enough, then we'll have some fun." Airron sounded confident that everything would turn out fine. April wished that she had the same positive attitude, but she didn't. Too many bad things had happened to her during her short lifetime.

Peter walked along, as preoccupied as earlier. Airron did most of the talking until they arrived at the path leading to his treehouse. "Might as well go home, I guess, since Raina has disappeared. I've got a lot of homework anyway, haven't done any in days. Gonna help me catch up, Peter?" Airron shifted his heavy pack onto his other shoulder.

"Sure. April, check your room one more time, for the vial," Peter said and went with him.

April didn't hurry home, and rather wished she hadn't arrived when she saw how upset the Pooles were. April took one look at their broody faces and started apologizing before either parent got a word in edgewise. "I'm really sorry about this morning. I should have left a note before I left for school ... I didn't even think - "

Mr. Poole cut her off. "That seems to be the general problem." He really was upset. "You didn't think about how we would feel when we discovered you were gone – do you have any idea how many elves were inconvenienced? Searching for you when you weren't even missing? I felt like an utter fool, sending half of New Haven to scour the forest for you while you were sitting in school!"

Mrs. Poole placed a restraining hand on his arm, "Marsh, please. April didn't mean any harm. She is still getting used to living amongst other elves. It hasn't been so long, less than one year after all. Ten short months."

"But she still has to be aware of how her actions impact other elves, more so because she has enough magical power to do untold damage. Our home could have been incinerated the other night, not merely her bed. Salm and Raina could have been seriously injured by the explosion," he stressed. "Even Raina is upset over April's behavior."

"Marsh, we don't know anything about that. They're teenagers, it is normal to experience heightened emotions and ... and emotional turmoil." Mrs. Poole smiled rather desperately at April.

"Yes, but we're dealing with more than that here, aren't we, Shelly. Normal teenage elves can't destroy a whole world because they experience heightened emotions. I know what happened the other night was because of this magical spell, but it won't always be so. And there has been more than one report of thunder in the distance. April cannot let her emotions get the better of her. She has to think about the repercussions of her actions and exhibit full control over herself at all times. She does not have the luxury of letting her emotions rule her, not like other teenage elves. She could cause serious damage, harm elves, even shut down the forcefield." Mr. Poole tossed his hands in the air. "And now this hazardous vial is once again lost in our world. What next?"

The words were like blows. April felt lost where she was standing. Until recently, she had thought that she was fitting into her new world very well. Apparently she wasn't. She should have realized. Even Raina wasn't talking to her and it looked like Mr. Poole would prefer that she didn't live with them anymore because she was so dangerous.

Deeply stricken, April ran for the shelter of her room. She shut the door, lay down on her bed and cried like she hadn't cried since she was a small elf and her parents had never come home again. April must have cried herself to sleep, a soft knock woke her up. It was almost dark.

April dried her damp face, sat up and called, "Come in."

Mrs. Poole entered, nothing more than a shadowy shape in the near-darkness. April didn't light a candle, she preferred not to be seen.

Mrs. Poole settled gingerly on the foot of the unstable bed. "April, are you okay?"

"Yes," April said, her hoarseness giving her away.

Mrs. Poole shifted to face her, even though April could be nothing but a dark blur. "Marsh didn't mean what he said, April. He was ... upset. We have all been under a certain amount of stress lately."

"Because of me." April sniffed and rubbed her nose on her covers.

"No April, because of the vial. We've been worried about how it affects you, we've been worried *about* you because we care about you. The fact that the vial is missing is also cause for concern, but that is not your fault." Mrs. Poole reached out to take April's hand. How she found it in the dark was something of a mystery, but she did. "Now, dinner is ready. Come and eat something. Marsh has calmed down."

"I'm not really hungry." April didn't want to be seen all puffy-eyed and blotchy-faced.

"I'll prepare a shell for you. Come down when you get hungry." Mrs. Poole rose and straightened April's covers.

"My thanks, but I don't want to come down, not like this," April said.

"How about I send a tray up, you need to eat."

April nodded, somehow Mrs. Poole saw that as well.

"But you will come down to breakfast tomorrow, and Marsh will no doubt apologize for letting his own emotions get the better of *him*," Mrs. Poole said firmly.

The words made April feel a little better. "Okay."

DewDrop carried the tray up and stayed to share it. April nibbled and DewDrop devoured April's dessert, bouncing around because she liked to make April's bed rock back and forth.

"I want your bed, can we trade?" DewDrop asked eagerly.

"You don't really want a three-legged bed, do you, Dewy?"

DewDrop bobbed her head. "Maybe you could explode a leg off my bed!" She was full of ideas.

"Your Dad would just love that." April grinned at DewDrop's freckled face, deeply glad of her sweet company. They finished the tray of food together and then DewDrop wanted to play a game instead of doing her homework. April was in complete agreement. They enjoyed a simple card game until Mrs. Poole called DewDrop for bed.

DewDrop scooted off the covers, gathering up the cards. She dropped half of them and sat down on the floor to collect her game. "Hey, something shiny is under your bed." As quick as a millipede, she wiggled underneath.

"What is it, Dewy?"

"I got it! I think it's that vial."

That didn't seem possible. April had searched everywhere, including under her bed. "Don't open it, Dewy. Don't touch it," April cried anyway.

Her heart clutched when DewDrop said, "Oops." A wave of hot rotten air welled up from below. The whole bed bounced high and slammed down again.

"Dewy, Dewy!" April screamed and shot under the bed. Holding her breath, she grabbed Dewy with one hand and the vial with the other, yanking both into the light. The stopper had come undone.

Her eyes burning, April twisted and pushed as hard as she could, resealing the vessel. She jammed it in her pocket and lifted DewDrop toward the fresher air near the window. The little elf was still and white. Before April could scream for Mr. Poole, Raina appeared in the doorway.

"What happened? What was that big bang? Dewy? What's wrong with Dewy?" Raina demanded.

"She opened the vial, just a bit," April said helplessly, leaning back so Raina could check her sister.

"Cripes April, I thought the vial was lost. Where did she get it?" Raina brushed DewDrop's hair off her forehead.

"It was under my bed."

"And you couldn't find it there?" Raina's scathing tone cut like a knife. "She's getting a big bump. Did something hit her?"

"Maybe the bed, it sort of bounced around. It might have hit her."

Raina didn't answer, she shouted urgently for her father.

Alerted by her tone, Mr. Poole was quick to arrive and take charge. He examined DewDrop while April described what had happened. She felt awful that DewDrop had been harmed while under her supervision.

There was no reprimand. Everyone was focused on DewDrop's condition.

The little elf was carried to her room by Mr. Poole. Mrs. Poole shooed the rest of them out. They hovered outside with Salm until the parents announced that DewDrop appeared to be recovering and should be fine.

Only then did April flee to her room, to be miserably alone with her guilt and the scummy vial. How had it gotten back into her room? April pulled the cursed object out of her pocket and examined it. The stopper was secure again and it didn't look like any of the gross fluid had leaked out. "How did you get back in my room? Where were you?" she asked it. The vial didn't have an answer but April knew what she had to do. At the first opportunity, she was going to carry this vial through the barrier and leave it outside, where it could harm no elf ever again.

Unsure what to do with it in the meantime, April scrambled back on her window ledge and replaced the vial in its original hiding spot, where it should have been unreachable and unfindable. She went straight to bed, and tossed restlessly for most of the night.

Early the next morning, after a quick peek at the comfortably snoozing DewDrop, April fled the house. She felt a bit like a shadow that had lost its body. At least she remembered to leave a note on the kitchen table saying that she had gone to school. She made sure to write down in extra big letters that it had nothing to do with a magic spell.

The Pooles must have stayed home all day with DewDrop. They were both in the kitchen when April got back from school with Salm. Mr. Poole asked to see the vial immediately. Terrified it would be gone, April went to check. It was still on the roof above her window. She carried it down to Mr. Poole and he examined it without opening the container.

Everyone watched when he placed it over his neck and sat like a stone. "Nothing," he announced and handed it to Mrs. Poole. She tried it on. Neither did it have any affect on her. Even Salm was volunteered, without any reaction.

"Now you April." Mr. Poole placed the chain around her neck. She turned toward the door and started walking. Salm blocked the exit and Mr. Poole lifted the chain off.

April stopped dead. "Oh, I did it again, didn't I?"

"I think we have located the culprit," Mr. Poole said with

satisfaction. "This vial must only work on a magical elf," he deduced.

"Yes," April agreed. "Maybe I should take it through the barrier and leave it outside New Haven. It's caused nothing but trouble."

"Good idea," Mr. Poole nodded. "Hide it safely until the weekend, then you can get rid of it." He patted her on the shoulder and didn't seem mad anymore. He simply seemed tired.

The rest of the week passed quickly. April didn't take anymore midnight trips. Raina continued to avoid April as if she was a stinkbug. And suddenly it was Friday, the day of the scavenger hunt.

As soon as her class sat down after lunch, Ms. Summers announced that she was going to draw partners for the contest. She reached into an upside-down acorn cap and started reading names. "First team will be Rosemary and Tinka. Second team, Daisy-May and ... Woody. Third team, Craig and Herb. Fourth, Violet and Peter."

Ms. Summers shook the cap around and Peter shrugged apologetically at April, even though the partnership with Violet wasn't his fault.

"Next, Heather and Willowna, Marigold and Barkly, Perriwinkle and Pansy." Pansy didn't look pleased with her partner, Perriwinkle rarely spoke and was inclined to be clumsy, very clumsy. Ms. Summer paused to say, "Did I mention that I will partner the last student, since we don't have an even number? But I won't find more than half the plants." Since the teacher was almost finished choosing teams, April would either get partnered with Ms. Summers or one of the two remaining students. She hoped it wasn't Ms. Summers or the teacher was sure to find out how little April had learned in her class.

The cap was jiggled around one more time before the teacher pulled out another scrap of bark. "Cherry Pitt and ..." The hand went in again. "Oh, oh dear ... and April." The class gasped. April and Cherry's feud was legendary. Everyone knew they would rather fight than talk. Even the teacher looked uncertain about their partnership. "Hmm, well, I guess that leaves Ginger and myself, doesn't it?" She stood indecisively in front of her desk. Was she considering switching at least one pair of partners?

Peter put a hand on April's arm. "April, ask the teacher if you can switch. I'll take Cherry if you want Violet. Violet's smart, she'll do a good job." It was a generous offer since Cherry hated Peter almost as much as she hated April. Or maybe she didn't, based on what April had seen earlier in the week.

"No, Peter. I can handle Cherry. It's only for a couple of hours. We're only picking plants." His kindness made her feel as weepy as a willow tree. Maybe it was more of those heightened teenage emotions that Mrs. Poole had mentioned.

"Now the lists. No two are alike," Ms. Summers said and handed out the squares of bark at random.

Cherry grabbed their list and Ms. Summers issued some last minute instructions. "Remember class, meet back in this room as soon as you have all twenty samples. Be careful when you handle the more dangerous vegetation. And don't forget to sign in with Ms. Figwart when you return or your team will forfeit any chance of winning. Everyone have their storage sacks? Good! Okay - have fun!"

Most pairs rushed out of the room in a hurry to get started and win. April and Cherry did not, they eyed each other with mutual distrust. Peter lagged behind until Violet yanked him away, she didn't let go of his hand.

As soon as they were alone, Cherry sneered, "April-May June."

"Just April," April said tiredly, knowing it was useless.

Cherry strutted out of the room; April trailed at a safe distance. They entered the undergrowth on the north side of the meadow and Cherry kept walking. April kept following, but not too close.

"Here, you carry the list." Cherry tossed the piece of bark over her shoulder and April lunged to catch it. Twenty plants were listed neatly - the first twenty plants that Ms. Summers had taught them about. At least April had been present that day, she might remember some of the information.

"Okay, I want to win and that's going to be tough with you as my partner, so stay out of the way and I'll find the plants. Got it?" Cherry laid out the terms of their partnership.

"Fine with me." April didn't mention that she wouldn't recognize most of the plants if they pulled up their roots and chased her.

"The teacher didn't say if we could still win if our partner disappeared on the hunt, never to be seen again. Wonder if I could still win if I came back alone," Cherry taunted.

"Maybe I'll come back without you and find out," April retorted.

Cherry actually laughed, then got to work. She found the mint, red clover and rose hip right off. They were common and not dangerous. All three were edible and April chewed on a mint leaf since she hadn't eaten much of her lunch.

When they found a healthy patch of sneezeweed, Cherry instructed April to pick that sample, then she shoved April headfirst into the greenery. April began to sneeze nonstop since she had gotten it up her nose and all over her clothes and hair.

"Water lily next," Cherry said.

"Are we near a ... achoo ... a .... achoo ... a lake? Achoo!" April was thoroughly lost following Cherry.

"We need a swampy shore, not a lake. Don't you know anything? Oh, that's right, you're not very bright, are you?" Cherry turned left to lead them unerringly to a swampy shore. She pointed to the beautiful white blossoms. "We have to collect a petal. You have gills so you can get it. I've already picked most of the samples." She had, but those had been the easiest ones.

April handed Cherry the list and waded in willingly enough. At least the water, scummy though it was, washed off the sneezeweed. She had to fight to detach one of the big, firmly attached petals. The thing finally came free with a snap and April splashed backwards into the slimy water, coating all of her in gooey sludge, especially her hair.

When April waded out, Cherry was laughing so hard that she was in danger of falling into the swamp herself. Tempted to give her a helping hand, April resisted the impulse. She didn't want to risk a storm.

"That's five done." Cherry glanced at the list before tossing it to April and stuffing the lily petal into their sack. It was so big, only part of the bottom fit.

"What's next?" April asked, since Cherry seemed to be in charge.

"Touch-me-not."

"I wouldn't touch you if you were dipped in honey and rolled in gold," April ground out. "Now what's the next plant?"

"Touch-me-not - that is the next plant. Just when I think you can't get any dumber, you prove me wrong." With a triumphant smirk, Cherry strode away.

April squelched after her, feeling as dumb as a stump.

When they found the large yellow-orange spotted flowers of the touch-me-not, Cherry ordered April to pick that sample, too.

Resigned, April reached for a petal. She must have brushed the capsule hanging underneath the flower because the capsule burst, covering her in seeds and fluff. Everything stuck to her, because she was still sticky with pond scum.

"Why do you think it's called a touch-me-not?" Cherry crowed. Thus far, she seemed to be enjoying the scavenger hunt. That made one of them.

April sneezed and handed over the petal.

The flax, yarrow, tansy, feverfew and mullein samples were retrieved and stored without incident. Then they scavenged for the medicinal plants: boneset, woundwort, and ironweed, bringing their total number of samples to fourteen of the twenty. The hunt was going better, all things considered. But Cherry was saving the more dangerous plants for last.

"Six more. What's next, April-May June?"

April consulted the list. "Fireweed."

"Fireweed. Isn't that fireweed?" Cherry asked brightly, pointing to something on the ground between them.

"It's not burning. Is it fireweed?" April said stupidly. She had no idea what the plant looked like.

Cherry plucked up the sample and stuck it in the sack. "What now?"

"Pokeroot."

"Oh, that should be in a shady area." Cherry surveyed the surrounding forest with narrowed eyes, turned left and pushed through some dense undergrowth

April lost sight of her and hurried to catch up.

She found Cherry lounging on moss beside a spindly plant, eating a berry. "Pick another berry for the sample sack," Cherry said, not bothering to move. April picked a couple, hungry from all the walking. She tossed one to Cherry and bit into the other. She hadn't even swallowed the second mouthful of the small dark berry when she began to feel sick – really really sick. April barely made it behind a fern before she vomited, cursing bitterly when she could.

Her stomach under control again, April stormed back to Cherry, rather surprised to find her waiting. "That was ... that was a poisonous berry," April sputtered, almost too mad to talk.

"No kidding," Cherry agreed smugly.

"But ... but you ate one." April had seen her eating a berry.

"That was a berry left from my lunch. I'm not stupid enough to eat poisonous fruit." Cherry rose gracefully and brushed off her skirt.

"But you let me eat one," April cried hotly, fighting to keep her temper.

"Hey, you ate it all by yourself, I didn't tell you to eat it. I had nothing to do with you eating it. Too bad it wasn't fatal." With that parting shot, Cherry took off. April had no chance to strangle her.

After she caught up and called Cherry every foul name she could think up, April felt a little better. Cherry let her rant, a supremely superior smile on her face the entire time.

When April ran out of names, Cherry asked, "What's left?"

"Four plants. Mayflower, bloodroot, pokeweed and Jimson weed," April listed. "Is there any water around here? I need a drink." Her mouth tasted gross.

"Don't think so."

"What about a mint leaf? You have some in the sack."

Acting highly put upon, Cherry hauled out half a green leaf and shoved it at April. "That's all you can have, we need the rest for the scavenger hunt. I think we passed some mayflower back there." Cherry turned toward their original path and started walking briskly. April shoved the leaf in her mouth and tried to keep up. It didn't take long to realize that the leaf she was chewing on tasted nothing like mint.

April spat the green pulp out quickly, but it was already too late. Her mouth was burning and her tongue was erupting in sores. What had Cherry given her now? Maybe this latest snack was fatal. Terrified, April started running. She almost slammed into Cherry; the elf had stopped beside a plant with waxy white petals topping large yellow berries. Mayflower.

"Cherry, what did you give me? That wasn't mint, what was it?"

"I'm sure I gave you mint leaf. Did I make a mistake?" Cherry asked with false innocence.

Desperate for answers, April grabbed the sack off Cherry's shoulder and dumped it out.

"Don't lose anything," Cherry sniped, standing well back.

April ignored her, frantically sorting through the samples. She found the half a leaf still in the sack. Closer examination proved that it came from the feverfew plant. April couldn't remember anything about that plant

"Is feverfew poisonous?" April demanded.

"Feverfew? Not sure, we'll have to wait and see, won't we."

"You must know. Tell me," April shouted, standing up to face Cherry as best she could from her much shorter height.

"Fine then. No, feverfew isn't poisonous. It causes mouth sores if you chew it, nothing serious. Now shut up about it so we can collect the last plants. I'm sick of hanging around with you."

"Likewise." April had no better comeback.

"We need one of the mayflower berries, right?" Cherry asked impatiently, getting back to work.

"That's what the list says."

"Why don't you grab three, they look really yummy," Cherry said.

While April climbed the stem and knocked down three berries, Cherry stored their collection of samples back in the sack, adding one of the berries. She handed a second to April. Cherry was acting a little too considerate. Normally she would have left April to pick up the berries.

"Are they edible or are they poisonous?" April demanded pointblank.

Cherry paused and twirled a golden curl around her index finger. "Mayflower berries? I think they're edible, might make your mouth feel better."

"Why don't you eat one first," April challenged.

"I'm not hungry, that's why." Cherry walked away without her berry. April tossed hers aside. It looked like Cherry was trying to poison her for a third time. And not just that, April's skin was starting to itch and burn. Even touching the mayflower was dangerous, it seemed. And it was getting worse. April's arms and legs were erupting in red patches and spots.

"Cherry! We need to find a lake. Where's a lake? My skin is burning," April cried.

Cherry swung around to stare at April and she started laughing again. "Aren't you a sight, all slimy and fluffy and puffy and spotted and red and disgustingly filthy. I'm embarrassed to be seen with you. Don't know how Raina does it."

"Shut up, Cherry."

The elf had hit a nerve and she knew it. "Trouble in paradise? The novelty of hanging out with a mutant elf worn off for Raina?"

"Go suck slug slime." April held her temper, barely. She thought she heard faint thunder.

"There is no lake nearby and we still have three more samples to collect if we're going to win, so live with your rash. It's not going to kill you. If I wanted to kill you, you'd be dead already. Next?" Cherry prompted.

"Pokeweed," April bit out. "Is that the same as pokeroot?"

"No, it's a completely different plant. You really don't know anything, do you?"

It took twenty minutes to find the pokeweed. The dark purple berries blended into the shadows and were hard to spot. "Hungry, April-May June. Those berries look good," Cherry taunted.

April wouldn't have eaten one of those berries if she hadn't tasted food in a year. She waded into the middle of the plant, picked a berry for the sample sack and tossed it to Cherry, then she noticed something interesting – she stank, almost as bad as a skunk. The plant had transferred an offensive odor onto her body.

Cherry plugged her nose and backed off.

Two more, April might live through this scavenger hunt yet. Only two left – bloodroot and Jimson weed. At least April knew that Jimson weed was highly dangerous, Ms. Summers had put three warning checkmarks beside it when she had written the name on the slate board.

Cherry didn't ask about the last two plants, she must have memorized them. She started hiking in more-or-less the direction of the school. After a long hostile silence, Cherry stopped beside a white flowered plant with rhizomes sprouting out around it. "That looks like bloodroot right there."

"Does it?" At least it wasn't dripping blood. The ground shoots were abundant, starting a whole new crop of the plants.

"We need one of the small starter plants," Cherry mentioned, tapping her toe impatiently.

"Why don't you pick it?" April was leery after her close encounters with vegetation.

"I found it, you can pick it. I'm not going to do all the work."

April couldn't argue, even though she wanted too. She leaned over and pinched off one of the baby plants. Instantly, her fingers began to burn ten times worse than her previous condition. Her fingers were covered with red sap, it felt like a fire ant was gnawing on them.

Blinking back tears of pain and frustration, April rubbed her hand on the damp earth, trying to get as much of the sap off as possible. Blisters were already forming, and it was her writing hand. April couldn't even blame Cherry for this day, not really. April was supposed to know how to handle the dangerous plants properly.

"Jimson weed, and we're almost back at school," Cherry said, resuming course in the same direction. After only ten minutes, she stopped and pointed at a beautiful flowering plant with trumpet-shaped violet blossoms. It had a strong, not terribly pleasant odor. "That's it, we're supposed to collect one of the prickly, egg-shaped capsules."

"You can pick it. I can't use my hand," April said belligerently.

"I'm not going to pick it. This is the most poison plant on the list. You can pick it."

But April had reached the end of her vine. "Forget it, if you want it

57

so bad, you can pick it." At least April knew where they were now, more or less. She marched ahead. If Cherry wanted to win so badly, she could get the sample herself. April couldn't care less if they won. She just wanted to go home.

When something hit her in the back, April swung around to find one of the pods lying by her foot.

"You have the sample sack," April pointed out, unwilling to touch the thing.

"I hate you," Cherry shouted, which had nothing to do with the pod.

"I hate you more!" April shouted back, tempted to kick the pod at Cherry. But it was highly toxic. It could cause serious harm, to her toes as well as to Cherry. April was pleased that she had thought twice before she reacted in anger. She hauled in a shaky breath and resumed course, almost calm. Cherry must have retrieved the seedpod because her footsteps kept pace and nothing else hit April in the back.

When Cherry pointed out a shortcut to the school, April veered off the path without a word. Cherry didn't follow. She remained exactly where she was until April was hemmed in by waxy leaves and white berries. Trapped.

"Oh, wait, I was wrong. It isn't that way at all, it's this way." Cherry pointed in the direction they had been following originally. Even April recognized the poison ivy surrounding her. She screamed in frustration and edged out of the ivy patch as nimbly as she could. It was already too late. When she caught up with Cherry, April was scratching like a squirrel with a bad case of fleas. Scratching only made her condition worse.

"Thanks Cherry, thanks a lot," April said bitterly, rubbing at her knee.

Cherry smiled so sweetly, she must have sipped a mouthful of honey. "My pleasure."

New Haven Academy appeared over the next hill. April hurried down the slope and stepped into the meadow deeply relieved to be back, except that it was hailing in the school meadow. It had never hailed in New Haven before, but it was hailing now – hailing ... rocks?

One barely missed her, whizzing by her ear. April leapt away from it, covering her head with her hands. She didn't see the rock that came down on her shoulder, the impact made her legs buckle. She had blundered right into the middle of the rockput class!

"Stop, stop, stop," Mrs. Myrrh screamed.

Afraid to move, April crouched with her hands over her head until the stones stopped falling.

When the coast was clear, Cherry waltzed into the meadow. "Look, April-May June. The rest of our class. Oh, are you hurt?" She sounded jubilant.

"No," April lied, shoved to her feet and started walking again. If she didn't put some distance between Cherry and herself, the class was going to be highly entertained by another spectacular fight. They were watching keenly and

April knew she was a sight to behold, all slime-coated, red and patchy, rashy and scratching, covered in seed fluff, and she stank. When it became clear that she was unharmed, her classmates started laughing and pointing. It was almost a replay of the first day she had arrived in this world.

April closed her eyes, feeling defeated. Maybe she never would fit in, maybe she never would be a proper girl. The laughter seemed to grow louder and louder. April opened her eyes, fixed them on the front door of the school and found she still had some pride, even if it had taken a beating. Head high, she started moving, past the class to the front door of the school. Let them laugh and get a good look, April told herself she didn't care.

When someone moved to walk with her, it was unexpected. April glanced sideways and found Raina by her side. Raina wasn't laughing. "Ignore them," she said simply. Together they passed through the front door. "April, are you hurt? That rock must have really hurt." Raina tried to check her shoulder.

"It hurt, but I'm okay," April said.

"But you almost weren't. The rock nearly landed on your head, it could have killed you!" Raina seemed deeply distressed, then April found out why. "It was my rock that hit you. Mine. I almost killed you. Me!"

April welcomed the show of concern, it meant Raina still cared about her. "It's okay Raina, it was an accident. Please don't feel bad."

"But I do feel bad, and not just about the rock." Raina bit her lip and surveyed April from head to toe. "What happened to you?"

"Scavenger hunt, Cherry was my partner," April said shortly.

"Oh no. Bad luck."

"Yes."

"April, I'm really sorry, about ... how I've been acting," Raina apologized, as if she couldn't wait to get the words out.

It was time for April to confess her own crime and clear the air between them. "Raina, I have to tell you something. I ... lied about Skylar asking me on a date. He really wanted me to ask you - "

"I know, he left a note on my window ledge last night - an invitation."

"He did? So you know ...?"

Raina nodded.

April flushed with disgrace. "I should never have lied, especially to you. I kind of thought that the girls - and you ... would like me more if I was dating too, dating Skylar."

"Oh April," Raina said rather lamely. She peeked into Mrs. Merry-Helen's class. It was empty. She motioned April inside, then said something unexpected. "That's actually a good idea. You should let the other girls keep thinking that you are dating the Prince, they were very impressed. We won't tell them any different."

"We won't?" April asked uncertainly.

"No! Skylar is cute and nice, and the Prince and everything! Lots of girls want to date him, most girls. So let them be impressed that you're dating him."

"Are you sure?"

"I'm sure." Raina did seem sure. "And if everyone thinks you're dating Skylar, Airron will stop being mad at me. It helps me out, too." Raina wrinkled her nose, looking a bit guilty.

That reminded April of something else she had to tell Raina. "Oh, and Airron was only trying to make you - "

"I know, he told me he was trying to make me jealous. I should have realized ... I only got so upset because I don't know what to do, about Airron and Skylar. And that's not your fault, that's me. I guess it was easier to blame someone else for my troubles, and I blamed you. I'm sorry April."

"Is that all it was? You seemed kind of fed up with me before the situation with Skylar and Airron got worse." It seemed the best moment to bring this up, since they were having a heart-to-heart talk.

Raina's eyes dropped to study the floor. "I guess I was maybe sort of embarrassed before."

"Embarrassed?"

"Lots of the girls were making fun of you, because you don't dress properly, or fix your hair, and sometimes you say or do childish things – stuff like that."

"Oh. I get it." April didn't need to know more. She rather wished Raina hadn't explained. "So you were embarrassed to be my friend?"

"No! Not really. Well, maybe a bit, but it was more than that. I don't know what to do about Airron and Skylar. I like them both, so I wanted to talk to some of the girls about ... about dating, and other girl stuff."

"I'm a girl." April sounded more like a little girl when she said that.

"But you don't know about this stuff," Raina stressed. April couldn't disagree. "And I was mad at you about Skylar and then Airron, but only because I was already confused, and that made me unhappy and grumpy, and I kind of took it out on you. And even if Skylar had asked you on a date, you have every right to accept. You had no reason not to date him," Raina stressed.

"Well, he would never ask me, so it really doesn't matter."

"But I should have defended you, like a friend, instead of being ashamed and avoiding you. That was a mean thing to do. Can you forgive me? Can we still be friends?" Raina sounded as upset as April felt inside lately.

There was no denying that Raina's words had hurt, but April could understand how her friend felt. She knew that she didn't fit in sometimes. She still had a lot of catching up to do after missing five years of growing up. She privately vowed to make more of an effort to be like the other girls and said, "Of course. We're always friends, aren't we?" April needed the reassurance.

"Always, I've missed you," Raina confirmed.

"I've missed you, too," April said.

"But I'm not going to hug you right now."

"That's okay, I wouldn't hug me either." That was all the words it took to fix things. "I have to check in with Ms. Summers before I can go home and clean up."

"You have looked better. I'll come with you."

Raina accompanied her right to the pixie class. April was the last elf to walk in, Cherry was already at her table, her face set in dissatisfied lines. They hadn't won, they had lost. Peter and Violet had won, Ms. Summers was congratulating them.

Everyone stared when April stepped through the door, then the class burst into laughter. Even the teacher hid behind her hand, her eyes crinkled and watery. It was funny how the laughter didn't sound mocking and cruel anymore. Now that Raina was her friend again, the whole situation seemed comical. April smiled too, because she couldn't help it. Good humour was something to be shared, even if it was at her expense.

"Can I leave?" she asked, as soon as everyone stopped laughing. The gong was about to sound anyway.

"Yes, in a moment. But this opportunity is too good to pass up." The teacher crooked a finger. April walked to the front of the room where she was used for a quick lesson in the mishandling of dangerous plants.

Ms. Summers pointed to the red patches. "Mayflower." She removed a seed attached to fluff and held it up. "Touch-me-not." One finger traced up April's arm, collecting a sample of slime. "Pond scum?"

April nodded ruefully. "Getting the water lily sample," she explained.

Ms. Summers plugged her nose. "Pokeweed and poison ivy." She indicated the knee rash that April was scratching. "Anything else?" she checked.

April didn't mention the vomiting and she kept her sore tongue hidden, but she held up her palm.

"Ah, bloodroot. Nasty plant. That will need treatment. Thank goodness there is no Jimson weed on you. Thank-you April, you may go now. If we do this again, please review your notes more thoroughly."

"I will."

April left with Raina, who made a quick stop to retrieve her pack and tell Ms. Myrrh that she was leaving. She had a quiet word with Heather and Willowna, then hurried April away.

April was happy to be hurried, she wanted to be as far from the building as possible when the gong released the rest of the students, the ones who hadn't already gotten an eyeful of April's new look.

While they walked, Raina talked as if they had never had a fight at all, as if they were still best friends.

She shared something DewDrop had revealed to her, something she had been wanting to talk to April about. "This is weird, DewDrop said she saw Peter leaving our house that day the vial reappeared."

"Elder Scarab said he saw Peter at your house the day the vial disappeared. But I don't think Peter would have removed the vial, although ..." April stopped walking when two separate pieces of information suddenly fit together. "I had the vial really well hidden where no one could find it – except Peter, who can sense gold!"

"Peter can sense gold anywhere," Raina said significantly.

"Peter," April echoed. She didn't want to believe he had snuck into her room and taken the vial.

"But why would he take it? Why wouldn't he ask you if he wanted to see it? You would have given it to him," Raina said.

"Without question," April agreed, recalling that Peter had told her she should search her room again, for the vial.

"We'll have to ask him if he had it," Raina said decisively.

April nodded. "Yes, he'll tell us. If he took it, he must have had a good reason." She had no doubt. Happy to be friends with Raina again, she decided not to worry about it until she got answers from Peter.

The two girls talked and laughed all the rest of the way home, and it was Friday! April ran straight into the waterfall before she stank up the house and got slime everywhere. By the time the rest of the family arrived home, April looked almost like her old self. Almost but not quite.

Mr. Poole took one look at her when he sat down to dinner and stood back up, motioning for her to follow. April did, silently. He brought his medical sack into the sitting room. She sank into a squishy cushion and he took the one beside her, rooting around in his sack. He pulled out a vial of white cream and handed it over. "For the red patches." He added a second vial. "For the poison ivy. Anything else?" April extended her hand. He examined it closely. "Bloodroot?" he checked.

"Yes."

"That must be painful. It is slow to heal, I'm afraid." He searched for a different cream and applied it himself, then wrapped a strip of cloth slowly and carefully around the burn with gentle hands. When he was finished, he leaned back on his cushion. "Anything else?"

The rest of her injuries would heal with time. April said, "No, my hand feels better already. My thanks."

He didn't move, he looked into April's eyes gravely. "April," he began, then stopped.

"Yes?" April hoped she wasn't in trouble again, she knew she had made thunder at least once this afternoon.

"April, I was out of line the other day and I took it out on you. Lost my temper, hadn't had a lot of sleep." He smiled self-depreciatingly. "I overreacted to your absence because I was very worried. You are part of this family and I do think of you as a daughter. I should have verified that you were not at school before sending elves to search for you. I accused you of not thinking about the consequences of your actions, but I am guilty of the same thing, in a different way. I overreacted because I assumed that you were missing and then ... well, I felt very foolish for sending so many elves out to search. Very embarrassed - and you bore the brunt of that. I fear I said some hurtful things, I am sorry," he apologized solemnly. "Even adults aren't perfect, you know. Even adults make mistakes."

"No." April didn't want him to take the blame. None of this was his fault. "I do a lot of things wrong, almost everything sometimes. It was me, not thinking. I'm sorry for causing so much trouble. I'll be more careful, I promise."

Mr. Poole leaned forward to take her undamaged hand in his. "I know you will. We all mess up, at times. It doesn't mean our family stops caring about us," he emphasized. "Families are forever, for better or for worse. Understand?"

April nodded, her throat too tight to release words.

"Good. Now, let's go and eat dinner." He pulled her under his arm and steered her back to the kitchen.

April sat down to eat, absolutely starving. It had been both the best day and the worst day, but it had ended up the best day. And it was Friday! Maybe Raina would come for a sleepover.

As it turned out, April slept over in Raina's room while Raina fussed over what they should wear to the King's Keep the following night. April had all but forgotten about the invitation. But now that Raina was coming with her, April was looking forward to it - except for the flying. April was dreading that. Maybe Skylar would be willing to postpone the lesson. She could ask him or beg him. He was sure to agree.

As much as April wanted to take the vial outside of New Haven, it didn't look like it would happen this weekend.

4 – To Fly or Not To Fly

Raina popped into April's room and asked, "Ready to go?" She looked great, her hair was shiny with small flowers woven above one ear. Her dress was the lightest pink silk and short. And she smelled great, like roses.

"Wow." April raised her eyebrows. "No wonder Airron and Skylar are fighting over you."

Raina flushed and tried not to look too pleased. "So I look okay?"

"You look a lot more than okay."

"But you're wearing overalls," Raina decried, as if April didn't know what she had put on.

"Only because I have to try flying. I can't do that in a dress."

"Oh, right. That wouldn't be good. Are you bringing a dress? For after?"

"Yes, the one you picked out. It's in the sack." April pointed.

"But it will get all wrinkled. April, you should wear the dress to the Keep, change into overalls before you fly, then change back into the dress."

"But I'm only walking to the Keep."

"April, everyone knows that you have a big date with the Prince tonight, I told Heather and Willowna and you can bet they'll tell everyone! So put on a dress and be quick about it." Raina was getting bossy.

April hauled the dress out of the pack and did as she was told, Raina added flowers to April's hair and dabbed flower perfume on her neck. Only then did she nod her approval to proceed downstairs. Salm raised his eyebrows when they walked into the kitchen. "Nice," he commented. April wasn't sure if she was included in the compliment since Raina was so much prettier.

Mr. Poole, on the other hand, frowned at Raina's attire and glanced at his wife. "Isn't that dress a little short?"

Mrs. Poole shrugged and handed him a steaming cup of tea. It was Saturday, they were relaxing.

Salm looked good himself, fancier than usual. "Let's go!" He jumped up as if he had been waiting for them.

"Are you going, Salm?" April was unaware that he'd been invited.

"Yup. Can't wait. I've never been inside the King's Keep."

"We've also been invited, we will walk over later for the dinner," Mrs. Poole mentioned. The gathering was growing bigger and bigger.

"You'll miss April's flying lesson. I can't wait to see your wings again. Are you going to fly in that?" Salm arched an eyebrow at her dress, a teasing grin on his face.

"No! I'm bringing overalls, in case I do try flying." She patted the sack.

Mr. Poole frowned again. "April, perhaps you should postpone the flying lesson. You had a rough day yesterday. And are you absolutely certain that your wings will appear again?" It was nice that he was worried about her.

"I'm positive. But I might not fly today, I don't really feel like it." In truth, she would never feel like it.

"You can decide when you get there. Come on!" Raina prompted.

The afternoon was warm and sunny, as always. The elves that they passed weren't hurrying anywhere. Saturdays weren't for rushing around, that's what school days were for and there were more than enough of those.

When they passed through the town square, a few of their classmates were relaxing around the fountain, including Heather and Willowna. April felt their scrutiny, and was suddenly glad that Raina had insisted she dress up. The girls rushed over and gushed excitedly about April's date with the Prince. April didn't correct their wrong impression and Raina made a point of reinforcing it. Salm held his silence with a suspicious expression.

Saying that they couldn't be late, Raina didn't let them linger.

As soon as they were out of the square, Salm said, "What was that all about?"

"We're improving April's image," Raina said pertly.

"Her image is fine," Salm countered.

Raina looked at him pityingly. "You're a boy, you wouldn't understand."

"I understand more than you realize," Salm alluded, darkly.

Raina flushed and held her tongue.

The guards nodded them through to the King's Keep, since they were expected. And Skylar was waiting. "Greetings, Raina. You look lovely, well worth the wait. It is wonderful to have you all to myself for a change." April and Salm must have been invisible. Or he meant without Airron – that was probably it. "Let us start with a tour of the Keep, I'll show you my room, then we can have some refreshments before the flying lesson." Skylar tucked Raina's arm eagerly through his.

"About that," April began.

"We will discuss it over refreshments." Skylar cut her off. April did feel invisible.

Salm winked and they trailed through the Keep for the impromptu tour. The King's residence was even bigger than it looked from the outside and each room was as elaborate and perfect as the one before. The dominant colours were red and gold, of course, in every single room. Skylar ended the tour prematurely when they reached his bedroom, stating that once you had seen half the Keep, you had seen all the Keep.

Skylar's room suited his important position. Everything was larger than life, red and gold and fancy. He had enough robes to clothe an entire classroom of elves, all hanging perfectly straight and evenly spaced in a closet that was spacious enough to masquerade as a room.

"Great bedroom," Raina commented. "Very luxurious."

April crossed to peer out the window. They were ridiculously high up on the prominent hill with a clear view of the town square nestled below, and beyond that, at least a mile of rolling hills. As Skylar had once mentioned, his window had bars for his own protection but he pried them opened whenever he wanted to sneak away. April leaned closer. Yes, there were deep indentations from repeated prying around the base of two bars. April pointed to the marks and Salm chuckled.

"Lots of escaping from your room, Skylar?" Salm asked.

"Enough. More so in the past. My father grants me greater freedom now and employs O'Wing to keep an eye on me. Come, the cook will have a small feast ready for us."

They settled outside on a wide balcony rimmed with flowering vines; several golden platters of snacks were waiting. They were fancy concoctions, more like cocktails. It was to be expected if the King had an elf that did nothing but cook.

The four friends lounged around on the patio, nibbling and talking. April felt happy and relaxed after the lonely week that preceded this day. They stayed there so long that April began to hope that Skylar had forgotten all about the flying. He did seem preoccupied by Raina's conversation.

When the King appeared, Raina and Salm leapt to their feet as if their pillows had caught on fire. Everyone bowed, except Skylar.

"Greetings. You may rise." King Skylar motioned them up. Skylar introduced Salm and Raina, although the King had met Raina on several occasions in the past.

"I have come to watch the flying lesson. I am most eager to see these magical wings of yours, April. Skylar tells me they are quite something." The King sat right down and joined them. "This balcony will provide an ideal view if you start from the highest tower. So I will sit right here and watch, with Raina and Salm. Head-Elder Falcon and Elder Scarab should be along directly, as well as a few other guests. Many elves have expressed an interest in the spectacle." The King reached across Salm to snag a bite of truffle, his elaborate crown flashing in the sunlight. April wasn't sure she liked being called a spectacle.

"I guess we should get started then. It is a long walk up the tower, unless you would prefer me to fly you to the platform." Skylar motioned to a jutting turret which loomed high over everything in sight.

April swallowed hard when her stomach performed a series of somersaults. "No, no, that's okay," she stammered.

"We will have to walk up then. April, are you ready?" Skylar extended a hand and tugged when she didn't move.

"As ready as I'll ever be," she said, which meant 'no'. But April allowed him to pull her into a standing position. The King and possibly a small audience would be turning up to see her magical wings. She couldn't refuse without a good reason. Paralyzing fear wasn't a good enough reason, was it?

April looked way, way up at the highest tower of the King's Keep. It had to be the highest elf-made site in all of New Haven. April stopped looking up when she tilted over, too dizzy to stay properly upright. She definitely shouldn't have sampled so many of the refreshments.

"April?" Skylar was waiting.

"Coming." If she could get her feet to move. It was almost as if they were under a standing-still spell, but they weren't. "I have to change," she remembered.

"You can do that on the way. You have something to change into?" Skylar prompted when she continued to stand dumbly.

"She does." Raina pushed the pack into her arms. "Bye April. Have fun and do a diving somersault just for me."

"Diving somersault?" April swallowed hard and allowed Skylar to guide her off the balcony. She changed in a handy room on the way to the tower, and then they climbed up, up, up.

"We only have to do this once," Skylar reminded her in the middle of the endless spiraling staircase. He could have flown to the top in no time, it was thoughtful of him to walk and keep her company. Then again, if she had been alone, she definitely would have run away. They kept climbing.

"Ah, here we are. Isn't this exciting?" Skylar stepped out onto the ridiculously high balcony. He unbuttoned his robe before he moved to the edge. The railings around the wide, circular platform were low and spindly, they looked useless to stop an elf from plunging to their death. April stayed against the tower wall, her head spinning.

"Do I look all right? Do I look ... strong?" Skylar asked, almost preening.

"What?" April gulped. Her ears were filled with a rushing sound, it was hard to hear Skylar's voice.

"Do I look all right? Strong?" he repeated, louder.

"I guess," April looked him over, it was better than looking down. "You look ...fine. Why?"

"*Fine*? That is all you can say? And hesitantly, at that?" He might have 'harrumphed'. "Raina will be watching me fly. I want to look impressive," he explained curtly.

"Oh. But she's seen you fly before. She knows what you look like," April pointed out. Skylar was acting weird. He scowled and moved April toward the railing as if he was considering the benefits of tossing her off the platform.

"Sometimes I need to be reminded that you are unaware of certain aspects of elvan life. Sometimes I forget that you spent five years alone," Skylar said, but not unkindly. "Now, are you ready?"

"No. I'll never be ready for this. And I have to tie my overall straps around my neck, don't I? Or my wings will be trapped."

"True, turn around." Skylar rearranged her straps. "There. That will work. You shouldn't lose your clothes in midair. Now, I think it is best if I go first, catch you if necessary."

"Skylar, I *really* don't want to fly," April choked out, now that the moment was upon her.

He did not heed her words. "You'll be fine once you test the air. Follow me." Skylar stood taller and stepped off the balcony where there was an open space between the frail railings. He lifted his arms and soared away in a slow circle, staying even with the platform. "Come on April, jump. I mean fly."

April stepped up to the edge of the platform and peeked down. If Skylar had told her to stick her head into a snake's mouth, it would have been an easier thing to do than jump off this platform. April swayed and stumbled back, shaking her head to clear it. Wings or no wings, King or no King, she couldn't do it. She was not that brave.

"I can't Skylar, I really can't," she cried.

The choice was taken away from her. O'Wing came out of nowhere, swooped over the platform and scooped her up.

"O'Wing, what do you think you're doing? Put me down." He didn't, he carried her higher. "Put me down, please," April begged.

"Are you sure?"

"Yes, I'm sure!"

"As you wish." O'Wing did put her down then, but not in the way she wanted. He dropped her out of the sky.

Too petrified to scream, April slammed her eyes closed and

plummeted until she felt something pressing against her shoulders. Wings.

"April, open your arms, damn it!" O'Wing sounded frantic. April stiffly lifted her arms as if they were two sticks and heard a whoosh of air. She slowed down and opened her eyes. She had almost hit the ground.

"Flap," Skylar instructed from beside her, he looked white. April moved her arms weakly.

"Not like that. Harder, faster, bigger," O'Wing shouted. April tried to do all those things, she spun sideways and lurched down instead of up.

"Both arms exactly the same, move them in unison. You should know how to do this instinctively," Skylar said from her other side. The boys had moved to flank her.

"Well I don't. I never wanted to fly, elves from my world aren't supposed to fly," April retorted, but she moved both arms exactly the same and she went a little higher and breathed a little easier. It was her first breath in ages.

"Better. Try and follow me left then right. Steer with your arms, tilt one then the other. You'll see what happens." It was O'Wing again, he had taken over the flying lesson.

April did as she was instructed and followed O'Wing, swooping left then right. She actually did a pretty good job. She could steer herself like a bird. "Now a circle, one direction then the other. We'll do a figure eight, follow me."

April followed O'Wing, lurching in both directions.

"Great! You're getting the hang of it. Fly up to Skylar now. I'll stay below. Arch your back and lift your arms while you flap. More arch, more flap, a little bend in the elbow." It took a lot of effort to fly up to Skylar. April's shoulder muscles were not used to the strain and the bruised one was making itself felt, but she reached him.

"Wonderful," Skylar congratulated her. "Follow me around now." April did, and he glided closer to the balcony to wave. More elves were sitting beside the King. Head-Elder Falcon and Elder Scarab had arrived, and there was a crowd of faces that April couldn't identify. She didn't try waving, she would have lost control. She followed Skylar around the tower and over the royal flower gardens and back over the balcony again.

"Are you having fun yet?" Skylar asked, flashing his dimples.

"No," April said honestly.

"Raina asked a favour of me. O'Wing, get lost. April, take my hand." Skylar extended his.

"Not while we're flying! We'll crash."

"Of course we won't. Our arms will still be free for flying." Skylar glided closer and took her hand in his. "See. Now stay with me."

Joined in flight, Skylar banked them toward the town square. April had no choice but to go along, gliding by his side. Far below, another audience of elves was watching. Most of April's class, it seemed. Had they come to see her magical wings? Or her supposed date with the Prince? April had no doubt that Raina had orchestrated this.

Elves waved and shouted. April felt like a fraud. "Skylar, why are you doing this?"

"Raina said the girls at school were teasing you, she said they would be impressed if they saw us together. They do seem impressed." Skylar tugged April close enough that they almost collided. "Had enough?"

"Yes." Her arms and shoulders were cramping. "My muscles aren't used to this."

"Okay. I'll demonstrate how to land. It's the hardest part." Skylar released her hand and angled back toward the Keep, soaring lower. "Now, follow me down." Skylar flashed by on his way toward the ground in a showy, twisting spiral. It was for Raina's benefit.

April descended, but without the fancy moves. She opened her arms wider and peeked backwards to see her wings. They looked the same as the last time she had seen them – rainbow-coloured and shimmering with brilliant magical light. They really were fabulous wings. They were definitely her best feature.

Feeling giddy, April descended in a circular pattern, trailing Skylar. When he neared the ground, he lifted his arms slightly and bent them at the elbow. He touched down as gently as a butterfly.

April tried to copy his movements, the lifting and bending and landing like a butterfly. She made it to the ground without crashing, but she felt more like a clumsy, three-legged toad.

O'Wing floated down beside her, as gracefully as an autumn leaf settling to the ground on a still day. He made it look easy, too. "That was great, April. Super!" O'Wing looked proud of her.

"Really? The landing needs work, but it went okay, didn't it?" April smiled at O'Wing until she remembered how the lesson had started. "Hey, wait – you dropped me! That wasn't fair!"

O'Wing had the grace to blush. "I did drop you. It wasn't really fair. Skylar thought you might back out and asked me to stand by. You can blame him."

"Yes, you can blame me," Skylar agreed willingly. "It was not fair at all, but I did so want you to experience flying. I knew you would love it once you got into the air. Will you forgive me?" He was too charming and cute for his own good.

"I'll think about it," she said grudgingly, but she wasn't really mad. "And I didn't love it," she said to be clear.

Skylar laughed and hugged her as if she was his little sister. April was simply glad that the whole ordeal was over. And there was a wonderful feast to look forward to, once her stomach settled back into its proper place.

"April, your wings are gone already. Amazing." Skylar turned her around and stared intently at her back. "How does that work? There isn't even a mark, well, maybe a faint line here, but it is hard to see." He traced across the top of her shoulder and down her arm. "They truly are magical wings, aren't they?"

"Wish mine could disappear when I wasn't using them," O'Wing said. "They get in the way sometimes."

Skylar nodded in agreement. "Don't they? Come, we should join my father and his guests. We can change and freshen up for this evening a bit later." Since both boys were bare-chested, they would have to dress before the banquet. Apparently O'Wing had also been invited to the gathering.

On the large balcony, the King was waiting with his audience. When April appeared, he clapped his hands together in delight, as if she had provided special entertainment. Everyone did, it was embarrassing.

"April, my dear, your wings are beyond description. I have never seen a lovelier pair. And to appear and disappear, it is truly miraculous. You flew very well for a first time." The King beamed down at her as if she was truly special.

"My thanks." April looked shyly around the table. Head-Elder Falcon and Elder Scarab nodded their greetings. She could identify faces now. Some she knew, some she didn't. Everything was a bit of a blur under the bright sun.

"Great wings, need to work on that landing," Elder Scarab muttered, high praise from him.

"At least it wasn't crashing." April sank onto a cushion, her legs barely supporting her now. She didn't move from her seat until the sun brushed the tops of the trees and King Skylar decreed it was time to move the evening along.

"Skylar, you may show April to the guest room. The pink one I think, so she may prepare herself for dinner," the King said.

April had forgotten that she was still in her overalls.

"I'll go and freshen up, too," Raina said, even though she already looked as fresh and perfect as a budding rose.

There really was a pink room with not a speck of red, but enough gold to remind them they were still in the Keep. Even the ever-flowing water basin looked like solid gold, inlaid with a pattern of sparkling crystals.

Skylar left them alone and April fell onto a puffy pink cushion. "Am I ever glad that's over," she told Raina, heartfelt. "Did you arrange for the class to see me flying with Skylar?"

"Not really. I simply mentioned it to a few of the girls, you know how news travels," Raina said with a twinkle in her eye.

"It certainly did this time," April said.

"Good." Raina was smugly pleased with herself. "Wasn't the flying fun? It did look fun, and everyone got to see your great wings. I would love to be able to fly," she said enviously.

"I guess it wasn't as bad as I thought it would be. Flying might be fun, if it wasn't so high up. I wish I could give you my wings, I don't think I'll ever use them again." April leaned her head into the soft pillow, yawning widely.

"I wish you could give me your wings too, then I could date any fairy I wanted." Raina's voice was light, but her words were revealing. With a valiant smile she added, "And you better keep your wings, you might need them someday, you never know. Time to get up and get dressed, the evening is only beginning."

"No time for a nap?"

"No time for a nap." Raina urged April to her feet and handed over her dress. Pre-flight, it had been stuffed haphazardly in the pack and was thoroughly wrinkled now. In spite of her private vow to be more presentable, April didn't seem to be managing it. Raina fussed, trying to smooth the material with a damp cloth. April's blue dress was getting all wet.

"Raina, my clothes are fine, better than usual. Please don't worry. Let's have fun tonight. I've got the flying lesson over with, now I can relax. And the food will be great. Forget about wrinkles," April pleaded.

"Oh, I guess. King Skylar was so impressed with your wings that he probably won't notice a few wrinkles. He couldn't stop raving about them. You're lucky he's not a lot younger, he would probably want to marry you for your wings." Raina picked up a golden comb and handed it to April, pointing at the mirror. April took a look, her hair had gotten awfully knotted from flying. She tugged the worst of the tangles from the end of her braid, then announced that she was ready. Her damaged hand hurt too much to do more, and her shoulders felt like grape jelly.

"April, we're at the King's Keep," Raina chided and claimed the comb. She took over and undid the braid. "You'll wear your hair loose tonight."

"I will?" April sat resigned, until it felt like Raina had tortured every single strand of hair on her head and it was a cloud of hair. Only then was Raina satisfied. When a melodious gong sounded, April thought she was back in school.

"Oh, dinner's ready," Raina said. "We better go."

Once downstairs, they were escorted to the dining room and found even more elves in attendance than when they had left. O'Wing was seated beside a girl of his own age that April had never met. And Head-Elder Falcon was partnered with Elder Rose. She had lots of white hair piled up on her head, and wore a robe, even though she wasn't a fairy. She probably wore the robe because she was an Elder. It seemed to be the uniform for the position, at least on special occasions. The Pooles were comfortably installed near the King, on his right side. At the farthest end of the table sat several important looking elves that April recognized as members of the High Court, but she didn't know their names.

"Skylar, April, you may sit here." The King indicated two adjacent cushions on his left side. He had partnered them together. Skylar assisted April to sit as if she needed help. Raina was seated beside her brother and she didn't look thrilled with the arrangement, but she wasn't about to complain, not in front of the King.

The elaborate food was almost too good, it was hard to stop eating. After the last course had been cleared, the King indulgently excused the youngest elves. They bowed and thanked him for his hospitality before they escaped to walk around and stretch their legs.

"The flower gardens," Skylar said, taking Raina's hand and leading the way. Salm and April followed, with O'Wing and his date, Jay. Skylar must have planned to end the evening in the picturesque setting because fireflies were already lighting the area, feasting on golden shells of nectar. Enormous blossoms crowded both sides of the meandering path.

Skylar stopped beside a cluster of trumpet-shaped white flowers. Moon flowers. Unlike normal blossoms, these opened up at night and closed during the day. Skylar lifted Raina inside the largest flower before he climbed in to join her. "Salm, make yourself useful. Give us a push and then get lost." It did sound like a royal command. Salm took hold of the strong stem, straining to push and pull until the blossom was swaying gently back and forth. Skylar and Raina looked too cozy together inside the flower.

Salm took April's arm and they strolled further along the path. O'Wing and Jay stopped to sit beside a trickling fountain as if they were alone. April glanced back at the gently swinging white blossom with a tight feeling inside. She thought it had to do with Airron. He would be very upset if he could be a fly in the flower garden right now. He would be hurt, April could almost feel the emotion for him.

"April?" Salm was watching her, following her troubled gaze. "Raina has to decide for herself."

"I thought there was no decision, with Skylar being the Prince. Raina doesn't have wings."

"There isn't a decision, but there is." Salm might as well have said nothing.

"Are you going to explain that?"

"I can try. Even if Raina can't date Skylar, she still has to want to be with Airron more than she wants to be with Skylar," Salm explained softly.

April frowned and thought about that. It did make a kind of sense. "True to your heart," she murmured. Raina would not be happy and Airron would not be happy otherwise.

"Yes, that's it. Couldn't have said it better myself."

"But someone is going to get hurt." And April was scared it was going to be Airron. She didn't want him to get hurt.

"Someone will probably get hurt," Salm confirmed. "But they'll get over it. I don't think anyone can grow up without getting hurt at some point, in some way. That's part of growing up, isn't it?"

"Oh. Well, I'm not ready to grow up then," April declared. She'd had enough hurt in the Outer-world to last a lifetime.

"I think you are already grown up, in the ways that count," Salm said seriously. April might have debated the point but the night was too lovely. And she didn't mind Salm thinking she was grown up.

The flowers filled the air with lovely scents and the fountain provided a background of musical tinkling. The sky was overflowing with stars, and the gentle breeze was as warm as the softest downy blanket. April slowed her steps and looked back along the path. O'Wing and Jay were very close together. They were ... kissing, on the lips! April gasped softly and swung back around, she shouldn't be spying. The moment was private. She pressed her hands against her hot cheeks in embarrassment. Salm was watching her again and he was having a hard time controlling himself.

"It's not funny," April hissed.

"Yes, it is," he chuckled, his eyes dancing with mirth. "April, it's just a kiss. Nothing to panic about."

"But ... but I've never seen two elves kiss – quite like that! Right on the lips and ... and ... they look like they're stuck together! I almost kissed once, with Figgy that time, but we didn't. Oh no, what if Skylar and Raina ...? We should go back." April swung around to retrace her steps. Except O'Wing and Jay were still kissing. She covered her eyes and turned back to Salm. "Oh no, what should we do?"

It was the last blade of grass. Salm burst into laughter. She'd never seen him do that. He laughed so hard and long that he had to lie down on the moss. "Salm, stop that! It's not funny," April insisted. He didn't agree, he laughed even harder.

He completely wrecked the romantic mood in the flower garden. Raina and Skylar wandered up to see what was going on, even O'Wing and Jay unlocked their lips to investigate.

"What's wrong with Salm?" Raina asked. April peered closely at her friend's lips. It didn't look like they had been kissed. Raina's lips looked completely normal.

April smiled in relief and shrugged. "I can't really say." And she couldn't. She would die of embarrassment if she tried to explain about the kissing. Salm eventually gained control of himself. He struggled to his feet, dusted himself off and the six elves finished walking around the flower gardens together. Then Skylar called for the mouse cart and drove them all home, they took the long way.

As soon as they arrived at the Pooles' house, Salm hustled April inside, leaving Raina alone with Skylar again. "But Salm ..." April protested, trying to dig in her heels.

"It is Raina's decision," he reminded her. "Let her make it." He was probably right, he knew more about this stuff, but April didn't have to like it. "Want a snack?" Salm asked.

"Are you kidding? I'll never be hungry again after that meal." But

April trailed him into the kitchen, to wait for Raina. Her friend took all too long to come inside and when she did, Raina made a beeline for her own room and shut the door, a clear signal that she wanted to be left alone. As tempted as she was to invite herself into Raina's room, April respected her friend's desire for privacy.

April and Raina slept late and shared a leisurely breakfast. Afterwards, they walked outside to lie in the sand and bask under the sun. April was bursting with questions about what had happened with Skylar and couldn't wait to talk to Raina alone. She didn't have a chance to ask even one question before Airron and Peter turned up.

One look at Airron's face was all it took to know that he was in a foul mood. He lowered himself to the ground so stiffly, he might have been a tree branch.

"Hey," Peter greeted them. Even he looked uncomfortable.

"Hi, did you have a good weekend?" April asked, when Raina didn't say a word.

"It was okay. Got all my homework caught up. Not very exciting," Peter replied.

"I haven't even started mine. Do we have a lot?" April said.

"We have enough."

"Oh. Friday was a disaster," she recalled all too clearly. "Except you won the scavenger hunt, with Violet. Congratulations!" April hadn't had a chance to tell him that yet.

"Thanks. Violet was a really good partner, she remembered everything about the plants, and I was able to find them all. We made a good team." Peter kept talking when both Raina and Airron held their silence. April wanted to ask Peter about the vial, but it didn't seem the right moment.

"I'm really glad you won," April said instead. "I think Cherry and I came in last."

"Well, you look like you've recovered ... from Friday," he said. "I'm glad you're okay. I can't believe you got partnered with Cherry. Talk about rotten luck. Was it horrible?"

"It could have been worse, I suppose. She didn't try to kill me outright, although there was some minor poisoning. I didn't know the plants and she wasn't much help ... well, you saw. Everyone saw." April pulled a face. They had almost run out of things to say when Airron burst into speech.

"So, how was Saturday night? At the Keep? Raina, did you enjoy yourself?" His tone was accusing, almost as if he knew that Raina had been the one with Skylar, not April. News did travel around New Haven in the most unexpected ways.

"It was nice," Raina allowed vaguely.

"Nice?" Airron made the word sound like a curse.

"Yes."

"Yes? What do you mean – yes?"

"Yes, it was nice," Raina stated more confidently. "April flew ..."

"I don't want to hear about April flying. You know what I want to hear about. I want to hear the truth – about you and Skylar!" Airron was starting to shout. Shouting always seemed to be contagious. "I want to hear the truth about what I saw when I flew by on Saturday night."

Raina gasped in indignation. "You were spying on me?"

"I was not spying! You and Skylar were in plain sight, cuddling in his carriage," Airron bellowed back. "Is that what was so nice about the night? Tell me about that!"

"Well ... well maybe I don't want to talk to you when you're yelling at me. Maybe what I do with Skylar is none of your business," Raina shouted back. The words were harsh.

Airron blanched. "None of my business? I thought I was your boyfriend but if you're sneaking around kissing with Skylar, I guess that says it all. Answers my question, doesn't it. Good-bye Raina," Airron said with an unmistakable finality. He looked more hurt than mad when he turned his back and walked away.

Peter was too good of a friend to let him go alone. "See you tomorrow," he mumbled and caught up with Airron at the edge of the undergrowth.

"Raina?" April said uncertainly.

Raina burst into tears and ran into the lake. She dove under the water and didn't come up again. April didn't follow. It was impossible to talk underwater and it was clear that Raina wanted to be alone. She could cry her heart out in the lake and no one would hear a sound. April only wished she knew why Raina was crying, she had been the one to hurt Airron.

April went inside and retrieved her school pack from her room. She sat on the shore and finished all her Environment Studies homework, and even some of her math before Raina waded back out, dripping wet and hiccupping.

April shoved her work aside and handed over a sun-warmed towel. "Would you feel better if you talked about it?"

Raina sniffed and dried her face. "I can't decide," she blubbered, fresh tears wetting her cheeks.

"Decide? If you should talk about it? Or between Airron and Skylar?" April guessed, at a bit of a loss. She wasn't good at this stuff.

"Between Airron and Skylar. I like them both, a lot. And when I thought Skylar wanted to date you, it made me want to date him even more. It's funny how we always want things more when we think we can't have them." It didn't sound funny to April. Raina bit her lip and confided, "Skylar told me ... he said that he didn't need to follow tradition. He said he would date me no matter what his father thought. Skylar said the tradition of arranged marriages and only dating other fairies was old-fashioned and stupid and it was time to ... time to change it," Raina sobbed. "He's willing to do that for *me*! Can you believe it?"

"Yes." April could believe Skylar would do that for Raina.

"Last night, I thought if I kissed Skylar, that I would know. And I kissed him," Raina confessed, meeting April's eyes and looking deeply tragic. "And Airron saw."

"But Raina, it was just a kiss," April tried, using Salm's words.

"A kiss says a lot, a lot that words can't. Skylar's kiss was supposed to decide for me, decide who I wanted to date, but it didn't help at all. It only made things worse. Kissing Skylar was wonderful. As good as kissing Airron, I think. Now I don't know what to do." Raina literally wrung her hands. "Not knowing what to do is the worst thing." She flopped back in the sand and closed her eyes. She was all cried out and exhausted.

April remembered what Mrs. Poole had said about young elves experiencing emotional turmoil and it being normal. It might be normal but it also looked painful. April wished she knew what to say, she wished that she had some good advice to help Raina, but wishing didn't make it so.

"I'm sorry, Raina. I'm sorry you're sad. I'm sure you'll know soon, I'm sure you'll figure it out. There must be some way." As far as advice went, it was pretty lame.

Raina must have thought so too, but seemed to appreciate April's effort. She nodded and made a visible attempt to pull herself together. "I have homework, don't I?"

"You can copy mine, I'm finished some of it," April offered. At least she could help that way.

"Umm, that's okay. I need something to keep my mind off ... you know. I'll do it myself. And I have to think about my marks." Raina always got higher marks than April.

Raina walked slowly into the house looking lost and forlorn. April stayed where she was, deeply disappointed in how the weekend had turned out. After she and Raina had sorted out their own problem, April had assumed that everything would be fine – back to normal. But it wasn't.

With a heavy sigh, April went for a swim in the lake. Chasing fish was a great way to wash all the troubled thoughts out of her head.

The situation didn't improve on Monday. At school, Airron acted like Raina was invisible but looked wounded whenever he dropped his guard. Airron and Peter sat elsewhere at lunch and left school immediately after the final gong. That set the pattern for the rest of the week. Peter and April barely had a chance to talk to each other, except in pixie class. April missed both boys' company and had no chance to ask Peter about the vial. It was still on April's roof, she was procrastinating about taking it through the barrier. It was such a long trip there and back that it was difficult to find a convenient day. And it was safe for the time being.

Raina remained quiet and withdrawn. As much as April tried to cheer her friend up, she failed miserably.

At least the other girls sat with April and Raina at lunch everyday.

April was included in their girl talk and felt like she was welcome. Raina had known what she was doing when she had broadcast that April was dating the Prince.

Another bright spot at school was the coming field trip. Mrs. Merry-Helen had taught the class all they needed to know about the eggstone caverns and they would have the whole day off for this expedition. No school on Friday sounded a lot like a holiday. April was looking forward to the adventure. Any unease she experienced was ignored. There was no such thing as a field trip curse, such a thing simply did not exist.

5 – The Eggstone Caverns

Friday morning bloomed as bright as a daisy. The class met in the meadow at first light. Elves chattered excitedly about the caverns and the eggstones. Mrs. Merry-Helen was more excited than all of her students, her head was happily tilting back and forth to the music only she could hear.

As soon as they left the meadow, Airron strode to the head of the line and stayed there. Raina dragged along silently at the back and April stayed by her side even though it wasn't any fun. Raina needed April's support right now. That was more important than having fun. Heather and Willowna soon joined them, but April didn't mind. They were better at cheering Raina up than April.

It took almost three hours of brisk walking to reach the only entranceway to the caverns. The dark hole was poked into the side of a rocky hill, and shaped chillingly like Giant's opened mouth.

The entry was flanked by two exceptionally large, scruffy elves. Mrs. Merry-Helen approached the pair with an eager smile and verified that the class was expected and would be allowed inside.

They were expected. One guide turned up to take them on their tour. The elf was as large as his mates. He seemed very shy when he faced the class; he had to clear his throat twice before he could speak. "More of you than I expected. Well let's get started. Call me Mica, that's my name. Now, you all got to be real careful in there. Dangerous place. We'll be the only elves down there, whole mine's closed for the week. So got to stay together. No wandering off, tunnels run everywhere – some are natural, some we excavated ourselves. More excavations are about to begin. Lots of tunnels, could get lost forever. Questions?"

Not one hand went up but a number of pale faces looked newly apprehensive.

"Okay. Let's go then." Mica stood aside and waved the class forward, then he thought better of it. "Uh, I better lead the way. Only one that knows it. Teacher, you come last. Make sure you don't lose any stragglers." He slapped his cap back on his head and stepped into the blackness.

Airron finally gave up his position at the head of the class, he moved to the side and stared fixedly at the hole, his dilated pupils making his eyes look even blacker than the tunnel entrance. Peter stayed by his side. Raina stepped right past both boys, she didn't spare them a glance.

April stopped. "Airron, are you going to be okay?"

He nodded but didn't speak. It didn't look like he was going to be okay.

"I could wait outside with you, Airron," Peter offered. "I don't care if I see the eggstones." He was lying. April knew exactly how much he wanted to tour the cavern; he had talked of little else in pixie class, all week long.

"Or I could stay with Airron. I don't mind," April offered.

"Hey, I can do this. I'm not a ... what's that scared bird again, April?" Airron asked in a choked voice.

"Chicken." She had explained the expression months ago.

"Chicken, I'm not one of those chicken birds." But he faced the black hole as if it was a monster. April knew exactly how Airron felt, she had experienced the same emotion when she couldn't step off the raised platform at the King's Keep.

"Airron, why don't you wait outside? You don't have to do this. I'll stay here." April touched his hand. It was cold and clammy.

"Ya, so you can tell Raina what a baby chicken bird I am. Not a chance." He took a couple of steps forward.

April gasped. "Airron, I would never do that."

"She would know anyway, if I didn't go in." Airron gripped April's arm tightly in his hands. It was like being held by ice. "Lead the way," he ordered. "Can't hold Peter like this, elves would laugh."

"Airron, you don't have to - "

"Move, before I lose my nerve," he commanded.

April started walking. Airron closed his eyes and let her guide him. Peter moved to Airron's opposite side and mouthed the words, "He's been a nightmare."

April nodded emphatically. Raina had been the same way.

"A little faster please," Mrs. Merry-Helen sang from behind.

April honestly hadn't believed that Airron would walk into the black hole, but he did. He was determined to show Raina he was brave. Once inside, he stumbled along with his eyes squeezed tight, humming under his breath. His icy hands turned hot and sweaty and began to tremble. April had to admire his will.

They soon caught up with the tail end of the class. Mica had stopped to talk about the cave wall, holding his torch close to the striated surface. The compressed layers of rock held small sparkly crystalline flakes that brilliantly reflected back the light.

Then Mica marched off again. He turned left into a smaller tunnel that angled more steeply downward; countless passageways branched off in all directions. The air grew cold and damp with an overpowering smell of musty clay. Flickering torches were mounted on the wall at every tunnel juncture.

Airron kept moving along as if he was in a trance, as if he didn't know where he was. And April kept leading him. Raina stopped at one point for April to catch up with her, but she took one look at who was attached to April's arm and hesitated.

With his eyes still closed, Airron didn't see her.

April shrugged at Raina helplessly, she couldn't leave Airron. He would probably have a heart attack and they were a long way from open space now. Raina's face tightened briefly when she watched Airron confront his worst fear. She didn't think he was a chicken. She looked like she wanted to hug him or smack him, but she didn't do either. She waved understandingly and stepped ahead to walk with Heather and Willowna.

All things considered, the tour of the tunnels progressed smoothly. The class continued to descend into what felt like the middle of the earth. The primary passage narrowed around them and even April began to feel claustrophobic. It was lucky Airron had chosen to be temporarily blind.

"Getting close to one of the main eggstone caverns," Mica called back, his voice overloud in the silent underworld. Reacting to the disturbance, Airron strangled April's arm convulsively, then he relaxed back into his withdrawn stupor.

"Is he okay?" Peter asked in concern.

Airron didn't appear to hear the words.

"Not really okay, but sort of okay, I guess." April examined Airron, his skin was as pale and waxy as a mayflower petal. It might have been tinged with gray, it was hard to tell in the faint unnatural light.

"Well, once we tour the main cavern, we'll start ascending again, I think. Won't be long. I'll breathe a lot easier when we get Airron out of here," Peter said softly.

"Me too. Peter, can you sense gold around us?" April asked. Peter's magical ability was new to him, and still developing. Cherry Pitt's father had possessed the same ability to find gold, but his magic had been overshadowed by his dark and evil nature.

81

Peter answered without hesitation. "No, my magic doesn't seem to work down here. But there is gold. The elves mine a wide variety of metals and minerals from this area, in addition to the eggstones. But the eggstones are the most famous product of the caverns." He sounded like a leaflet, he always did when he was explaining things.

And then they arrived at the cavern. The open space was impossibly vast, it felt like they had stepped outside again. The ceiling was so high that you couldn't even see it, except for the stalactites that poked down like deadly fangs.

"Wow," the whole class gasped as one.

"Impressive, first time you see it," Mica beamed. "Take your time, have a good look. Then come with me to the far wall." Eager for the next sight, the class soon followed on his heels. It was quite a distance to reach the opposite rock face. Once there, Mica lit extra torches and handed them out at random. "You won't want to miss this. Real treat for you. Flash your lights this way! Closer now."

Mica looked like a proud father bird when he revealed one egg-shaped gray rock. It came up to his thigh and had a smooth oval exterior that really did have more in common with an egg than a stone.

"Is there something alive in there?" April gasped quietly to Peter. She hadn't been paying a whole lot of attention in class lately.

"No, it's a stone, nothing more. But the inside is very special." Peter leaned forward and smiled with excitement, looking truly happy for the first time in weeks.

Airron didn't like standing still, he began to rock back and forth. April stroked his hand reassuringly.

"Now, this is the latest find," Mica announced. "Hasn't even been cracked open yet. That's the treat. I'm going to open it for you right now. You'll all be witness to the discovery inside. And no two eggstones are alike, as I'm sure your teacher has told you." Mica grabbed a long flat metal tool and a large wooden hammer, he held them up on display. "Chisel and mallet, that's all it takes. And one heck of a strong arm, of course. Pay attention now. Listen hard. The sound you hear is the most important clue."

He tapped the mallet around on the top surface of the eggstone and the class listened as if their very lives depended on the sensitivity of their pointed ears. April could discern the different tones as the mallet moved around, some areas sounded hollow, others sounded dense.

"There now. I want to crack the shell of the stone where it is thinnest. I can hear that with my ears. Right here," Mica pointed and tapped with the mallet again. It did sound the most hollow in that spot. "Ready?" After a deliberate pause to build suspense, he placed the sharp edge of the chisel on the exact point he had indicated and raised the mallet high over head. With dynamic force, he brought it down on the handle end of the chisel, again and again. The impacts sounded like explosions. The noise echoed around the cavern like a hundred hammers, building in intensity. Airron's eyes flew opened as the eggstone split into two equal parts, falling away from each other.

April glimpsed a flash of hollow interior lined with what looked to be closely packed crystals at the same instant that the floor of the cavern shook hard and a vigorous gust of wind blew by, extinguishing every last torch in the chamber.

Something enormous yet intangible surged past April with a rush of prickly hot air. It seemed to pass right through her and surround her. It even felt like her feet left the ground before she dropped back to earth, too dizzy to stand. She fell down, completely discombobulated.

Mica was shouting to be heard over the frantic voices of frightened students. Lots of feet moved around April, it didn't sound like anyone else had fallen down. "Steady on now. Don't move. This happens every so often down here when some of the eggstones open, bit of a mystery why. But no need to panic."

April wasn't so sure about that, and she had an even greater fear. Airron had released her arm and she didn't know where he was in the pitch blackness of the deep underground.

"Peter, find Airron. Airron! Airron!" April cried, struggling up. But so many students were shouting, her voice was lost.

"I've got a flint stone somewhere, sure of it, settle down," Mica thundered, trying to calm the class.

April couldn't wait. She concentrated hard on the torches attached to the walls, picturing their location. Nothing happened, then she remembered - magic didn't work deep underground or if it did, it was the smallest magic produced with the greatest effort. Lighting the torches would have taken her an hour and the effort required probably would have killed her. By the time Mica located his flint stone and provided light, too many minutes had passed. Airron was no longer in the cavern.

"He could have gone anywhere," Peter said. They stared at each other helplessly. Mica resumed his talk about eggstones as if nothing had happened and students crowded closer to have a look at the interior of the stone he had just cracked. But not Raina, she made her way towards them carrying one of the torches.

"April, where's Airron?" she gasped. "Did you lose him?"

"Kind of, he disappeared when the torches went out, when I fell down," April said.

"Why did you fall down? Oh, tell me later. We have to find Airron, fast," Raina cried. "I'll tell Mrs. Hairy-Melon - I mean Merry-Helen, that he's missing. We need to start the search immediately, before he gets too far. Oh, April, can you sense him?"

"No, magic doesn't work down here. Well, barely. But I can give it a try, sensing is a different magic than lighting torches. You never know, maybe it will work." April had to try.

"See if you can sense him. I'll tell the teacher that he's lost." Raina was already starting to organize the search and Mrs. Merry-Helen hadn't even realized that one of her charges was missing, she was enthralled by the glittering eggstone crystals.

April moved further away from the crowd of students and closed her eyes. She knew instantly that trying to sense Airron was futile, she couldn't even sense the whole crowd of students standing in full view.

Peter was watching her hopefully when she opened her eyes. "It won't work down here," she told him. Raina was not having any better luck. She came back looking mad.

"Hairy-Melon says 'not to worry'," she snapped in disgust, using the nickname deliberately. "She says he'll find his way up the main tunnel and be waiting for us. She doesn't realize how incapacitated he is down here, or else she doesn't want to be distracted from her precious eggstone. I think she's in love with it," Raina finished with a huff.

"Airron did keep his eyes closed the whole way down, he won't have any idea which tunnel goes back to the surface." April scanned the cavern. Five tunnels led into it, marked by five extinguished torches. No one had bothered to relight those and most of the cave was gloomy at best. Some of the other passages probably went even further underground. What if he had taken one of those? According to Mica, it was possible for elves to get lost forever in the maze of the mine.

"Oh, we have to find him," Raina sobbed. Her disagreement with Airron had been forgotten.

"We will find him." Peter sounded positive. "And it is possible that he chose the right tunnel and ascended to the surface."

"But we can't wait to find out. I'm not going to wait for the stupid tour to be finished before we start looking, I'm going to search now. I don't care if I get in trouble!" Raina declared, swinging around to leave. "Uh, which tunnel did we take?" Even she didn't know.

"Come on. First we'll check if Airron did reach the surface." Peter led the way and kept going, even when Mrs. Merry-Helen noticed their hasty departure and started shouting for them to come back. They jogged, ascending steadily until the outdoor light nearly blinded them. The same two elves that had allowed them entrance were still posted by the hole in the rock.

"Hey, what are you doing here?" the larger of the pair asked, puzzled by their appearance. "Not supposed to be roaming around without supervision. Too dangerous."

Raina stepped forward. "Umm ... actually, we are looking for a lost classmate. Did any students come out of the cavern, before us?"

"No, course not. Been here the whole time. Lost student you say? That's not good, not good at all, might be gone forever," the elf declared. It was not a very tactful thing to say and Raina's face crumpled.

"But, how do you usually go about finding a lost elf?" she asked.

84

The two miners shared a glance. "Well, never had students in the mine before. Never will again I'm guessing, since Mica went and lost one of you. Never had a lost student in the tunnels. Going to be tough to find." The miner lifted his cap and scratched his head.

"Well, thank-you. We'll return to our class now," Raina said, shoving April and Peter back into the mouth of the tunnel.

"Wait, you shouldn't go alone," the miner hollered, but Raina kept pressing them forward until they were running. The miners did not give chase.

"They don't have a clue, do they? We need to start searching on our own before Airron goes too deep. Oh, he must be so scared," Raina wailed.

They raced down the main passage, going faster and faster.

When they heard a crowd of voices approaching, Raina skidded and dodged into the nearest smaller branching tunnel. April and Peter ducked in after her. They all pressed themselves against the wall and didn't make a sound while the class straggled past. April kept a close watch to verify that Airron was not with the other students. He wasn't.

As soon as the coast was clear, they finished their mad dash down to the cavern. The vast space echoed eerily now that it was deserted, save for themselves. "Wow, it feels different down here when it's empty. Creepy! Okay, Airron obviously took one of the other tunnels. Which one?" Raina asked.

April didn't point out that Airron also could have taken the main tunnel and branched off anywhere. Raina was upset enough.

Peter grabbed a torch off the wall. Someone had relit all five. "Let's see if we can find a clue, a sign that tells us which tunnel he took." Peter strode with purpose to the nearest hole in the rock.

Together, they thoroughly examined the entrance to each of the four remaining smaller tunnels and shouted Airron's name loudly into each. Nothing but silence answered them. And Airron had left no clue as to the direction he had taken.

"Well, I suggest we each pick a tunnel and go a little way down it," Peter said. "If we split up, it will save us a lot of time. After five minutes, turn around and come back. We'll meet right here." Peter sounded stern when he issued the instructions. "Even if one of us finds a sign that Airron is in a tunnel, we'll still come back so we can continue the search together. Okay?"

"Okay," Raina nodded, allowing him to take charge.

April borrowed a torch off the wall and they each picked a tunnel at random. As soon as she moved out of sight of her friends, April experienced a swamping sensation of isolation and claustrophobia. The underground didn't bother her in the same way that it paralyzed Airron and even she was frightened. This route was much narrower and lower. As short as she was, April's head kept brushing the overhead stone. The weight of the earth felt crushing.

After five minutes, there had been no sign that Airron had taken her passage. April shouted loudly ahead and listened hard - nothing. It was time to turn around. Before she backtracked to reunite with the others, April sat down on the cold rock and leaned against the damp wall. She would try once more to sense Airron, while she was alone. Her eyes squeezed tightly shut, April drew on all her energy and ability. She held her breath and pressed on her temples with her fingers, fighting to sense anything at all. She couldn't sense an elf, but there was something else ... a sort of magical tingle, in the earth below.

"That's not possible," April whispered. It wasn't, was it? She was far underground, magic didn't work here, so why was she tingling? April lay flat and pressed her ear to the hard-packed floor. Yes, the magic was so strong it almost hummed. But it was not the kind of magic that would help find Airron. April couldn't even guess what kind of magic it was. It didn't feel like the Echoes that protected New Haven. It felt like something else entirely. Not elves and not Echoes. What could it be? And where was it coming from? It was certainly a mystery, and every bit as peculiar as the rushing force that had knocked her down after the eggstone was cracked. Deeply disturbed, April stood up and brushed off. Finding Airron was the first priority, this other thing could wait.

When April reached the main cavern, Peter was already there, examining the newly opened eggstone. "April." He looked relieved to see her. "Anything?"

"No, and I tried to sense him again. Nothing. You?"

"Nothing. Let's hope Raina found something." Peter looked ghostly in the torchlight as he bent over the treasure. "These are pretty amazing stones." The crystals were sharp and perfect, completely lining the hollow interior or the eggstone.

"They are extraordinary. What do elves do with them?" April asked.

"Depends. The most perfect stone shells are left intact – well, in half. There is one on display in the museum. The rest are shattered into separate crystals, those are used for all kinds of things, both functional and decorative." Peter straightened and paced nervously. "Raina should be back by now."

"Peter, I'm going to start down the last unexplored tunnel while you wait for Raina, I'll be quick."

"Okay. Don't go far and be careful." Peter sat down on the eggstone to wait.

As well as searching for Airron, April wanted to find out if another passageway also hummed with magic. The second tunnel angled more steeply than the previous one, invading deeper into the earth. After the requisite five minutes, there was still no sign of Airron. April stopped and lay down with her head pressed to the ground. Yes, the tingle was here and even stronger. April was surrounded by the same peculiar magical hum.

The New Haven elves probably didn't know about it, since she was the only elf who could sense such things. But what did it mean? It felt like something she had never encountered before. Was it the non-elvan part of the magical union that formed the forcefield?

"Airron first," April said. It was time to return to the cavern. Peter was still alone. Raina had been gone much too long.

Together they jogged into Raina's tunnel. Now they were searching for both of their friends. If they had been anywhere but New Haven, April might have suspected them eaten or attacked by any number of burrowing creatures. Luckily, no such animals existed here.

Five minutes in, they trotted around a sharp bend and almost tripped over legs. April gasped in shock, covered her eyes and swung around into Peter. Raina had found Airron all right. She had found him with her lips. They were sitting hip to hip, leaning against the wall - kissing! April was too embarrassed to look again, it felt like her face was on fire.

"April, are you okay?" Peter sounded puzzled. Had he not seen?

April shook her head, then she nodded. She still wouldn't turn around.

"She's embarrassed," Raina supplied, sounding perfectly normal. In fact, she sounded amused. "I think April has a ... a ... kissing phobia," she giggled. If Raina was talking, she couldn't be kissing. April edged around and peeked between her fingers. It proved safe, so she dropped her hands.

"I do not have a ... that thing phobia," April declared indignantly, blushing hotly. "You found Airron." She stated the obvious.

"I did." At first glance, neither elf was in the best condition. Raina had been crying and Airron had blood all over his robe and his nose was larger than normal. At second glance, they both looked kind of happy and goofy.

"Oh Airron, did you break your nose again?" April asked. She had broken his nose not so long ago, by accident. Or unintentionally, at least. His nose had looked about the same then.

"Think so, got disoriented in the dark, ran into a wall." He sounded perfectly content, in spite of it all.

"Oh. Your nose looks really sore. Does it hurt?"

"Not anymore. Raina kissed it better."

April didn't know what to say about that, she said, "Oh."

"How come you didn't lead Airron back to the cavern?" Peter asked Raina.

"We were talking and stuff," Raina replied easily.

"And I hurt my ankle. Not broken but can't walk on it." Airron smiled as if he was delivering good news.

"Umm, do you want some help? Or do you want to stay here?" Peter asked. Airron was all too comfortable, given their present location. And much too happy. Maybe it was the blow to his head, or maybe it was the kissing. Kissing could make elves behave in the silliest ways.

"I wouldn't mind getting out of here," Airron admitted.

Raina scooted up and offered him two hands.

"Wait a minute. Don't get up yet, Airron. I need to check something." April could not miss this opportunity to sense another tunnel. She dropped flat to the earth and pressed her head to the ground. Yes - this third passage proved to have the same mysterious magical hum as the previous two.

"Why do you need to lie on the ground? April, what are you doing?" Raina asked, nudging her with a toe.

"I've discovered something weird down here, in all the tunnels. I'll tell you while we walk."

They made slow progress assisting Airron to limp out to the cavern and April described the inexplicable floor of magic beneath them. Her friends hadn't noticed anything, not even Peter. Neither had any of her friends experienced the surging force that had knocked April down after the eggstone was cracked open.

When they reached the main cavern, they were met by the three miners organizing their own search party. Two of them lifted Airron between them as if he weighed no more than DewDrop and carried him all the way up the main passage. Mica scolded them for getting lost in the caverns and warned them that their teacher was in a tizzy about their disappearance.

"But is she still smiling?" April asked.

"Uh, ya. She is, actually." Mica grinned crookedly. "Never seems to stop."

Maybe they weren't in too much trouble after all.

While she had the chance, April asked Mica about what lay beneath the caverns and how deep the tunnels ran. He reported that there was nothing but rock, clay and earth below. He also said that the class had traveled to the very deepest cavern, only some of the tunnels burrowed any deeper.

"And the wind that made the torches go out, and the shaking before? What was that?" April pressed.

Mica doffed his acorn cap and shook his head. "Can't explain it. Happens now and then when we open some of the eggstones. Don't know why. Bit of a mystery." He didn't seem concerned.

"Does anyone ever fall down or faint when the stones are cracked?"

"Course not, miners are tough, strong – no weaklings down here. No fainting allowed," he declared, suddenly sounding rougher and tougher. He also didn't know very much so April stopped quizzing him.

The entire class greeted them with cheers when they exited the black hole. It was wonderful to step into the light and fresh air after being deprived of both for so long. Airron couldn't walk easily but insisted that he was fine to fly home. Raina whispered something in his ear and he nodded.

Mrs. Merry-Helen reprimanded them all, then assigned Cosmo and Ray to accompany Airron on his flight, in case he got woozy from his injuries and fell out of the sky. The rest of the class had to hike back; the three hour walk seemed a much greater distance than it had that morning.

As soon as they reached the school meadow, they were dismissed, even though the final gong would not sound for another half-hour. No one minded starting the weekend early.

"Come on." Raina motioned for April and Peter to follow her.

"Where are we going?" April asked.

"Home. Airron is going to meet us there. My father can treat him when he gets home." Raina was looking joyful and excited, her face was positively glowing.

April didn't need to be hit on the head with a stick to know that Raina had made up with Airron. His disappearance must have been the catalyst that helped her decide who she truly cared about. It was Airron.

They found him lounging on the shore of the lake, soaking his ankle. He had washed the blood off his face and managed to clean his robe. It was hanging over a nearby branch, drying out.

"We'll get snacks," April offered in case Raina started kissing him again. Peter came along to help. He didn't have to be hit on the head with a stick either.

They took their time searching through cupboards. They even tried to make fancy snacks, kind of like party food.

While April was alone with Peter, it seemed a good time to ask him about the vial. In an awkward rush, she said, "Peter, when the vial was missing, did you have it?"

He froze for a moment, then resumed drizzling honey on berry slices with full concentration. "Why would you ask that?" he said evasively.

"A couple of people saw you near the house on the day the vial disappeared and the day it reappeared."

"Really?"

"Yes."

Peter kept drizzling honey, eyes on his task. He didn't say a word.

"And you can sense gold, the vial was hidden where no one could find it. And you told me to search my room again, to find the vial. Did you take it, Peter? Then put it back?"

He kept working, still silent.

"Peter, you didn't say 'no' and that sort of means 'yes', doesn't it?" April asked uncertainly.

"I guess it could." With a self-depreciating smile, Peter finally looked up. "I don't want to lie to you, April, so I would rather not answer your questions, not yet."

"But ... but why not, Peter? What's going on?"

He slumped down on a cushion at the kitchen table, looking heavily burdened. "April, this magic stuff is new to all of us, except you. I'm just trying to figure out my magic. You said that you thought the vial would only work on a magical elf, so I wanted to test it – on me."

April sat down beside him. "Why didn't you just ask me for it?" That would have been the logical thing to do and Peter was normally the most logical of elves.

"I can't really say. It's complicated. Some aspects of my magic are bothering me, I'm trying to figure things out." Peter stared into her eyes, grimly. Was fear lurking in the dark depths?

His answer still didn't make sense to her. "Peter, why don't you ask me questions about your magic?"

"Because I think this is magic that you don't know about and I don't want to discuss it," he said curtly.

There was a lot that Peter wasn't telling her, too much. "Did the vial work on you?" she asked.

"No."

"Is that good or bad?"

"I don't know."

"Peter?" April took his sticky hand and he jerked it away. "Peter, what's going on?"

"Drop it, April, please." Peter returned to making snacks.

"But -"

"Drop it."

April didn't say another word.

When Salm bounded into the kitchen, he joined them in the snack-making, eating as much as he prepared. They carried the food outside to share by the shore of the lake.

Skylar dropped out of the sky unexpectedly to see if they had plans for Friday night. It didn't take him more than one look at Raina and Airron to know that they had their own plans. He smiled without giving any sign of the effort it cost him, sampled several bites of the sloppy snacks, insisted they were delicious and said he had to be going. He nodded to everyone and gracefully soared away, just like that. Not many elves could have masked their heartbreak with such aplomb, then again, he was the future King of New Haven.

6 – Hammer

A quiet weekend was followed by a quieter week. There were no scheduled field trips, although there was lots of work and even more homework. Salm was being increasingly pressured by his parents to decide the course of his future with only three months remaining before he left school for good. The family could not eat dinner without some discussion on the subject. Mr. Poole continued to stress that he would be delighted if Salm would apprentice with him as a Healer and follow in his father's footsteps. Mrs. Poole suggested a number of alternatives when it became clear that Salm was not jumping at the offer. He still didn't know what he wanted to do, but whatever it was, it would have nothing to do with blood, broken bones, and mysterious rashes.

Traditionally, merrows often worked around water or in water. Some caught minnow fish and delivered them to elves in the same way that Mr. Tilly delivered vegetables. Some merrows harvested lakeweed, another popular food source. A small number of merrows hunted along the bottom of lakes for clams, always hoping to find a rare pearl. Merrows also worked on land, of course. Neither of the parent's careers had anything to do with their merrow status.

"It's really hard to decide," Salm insisted over dinner on Thursday. "I mean, some elves know what they want to do. And some elves have it decided for them, like Skylar. But I don't know what I want to do. I might take some time off, you know, before I decide, to help me decide," he mentioned casually.

Mr. Poole slammed his cup down, rather hard. "School doesn't end tomorrow. You still have some time to reach a decision. Keep thinking." It was an order. "And Raina, it wouldn't hurt you to consider your own future, then you won't be in the same quandary as your brother when you finish school next year, and it will come sooner than you think."

"Do you know what you want to do?" April asked. She thought Raina would make a great mayor. She was very organized and liked meetings.

"She could have been Queen," Salm griped. "We could have moved into the Keep, been bowed to. But no - "

"Salm! Shut up. And being Queen isn't a career or a job, is it? I would still want to do something. I wouldn't mind being an Elder, but I'd have to get old first, start out as an apprentice and work my way up, but that seems really boring. I don't know what I want to do either, but I don't want it to be boring. I want it to be exciting."

"April, what about you?" Mr. Poole asked. "Any thoughts about your future?"

"No. Not really." April didn't even know if she would be allowed to finish school with Raina, considering she had hardly gone to school at all.

"I know what you should do, April," Salm declared. "You should lead tours into the Outer-world. Take elves on camping trips. That would be fun. Hey, I could be your partner and Raina could organize the expeditions. We would have our own business. I bet lots of elves want to go and see the sights in the Outer-world but they're too scared. They could go with you and feel safe." Salm sounded serious.

"No one is safe out there," April countered. Even she wasn't safe out there.

"And Salm, the barrier doesn't allow elves to leave New Haven anymore. Your stupid plan won't work," Raina said. Sisters could speak frankly.

"Hey, the barrier could be altered to allow elves exit. It's happened before," Salm argued.

"Once. Once in two thousand years! And look how that turned out," Raina retorted. It had resulted in Brag, the imp.

The pair continued to bicker back and forth while April enjoyed her second serving of dessert - diced crab apple and crushed acorn boiled in maple syrup. In her opinion, it was every bit as good as the food at the King's Keep. DewDrop was sharing off her shell, but that was okay.

As soon as dessert was finished, Mr. and Mrs. Poole rose with purpose. "You three can clear up. Your father and I must attend a meeting with Head-Elder Falcon. I don't know why he wants to see us, he said something rather odd about the King requesting our presence at the gathering. Anyway, we should be home before bedtime. If we're not, make sure DewDrop gets to sleep at a decent hour. It is not the weekend yet," Mrs. Poole emphasized. The bedtime applied to all of them, not only DewDrop.

After cleaning up the dinner mess, Raina insisted they finish their homework. April had been planning to forget that she had any schoolwork. Raina didn't let her get away with it. They put DewDrop to bed then Raina pointed April upstairs, she brought her own books along to April's room. April tried to discuss her concerns about Peter, but Raina cut her off. "We'll talk after we've finished our homework."

They scribbled with concentration for an hour.

Raina was the first to thump her book closed, she was finished first. "Thank goodness tomorrow is Friday. I don't know why the teachers are piling on the work. They get in the mood to torture us every so often, for no reason. Are you done yet?"

"Almost." April hadn't been able to figure out the math.

"Let me see." Raina grabbed April's bark. Most of her answers were scratched out or wrong. April stood up to stretch her legs. She wandered over to the window, yawning. The moon was rising brightly over the lake, it was full. It was getting closer and closer. April rubbed her eyes to clear them.

"April, come here. Not one of these answers is right," Raina called.

The shimmering sphere that was masquerading as the moon appeared to be on a collision course with April's tower. She threw herself to the ground when an enormous bubble sealed the window, trying to squeeze inside. "Get out!" she shouted at Raina.

"Well, there's no need to get upset. I'm only trying to help, you're not very good at math, you know." Raina sounded highly insulted until she looked up. "Oh. Oh, I see. Okay, I'm getting out. April, hurry!" she screamed and tumbled frantically across the floor.

The bubble was determined to force its way inside with whatever it was carrying. The bubble wouldn't fit, neither would its contents. When a crack snaked across the wall from the corner of the window, April rolled to her feet and ran towards Raina. The floor shook and split behind her. The bubble was demolishing her room.

Raina grabbed for her hand and they made the doorway with not a second to spare. The walls collapsed behind them, loudly and violently.

"Faster," Raina screamed, hurtling down the spiral staircase as fast as if she was freefalling. April stayed on her heels while fragments of wall and floor rained down on them.

Salm was running for the front door, holding DewDrop tightly. He couldn't know exactly what was happening, but he knew they needed to escape the house. They raced outside together and made it safely into the front garden. The grinding and banging reached a climactic crescendo, then faded to silence.

It had all happened so fast, three minutes ago April had been doing homework. Now it looked like her room was destroyed and the school work was gone. April said the first dumb thing that popped into her head. "We did all that homework for nothing."

Raina turned to her with a dropped jaw and cried, "How can you even think about that? Look at your room, it's gone!"

Dust and debris were settling in the light cast from the house and April's room was gone. The very top of her tower was nothing but a pile of rubble. At least the destruction had stopped there, the rest of the towers were still intact.

"What happened?" Salm asked. "You didn't get mad about something, did you, April?"

"No, I didn't do it. It wasn't me. I think Brag sent another bubble." April stared numbly up at her room – at her lack of room. "It was much too big to fit through the window."

"A bubble did that?" Salm gasped. "Good grief."

"The bubble had something inside it." April tried to see what it was by standing on her tiptoes and straining her neck. Something large and lumpy was perched in the wreckage of her tower, it was impossible to tell what it was from below. April closed her eyes and concentrated, she couldn't sense anything. Whatever it was – at least it wasn't alive.

"Brag's last bubble caused enough problems," Raina muttered, putting an arm around DewDrop who was sobbing softly. "This one looks so much worse. What do you think was in the bubble?"

"I don't know. I better go and see. Wait here, just in case." There was a chance that the thing was not as inanimate as it appeared.

"April, you know I'm not going to let you go alone," Salm said steadfastly.

"I was hoping you would," she appealed.

Salm simply shook his head. "Raina, stay with DewDrop. We'll check it out." He linked their hands and started forward, and April couldn't stop him. She knew well enough by now that her friends always stood with her, no matter what the danger or risk to themselves.

They grabbed two torches from the sconce inside the front door and April created light before they crept forward, listening hard. The interior of the house looked mainly undamaged. There was a pile of debris at the bottom of April's staircase, nothing more.

April took the lead, scrambling awkwardly over rocks and what looked like the wreckage of her three-legged bed. The staircase wobbled loosely but stayed upright. At the top, what was left of her room sat exposed to the sky. The big dark thing didn't move. April extended her torch closer, heart pounding like a herd of stampeding grasshoppers.

"What is it?" Salm whispered into her ear. He leaned forward, raising his light. "It just looks like a big rock."

It did, from this perspective anyway. But they couldn't see everything. They picked their way around the exposed and cracked edge of the tower wall to the other side, sending loose debris splashing into the lake below.

The hidden side of the boulder revealed chilling details. This boulder wasn't merely a boulder, it had another name and another purpose. April wasn't in the least prepared for the thing she faced. The smell alone almost knocked her off the tower. The object still reeked of the filthy hand that had once wielded this weapon. Her torch fell from nerveless fingers and rolled off the tower to sizzle into the lake below.

"April? What is it?" Salm asked

She couldn't answer, she had lost her voice.

"Hey! Are you okay?"

April opened her mouth to speak but still no sound came out.

"Do you know what this thing is?"

She nodded.

"Do you want to go downstairs and talk about it?"

She nodded emphatically.

"Come on then." Salm took her hand, he led her downstairs and back to Raina. April sat down hard on the ground, her arms wrapped around her knees. The foul smell still filled her nostrils and she couldn't stop shivering.

"April? Salm? What is that big thing?" Raina asked impatiently.

"I don't know but April does," Salm said. "She's been freaked out since she looked at the big rock that wrecked her room. It only looked like a boulder. April? What is it?"

April had to get a grip on herself. She tried again to talk, it took several attempts but her friends were patient, for the most part.

"April, what did you see? Tell us!" Raina pressed.

"DewDrop," April whispered. She couldn't say it in front of her. Raina guided her sister over to the shore of the lake and ordered her to stay put, then she hurried back.

"April," Raina said, "Tell us."

"That thing belongs to a ... a Giant," she stammered.

"It does not!" Raina denied reflexively.

"Does it really? But what is it?" Salm sounded skeptical as well.

"A hammer, sort of. Giants ..." she swallowed sickly, "Giants attach pointed boulders onto thick sticks and use them as hammers, to hit and ... crush things. The handle on this one is broken but part of it is still there. It's decorated with ... teeth." They would see for themselves in the light.

"Are you sure?" Salm asked.

"Yes."

"But why did Brag send you a Giant's hammer?" Raina gasped.

April could guess but she wasn't going to say. DewDrop hadn't stayed put, she was probably too scared to sit alone after what had happened to her house. April pulled DewDrop down beside her and hugged the little elf. She needed the contact as much as DewDrop. More.

Mr. and Mrs. Poole found them seated in the garden when they turned up several minutes later. They didn't notice the house at first, in the dark.

"What are all of you doing awake at this hour?" Mrs. Poole scolded as she walked up. "Raina, I asked you to put your sister to bed."

"I did, then that happened." Raina pointed up.

"The house? What happened to the house?" Mr. Poole asked calmly, it hadn't sunk in yet.

"It wasn't me," April said, to be clear.

He squinted. "But your room is destroyed."

"Yes," April said sadly. It had been a very nice room, too. She would miss the only room she had ever known. Most of her things were probably gone, too. And she'd never had things before. She would miss her room and her things.

"It has certainly been a night for surprises. First the King's proposal and now this." Mr. Poole didn't explain his remark, he simply peered up at the damage.

"But this is awful! How did it happen?" Mrs. Poole sounded properly upset.

Salm explained about the bubble and the boulder. He omitted any mention of the Giant's hammer, since DewDrop was all ears.

"Wait here while I have a look at the rest of the house, make sure it's sturdy," Mr. Poole said and strode off. Salm went with him, creating an opportunity to tell his father everything. Long minutes passed before the pair emerged from the house. Mr. Poole declared the structure safe for sleeping in, and Mrs. Poole took DewDrop off to bed.

As soon as the pair was out of sight, Mr. Poole asked, "April, are you sure about this Giant's hammer?"

"Yes," she said; there was nothing else to say.

"Well ..." His hand thrust through his thinning hair "This is certainly unexpected, and unwelcome. We will have to investigate the object thoroughly in the morning, I suppose. Too late now, too dark. The hammer isn't going anywhere, is it." He hadn't meant the words as a question but April shook her head, she sure hoped not. Only one hand could lift that hammer, a hand that should never be in New Haven.

"Come on, April. We'll have a sleepover." Raina urged April up to her room. It wasn't much of a sleepover, April was dead to the world as soon as her head rested on the borrowed cotton ball pillow. There was something about deeply shocking events that could put April to sleep almost instantly. She dreamed about Giants.

Mrs. Poole shook April awake. She didn't know where she was for a minute, she had gotten used to waking up in her own room. Not anymore, she remembered with a sharp pang of regret.

"April, come have breakfast. Someone is waiting to talk to you," Mrs. Poole said. Her voice was enough to waken Raina. The girls pulled on clothes and stumbled rather groggily downstairs.

"Do we have to go to school, Mom?" Raina yawned. "All our homework is destroyed. We'll get in trouble."

"Yes, you must attend school. You will be much better off there, than here, although you have permission to be late and I will send a note." It was the best deal that they were going to get.

Head-Elder Falcon and Elder Scarab were waiting. Brief greetings were exchanged before the Head-Elder got straight to the point.

"April, I do have an important question before I see for myself this object that you believe has been sent by the imp," he began, tension roughening his aged voice. "Do you know why Brag has delivered you a Giant's hammer?"

"I don't know for sure, but I can guess."

"Yes?" He had probably guessed as well.

"I think it means that Brag has found some Giants – alive. I think the Giants can't be very far away, I think they are close to New Haven," she warned. "But I could be wrong, imps aren't very good at communicating. I still don't know what he meant to tell me when he sent the vial filled with brown scum, unless the vial was enchanted to guide me east because he wanted me to go and see the Giants. But he could have just come and told me about the Giants himself, and he hasn't turned up. I don't know what it all means."

Head-Elder Falcon was twisting his beard, as he was wont to do in troubled times. "I suppose anything is possible," he murmured, as if to himself. "At least we should remain protected by our forcefield. According to myth, it is supposed to keep us safe even from Giants. Now, let us have a look at this hammer, shall we?" The Head-Elder rose stiffly and patted his beard back into place as if he needed a moment to compose himself.

Raina had to wait below while April led the way up the shaky staircase - her father wouldn't let her come along. In the clear light of day, the destruction of April's room looked so much worse. At least this time April was prepared for what she would find.

"You need to go to the other side, to see the … the details," she said, when a wall of rock faced them at the top of the stairs.

The Head-Elder touched her shoulder and said, "Lead the way."

She did, around the huge boulder with a grumbling Elder Scarab close on her heels. "You're not saying a Giant can pick this up and bang it around?" Elder Scarab demanded, disbelief deepening the wrinkles in his face.

"As easily as you can lift a cup of water," April told him.

"You don't say. What's that sticking out thingy?" They had reached the other side of the boulder, the side with the details.

"The handle, most of it is broken off." The stump of wood was affixed to the rock with ragged strips of badly cured leather. Bloody fur still clung in places.

"And the stench?" he choked.

Head-Elder Falcon made good use of his beard to cover his nose.

"A few smells blended together. Sweat of a Giant, rotten blood or meat from the leather strips. Maybe other stuff, like the teeth." April had avoided looking at the white nubs banged into the handle.

Elder Scarab peered close and pulled a gruesome face. "Cripes. What animal has teeth that big?"

April took a look. "Those are Giant's teeth. They keep the teeth as trophies if they knock them out of another Giant in a fight. Giants aren't very civilized." April edged closer to the handle, gritted her own small teeth and climbed up onto it. This handle proudly displayed two Giant's teeth. They were more than half her height and a lot wider. The New Haven elves would probably be very interested to study them. "There are two Giant's teeth, if you want to keep them," she said.

"Larger than I expected," was all the Head-Elder said, grimly.

"Yes, they always look bigger up close." At least these teeth weren't trying to eat them.

Mr. Poole stepped up and poked at one of the teeth. "It will take some work to free them from the wood. And the other teeth? Do you know what creatures they come from?"

"I can guess. The pointiest ones, like those," she pointed, "Come from large forest cats or bears, while the flatter ones come from moose, deer, and animals like that, animals that grind vegetation between their teeth, rather than ripping meat."

April was still identifying teeth when Skylar and O'Wing glided down and landed on the boulder. They turned in a circle, taking in the scene of destruction.

"Wow. Lucky you weren't asleep when this arrived, you would have been crushed," O'Wing concluded. "I heard this thing floated here? But it must weigh about a hundred pounds. A hundred pounds can't float, can it?" He walked around on the top of the stone, a bit bug-eyed.

Skylar was more concerned about the occupants of the house. "April, you were unharmed? All of you …?"

"I'm fine. We're *all* fine," she stressed.

"Well, that is a great relief. Please pass my regards along to Raina."

The longing look in his eye had her saying, "Raina is downstairs, if you want to tell her yourself."

"No." Skylar turned his back, the defeated line painful to see. April felt so bad for him, her own heart hurt.

O'Wing and Skylar were the start of an endless stream of fairies that flew overhead to view the damage with their own eyes. As soon as she was able, April slipped downstairs and left for school with Raina and Salm.

By the time they stepped inside New Haven Academy, they were so late that Mr. Parsley's class had started. He was already in a bad mood before they walked in. He yelled enthusiastically at both girls; Raina had forgotten to get a note from her mother excusing their tardiness.

When he discovered that neither of them had their homework

completed, Raina tried desperately to explain. "But Mr. Parsley, we did our homework. We finished it. But a Giant's hammer fell on my house and destroyed it. It's lucky we weren't flattened!"

It must have been too early in the day for the news to have traveled throughout all of New Haven because Mr. Parsley didn't believe a word, and April couldn't blame him. It did sound highly implausible. The teacher renewed his tirade and concluded it by assigning them five times as much extra work for lying, not doing their homework and being late. It could have been worse, they could have gotten a month of detentions on top of all the extra work.

Peter and Airron couldn't wait to find out what had happened. When Raina confirmed the tale at lunch, Airron flew off for a quick peek at Raina's house. He returned and declared that a Giant's hammer had indeed destroyed April's tower room. He reported it to the meadow at large when classmates crowded close, eager for exciting details.

After school, Peter and Airron weren't the only elves who came by to view the demolition. The entire student population turned up. No visitors were allowed up on the tower, it would have been too hazardous, but the spectators had a great view from the ground. And something was happening - something exciting.

The hammer had been deemed too dangerous to stay perched on top of the cracked tower and a determined group of elves were working to bring it to the ground without flattening more of the house.

It was an enthralling show and the number of spectators swelled while elves on the tower arranged vines, fulcrums, long poles and pulleys, all in an attempt to shift the hammer and lower it down to the back garden. April had her doubts when she studied the complicated arrangement. The hammer likely did weigh an incredible one hundred pounds, if not more.

The elves on the top of the tower were at the most risk, but safety precautions had been taken. Each worker had a vine knotted around his waist. The opposite ends of the vines were held by fairies flying overhead, ready to yank elves to safety if the tower should collapse. O'Wing was one of those flying fairies, his distinctive leaf green wings were impossible to miss.

"Stand back, stand well back," a hefty elf thundered, waving at the crowd. "We're going to try and bring the hammer down now. Stay back!"

The audience edged closer and held a collective breath when a flurry of frantic movement took place up on the tower. Vines strained and wood creaked and elves groaned with great effort. The hammer shifted, causing the tower to crack ominously. When the massive boulder tilted too far and something snapped, the elf in charge blasted a warning and the fairies in the sky yanked their charges to safety, dangling in mid-air. With a harsh grinding noise, the hammer tumbled slowly over the edge of the tower and thudded to the ground in the front garden, right beside the main door of the house. The boulder had landed awfully near one edge of the crowd.

There was a profound moment of silence before the air filled with cheers. The hammer was down and elves were safe, not to mention that the beautiful house was still in one piece, for the most part.

"Come on. We can go inside now," Raina said. There was not enough room for everyone, so the four friends slipped into the kitchen while elves lined up to have a closer look at the Giant's weapon.

Salm met them inside, dragging his friend Paddy along. "It's like having a monument in our garden," Salm said, helping himself to their snacks. "It's probably there forever, too heavy to move. Did you see the size of some of those teeth?"

"If they can't move the rock end, I'm sure they will cut loose the handle and cart that away," Paddy said. "Although the boulder is movable, with the proper leverage. They did get it down from the tower, after all."

"Sit down, Paddy. Eat something," Salm ordered. "Enough about leverage." It sounded like he'd already had an earful about leverage.

Paddy sat down and April slid the shell of corn cakes closer so he could help himself. Paddy was tall and skinny, he looked like he needed feeding. The snacks ended up being dinner; the parents were too occupied with clearing up the wreckage to sit down that night. And the front lawn was a main attraction until well past moonrise. When Airron and Peter left for home, there was still a line-up to examine the already famous object.

"Should have sold tickets. Night, sleep well," Salm called, going off to his bed.

"Sleep well, Salm." April envied him his bed. "Raina, I want to go look at my room now that the hammer is gone. I want to see if I have any clothes left. Or anything left." She was wearing Raina's dress and it was too large. It kept falling off her shoulders.

"I'll come. I want to see your room, too. I haven't been up there yet."

April mentioned something else that was on her mind. "The vial must have been broken when the hammer crushed my room, but since nothing bad happened, I guess the contents weren't dangerous after all."

"Good thing! I forgot all about the vial." Raina lifted a burning candle and April grabbed a torch. They ascended cautiously through the remaining debris. There was a lot more rubble on the stairs than before the hammer had been removed.

If April had possessed even the smallest talent for seeing things before they happened, she would not have set one foot on the shaky staircase. She would have run a mile in the opposite direction. Sadly, she did not have such ability. Only Ms. Larkin-LaBois had the rare gift of foresight and she had not come to visit the hammer.

The top of the tower was deserted now. All the equipment had been tossed down to the ground and carted off. The stars twinkled cheerfully overhead, April wasn't used to seeing stars overhead in her room. She sighed sadly. "Not much left, is there?"

"No," Raina put an arm around her shoulders. "But you can stay in my room until this one is rebuilt."

"Can it be rebuilt?" April had assumed that she would never get another room.

"Sure. They built it once, they can build it again. You can even pick what colour you want the walls. Let's see if you have any clothes left." The closet had been flattened and everything was squished, wrinkled, dirty and torn. And the cloth smelled like Giant. April dragged everything free for a closer look. Some items were repairable, others were not.

"I still have overalls, at least," April smiled, yanking them out. They had survived on the bottom of the pile.

"Some of the dresses will be okay. We can wash them in the creek tomorrow and they'll be as good as new, well – almost. It's time you learned to sew anyway." Raina grinned.

"It is?" April walked to the far side of the room to check her box dresser. It had held her most special possessions, scant that they were. She had arrived in this world with nothing, but had collected a few treasured items.

The dresser had been crushed flat. The hammer must have landed right on top of it. April bent down to lift aside fragmented splinters of wood, hoping that something had survived. Her small fortune of gold coins were scattered throughout the debris. Raina helped to collect them and they tied the coins into a ruined skirt.

They toured the perimeter of the round room one last time. Raina leaned over where the window used to be and looked down at the lake. "Some of your room must be under the water," she mused. "Maybe we can make an underwater fort with the stones. That would be fun. Hey look, what's that?"

April leaned cautiously over the edge with her light and could not believe her eyes. Dangling from a jut of stone was a golden chain. She crouched down and lifted the vial cautiously. It looked unbroken.

Raina held her candle close. "It doesn't look like it's even cracked, does it?"

"No. It's undamaged."

"Imagine that." Raina extended the makeshift sack. "Here, put it in with the gold coins. We'll hide it in my room until you get rid of it permanently."

April laid the vial carefully on the coins and had a final look around. Everything else had been demolished. But she and Raina hadn't been harmed. "Bright side," April murmured. Everything else could be replaced but Raina was irreplaceable.

Happy all of the sudden, she started after Raina. Her foot slipped on a piece of birchbark. What was left of their homework? It was probably her useless math. April picked up the torn fragment and held the torch closer. No, it wasn't math, it wasn't even homework – it was old script, the script from her former world. This message was written in … was it blood? It did seem so.

This bark had not been in her room before Brag's bubble arrived. That meant only one thing, the bubble had held more than the hammer. It had also held this small missive, written in old script by an elf from the Outer-world.

Ignoring the strong sense of foreboding that gripped her, April read the words where she stood. The communication was short. She only had to read it once, but she read it twice. Then she held the bark over her torch, burning it away to nothing but ash. Brag hadn't needed to send the stupid hammer, the note would have been clear enough.

"April, are you coming?" Raina called from downstairs.

"Yes." April tried really hard to sound normal, she almost did.

The parents were sharing tea in the kitchen with DewDrop. The little elf had stayed up late. April had forgotten that it was Friday. Salm must have forgotten too, because he had already gone to bed. Raina handed April a cup of honey tea and she sat down, joining her family.

The tea was soothing, April tried to hold the cup but she had to put it down, her hands were shaking. She listened to everyone talk and felt like she was in the middle of an awful nightmare. When Raina rose to go to bed, April didn't accompany her. She didn't think she could talk with Raina alone and not confess the contents of the note.

When enough time had passed for Raina to fall asleep, April yawned pointedly and hugged everyone good-night. She didn't cry or anything.

Raina was breathing deep and slow when April got upstairs - sleeping. Sadly, there had been no chance to say good-bye to her best friend, or Salm.

Knowing it was going to be a very long night. April sat on the floor and waited, biding her time. When the house was so deeply still that it almost echoed with silence, April tiptoed downstairs and filled a sack with food, then added a torch. She changed into her overalls in the middle of the kitchen and tied the straps around her neck. She had to be prepared for anything, even flying.

Her thoughts were so scattered that she had almost forgotten the most important item - the vial that would guide her to the Giant that held an elf captive in the Outer-world. Raina had taken it away with all the gold pieces.

April tiptoed back upstairs to Raina's room to search for the vial. She slunk around in the dark, feeling with her hand. She checked in Raina's closet, in her dresser, under her bed, and even in her school pack, but the search proved fruitless. Raina must have hidden it really well. Maybe it was even under Raina's pillow. Only one way to find out.

April took a soundless step closer to Raina's bed, then a second. Her hand slipped like a snake under Raina's pillow, weaving back and forth. Her fingers touched something hard. Except it didn't feel like metal, it felt more like fingers. Raina's fingers. They were tucked under her pillow.

Raina sounded wide awake when she said, "April, what on earth are you doing?"

"Umm … nothing. Looking for something. Looking for my gold coins," April whispered back. "Where did you put them?"

"Why do you need gold coins in the middle of the night?" Raina's question was infused with suspicion.

"No reason. I was just wondering. Where did you put them?"

Raina didn't answer, she sat up and said, "April, light a candle."

April wasn't about to do that. "No need. Just tell me where my things are and go back to sleep."

"If you want to know where your things are, light the candle."

Reluctantly, April did.

"Hey, why do you have a pack?" Raina asked sharply.

"Pack? Oh." April should have hidden the pack before she created light, but there it was, slung over her shoulder and obviously stuffed.

"And why are you dressed in your overalls? You look like you're going on a trip."

"Umm …" April didn't have a believable explanation ready. She couldn't think that fast. "Raina, please tell me where you put my things. It's important."

"Not until you tell me why you want them. The truth. I can tell when you lie." Raina issued the ultimatum firmly.

April clamped her lips shut and scanned the room now that she could see. Her things still weren't visible. With a flare of light, she magically lit all the other candles hoping that would help. The makeshift sack was not revealed by the brightness.

"April, if you leave without telling me where you're going, I'll feel worse than if you tell me. Not knowing is always worse than knowing, no matter how bad it is. We're best friends, you have to tell me what's going on. Maybe I can come with you," Raina appealed. She already sounded distressed and she didn't know how awful the situation was.

"No, you can't come with me." April sank onto the edge of Raina's bed. "You can't come with me. No one can come with me." She might as well have told Raina exactly where she was going.

"The Outer-world?" Raina wailed. "You're going through the barrier! But why?"

It was time to confess. "The bubble held more than the Giant's hammer. It held a note, written in old script. My script. I found it when we were in my room."

"Oh. Brag located the lost elf, and you're going to meet them?" Raina said. "That's not so bad. Why didn't you tell me? Oh – the Giant's hammer. Why did he send that?"

"There's a problem." April honestly didn't know how to say the words. She could barely conceive of what she was going to do. Talking about it was like trying to speak with a mouthful of thistles.

"The Giant?" Raina looked at her tragically.

"Yes, the Giant. The Giant is keeping the elf prisoner. Sometimes a Giant will use an elf ... force an elf," she amended, "To perform magic to benefit the Giant. Giants don't have magic, they're just really big, so they use elves for magic. Anyway, the elf must have slipped the note to Brag who used his magic to send it, along with the hammer. The vial will guide me to the Giant so I can try and free the elf. I need the vial, Raina. Where did you put it?"

Raina didn't answer April's question, she yelled, "You're going to the Outer-world to take on a Giant? Are you nuts?"

"Yes, no, shush! I'm not going to confront the Giant directly. I'll be sneaky to rescue the elf, so the Giant will never know I'm there. I'll be safe, I'll come back. But I can't do nothing, the Giant has the elf trapped!" April sobbed. She wished she could do nothing, but she couldn't live with this knowledge and not act upon it. Even Brag had gotten involved to help this elf, and he was an imp. How could April be less worthy than an imp?

"April, you can't go take on a Giant. That's stupid, it's suicide. I'm not going to tell you where the vial is." Raina was shouting again.

"Raina, where's my vial? I need it to find the elf and it is my decision, my choice. I don't want to go, but I have to go. Please tell me where the vial is," April pleaded, hoping Raina would understand.

"No, you don't have to go. You can stay here! You can choose to stay here. This is your home now." Raina trailed off into a whisper.

"I can't do nothing, Raina. I know what the elf is going through. The elf is suffering! I have to help."

They both jumped when Salm stepped into the room. His tower was the closest.

"Hey, what's going on? Why all the shouting?" Salm blinked owlishly with his hair standing up on his head. He spotted the pack around April's neck immediately. It wasn't what an elf normally wore to go to bed. "April, are you going somewhere?" He managed to sound every bit as suspicious as his sister.

"She's going to the Outer-world to take on a Giant," Raina wailed. "She's being unreasonable."

"No, I'm not. I have to go. You're acting like I *want* to go. I don't, but I have to go." April almost lost her voice, she wanted to cry like a baby at the thought of leaving her friends and her home and her family.

"Have to go where?" Salm wasn't awake enough to take in the words.

Raina explained and April paced across the room and back again. Frustrated, she kicked her pillow in passing and heard a distinct clink. Raina stopped talking.

April bent down slowly and stuck her hand under her own pillow. If she had laid her head upon it, she would have found her vial. She lifted it free, now she could leave.

"April, please don't go," Raina sobbed. "You won't make it back, not against a Giant. I saw the hammer and the ... the teeth."

April sniffed and wiped her eyes. "I will come back." She donned the chain.

"Be careful April." Salm was a lot calmer than Raina, almost too calm. He stepped closer, as if to say good-bye. Or was he going to take back the chain? Unsure of his intent, April stepped up to the window. She couldn't chance being stopped; it was her choice and she was choosing to go.

"Sorry Raina. Sorry for making you sad. Bye Salm." In one motion, April leaped over the window ledge and started to fall. It was fortunate that she had taken the flying lesson with Skylar. When her wings appeared, she spread her arms and skimmed over the dark lake, leaving her wonderful new life behind to return to the nightmare she knew all too well.

7 – Big Foot

The vial's spell guided April east as if she could already see the rising sun. Flying was so much faster than walking and April used her wings as long as she possibly could. When her arms and shoulders cramped badly, she was forced to land before she fell out of the sky. By such time, she was through both the inner and outer layers of the barrier and no elf could follow her. And it was freezing.

The Outer-world was slipping into winter. It wasn't the frigid middle of the season yet, but after almost a year of eternal summer, the frosty breeze nipped sharply at April's skin. She wrapped a dry autumn leaf around her shoulders, and another around her head while her legs marched her along as surely as if she was a migrating animal irresistibly drawn to another home.

The sun appeared on the horizon ahead and she walked without pause, occasionally checking the forest for dangerous creatures. Since she couldn't change direction anyway, the safeguard was rather pointless.

At high noon, April began to search for something high to jump from, she wanted to fly again. She wanted to travel faster and the sky was generally safer than the ground in this world. Sadly, her feet would not allow her to detour up a tree. Her feet were being stubborn and thoroughly unreasonable again.

April had never tried gaining her wings by running and jumping, but she tried it now. As soon as she reached a sharp downward slope, she ran as fast as she could and leaped into the air with her arms wide. It didn't work at all. April crashed into the ground with enough force to rattle her teeth loose. She wasn't allowed even a minute to recover, her feet stood her up and kept on going and going and going. Her feet were a worse taskmaster than any teacher she had ever met. If her destination was a week or two away, April would be nothing but a wispy forest spirit before she even got close.

Exhausted, April touched the vial and closed her eyes. Maybe she could really sleepwalk. Or maybe she could take the vial off and have a rest. Her eyes snapped open when the hazy thought struck with the force of a hailstone. Why couldn't she take the vial off to have a nap? What was stopping her? Shaking her head to clear the fog, April lifted the chain off and collapsed to the ground.

For the first time, she was glad that she was alone so no one could witness her extreme stupidity. Whenever she wore the vial, she lost her clear thinking. April stuck the thing into her pack, collected an armful of fallen leaves and climbed into a tree for some much needed rest. With the vial off, she could climb any tree she wanted and jump to gain her wings. This journey had just gotten a whole lot easier.

April formed the leaves into a nest, pulled a couple on top like a blanket and slept until moonrise. Upon waking, she ate some rations out of her pack, replaced the vial, and jumped, planning to fly through the night if her arms could last that long.

She flew close to the ground in case any owls were hunting for their dinner. At least the bats would be hibernating in their underground caves, so she didn't have to worry about those predators. April kept her senses alert for dangerous creatures, but they were all on the ground. She flew over enough of them that first night, even a pair of forest cats, but she was safe in the sky.

When the sun rose again, April had no choice but to return to the ground. Her arms were failing. It was the start of her second day away from New Haven; it was Sunday. She had missed the whole weekend, but she would get to miss some school days, too. "Bright side," April said, trying to cheer herself up. It didn't work.

She walked until noon, then repeated the previous day's routine.

That night, April finished her rations. She hadn't brought nearly enough but at least she could find some food at this time of year. If the ground had already been buried under thick snow, she would have spent her days nearly starving. "Like old times," April murmured.

After she ate, she flew until the sun rose again and she was shivering with chills. It was time to walk. "Monday." She had to remember what day it was. Raina and Salm would be getting up for school. April pictured them walking beside her. She had thought it would make her feel less lonely; it made her feel worse because they weren't really there.

Around midmorning, April stumbled upon an old apple tree. A couple of shriveled brown apples clung stubbornly to the twisted branches. She climbed the tree and feasted on the mushy brown pulp, then napped right there.

That night, she started flying earlier than on the previous two days. Her wings held out until the sun rose; her arms and shoulders were getting used to flying. She would be an expert by the time she got back to New Haven. She couldn't wait to show off in front of Airron and Skylar and O'Wing. The thought made her yearn for home.

As soon as her feet touched down, April yanked off the vial, needing a small rest before she continued walking. "Tuesday. It's Tuesday," she declared to the empty space around her. Raina and Salm would be getting up for school again. April scavenged for food but came up empty. There was nothing to do but continue trudging along, wrapped in her coat of leaves.

By Wednesday, April was starting to resent the vial. Whoever had invoked the spell or charm should have included some sense of proximity. It was frustrating to have no idea if she was walking for one more day or a week or a month. Thanks to her new wings, April was making very good time and staying safe, but that didn't tell her anything about how long this journey would last.

When the sun rose on Thursday, April landed and started walking automatically. She checked the forest, avoided a trio of rambunctious raccoons, found a decent supply of seeds and ate them while she hiked until noon. When she settled into her leafy nest, at least she had a full stomach. It was a small comfort.

She slept later than sunset. April didn't know what time it was when she woke up, since it was fully dark and she couldn't see the moon. It was hidden behind a thick layer of cloud. The air smelled damp and froze her nostrils. "Snow." April could feel it in the air. It was the start of December, after all.

April placed the vial over her neck, jumped out of the tree and started flying. She learned something interesting about fairy wings when wet, heavy snowflakes started pelting down. Faster than she could shake them off, the flakes kept coating her wings and weighing her down. April was forced to land and walk long before sunrise. Then the wind picked up and started tossing her about willy-nilly on the ground. If she had been feeling less stubborn, she would have sought shelter. Instead, she tied a double layer of leaves around her feet and wrapped leaves all around her body and over her head, and kept on trudging. When the sun rose, she could barely see the light through the thick snow.

"It's Friday," April hollered angrily at the leaden gray sky. "Friday, Friday, Friday!" This was her seventh day of traveling and the worst by far. She was frozen and she was going to miss a second weekend in New Haven.

Determined to get wherever the heck she was going, April struggled through the snow, dreaming of home. Home was warm and home had food and home had all the elves she cared about. It was only the seventh day but April felt like she had been alone for a year. She made poor progress that day.

When she passed a thickly branched evergreen tree, April climbed into the sheltered center beside the trunk. She curled up in her wet leaves and instantly fell into a sleep of exhaustion. She slept for hours and hours; the sun was halfway to high noon when she opened her eyes to find the storm over. The world was wrapped in a blanket of pure untouched snow and profound silence.

It was Saturday - the weekend. April yawned, slipped the vial over her neck and jumped. She didn't get far, she had arrived at her destination. The vial didn't have a proximity warning but the snow held a shocking message. Enormous footsteps had walked right past her tree while she slept like the dead. They told her everything she needed to know. A Giant had marched past, heading west. As if it could read the snow too, her vial stopped guiding her east and turned her west.

"Not yet," April said, and yanked it off. She coasted down and landed in the nearest impression. In her world, it was considered very bad luck to walk in a Giant's footstep, but April needed to know when the monster had marched by her. The snow had been packed solid beneath the Giant's massive weight; April bent down and gingerly touched the icy surface. No fresh, loose flakes lay on top, it had not snowed at all since the Giant passed by. The storm had been over. Unfortunately, April didn't know when the storm had ended. She had slept through that, too.

"Hmm," April murmured, pacing from the back of the heel to the tip of the biggest toe. "Massive Giant," she murmured, not that it mattered. All Giants were so enormous that an extra yard of height didn't matter.

April closed her eyes and concentrated. The Giant was not within sensing range, neither was the elf, if the elf was still alive and in captivity.

Tracing the monster's trail was going to be as easy as following a river. April struggled through the soft snow towards the nearest tree, climbed high enough to leap and started flying again. She didn't replace the vial, she didn't need it now.

The longer she followed the tracks, the more terrified April grew. If she wasn't mistaken, this Giant was making a beeline for New Haven. Was it chance or did it know something? And would the forcefield truly work against a Giant? It was supposed too, but a Giant was so very big, it might not.

April struggled on all day without rest, determined to catch up to the monster and learn what she could. When the sun started to set, April concentrated yet again and faltered. The Giant was near enough to sense now. His aura was big and black and thick, almost suffocating. He wasn't moving.

The very last thing that she wanted to do was fly closer, but she did, until she could see the flames of a bonfire and smell wood smoke.

Dusk masked her small presence. April flew higher and closer, and suddenly there he was, silhouetted against the sparking flames. Somehow, over the years, April had forgotten exactly how big and thick and tall a Giant truly was. How could she have forgotten that? April landed clumsily in the branches of an evergreen tree with a clear view of the scene below.

"Look at what you are facing," April ordered herself and leaned forward. The Giant was an enormous lumpy shape, with lank hair hanging over sunken pits of eyes. He was tall, taller than most of his kind at about twenty-two feet. He growled and grunted when he poked his finger into the flames causing sparks to spring into the air and rain sizzling into the snow. April closed her eyes. She knew what she was facing, she didn't need to see more.

April burrowed deeper into the tree and tried to sense if an elf was down there somewhere. She concentrated hard but could sense no other living thing, only the Giant. His presence was so overpowering, it blocked out everything else. She would have to search with her eyes since her magical senses were blinded by the Giant.

Trying to feel brave, April jumped out of the tree and glided lower. Her wings kept her safe from the Giant in a way that she had never been in the past.

At about the level of the Giant's head, she landed and crouched hidden on a branch. The Giant did have a bulky pack created from an animal skin. It matched his tunic, dark brown and reeking even from afar. And he had dinner - half a carcass. It looked like the front end of a boar, complete with mangled head and glassy staring eyes. When the Giant picked it up and heaved it on top of the fire, the sparse fur and thick layer of fat caught on fire and flared brightly. This meat was far from fresh, April was almost sick from the stench, her stomach flip-flopped like a beached fish.

The flickering light revealed something else, a small rectangular shape nestled in the top of the pack. April focused on it and concentrated. As before, she could sense nothing but the smothering Giant. She would have to fly down to the campsite to know if an elf was in the box.

April pressed her hands together to stop them shaking and curled up on the branch to wait. "Wait for what?" she whispered sickly. But she knew. The Giant would feast on the meat of the boar and afterwards he would sleep. That was when she would fly silently down and look for the elf. It was a simple plan. There was little risk, since the Giant would sleep like the dead after filling his belly with pork and fat. Knowing those facts didn't reassure April about what she planned to do.

Before it was nearly cooked enough, the Giant hauled his gamey meal out of the fire, dragging it by one hoof. His mouth slack and dripping drool, he rolled the carcass around in the snow to cool the charcoaled skin. April looked quickly away when he ripped into the pig. Elder Scarab might have appreciated this spectacle in a way that April couldn't; she wished he was sitting beside her.

The Giant ate the entire half a boar. When the meat was gone, he sucked on the bones – his dessert, and tossed them aside like sticks. The meal had made the monster drowsy, he yawned widely enough to swallow a house, tossed another tree on the fire and approached his pack.

When the Giant grabbed up the small box, April had great hope that he would reveal the contents to her. He did nothing of the sort, instead, he shook it roughly and held it to his ear. With a throaty grunt of displeasure, he shook it again. Then he did something truly disgusting, he picked a chunk of meat from between his teeth and pushed it through a small hole in the box. April swallowed hard, thrice.

Still holding the container, the Giant dragged his sack closer to the fire. The lumpy smelly pack became a pillow. And the box stayed clutched in his fist, pressed against his ear. April didn't understand why the Giant kept the box in his ear, but he fell asleep that way, soon snoring loudly enough to shake loose the last few autumn leaves clinging stubbornly to bare branches.

It took every scrap of April's ragged courage to abandon her tree and fly toward the hill of Giant. She glided near enough to hear a rusty voice humming from inside the Giant's ear, but she didn't dare go any closer. She couldn't help the elf in the box while it was sitting in the Giant's ear and covered by the Giant's hairy fist. She would have to wait for a more opportune moment.

April glided back to her perch to spend another cold night alone, too sad to sleep. The elf in the box was suffering but she would find a way to help. Soon. Tomorrow.

She dozed fitfully, keeping an ear on the Giant. She woke with the sun but the Giant slept late. The box did not move from his ear until he lurched up and stuffed it into the top of his pack. Worse yet, he resumed walking west with purpose. He did seem to have a destination.

Trailing at a safe distance, April shadowed the Giant. She flew as fast as she could and managed to keep his back in sight. The sun was melting the carpet of snow and his footsteps were no longer clear impressions, but muddy blobs staining the pristine white. The temperature in the Outer-world was not yet consistently cold enough to hold a blanket of snow as a winter cover.

The Giant walked west all the long day, scattering every living thing before it. All forest creatures knew to avoid Giants, even if they had never seen one before. The sheer size and shaking ground scared them far and wide. And this Giant moved fast, his powerful legs gobbling up the miles.

By the end of that awful day, April was convinced he was closing in on New Haven, and she was having a terrible time matching the Giant's speed. Her shoulders were burning and her whole body was aching. She was cold, hungry and weak; it was a trial to keep going. When the Giant finally stopped before sunset, April almost glided down to thank him personally. She wisely headed for a tree instead.

As before, he started a fire with his flintstones, but he had no food. In a petulant mood, he kicked at the burning branches with his bare toes. His skin was so thick, he didn't feel any pain. His shoved his greasy hair out of his eyes and scanned the area, sniffing for food. He must have scented something of interest, because he grunted with excitement and took off running. April wasn't in the least prepared for his sudden departure, and he had left his pack behind.

With not a second to waste and no time to even think, April leapt and coasted down to the pack. As soon as her feet landed on top, she stumbled towards the little box. Up close, it was a creepy cage. The outer shell was ribbed with slats of bones. Were they Giant's finger bones? If so, there were a whole lot of them, decorating all four sides and even the top. The gaps between bone showed glints of silver metal. Small air holes didn't allow April to see more than the blackness inside. When she banged a fist on the metal, something scurried around.

"Hey!" April's voice almost failed her, it was a croak. "Hello! Who's in there?"

"Out," a voice whimpered back. Nothing more.

"Okay, okay. I'll try." April circled the box, searching for a way to open it. The sides were impenetrable, metal inside and bars of bone outside. She hauled herself up on the top, it was the same as the sides. This prison must open from the bottom. "Hang on," she hissed urgently, hopped down and shoved with all her strength. The box tilted slightly, but April wasn't strong enough to tip it over. She stepped back, feeling hopeless until she remembered how the New Haven elves had moved a great boulder. April needed a lever and a fulcrum!

She slid down the pack to search for tools. There were enough broken branches lying around, thanks to the Giant. One of those would be ideal. April dragged a sturdy stick up the side of the pack, desperation granting her strength.

Beside the box, a hard lump jutted out of the pack. April could use the lump as a makeshift fulcrum. It was a stroke of luck.

She centered the branch on the lump and worked one end under the box. "Perfect!" April ran to the opposite raised end and pushed it down with all her strength. This time the cage tipped right onto its side, exposing the bottom.

There were no bones below, only a hinged trapdoor, closed with a metal latch and hook. The Giant had not constructed this box, large fingers had no such ability to work finely with metal. Something much smaller had constructed the box long ago. The underside was tarnished black with age and scarred by countless marks and unsavory stains.

The trapdoor was simple to open from the outside. April shoved the metal hook free of the eye and pulled the door wide. "Quick, we have to get out of here," April cried, standing back.

Something climbed out of the box and April honestly could not believe her eyes. The body was gray, wiry and hunched, and covered in patchy coarse hair. A droopy soiled loincloth hung from bony hips, and too many crowded pointy teeth grinned widely at April. It was an imp – an imp that she knew rather too well.

"Brag? Brag! Brag? What the heck are you doing in there? Where's the elf? In the box with you?"

"April friend!" Brag hugged her joyously. He was rank enough to make an elf's eyes water. "April save Brag."

"I guess I did. But Brag ...where's the elf? You sent that note, didn't you?" she asked faintly.

"Note!" he beamed. "Bad elfie write note. Brag send hammer and note in bubble." But that was not the only news he had to share. "Elfie escape. Brag not escape."

"Good grief! The elf already got away?" she cried in dismay.

Brag nodded. "Bad elfie escape."

"But ... but ..." April had so many questions, she chose one at random. "How did you send a bubble anyway? Your magic doesn't work around Giants, does it?"

"No work. Giant go hunt. Kill beast food. Brag send bubbles. Vial first!" he declared, pleased with his cleverness.

April barely attended his words, urgency to flee distracted her. "You have a lot to explain Brag, but you can tell me the rest later. We have to get out of here before the Giant comes back. That way, Brag!" She pointed at the nearest edge of trees.

"Okey dokey!" Brag scurried down the side of the pack. April slid after him, the Giant's sack wasn't high enough for her to jump off and get wings. Together, they trudged away from the fire. The heat was melting the last of the thin layer of snow, turning the ground to soft sludge. It made for slow going.

April had too many questions in her head to stay quiet once they were on the move. She started with the most pressing one. "If you could make a bubble, why didn't you float the box away to somewhere safe? While the Giant was hunting?"

"Box not float. Giant bones not float." Brag squished his face up and sniffed the air.

"Oh. But how did the elf get away?"

Brag tugged his droopiest ear. "Not remember."

"You're going to tell me everything once we get out of here. How did you let a Giant catch you anyway?" Imps weren't smart, but they were a lot smarter than Giants.

"Bad Giant Loug get lucky," Brag said belligerently.

"Well, you caused me a lot of trouble, Brag. Now tell me all about this elf. But first, why don't you make a bubble and float us out of here!"

Talking about his bubbles has given April the idea, and slogging through the sucking snow was taking too long.

"Very bad bad bad elfie, badder than Loug," Brag ranted, wiggling his fingers as if to loosen them up to perform his magic. Since he thought all elves were bad, his opinion was questionable.

"How do you know the Giant's name anyway? I didn't know Giants had names."

"Loug good name." Brag had probably christened the Giant himself. The name suited the monster somehow. With a concentrated expression, Brag waved his fingers around, but nothing happened.

The knot in April's stomach tightened. "Why is the Giant Loug walking west, by the way, toward New Haven?"

Brag winced. "Brag point west. Brag say find whole world of elfies." He ducked his head. Even he knew he had behaved badly.

"What?" April's feet stopped walking. "Brag! Why did you do that?"

The imp looked at her as if she should have been smart enough to figure it out for herself. "April in Haven. April save Brag from Loug," he explained.

"Good grief, you were leading the Giant to New Haven so I could save you? That wasn't smart Brag. That was dumb, even for you!" she burst out. After more than a week of freezing and starving and missing her friends … only to learn that Brag was leading a Giant towards New Haven and there was no elf to rescue - it was too much! April was tempted to stuff the imp back in the box and leave him there, forever.

"Haven safe. Haven protected," he said sheepishly.

"Maybe it is, but maybe it isn't. We're talking about a *Giant*! You can't take chances with a *Giant*. Now make a bubble, I want to get away from here."

He pouted. "Brag try, bubble not work."

"Try again!"

"April bossier than Brag remember." He scrunched up his face and jabbed the air with all ten fingers. Still no bubble appeared. "No magic. Giant too close," Brag whimpered, and then the ground trembled.

Loug was returning. Brag's magic would not save them now and the edge of trees looked much further away than it had a second ago.

Brag leapt forward as if he had been prodded with a burning stick. April tried to race after him, but her smaller feet kept sinking in the melting snow. She tripped over something hard and lost precious seconds. As soon as she regained her feet, she tried to run but it was as if she was moving in slow motion. The next time she stepped forth, she sank up to her armpits.

"Ahhhh!" The frigid dunking was a shock.

In the muted dusk, April hadn't spotted the Giant's deeply pressed footstep, filled to the brim with a mixture of watery mud and snow. The submerged print had proved as effective as any deliberately dug pit trap. April flapped her arms trying not to sink deeper, her gills could not breathe this sludge.

"Brag," she yelled, "Come and pull me out! Help!" But the imp had already gained the shelter of the trees. His frightened face shook back and forth, barely visible.

"Brag no help. Giant come." His teeth chattered with nerves.

"Hey, I saved you!" April wailed and fought for the edge of the footprint, kicking as hard as she could, sadly her movement only drove her deeper. She was up to her chin when she reached the edge, but it was too late to climb out. Loug had returned.

April cowered in the heel. She was very small and submerged in soupy slush; the light was fading fast. There was every chance that she was completely camouflaged. Every chance.

Loug had not captured any dinner. His hands were empty and he looked mad. He also looked a thousand times taller from April's perspective. He stomped up to the campfire and tossed on another evergreen branch. It flared brightly and he turned back to his pack.

He was quick enough to notice the empty box lying obviously opened. April spotted the error herself, she had forgotten to reseal the door after the shock of Brag's appearance. She would have kicked herself if she'd had any feeling left in her feet.

Loug poked at the box and wrinkled his bent wreck of a nose. He scratched some fleas from his hair, staring at the box as if he had never seen it before. He tried to force his finger inside. A Giant's finger is taller and fatter than an elf, but stubby, as if the last joint had been severed off. As much as he tried to make it, Loug's finger didn't fit.

An enraged roar rent the air. Howling, the Giant spun around in a circle, sniffing. He was trying to scent Brag. Then he stilled. April watched because she couldn't look away. His massive head swung in her direction and the nostrils flared. It had to be Brag that he smelled, not April.

Loug bent way, way down and pushed his face close to something on the ground, something disastrous. April could see them as well as the Giant – a line of tiny muddy footsteps leading away from the box and tracking across the white of the snow. April was sure a forest spirit slipped an icy hand inside her chest then, and squeezed.

It took the Giant three steps to reach the place where she and Brag went in different directions. Brag's tracks led into the trees, he would be long gone by now. April's footsteps didn't lead anywhere but to her.

The Giant sniffed again, and narrowed his black eyes in her direction. April held her breath and sank below the surface of the slush. When the Giant stuck his finger into the footprint and stirred, April knew that her luck had run out, not that she'd had much to begin with. The finger bumped her away from the side and crooked to scoop her up.

"It's only a nightmare, a really bad nightmare," April promised herself. It was a blatant lie.

Loug deposited her into his other palm and stood way, way up. April simply lay helpless and shuddering from cold and terror as she was carted toward the fire. When the Giant dropped her, she thought she was falling into the flames and screamed with abandon. Instead, she landed roughly in a puddle of melted water. It was actually lovely and warm from the fire. The mud came off and the Giant realized he did not have Brag, but someone else entirely.

April was plucked back up by the straps of her overalls and examined by an eyeball as big as the full moon in the sky. The heavy eyelid crinkled in dark delight. An elf was a much more valuable find than an imp, and generally a whole lot harder to catch.

Loug whooped and almost blew her out of his hand in a gust of hot, rotten breath. His hand closed around her with crushing force. When he opened it again, the first thing she saw was the little box. She stared at the black doorway with resignation. She could enter willingly or wait for Loug to stuff her into the cage. April climbed quickly inside, before the Giant tried to shove her with his finger and broke half her bones.

The door slammed shut and the latch snapped in place. April was replacing Brag in the filthy prison box. She knew she was in shock because she couldn't feel a thing, both her body and brain were blessedly numb. Minutes or hours passed while she sat unmoving, then the box was picked up and shaken. April banged roughly against the walls.

When the movement stopped, she peeked out through the small holes in the side, trying to see what was happening. The box was pressed against a familiar black hole – Loug's ear. She guessed she was supposed to sing or hum or something.

"Not a chance," April shouted, her voice cracking.

The box was shaken harder. It was incentive enough. She hummed, her throat was too tight to form words.

As soon as Loug started snoring, she fell silent and drifted into sleep, wrapped in soiled leaves. Sleep was the best place to be, sleep was so much better than a loathsome prison box perched in a Giant's ear. Just about anywhere was better than that.

Unfortunately, when the sun rose on a new day, she was living the same nightmare. "Sunday? No Monday," she whispered. She thought it was Monday, she was pretty sure. She was supposed to be in school, not in a Giant's stinking ear.

Loug rose long after the sun, mumbling incoherently as he stuffed the box into the top of his pack and started lumbering along. After five minutes, he put down the pack and lifted up the box. April stayed silent and didn't move a muscle. It wasn't long before he opened the door and shook her out into his palm. Was she breakfast? April swallowed the hot panic that rose up in her throat when Loug raised her to his face, but he didn't stick her in his mouth, he grunted instead in a questioning way.

"What? What do you want?" April cried, her heart beating so hard that she shook.

In answer, Loug pinched her between his thumb and finger, and swung her left then right. "Go?" he rasped and repeated the action.

"You don't know where to go?" April asked. Without Brag, the Giant was lost.

"Go!" he roared and bared his teeth. Up close, they had a fuzzy layer growing between them.

"Okay, okay," April choked out and pointed south. She could lead him around New Haven at least. Satisfied, he dropped her back in the box and the endless day began. Loug proved to have a more limited vocabulary than any other Giant she had ever overheard. Giants struggled to communicate at the best of times, and perhaps Loug had been alone so long that he had forgotten how to speak even a dozen basic words.

Every couple of hours, April was dumped out of her cell. She pointed south and got put back in the box, over and over. When the sun lowered towards the treetops, April was so hungry and thirsty that she tried to get that message across to the Giant.

The next time his guttural grunt demanded directions, she did not point south, she pantomimed drinking and eating, then rubbed her stomach. The Giant lowered his protruding hairy brow and surveyed the area around him, he had quite a view. He stepped towards a glint of water. It was merely a puddle, nothing deep enough to swim under and hide in, but it would quench her thirst. April drank the dirty water for a long time, not sure when she would have an opportunity.

Loug picked her up as soon as she stood. She pointed south with resignation and advised the Giant that he really needed to wash his hands. He didn't care or he didn't understand. As to the eating, no food was offered. Maybe that was a good thing. April had witnessed what the Giant fed Brag. She would rather starve.

As always, Loug stopped at sunset. He lit his fire and left immediately to hunt food. April used the time alone to try and escape; it shouldn't have been that hard. She was a lot smarter than Brag. She concentrated to learn if there were any nearby creatures that might be willing to cart off the box or paw it opened. Sadly, there was nothing large enough in sensing range. The Giant had scared the animals far far away.

Next, she tried to kick the door open. The latch was secure, she wasn't strong enough. Could she burn her way out of the box? April ran a hand over the wall. No, the metal was thick and solid. If she tried to melt an escape hole, she would probably cook herself or choke to death on the fumes. The risk was too great.

By the time Loug returned, April hadn't escaped or even dreamed up a crazy plan to win her freedom. She peeked out one of the holes and saw that the Giant had been successful in his hunt. He had captured a long brown snake, nicely plumped for hibernation. Loug must have invaded its winter den.

The Giant snapped the reptile sharply by the rattling tail and tossed it on the coals, where it crackled and sizzled and popped in the most gruesome way. April stuck her fingers in her ears, sickened by the sounds.

As soon as the serpent was charcoal black, Loug yanked it out of the coals and ate every bite, except for the morsel that he dropped into April's cell. That strip of snake had been peeled right off the bones, it hadn't come out of Loug's mouth. April was so hungry that she devoured the meat. She had never tried snake before. It was actually delicious, tender and steamed in its own juices. It was the best meal that April had eaten in well over a week, cooked by a Giant no less.

She hummed Loug to sleep and then couldn't stop her own tears. She hadn't cried yet, she was allowed. It was only her second night in the Giant's ear but it felt like forever. Brag would be long gone. With his fear of Giants, he would not risk returning to free her from her prison. He wasn't going to be any help. It was up to her to get herself out of this mess. And April would find a way to escape, and in the meantime, she would guide Loug far away from New Haven.

8 – Lost World

April's time with Loug blended into a gray fog of misery. She kept pointing south and Loug followed her finger. Nights were spent clutched in the Giant's fist and pressed against his ear. It stopped her from freezing to death when the temperatures dipped sharply.

It hadn't snowed again, although there had been a nearby thunderstorm a day ago. Loug had been very scared of the lightening and thunder, he had cowered under a tree and snarled at the sky until the booming noise faded away.

And April had all too much time to ponder her fate. She kept trying to think up an escape plan, but her brain didn't seem to be working very well. She hadn't managed to come up with anything and dreaded what would happen when Loug didn't find the world of elves that Brag had promised him. Maybe the Giant would keep April to do magic forever, or maybe he would crush her in anger. And there was always the being eaten alive option.

When Loug stopped at sunset on what April guessed to be Thursday, he paced restlessly and sniffed the air, growling low in his throat. Something was up. It had snowed on and off all day and the ground wood was white and wet. Loug kicked damp sticks together, tore dripping branches off trees and tried to light the pile by banging his flintstones together as if he was wished to destroy them. He had forgotten to find anything dry to put on top, all the sparks he created fizzled and died.

Loug reacted by throwing a Giant's temper tantrum. It was something to behold. He raged and roared and ripped trees up by their roots. He stomped to shake the earth and heaved loose boulders through the air. April covered her ears and cowered; if he landed a boulder on his pack, she was doomed. He really was in a foul mood about something, not merely the fire. Maybe he had expected to find his treasure of elves by now.

When Loug picked up the box and shook April roughly into his palm, it was unexpected. He didn't usually take her out of her cell at night. Loug pointed to his pile of uprooted trees and snarled, "Food."

"Get your own food," April shouted angrily, her own temper unpredictable after too many days as the creature's miserable captive.

Loug pushed his ugly face too close. His sunken eyes were black empty holes in the gloomy light. He curled his lip and stabbed his finger at the pile of soggy wood. "Food," he repeated.

"I can't make food appear with magic, not enough to feed you anyway! No elf can do that! Stupid lumpy brainless Giant." It felt good to call him names. And the Giant believed he needed her to lead him to the elves, he wasn't going to harm her yet.

Loug closed her in his fist and shook hard. Then he opened his hand and pointed at his flintstones. "Food."

April stopped cringing and stood as tall as she could, her temper taking over. "Do you mean fire? Fire isn't food. You can't eat fire! How dumb can you get?"

He shook her again.

"Okay, one fire," April mumbled, her head spinning like a whirling dervish. She fell down into his palm, it took a couple of minutes to regain her legs. When she could stand, April focused on igniting the wood and suddenly had an idea. It was a long shot, but maybe if she got really mad, she could generate her own thunderstorm, complete with lightening. Maybe lightening would come down and strike this beastly Giant. April wasn't inside New Haven and she didn't have the thunderwands, but it was worth a try. Any escape possibility was worth attempting now that Loug had bypassed New Haven.

April pretended that she was going to make fire by pointing at the soggy wood and wiggling her fingers while she fanned her own anger. It wasn't hard to prime herself into a temper, especially when Loug shook her again because she was taking too long. She got plenty mad then, she could feel the storm churning inside her, but nothing happened in the sky. Not one tiny cloud, not one low rumble - nothing. As she had suspected, creating a storm did require New Haven.

With a hopeless sigh, April channeled her energy to start the Giant's fire. It exploded wildly to life, fueled by her store of suppressed anger.

"There, happy now? You can make your own blasted fire next time! Unless you don't have a brain inside that big lumpy hollow overgrown head," April hollered and kicked his hand as hard as she could.

He either understood her words or he didn't like being kicked. Loug tapped her on the head with his powerful finger. The blow was hard enough to make her see one big exploding sun; April fell senseless into his hand.

When she woke up, she was back in the foul box. It was the dead of night, the fire was a bed of coals and Loug was snoring slow and deep. That must have been what awoke her, that and the bone-chilling temperatures. April hadn't been conscious to hum Loug to sleep and he had left her box on the ground beside his pack. It was preferable to sleeping in his ear, except for the cold.

"April? April? Say something. Are you alive?" Raina's voice came out of nowhere.

April realized that she was having a hallucination, maybe the Giant had damaged her brain. At least it was a lovely hallucination. It was wonderful to hear Raina's voice even though Raina wasn't really there.

"April? April, answer me!"

"Hey Raina," April obliged.

"Are you okay?"

"I don't think so, I'm having hallucinations."

"What?"

And then April heard more voices - Salm and Airron and Peter. They were all there. April said 'hello' to everyone. It was the best fantasy ever.

"How do you open the box?" Peter asked with great urgency.

"The bottom," April said. Her lovely dream wouldn't be complete without escaping from the Giant.

"Hold on," Peter warned. It really felt like the box tipped over. Within seconds, the door popped wide. April obligingly climbed out and hugged her friends. It even felt like they were really there. April touched Raina, her friend was soft and puffy. Peter was smart enough to relatch the door.

"Come on," Raina whispered in a shaking voice and tugged April by the hand. Silently, they ran from the Giant. As soon as they were safely away, Airron asked April to light a torch. She did. Then she could see her friends. Everyone stared at April in the flickering light and she smiled euphorically back.

"April, I really don't think it's a good idea to yell at a Giant. They're very big, aren't they?" Raina said first. Her eyes were rimmed with red and her teeth were chattering, but not from the cold. She was wearing too many layered clothes to be anything but warm and toasty.

"Couldn't believe my eyes, April yelling at a Giant," Airron said. "And to be honest, I always thought you were exaggerating about their size. They're bigger, aren't they?"

"April, what were you thinking?" Salm chided and hugged her against his chest. Peter was next. The boys were as puffy as Raina. All four elves were dressed for winter.

April didn't say a word, she simply gazed at her friends and tried to figure out if she had lost her mind forever.

"April, are you okay?" Peter asked.

"I wish ... I wish you were really here," she said and started to cry. She wouldn't have done that if her friends were truly there, but they weren't, so she could cry her heart out if she wanted. It had been a dreadful week.

"But we are here. We are here and there's a Giant. And I wish we weren't here. But we had to come and get you." Raina's voice faltered. "And ... and I want to go home now."

"But how can you be here? You can't be here. None of you can cross through the barrier - "

"Brag. He came and got us to help you," Salm explained. "We had to steal the thunderwands. Raina got Skylar to reveal the secret location." Raina looked appropriately ashamed. "And Brag altered the barrier so we could leave to come and save you from the Giant. My parents are really going to kill us this time."

It was a plausible explanation. April's fantasy was very creative with the proper attention to detail. "I wish you were really here," she repeated, and hugged each one of her wonderful friends once again because they felt so good and so solidly real.

"Do you think the Giant hit her too hard?" Airron asked.

"I wouldn't be surprised. We'll get her home and my Dad can check her head," Salm said. "I can't even imagine what she's been through."

"And all to save Brag. That imp is more trouble than he's worth," Peter growled.

They were talking about April as if she wasn't standing right beside them. Then Raina handed her a flatbread and wrapped a blanket like a shawl over her shoulders. April savored the food while they hiked through the undergrowth. They walked until the sun rose. At one point, they had to skirt around a sizable pond.

Raina glanced at April and sniffed. "Too bad the water is so cold."

"What? Are you saying I stink?" Of course she stank, after sharing Brag's filth and hanging out with a Giant.

"A bit," Raina allowed.

April removed the cozy blanket, strode over to the pond and jumped in. The water was as cold as it could possibly be without being frozen over. She gasped and lost her breath. After a thorough rinse, she waded ashore shivering hard, her teeth chattering uncontrollably.

"April, why did you do that?" Raina cried. "You're going to be frozen. We don't care about the smell. It's not your fault that you smell like ..." Raina stopped her words. "Here, I'll give you some of my dry clothes, I'm wearing about ten layers. We remembered that you said it was winter out here now so we came prepared." Raina guided April behind a tree trunk and all but dressed her. The borrowed clothes were dry, warm and best of all – clean.

Raina bundled up April's wet overalls, tossed the blanket around her again and hurried them back to the others.

"Do I smell better?" April asked.

"Well, you couldn't possibly smell worse, so you have to smell better," Airron retorted.

It was at that precise moment that April began to wonder if this was truly happening. The pond had been very cold, and Raina had told her she stank. "Are you really, really here?" April asked again.

"Is she still saying that?" Airron demanded. "April, we're here. What do we have to do to convince you? We've rescued you from a *Giant*! Do we have to thump you on the head ourselves?" He gripped her shoulders and shook gently.

If her friends were really in the Outer-world with the Giant running around, they were at great risk. "If you are here, you shouldn't be here. It's dangerous," April said.

"No kidding. I think she's finally getting it," Airron whooped. "We are here and it is dangerous and we're trying to get home. So let's get moving before that monster of a Giant wakes up and chases us. Okay?"

"Okay," April agreed meekly.

She started walking along as if she was in a dream rather than a nightmare. They really were here! April let the wonderful news sink in. She wasn't alone or trapped in the bone box. She was free and back with her friends. And soon they would all be safely home. It seemed too good to be true.

"Umm ... how far away is New Haven?"

"Not so far, another day or two. Is that right, Peter?" Raina checked.

"About right," Peter agreed.

April had steered the Giant dangerously close to New Haven. The last few days had been cloudy, hiding the directional sun and it was hard to see much of the world through the little holes in the box. Clearly, she lacked Peter's almost magical sense of direction.

They hiked at a punishing pace over the dusting of snow, with only brief rests when it was absolutely necessary. And they talked non-stop. April heard all the details of how her friends had engineered their own escape from New Haven, with Brag's help. It was an amazing story and April was very impressed. She said as little as possible about her time with Loug, she didn't want to remember any of it.

They finished all the food in the packs before the sun disappeared that day. April seemed to have ended up with the largest share, but she was too starved to refuse what was offered.

When the sky grew black, April assured her friends that it would be safe to stop for the night. Loug had never walked after the moon rose and rarely moved until midmorning, and he probably wouldn't change his routine. If he did, he would have an impossible time spotting small elves in the dark of night.

They climbed trees until they found one with a secure hollow to spend the night. It was so cold that they hauled a whole pile of leaves in and huddled under them. The cozy arrangement was so much better than being alone in the prison box. April fell asleep with a smile on her face. She woke up the same way. It was daylight.

Everyone was stirring and stretching. April yawned and sat up.

"Hey." Airron shifted his shoulders, adjusting his wings. "Sleep well?"

"Like a log. Best sleep since I left."

"Well, tonight we'll be home in our own beds," Raina said, trying to pat her hair into place. It was sticking up everywhere. "And my parents will be so happy to see us that we won't really get in trouble."

Salm snorted. "You're dreaming." He passed behind his sister and mussed her hair with both hands. There was nothing to eat so they started walking again.

By noon, there had been no sign of the Giant and they had managed to avoid anything truly threatening because the forest was almost empty of life. Brag hadn't shown his face, either. With his fear of Giants, he had probably gone home to his garden.

"Peter, when do you think we'll get home?" April asked for about the tenth time that day.

"In time for bed," he promised, again.

Everyone hiked with renewed energy. April continued checking the forest even though they should have been well into the outer layer of the forcefield at that point - the layer that warned everything large or dangerous away. She didn't sense anything alarming, but was disconcerted to spot paw prints tracking across the snow. A sizable forest cat had prowled by recently. Cats would not normally be scampering around so close to the inner barrier. A fission of fear tingled along April's spine and her feet slowed.

"Umm ... when Brag altered the forcefield, are you sure he did it right?" she asked, trying to sound unconcerned.

"I suppose. He said he knew how. He did do it before, and he did it right that time," Raina reasoned.

Peter shot April a keen glance, but he didn't follow it up with awkward questions.

They kept walking and darkness pressed in around them. The vegetation grew sparse and the land began to slope steadily downward. April magically lit torches and the small weary group kept trudging along. When she stumbled into a moose's hoof print, a chill settled deep inside her heart. According to Peter's estimate, they should be inside New Haven by now. There shouldn't be any raccoons around, not for miles and miles. And it should be warm and summery, it was all cold and wintry.

124

"Uh ... you don't think Brag turned the forcefield off by accident, do you?" April asked in the most conversational of tones.

Raina stopped walking, everyone did. "April, what are you saying?"

"I'm not saying anything. I'm asking a question, and I'm only asking because that was a moose print I just fell in, and I've never seen a moose in New Haven – and I've never seen snow in New Haven." She kicked the white ground. "We should be inside the pit of the peach, you know, inside the inner layer of the forcefield – inside New Haven. There should be a lot more vegetation, there's hardly any. I'm sure it's nothing," April tacked on lamely. "We probably aren't as close as you thought, right Peter?"

Peter didn't answer.

"Peter?" Raina prompted, a panicky edge to her voice.

"Listen," he said gravely, "It might be worse than that."

"How can it be worse than the forcefield being turned off?" Airron demanded. "Especially when *we* did it?"

"Let's sit down, I'll try and explain." Being told to sit down was alarming in itself. They sank to the cold ground and Peter paced.

"Spit it out," Salm advised.

"Okay. The barrier is not turned off. New Haven is ... gone," Peter said baldly.

"Gone?" Airron snorted with laughter. "Right! Pull the other one. Very funny joke! Can we go home now?"

"We are home. We are inside the barrier, except even that's gone." Peter sounded serious. It was dark, and he had said that they would be home in time for bed.

"Peter, you must have made a mistake," Raina insisted. "Anyone can make a mistake. Let's keep walking, I'm sure New Haven is around the next tree, although there don't seem to be any trees ..." She trailed off uncertainly.

By unspoken agreement, everyone stood up and started slogging again, it was better than sitting on the icy ground.

As discreetly as possible, April nudged Peter and slowed. He matched her pace and offered a pointed ear. "Peter, where is New Haven gone?"

"I wish I knew. But it is missing, I know that as surely as I know my own name." It was the worst news.

"But how is that possible? What are we going to do? How are we going to find a missing world?" April whispered in distress.

"You ask tough questions," Peter said. It was no answer at all.

Soon, walking became impossible. The angle of the hill increased until they kept skidding and sliding down the icy slope in uncontrollable fits and starts. They gave up on the walking and simply slid for the longest time, until they reached bottom. Back on level ground, Peter suggested they stop for the night.

They scoured for cover but couldn't find any. They might as well have been standing at the bottom of a frozen lake, if all the water had been drained out. There was nothing to do but keep walking, all night long.

The land eventually began to curve up and climbing the steep slope was a lot harder than slipping down such a surface. The sun was well up before they crested the challenging hill and found first some scruffy vegetation, and then some small scraggily trees.

Exhausted, they climbed into the split trunk of a long dead maple. The home away from home left a lot to be desired, especially since they had expected to be in their own beds by now, not lying with hungry bellies in a whistling wind.

Even though they had walked through the night, April could not fall asleep. It had nothing to do with the hunger or the wind, and all to do with guilt and fear. New Haven was gone and it was probably her fault. She had started the disastrous chain of events by leaving, inspiring her friends to alter the barrier and follow her. And all to save Brag, who probably would have managed to escape in his own good time. Imps were tough, a lot tougher than elves. There had been no need for April to go haring off in the middle of the night after all.

In her defense, the note had been misleading. It was written by an unidentified elf while he or she was being held captive in the box. April couldn't have known that the elf would escape, leaving Brag behind. And Loug had robbed her of any opportunity to gain answers from Brag.

Raina finally reached over to hold April's hand. "We'll find New Haven. Peter made a mistake, got lost, that's all," she murmured comfortingly, as if she could sense April's turmoil. It had probably been all the restless tossing and turning and almost rolling out of the tree.

"Yes," April agreed, not believing it for a second.

Around noon, everyone gave up on trying to sleep. Airron decided that he should fly around and look for New Haven. April didn't want him to go alone, it was too dangerous. She insisted on going, too. The rest of their party promised to stay where they were in the tree. April insisted on that as well.

It was the first time that April and Airron had flown together. Airron grinned at her and complimented her flying ability. She was not nearly as good as Airron, but she matched his pace.

"Not scared of heights anymore?" he asked, when they had gained an impressive altitude.

"Not so much. I've been flying for days and days. I think I've gotten used to it." And if she fell, she had wings and she knew how to use them. It wasn't the same now. Except for the stinging cold, April enjoyed flying with Airron.

They flew forward, then back the way they had come, and nothing looked familiar. They couldn't find nine hills ringing a world of bright green and sprouting smaller than normal trees. They couldn't find the town square. There were no elves or elf dwellings anywhere. What they did see below was a vast circular wasteland near their temporary campsite, with no vegetation or trees. It was the empty frozen basin they had walked through in the darkness. "What do you make of that?" Airron called, pointing down at the depression.

"I'm not sure," April replied uneasily. She had a deeply foreboding feeling about what lay below, or didn't lay below. The only landmark that interrupted the desolate space was a wild river surging away from the base of a violent waterfall that splashed down into the basin on one side, and cut deeply enough into the opposite side to flow back out.

"No New Haven," Airron concluded.

Too frozen to fly further, they glided down to their temporary home.

When they landed in the tree, their friends were impatient to hear some good news. "Well?" Raina demanded, as soon as they settled in the nook with blankets around their shoulders. "How far away is New Haven?"

April looked at Airron and Airron looked at April. She waited for him to deliver the awful news.

"Okay, here's the thing. We couldn't find New Haven. We flew far and wide, it does seem to be ... gone," Airron said gently, putting an arm around Raina's shoulder.

"But? But ... that's impossible. A world can't just up and disappear," Raina argued.

"I know," Airron agreed.

"It can't," she insisted.

"I know," he repeated, patiently.

"It really can't." Her voice wavered.

"It really can't, but it has. New Haven is gone." A wake of silence followed the fateful pronouncement. Bewildered eyes turned to April. She could do no more than nod, verifying Airron's words.

Raina asked, "April, do things like worlds just disappear in the Outer-world?"

"No," April said sadly.

"Never?"

"Never."

"Oh." Clearly, Raina didn't know what to say next.

Airron changed the subject. "Come on, let's find something to eat. I'm starved."

Raina cried, "How can you think about food at a time like this?"

"Hey, I've been flying all morning. I've been thinking about nothing but food for the last hour. We don't have anything else to do, we might as well find food." And it would grant them time to come to terms with the tragic situation.

Since they didn't know what else to do, they scavenged for food, automatically skirting the empty land that sat where New Haven should. Near the edge of a stream, April found a couple of dehydrated frozen raspberries and some edible roots. She stuck some raspberry seeds in her pocket for later and the five friends sat in a close circle. It was a subdued group that chewed the tough, coarse meal.

When they were finished choking down lunch, Salm asked, "What now?" It was time for a plan.

"I want to go home," Raina said, her lip quivering. "Do you think New Haven is invisible or something? But still here?"

Peter shook his head decisively. "If it was simply invisible, it would still be where it normally is but we wouldn't be able to see it. We did walk to where it was supposed to be, it wasn't there. It is gone, which is more than invisible."

"But gone where? Where are Mom and Dad and Dewy?" Raina's voice thickened.

"I don't know. I've been thinking about it half the night and I have no explanation." Peter looked around hopelessly. "Does anyone have any ideas?"

No one did.

"So, what should we do?" Salm asked. "Should we hang around here, where New Haven is supposed to be? In case it comes back?"

"That's probably the best idea for now," Peter concurred. "Does everyone agree?"

Four heads bobbed weakly. It wasn't much of a plan but it was something.

"If we are staying here, we should find the safest place to sleep and live," April said. "Large creatures might start roaming around again if Loug goes home. And it is getting colder."

"Colder than now? I thought it was winter," Airron said.

"It's only the start of winter. It will get a lot colder, depending on how long we're out here. Not that we are going to be out here that long," she tacked on hastily.

"Better not be. And what about food?" Airron asked.

"We'll manage. There is usually something to stop an elf from starving. It's not always good," April warned. "But we won't starve."

"Speak for yourself, I'm already starved," Airron shot back.

April recalled the last good Outer-world meal that she had eaten. "Maybe I can find a small hibernating snake. They're very good cooked over a fire. The Giant fed me some snake. It was the first time I'd ever tried it, but it was delicious." Her suggestion of a snake dinner was not well received.

"Snake? Good grief, I'd rather eat my pack," Raina countered.

"Considering that the Giant fed Brag some rotten pork picked from between his big grungy teeth, I wasn't going to complain about fresh cooked snake, believe me," April said.

Everyone looked kind of sick and Airron told her to 'shut up'.

"Fine, no snake then. It would probably be too dangerous to sneak into a den of snakes anyway, even if they are hibernating."

Salm raised his eyebrows. "Den of snakes?"

"Snakes often hibernate together, a whole squirming bunch of them, deep in the ground where it's not so cold. Sometimes in the spring, a big ball of sleepy snakes will roll out of a den, they look really funny all tangled up," April said.

Airron looked incredulous. "I'm sure you make this stuff up."

"I do not," she cried.

"If we're still stuck here in the spring, you can show me one of these snake balls," Airron replied, "Then I'll believe you."

No one wanted to think about being without New Haven until spring. Peter quickly suggested it was time to scout for a hopefully very temporary home. Searching gave them something to do, which was a lot better than worrying about New Haven.

As the afternoon drew to a close, the best site they had discovered was a deep hollow in the trunk of a fat tree. It was about ten feet from the ground, too high for anything to wander in without warning. And it was empty, sort of. Nothing alive was lurking inside now, but something had lived in the hollow until recently. The cave reeked, and it was littered with droppings and scraps.

Everyone helped to clear out the gross debris.

Peter was rolling a lumpy roundish object toward the door when he stopped and peered closer. "April, do you know what this thing is?"

"There are a couple of them over here, too," Airron chipped in, kicking one closer. It came up to his thigh. "Hey! Is that ... fur? And a bone sticking out?"

"Probably." April knew exactly what the gruesome packages were. "Those are owl pellets."

"Owl pellets? You say 'owl pellets' when you're cursing." Peter wiped his hands on his pants. "Does that mean this is owl dung?"

"Not really. It comes out the other end – the beak end," she explained.

The boys merely looked confused.

"Why would that thing be coming out of an owl's mouth?" Airron asked.

"Owl's swallow their smaller prey whole – things like mice. They can't digest the bones and fur, so they vomit that stuff up later, in pellets like these."

Airron kicked his pellet right out the door with gusto. "Don't think I want to cuddle up to those when I'm sleeping." He energetically got rid of all the rest. There were a lot of owl pellets in the hollow. When the whole space was cleared, Raina insisted they scrub the floor with snow, twice. Only then was she satisfied.

Finally, the boys dragged up armloads of clean dry leaves while

Raina and April scavenged nearby for as many seeds as they could find. The food was hauled up, too. Salm even stumbled upon one lonely acorn, probably dropped by a passing squirrel. He pounded on it with a rock until it crumbled, then shared out the pieces.

They settled down for yet another night in the Outer-world, safe and fed. It could have been fun, like a camping trip, except for the heart wrenching disappearance of New Haven. The missing world weighed heavily on all of them. Raina was the most homesick but she showed a brave face. Airron kept a comforting arm around her shoulder and talked nonstop, distracting all of them. When it was fully dark, he trailed off into somber silence. Last night they had only suspected that New Haven was gone, this night they knew it had truly and mysteriously disappeared.

Their optimistic hope that New Haven would pop up beside them faded when the days stretched into a week, and then a second week. The weather did get steadily colder and food grew scarce, especially after snow fell to thickly coat the forest floor. This time it didn't melt, it stubbornly held its ground.

April was kept busy teaching her friends all the tricks of survival that were second nature to her. They walked around with leaves wrapped over their clothes. Peter's pocket blade was employed to cut up a couple of their sacks, and the pieces were used to make much-needed slippers and mittens. April demonstrated how to tie slabs of bark under their feet, so they could walk over the surface of the snow on the days when it was too soft to support even their small weight.

And she worried. April was always saying 'don't touch that' or 'stay away from that' or 'quick, get in the tree' or 'don't stray'. Airron nicknamed her 'mother', he even accused her of nagging. April began to feel true sympathy for the Pooles after what Raina, Salm and she herself had put them through in the past. And this latest episode was the worst by far. After all this time, their families were probably thinking the very, very worst.

One afternoon at the end of the second week, food had been particularly elusive and everyone had reached a low point. Raina had cried herself to sleep the night before and hadn't smiled once all day. April was tormented by guilt for causing this terrible situation with her rash departure from New Haven. She was desperate to cheer her friends. When she found the forgotten raspberry seeds in her pocket, it gave her an idea. The least she could do was provide a decent meal before the ground froze solid.

At noon, April scraped the snow off a patch of soil in a sunny pocket between leafless trees and sat cross-legged in the snow with her seeds. Raina and Airron wandered over curiously. "What are you doing?" Raina asked.

"I'm going to make lunch."

"Lunch? Not snake?"

"No, not snake. A surprise. Well, I guess a snake would be a surprise, but this is a better surprise." Salm and Peter drifted over to have a look. None of her friends had ever seen this magic and she hoped it would entertain them as well as provide food. There was little risk that the magic would attract the nearest forest creatures, due to both Loug and the season. Anything larger than a rodent was still missing and they were beside their treehouse if they needed to seek shelter fast.

April buried the raspberry seeds in shallow earth and placed her hands over the mound. The magic wasn't complicated, but it did require concentration and effort, doubly so because of the cold ground and weak sun. If she had been inside the barrier, this magic would have been accomplished in short minutes, but not out here.

With closed eyes, April absorbed the small warmth of the sun and inhaled the moisture in the air. She focused all her attention on the spot of earth holding the seeds. As if time had sped up, the seeds sprouted. When the new shoots tickled her hands, she lifted them aside. The shoots slowly transformed into long stems, with leaves and then buds. April was being drained of energy but fought to keep going. The buds turned into small white flowers and then unripe pink berries. The newly grown raspberry bush was heavily laden with fruit; the berries ripened and turned rich red in minutes rather than days or weeks. April had seen the results in her mind, but when she opened her eyes – it was exactly as she had imagined. A quick check confirmed that no forest creatures had been drawn to her magic.

There were cheers all round.

"Lunch is served." April didn't have to say it twice.

Hands reached out and berries were plucked reverently. It had been too long since they had eaten anything fresh and delicious. Peter handed April a berry when she was not inclined to move. She had forgotten how draining it was to create magic outside of New Haven.

They feasted until they couldn't eat another bite and everyone smiled. The remaining berries were picked and stored carefully in the tree hollow. The cold would keep them fresh.

Throwing caution to the wind, April asked the boys to gather the driest wood they could find, and she started a roaring fire with the last of her energy. The smoke should not alert anything to their presence, since the magic hadn't.

Shoulder-to-shoulder, they huddled close and warmed up for the first time in days. Raina brewed bark tea over an edge of coals, in the upside-down cap from Salm's acorn. The drink was passed around; the shared sips of hot liquid were as welcome as the full bellies. They slept soundly that night.

The next day, Peter said they all needed to talk. It sounded like he was calling a gathering.

"Peter? Have you discovered something?" Raina asked eagerly.

"What? No, no. Nothing like that, nothing good, nothing bad. I simply want to reevaluate our situation. Talk. We've been here almost two weeks and New Haven hasn't reappeared, or shown any sign that it will. I think we might have to search for our world," he said in a rush.

"But Peter, how would we know where to look," Raina cried. "At least we're safe here and New Haven might come back. I don't think we should go anywhere else, in case it comes back. I want to be here when it comes back!"

Peter stopped pacing the small confines of the tree cave. He crouched down and looked Raina in the eye. "It has been two weeks, I don't think it is coming back," he said frankly. "I think we need to go and find it. All our families must be worried sick - "

"I know, I know that. Do you think I don't know that," Raina burst out, her face crumpling. "But what if they come back and we're not here? That would be worse. I'm not leaving." She started to cry in earnest.

"We'll think about it," Salm said quietly, pulling Raina against his side. "We'll think about it." His face had already grown thinner, the torchlight emphasized the hollows beneath his cheekbones. It made him look aged. His solemn eyes told Peter to be quiet. Peter didn't say another word.

Even though it wasn't mentioned again, the subject was on all of their minds over the next few days. April privately agreed with Raina, the rest of the world was too big to search and they didn't know where to start looking. April knew better than anyone exactly how big the rest of the world was. She had heard tales of lakes so large that it would take years for an elf to cross to the other side, and hills so tall that they disappeared into the clouds. It had taken her five impossibly long and lonely years to find New Haven the first time, and she'd had directions, sort of. April was inclined to think that their small group should stay put. On the other hand, Peter had very good instincts. Any opinion he held was worth considering.

Setting out to find New Haven was a difficult decision to make, and not one to be made lightly. As long as their present situation didn't change, they had all the time in the world to decide if they should stay or go.

It was fortunate that they did not pack up and leave because two days later, they had an unexpected visitor.

9 - Tracks in the Snow

April was puttering around the campsite, keeping her senses tuned on the surrounding woodland, so she was the most taken aback when a finger tapped her on the back of the shoulder.

"Ahhh," she yelled, leaping away as if she had been stung by a bee.

It was Brag. He blinked his bleary green eyes at her and rubbed his grizzled snout. "April scare Brag," he accused.

"Well, Brag scared April more," she gasped.

Everyone rushed over. Salm stepped protectively close, he didn't fully trust the imp. None of them did since Brag had almost killed them off one by one, not so long ago.

"April escape!" he declared happily. Had he just noticed?

"Yes, April's friends saved her, after you told them about Loug. Brag, where have you been?" She really had to stop referring to herself in the third person when she conversed with the imp.

Brag had something else to talk about. "Haven gone." He scratched his head and motioned at the bare land behind him. "Where Haven gone?" He'd had nothing to do with the world's disappearance, it seemed. And even the imp knew it was supposed to be *here*.

133

"We don't know. We can't find it. Do you know what happened to it?" April asked, hoping to jog his memory in case he had forgotten.

"Brag not know."

"But did you do anything weird to the forcefield, maybe? When you altered it?" April hinted.

"No weird, like before," he said.

April believed him, plus he seemed sincerely bewildered to find New Haven gone.

"Brag have surprise," he added with his hugest grin. She could see every last one of his crowded teeth, and he had a lot of teeth.

"Is it a good surprise?" she asked. You never could tell with imps.

"Bad surprise. Elfie surprise," he elaborated.

"Elfie surprise?" April didn't know what that meant?

"Have you found the lost elf?" Raina gasped.

"Elfie foots in snow." He pointed east. "Brag go home now. Giant Loug close." It was awful news and he hadn't prepared them for it. Brag turned to go.

"Brag, wait." Peter stopped him. "Before you leave could you maybe tell us exactly how close the Giant is, and where you saw these elf footprints."

"Okey dokey. Brag go east. Show elfie foots." He was offering to escort them, since he was headed that way.

"And the Giant?" April reminded him.

"Close."

"You already said that Brag. How close?" April really wanted to know, or maybe she didn't.

"Close close." He shrugged his bony shoulders with a twitchy jerk. "Go now."

The decision about whether to stay or move on had been made for them. They scrambled to gather their few belongings and shared the last of the raspberries, including one for Brag. They strapped bark on their feet since the latest snow was fluffy, and then they were ready to leave. Brag didn't need bark, his feet were big and flat all by themselves. The imp led the way, cheerfully chattering his teeth.

It felt strange to leave their temporary home so abruptly, but if Loug was approaching, it was best if they went somewhere else. New Haven had been smart enough to leave, they should too. And the footprints had to be examined.

"April, do you think it is an elf from your world?" Raina asked, staying close, hunched inside her puffy layers.

"It's the most likely explanation. I've never met another elf in all the years I walked west. Except for New Haven, there don't seem to be any elves around."

"I guess you would be happy to meet another elf from your world," Raina said hesitantly. "I mean, you haven't seen any since you were little."

"She's still little," Airron interjected.

"I'm not little. I'll turn sixteen the same day as you."

"I meant small." Airron smirked condescendingly, patting her on the head. He was distracting Raina from her sadness at April's expense.

While she had the chance, April pressed Brag for answers about the elf that had shared Loug's box with him. Even for Brag, he was surprisingly uninformative. He said the elf was either a girl or a boy, adding maybe, maybe not. From his account, the box had been dark, the elf had been covered in fur, and very very very bad. Since the elf had escaped and left the imp behind with Loug, his opinion did have merit in this case. Brag truly didn't know how the elf had escaped, he had slept through that. April asked him lots of questions, and he kept saying 'don't know' or 'maybe, maybe not'. She gave up.

They followed Brag until the sun started to set. April felt secure walking with the imp, his magic was extraordinarily powerful when no Giants were around. If anything had threatened them, he probably would have blasted it.

By the time Brag pointed out the footprints, it was almost dark. April crouched down to have a closer look and discovered something wholly unexpected. There was not one set of tracks, but two, walking side-by-side. The small impressions were the perfect size for elf feet. The length of the stride was about right, too.

"You didn't say there were two elves, Brag," Airron mentioned.

The imp looked dimly at the footprints and began to count on his fingers. Airron rolled his eyes but wisely kept his mouth shut. They did not want to offend their guide.

"It does look like elf prints, two elves," April confirmed softly. "But we'll have to follow them tomorrow. We should climb a tree for the night, without delay."

"Yes mother," Airron said with exaggerated patience.

A suitable evergreen tree loomed over them. They found some dry brown leaves in an area sheltered from snow and each hauled up an armful.

"Brag, are you coming?" April asked. He didn't smell as bad as usual, he must have been rolling around in the snow. They could probably sleep in the same tree.

Brag had other plans. "Brag go home now. Bye April friend. Bye bad elfies." And he left, just like that. Once the imp decided it was time to go, he never lingered. He had no fear of walking through the night, he could see well enough in the dark and could certainly protect himself from almost anything. April had been planning to ask him more questions, even though he didn't appear to have any answers. Now she would have to wait until the next time they crossed paths, and there probably would be a next time. She would have bet her mittens that Brag would turn up again, probably when they least expected it.

"Bye Brag," they called, shared a bemused glance and climbed into the thickest branches of the needled tree. It wasn't as cozy and comfortable as their former hollow, but it would do for one night.

The sky was barely light when a deafening noise vibrated through the still morning air. In a haze of sleep, April was convinced that the Giant had found them and was politely knocking on their tree. "You can't come in," she mumbled stupidly.

"April, what the heck is that?" Salm gasped, shooting upright.

"Huh? Oh. It's ... it's ...," April sputtered, trying to make the adjustment from slumber to panic. "It's ... oh, it's a bird." She collapsed back on the branch in relief.

Airron refused to believe it. "A bird? No. That is not a bird."

"A dangerous bird?" Peter crouched, ready to move fast.

"No, no. Not unless you're an insect," April said.

"But what's that noise?" Raina asked. The pounding vibration hurt all their ears. "How can a bird make that noise? Are you sure about this?"

"Yes. It's a woodpecker, it bangs its beak hard against a tree trunk. It has a really pointy beak that can make holes, so it can get at the bugs and larvae inside the tree to eat them. It also drums to communicate with its mate. We can probably see it." She stood up and walked along the bough, tracing the noise. No wonder it was so loud, the woodpecker was in the dead tree right beside them. The bright red head made it easy to spot. "There." April pointed.

Raina leaned over. "Good grief, it is a bird. I've never seen a bird do that."

"Most birds don't." April smiled at her friend's intrigued expression. Even though the majority of creatures had fled or were hibernating, Raina had still seen many interesting sights these past few weeks. Everyone had. There would be many adventurous tales to tell once they got back to New Haven. If they ever got back to New Haven.

Everyone watched the woodpecker for the longest time, quite fascinated.

When Peter nudged April, she pulled her fingers out of her ears. He turned his face up to the sky and said, "I think we should start following the footprints." The sun would not be showing its face this day. A heavy layer of cloud had snuck overhead while they slept. Snow clouds - and from the look of them, the flakes were impatient to fall.

"Slug slime," April swore. There wasn't a second to lose.

They scrambled down the tree and were soon jogging on top of the snow. The footprints were clear enough, heading east, then south, then west. The two elves were leaving behind a path so twisted and turning, it might have been made by a blind, tongueless snake.

The snow held off and they followed the tracks all morning. At one point, the trail crossed itself and they were able to pick up a much fresher set of prints. The elves must have spent hours walking, only to return to their original location and cross their own path. It confirmed something that April was starting to suspect.

"I don't think these elves are from my world," she told her companions. The fresher prints were leading them west, back towards where New Haven used to be.

"Why do you think that? Elves from your world have different feet? I've noticed your toes are unusually knobby," Airron said.

April smiled. "They are, aren't they? But no, that's not it. Elves from my world know about traveling in the woodland. These elves don't. It looks like they don't have a clue about how to get anywhere."

"They did walk in a big circle," Raina agreed. "Even I know not to do that. But who else could it be?"

Salm squinted up at the sky with dismay. "Whoever it is, we better find them soon." The first few flakes were wafting down.

"If we don't, the trail will be gone. Pick up the pace!" Peter started jogging. April checked the forest again, as she did every five minutes. There were still no elves within sensing range.

"April, should we fly ahead? It would be faster." Airron had suggested the action earlier but April didn't want their group to separate. She didn't want to risk losing each other with the snow coming.

"No. We should stay together Airron," she repeated, expecting to be called mother again.

"Run faster then. We have to keep up with Peter." Airron gave her a small shove. Peter had the fleetest feet of all and was almost out of sight. They gave chase.

The next time April checked the forest, she finally discovered something. Elves – two elves.

"Peter, they're up ahead!" Now that April could sense the elves, the footprints were irrelevant. She jogged directly towards them through the thickening snow, taking the lead.

"Almost there," April shouted back. "Almost." She dashed between two wet mossy rocks and came face-to-face with the two elves. Their identity was so unexpected that she skidded and landed on her behind. These were the very last two elves that April would wish to meet – anywhere!

Then everyone caught up. Airron still retained the power of speech. "Cherry? Marigold?" Then he lost it and his mouth hung open.

"Fancy running into you," Cherry drawled, with no sign of welcome. Both girls were filthy, scratched and bruised, yet Cherry summoned up a superior smirk and stared down her nose at April, who was freezing her behind in the snow.

"But ... but? How?" Salm stuttered. "How did you get here? Where is New Haven? What's going on?"

Marigold burst into hysterical tears. Babbling incoherently, she launched herself into Salm's arms. Salm patted her on the back and looked generally helpless.

"You are not who I would have chosen to rescue us, but I guess you will have to do." Cherry had not attended Salm's words.

"We're not rescuing you, Cherry. We're lost, too," April said frankly, struggling to her feet.

"Oh. Can't you find New Haven? I thought you knew how to do that sort of stuff. I thought you were good for *something*," Cherry huffed, brushing snow off her head with an annoyed flick of her hand.

"Actually, Peter has the best sense of direction and even he can't find New Haven because it's gone. So, you really don't know where it went?" April asked.

"It can't be gone. Even you aren't dumb enough to believe that, or maybe you are," Cherry sniped. She truly didn't know about New Haven.

"Come on, let's talk about this somewhere more comfortable, or less uncomfortable," Peter said. The snow was coming hard and fast now, blowing sideways on the wind. Anywhere would be better than standing exposed in the middle of an icy snowstorm.

Finding shelter proved difficult with the limited visibility. The best they could manage was a drafty cave beneath a congregation of fallen rocks, piled against a felled tree trunk. The interior was dank and chilly; it smelled strongly of rot and something that had died long ago. On the bright side, the space was large enough for seven elves and it wasn't snowing inside.

Cherry wasn't in the least appreciative of the accommodations. Her disparaging glance blamed April for the squalid shelter. They settled around the lumpy rock walls with a great deal of shifting, trying to get as comfortable as possible.

Peter was the first to ask the most pressing question. "So, how did you get out of New Haven and end up lost?"

"That's none of your business." Cherry crossed her arms over her chest and shifted sideways, still trying to find softer rock.

Her attitude was ridiculous given their dire predicament. It was amazing that Cherry and Marigold had survived in the Outer-world, but April strongly suspected Cherry had her own brand of magic, based on past events. Not so long ago, the elf had proven herself a dangerous enemy and now they were stuck with her. She might harm them if the chance presented itself. Although, Cherry did need their help to find New Haven, so she needed them healthy - as long as Cherry realized that.

"Cherry," Salm said patiently, "If we're going to survive, we have to work together. Listen to me! New Haven is gone, lost, missing, not where it used to be and certainly not where it's supposed to be. Clear enough? We're trying to find it and you might know something that we don't, something that could help us to find it. So how did you get out of New Haven and get lost?"

Cherry was still not inclined to say.

"Marigold?" Salm prompted.

Marigold swiped her dripping nose and shot a disgruntled glance at

Cherry. Marigold was willing to talk. "Cherry wanted to follow you ... when you were leaving. She said we had to follow you and the stupid imp. She said we had to find out what was going on."

That made sense. Perfect sense. "Okay, so you followed us when we left New Haven. And then what?" Salm asked.

"Then we lost you in the dark. And when we turned around to go home, we couldn't find New Haven again. We must have gotten lost, right Cherry?"

Cherry didn't respond.

"So, it was gone that fast?" Salm verified. "I think that's important to know." It did give them a timeframe.

"Are you saying it really is gone? Not that we simply couldn't find it?" Cherry demanded.

"That's what we keep saying. Ears not working?" Airron taunted impatiently.

"New Haven is gone? Well, that's great! Just great!" Cherry snarled. "So is New Haven gone forever? Blinked out of existence? And I'm stuck with you lot?" She had quite a way with words. No one else would have suggested that their world was gone forever, not out loud anyway.

"Of course it isn't gone forever," April retorted angrily. "We have to find it, that's all. And the Giant is close. That makes searching a lot more difficult." They could not risk leading the Giant towards New Haven, if they could track down their world.

"Giant? What are you talking about?" Cherry didn't know about the Giant either.

Airron couldn't wait to tell her. "Oh, there's a Giant wandering around, hunting for us and New Haven. More than seven yards tall and as nasty as you, Cherry. Maybe you want to make friends?"

She laughed at him. "How gullible do you think I am? Giant, right!" She got up and paced as far as the rock would allow. "How long is this stupid white crap going to fall?"

April was the best one to answer. "The sky is heavy with clouds, it will probably snow until tomorrow."

"Tomorrow?" Cherry scowled and slumped back against the wall. "You don't have food, do you?" She sounded a tinge friendlier when she asked that question.

"Not a crumb," Airron took pleasure in telling her. It was going to be a very long day. And an even longer night.

It was. They were trapped with Cherry and no food. Marigold wouldn't stop sniveling and whining. Her ceaseless high pitch was enough to grate on everyone's nerves and ears.

When night arrived, the snow was still falling thick and fast and the wind was howling through the cracks like a beast. They were all too cold and hungry to sleep properly and the chamber was filled with tossing and groaning.

139

April kept dozing off and jerking awake, fearful that Cherry was sneaking up to strangle her.

Finally, faint slivers of light showed through the spaces between rocks. It was morning. Silently, April slipped outside to find blue sky and sunshine, even the blustery wind had blown itself out. The accumulation of snow was impressive, twice her height in the open areas. They were lucky the entrance to their cave was sheltered or they would have spent the day digging a tunnel out.

April walked gingerly up a smooth slope of white, testing the surface. It was hard packed from the fierce wind which would make traveling easier, if they had anywhere to travel to. At the very least, they could travel to a more comfortable lodging.

But the first priority was food and shelter, it was the tiresome reality of the Outer-world. With most of the ground buried deep now, it was going to be difficult to find anything edible - difficult but not impossible or April would not have lasted five years.

"One elf." She sighed. Their group now numbered seven. Seven elves were a lot of elves to feed. It was going to be a challenge. Feeding Cherry would be a thankless task.

"April?" Raina yawned from behind. "We survived the night?" She leaned against April's shoulder, her eyes bleary.

"Yes." Now they had to survive this day.

"What's the plan?"

"Food and shelter. Avoid the Giant. Find New Haven." April smiled slightly. If they could do all that in one day, she would be the happiest elf in the whole world, the whole big world.

"Good plan, I like it." Raina smiled sadly back. "Should I wake everyone?"

"No, if they can sleep, let them. I'll scout around, see if there are any seeds not covered in snow." It was better than going back inside.

"I'll come too. I can find seeds." Raina linked arms and April checked the forest, it proved safe. It was almost a waste of time to keep checking, no large or dangerous animals had turned up in weeks. Except for Loug and because of Loug.

"But we can't go too far," April worried. She didn't want elves waking up and wandering away.

"Yes mother." Raina smirked.

"Not you too?"

"Sorry. Airron's fault. He started it."

"He did." They walked straight. Their feet were still wrapped in cloth robbed from the packs. It was too cold to ever remove their makeshift slippers now that winter was gripping the land in a cruel icy claw.

"But Airron's only joking, you know. You've been looking after us really well, April. You seem a lot older out here than you do in New Haven."

"Do I?" April wasn't sure what Raina meant.

Raina nodded and explained. "Now that I've lived out here, I can understand why you don't worry about small things, like clothes that match or … or fixing your hair, or doing your homework. Out here, everything is so *hard*, always trying not to starve or freeze to death." She pulled a face. "And trying not to get eaten - and even Giants, for goodness sake! Everything is life or death, isn't it? After this experience, stuff like wrinkled clothes and homework will seem awfully unimportant. You grew up differently from us, so you have different priorities," she summed up.

April had never thought of it quite that way, but Raina's words made sense.

And Raina wasn't finished. "I'm sorry I thought that meant you were too young to talk to about some stuff," she apologized. "I feel bad about before, about not being a good friend, especially now that I know what you went through for myself, and you were alone, and *little*." She was apologizing again for something that April had already forgiven and forgotten.

"Please forget it Raina. And I'm the one that's sorry - for leaving New Haven and leading you all out here, and now New Haven is lost." April felt so bad inside that she could barely voice the words. Raina had nothing to apologize for, but April certainly did.

Raina stopped walking abruptly. "Have you been thinking all this is your fault?"

"Well it is," April replied, shamefaced.

"Of course it isn't. You were being really brave to come and save the elf. You had no way of knowing the elf had escaped. And how could you ever guess we would follow you? Or even be able to leave New Haven? I was the one that came up with the brilliant idea of shutting down the barrier, so it's my fault we're stuck out here." Raina looked as guilty as April felt. "I bet everyone thinks this is their fault in some way, except Brag – and you know what?"

"What?"

"Brag is the one to blame," she declared. "Now, let's find breakfast!"

"Breakfast it is," April said, feeling lighter. Raina was right, Brag could certainly be assigned a bear's share of the blame.

They searched for food under the largest evergreen trees where less snow had settled. There wasn't much to find. It looked like the birds and squirrels and smaller rodents had long ago made off with anything worthwhile.

"Nothing here," Raina said, pressing a hand against her stomach and wincing as she kicked at an empty, rotted seed casing.

April stepped from beneath the overhanging branches and scanned the area, considering their options. Normally she wouldn't steal food from other creatures, but the situation was desperate. Her friends were starving.

"That is a whole lot of snow. April, what are you doing?" Raina asked.

"Searching for food in a different way."

141

Raina eyed her eagerly. "How?"

"Well ... I'm searching for food to steal," April confessed.

"Oh. From what?"

"Chipmunks, squirrels, mice. Small rodents store food for the winter. I wouldn't take much, only enough for breakfast," April said.

"Take more than that! Is it dangerous? Do the rodents get mad if you steal their food? Do they try and stop you?" Raina asked good questions.

"I'm not sure. I've never done it before," April admitted.

"Then why do it now?"

"There are seven of us. We'll need quite a bit of food."

Quite nastily, Raina said, "Don't feed Cherry and Marigold. They can find their own."

"That would still leave five." Five wasn't much better than seven. "Okay, I can sense a chipmunk in a ground burrow, pretty close to here." April pointed straight ahead. "It must have a store of food inside the hollow. Chipmunks spend months preparing for winter and this is just the beginning of the deep cold, so it probably has plenty of food. I'm going to go check."

Raina looked around. "Where is the burrow?"

"The entrance is under the snow, want to help me dig?"

Raina hesitated. "Won't the chipmunk be mad if you steal some food? Are you sure this isn't dangerous?"

"The chipmunk should be sleeping – hibernating. It only wakes up every few days to eat from its stores, and it doesn't stay awake long. It probably won't even notice I'm there." At least April hoped that was the case since all animals were territorial and would defend their home and food from intruders. As cute as chipmunks were, their behavior was no exception to that rule.

"I'll help you dig then, if you're sure it's safe," Raina said.

April led the way unerringly to the chipmunk's burrow and they began to shift snow with sticks. They didn't have to move too much snow, the chipmunk had been smart enough to dig its burrow in an area sheltered by trees and brush.

Once the mouth of the tunnel was exposed, Raina looked newly apprehensive. "How deep do chipmunks tunnel?"

"About two feet, not too deep."

"Is there another way out, if the chipmunk wakes up and tries to stop you from stealing food?"

"Most burrows only have one entrance. I'll be fine Raina. I'll be quick." April crouched down and then had to lie flat to slide into the tunnel, it was that small.

"I'll stand guard," Raina called. "Just be careful."

"Yes mother." April dragged herself along the downward sloping passage, using her elbows and toes to propel her body. It was a tight fit, in one spot she almost got stuck and her leafy poncho tore off, but she squeezed through. It was a great relief when the passage widened slightly, and then widened a lot more. She couldn't see a thing in the dark, but assumed that she had reached the rounded nest chamber at the end of the tunnel.

Silently, April crouched and felt the ground ahead of her. There was a lot of dried vegetation on the floor. She explored it by touch until her fingers felt a severed leaf stem. Perfect. She held it aloft and concentrated to create a small flame on the end of the stem; it took some extra effort because she was a little bit underground, but her magic still worked so close to the surface.

The rudimentary torch illuminated a much smaller chamber than April was expecting. She couldn't stand upright and was almost cuddling against the white stripe of a soundly sleeping chipmunk.

April didn't dare move a muscle as she surveyed the hollow. It was warm and cozy, well lined with grasses, shredded leaves and even seed fluff. Against the far wall, an impressive amount of seeds, nuts, dried shoots and even dead insects were piled. Two lovely acorns perched on top of the heap. The chipmunk had so much food it surely wouldn't miss a couple of acorns, April told herself, tamping down her thief's guilt.

Unfortunately, the rodent was between April and the food.

"Just get the acorns and get out," she breathed, heart pounding.

Ever so carefully, April tried to maneuver around the curled chipmunk. It twitched restlessly. Did it sense her presence? Or smell the smoke? Moving faster, April scooted between the rodent and the earth wall, then reached as far as she could with her free hand. Her fingers touched an acorn and she tried to roll it closer. She needed two hands. April propped her light against the wall and leaned over to grab the acorn.

With disastrous timing, the chipmunk twitched again, jerking its legs. A paw kicked the burning torch, knocking it flat onto the dried vegetation. The grass crackled to burning life before April could stomp on the torch.

Reacting, she leaped onto the burning floor and hopped around like a wild bunny, putting out the spreading flames as fast as they could ignite. The chipmunk wasn't about to sleep through that fuss. As April smothered the last flame, the chipmunk woke with a start. Glowing embers reflected off the accusing eyes of the rodent. It had spotted her.

April concentrated hard and fast, trying to communicate with the furious chipmunk. It wasn't interested in chatting, it wanted to attack the intruder in its hollow. April pressed along the wall, trying to explain that she wasn't an intruder, not really. She communicated how hungry she was, and pictured one acorn. Chipmunks were usually friendly creatures. April hoped it might even let her take a bit of food if she asked nicely, now that she had woken it up.

The chipmunk didn't understand sharing, it understood survival. The winter was long and it had found the food. The rodent was not willing to share; it was an animal, not an elf. And it was furious that April had almost incinerated its hollow and burned up every bite of its food.

It began chattering in an agitated tone, warning April to get out. It moved threateningly closer. It was past time to leave the nesting chamber.

"Okay, okay, I'm leaving." April dashed for the exit and tripped, over an acorn. She scooped it up, dove into the tunnel and fled, as fast as she could. It wasn't fast at all, clawing up the slope on her belly proved much more difficult than going down. She could hear the rodent coming after her, and it could move so much quicker through the tunnel than an elf.

April screamed when her face pushed into something. It was only her leafy poncho. She tossed the acorn ahead of her and wriggled past the tight spot in the tunnel. Something brushed her foot, teeth latched onto her slipper. The chipmunk had caught up.

Terrified that it would try to bite her toes off, and desperate enough to try anything to slow her pursuer, April scrambled past her poncho and concentrated to light it afire. The dried leaves exploded with flames, almost burning April with them. She surged ahead of the heat, fighting for the light at the end of the tunnel. Then she was breathing fresh air and two hands reached out to pull her free of the tight passage.

Raina picked up the acorn that had popped out with April and said, "How did it go? Why is smoke coming out of the tunnel?"

April said, "Run!"

They raced for the nearest tree and ducked around the trunk. April stopped and leaned against the rough bark, panting hard.

"What happened down there?" Raina asked.

April placed a finger in front of her lips, signaling for silence. Then she leaned around the trunk, peeking at the chipmunk's burrow. No more smoke was coming out. A disgruntled striped head poked into sight, little nose wiggling to scent the air. The body came next, but the chipmunk didn't venture away from its home. It wasn't about to leave the entrance unguarded, not with an intruder nearby. After a quick roll in the snow and what might have been a 'harrumph', the chipmunk wiggled back into its tunnel.

April sagged against the tree in relief.

Raina regarded her curiously, waiting to hear the tale.

"The chipmunk woke up, there was a bit of a fire," April said, no more.

"Is that what happened to your slippers?"

April looked down. Her rough slippers were singed and black and one was missing the tip, but they had protected her toes. "Uh, yes."

"But you got an acorn. And it looks delicious. Let's go eat breakfast."

April simply nodded, still recovering from her close encounter with the dangerous chipmunk.

Raina woke everyone up. She ordered Salm to hit the acorn with a rock and ordered Peter to find dry wood. He heaped his sticks outside the entrance to their rock hovel and April stirred herself to light the pile. Over an edge of coal, Raina boiled bark tea in the acorn caps. They had two now.

The seven elves huddled around the fire, crunching on acorn pieces and taking turns sipping the hot liquid. It was delicious. Marigold was appreciative; Cherry seemed to think she deserved such service and the largest share.

With full warm bellies, it was time to set out in search of proper shelter. "And New Haven," Raina reminded everyone optimistically. "Maybe it came back with the snow. Maybe it came back while we were gone!"

"Maybe it did," Airron agreed easily.

Wrapped up against the cold, they started the hike west, back toward where New Haven should be. They didn't know where else to go. The snow formed a solid surface beneath their feet and April checked the woodland regularly. They trudged along all the long day; there was no easy conversation now that Cherry and Marigold had joined their number.

The boys started singing at one point. Peter had a lovely deep and harmonious voice, April could have listened to it forever. Unfortunately she had to advise them against making so much noise and got called 'mother' again.

Late afternoon, they crossed an unusual path. At some point since the storm had tapered off, a wide assortment of animals had charged through the snow, almost like a parade. It was a peculiar trail, usually such a variety of animals did not make one path.

"How come you didn't sense these animals, April?" Peter asked.

"They were probably outside the range of my magic. And it doesn't look like they lingered." April studied the tracks, the strides were widely spaced and deeply pressed. These animals had been in a hurry to get elsewhere. She identified the prints for everyone, declaring the animals to be dangerous, safe or in-between. She made sure her companions would be able to recognize the prints again. It felt a bit like she was teaching a class.

After she had identified cloven deer tracks and declared deer perfectly harmless unless they accidentally stepped on you or chomped you in a mouthful of grass, Salm nodded in satisfaction. "See, you're good at this stuff. You would be a great Outer-world guide and now that the barrier is altered again, lots of elves are going to want to camp out here. I think we should seriously consider organizing Outer-world tours as a future career." It gave them something to talk about and everyone had an opinion, even Cherry who dismissed the idea as 'lame'.

They spent a short night in a tree, and resumed their trek at sunrise. Before the sun set that day, they reached the edge of the barren landscape where New Haven used to be. The magical world hadn't returned. The area was still a concave windswept wasteland, cut by the rushing river. There was not one speck of green as far as the eye could see, only white and more white. The disappointment was crushing. Raina sat down and refused to travel further. She wept bitterly and was inconsolable.

It was time to search for a new home.

April and Airron flew around a lot of trees before they located the perfect site in a leafless old oak. The cave was a little high off the ground, at about twenty feet, but the added height ensured safety. It was big enough for all of them, but not so big that they would lose precious heat. The entrance was smallish, no owls would fly in and surprise them or eat them. Best of all, it was clean and dry.

"Perfect," everyone agreed, except Cherry. So far she had disagreed with everything so it was no surprise, but it was annoying.

The boys used Peter's pocket blade to cut a birch bark slab off an adjacent tree, to act as a makeshift door. April and Raina searched for food, leaving Cherry seated in the hollow, telling the boys where to put the leaves they had hauled up. The boys were ignoring her directions. Airron had a suggestion about where Cherry could stuff some leaves. It wasn't at all polite, but it would have shut her up.

Before darkness settled around them, they found enough seeds for dinner. Everyone devoured their ration silently and went to bed, depressed over not finding New Haven. April slept until Raina's quiet sobs woke her. She scooted closer and stroked Raina's hair, fighting tears herself.

"What if we never find my Mom and Dad? Ever. I miss them so much. What if we're stuck out here for the rest of our lives?" Raina asked hopelessly.

April struggled to find words of comfort, and drew on her own experience for surviving alone in the Outer-world. "Raina, you can't think that way. Just ... just think of one day at a time. Make it through each day, and New Haven will be here one morning when we wake up. I know it will. Just keep believing that. We'll find your family, we'll find New Haven, we just have to survive each day until then."

"One day at a time," Raina repeated softly. It summed up life in the Outer-world.

"One day at a time, and think about all the great adventures you'll have to tell everyone when we get home." April hugged her close and kept talking about anything and nothing until Raina fell asleep.

10 – Loss

Their small, forlorn group spent several days feeling rootless. They had lost their world and didn't know how to find it again. They might have camped in the same location for as long as it took New Haven to return, but once again, the decision to move was taken out of their hands, this time in the worst possible way.

The day started normally enough. Everyone slept late, the hollow was insulated from light and sound. When April climbed aimlessly down the tree, the sun was high. If it were a school day, they would be eating lunch in the sunny meadow.

April wondered if elves were still attending school, somewhere. Or was the elvan realm in a state of crisis? If New Haven Academy was still running as normal, they were going to be ridiculously far behind in their lessons when they got back. April figured she had missed about one month of school so far. The way things were going, she might miss the rest of the year. Maybe she would have to repeat her whole grade.

April stopped thinking about school and magically sensed that the forest was deserted before she lit a fire. There were now enough acorn caps for each of them to have their own cup of bark tea. April was packing fresh snow into each cap when Raina turned up.

"Seven? I don't know why you're making seven." She yawned. "Cherry hasn't lifted a baby finger since we found her and you're serving her breakfast!" She sounded sleepy and exasperated.

"Keeps her quiet?" April suggested.

"She's never quiet." Raina was grumbling on about Cherry when April heard something charging towards them. Whatever was approaching was loud and fast and big.

"Raina, the tree!" April grabbed her hand and yanked. They made it as far as the trunk when a wolf flashed by, paying them no attention. It was a furry gray blur. The beast stepped on the fire in passing and didn't even notice.

"Fox?" Raina guessed faintly, eyes a bit bulging.

"No, wolf," April panted, leaning against the trunk. "It came so fast, I didn't sense it in time. Sorry."

"That's okay. It didn't try and eat us. It didn't even notice us, did it?"

"No." The wolf had looked preoccupied. They didn't have a chance to move before another disturbance reached their ears.

"What?" Raina gasped. Before April could sense anything, a trio of long-legged deer dashed by. "Deer?" Raina guessed, rightly.

April frowned. "Deer. Weird, usually wolf chase deer, deer never chase wolf."

"April? What's happening?" It was Peter, leaning out of the entrance to the hollow.

"A few animals are running by. You better stay up there. I think we should climb back up." They didn't have time. Raina grabbed her arm and squeezed as the biggest noise yet approached with much snorting and grunting. It sounded like … a bear. It was, the gigantic black shape galloped by, eyes flashing in terror. It was supposed to be hibernating, what was it doing running around the forest looking frightened?

"What … what was that?" Raina didn't even hazard a guess.

"Bear. Nothing frightens a bear," April gulped out. No, that was wrong. She could think of one thing that would scare the fur off a bear. She didn't say 'Giant' out loud, she said, "Quick, climb the tree."

Raina didn't need telling twice. She almost ran up the trunk and April matched the pace. Before they made the hollow, a pair of raccoon loped past.

Hands reached out to yank them inside and Airron slid the crude door closed.

"Airron, wait. We need to see what's going on outside." April pushed the door partially out of the way. "This is not normal, even in the Outer-world. Bear are supposed to be hibernating, not running around. Something has disturbed its den."

All of them crowded around the entrance to watch. A steady stream of creatures continued to race by their tree, fleeing something. April identified the animals for everyone while she tried to sense what was going on.

"But April, where are all these animals coming from?" Peter asked. "You haven't been able to sense any dangerous animals since we've been out here."

"It's like with that trail we found, the animals would have been outside my range. And they're running so fast right now, I barely have a chance to know they're coming," she stressed. "If it was summer, the animals could be fleeing a wildfire, but that doesn't happen at this time of year, and there's no smoke. They could be escaping a flood, but that's just as unlikely. It's not raining and it's not spring." April was trying to come up with any explanation for this wild exodus, anything except 'Giant'.

"What else would scare all the animals?" Peter asked, when another black bear hurtled past. If its stubby tail had been any longer, it would have been tucked. The tree trembled slightly and April closed her eyes in anguish. She hadn't wanted to believe that Loug was causing this. She hadn't wanted to believe that Loug was within a hundred miles of their provisional home.

"Something ... something really big," April stammered. And it was heading their way, hunting the animals. She could sense Loug now.

Salm said it. "Giant?"

"Yes," April murmured sickly.

"Can we close the door now?" Airron prompted.

"Yes, close the door tight." They were well hidden in their tree, they were safer hiding than running. And the stream of animals had obliterated any sign of their campsite and their scent.

"Giant, ya right!" Cherry scoffed. "Leave the door open, I want to see this with my own eyes." She shoved April roughly aside.

"Quit it." April pushed her back. "We have to close the door!"

"No way. I want to see your so-called Giant with my own eyes. You're always telling lies. Giants don't even exist." Cherry pushed April hard and everyone was jostled around. So was the birch bark door. It was knocked right out of the tree and floated down to the ground ever so slowly, sailing outward from the trunk. And then a very big voice rumbled curiously.

"Oh no," Raina whimpered, falling back.

Everyone tumbled away from the door and pressed against the walls trying to become part of the wood, trying to hide. Everyone except Cherry. Salm reached out a hand and yanked, Cherry shook his hand off.

"Cherry," April hissed. "Get away from the door! Get out of sight!"

"Why? What was that noise?" She foolishly peered out.

Their lodging was twenty feet above the ground. Twenty feet – a Giant's eye level. A Giant's eyeball is very big, almost as tall as an elf. When a pair of these huge orbs moved across the entranceway, blocking the light, Cherry screamed. An engraved invitation could not have been more inviting.

The glistening eyes crinkled and blinked in malicious delight. Salm leaned forward and grabbed Cherry's arm again, successfully jerking her back this time. The action was too late, she had been seen and heard. One of the Giant's eyes pressed up against hollow's doorway, peering into the dark interior. Loug couldn't see a thing.

The eyeball disappeared and one of the Giant's stubby fingers poked into the hollow. It could only reach so far. The finger wiggled around, unable to touch any of them.

But April knew it was only the beginning. The Giant would knock the tree flat to the ground and hammer it opened to capture an elf. Loug had only seen one elf in the shadowy cave. He might even think it was April. He didn't know about the rest of them, but he would find out as soon as he smashed the tree apart. If they survived the demolition, they would not survive Loug.

One elf - he would be satisfied with one elf. As tempted as she was to shove Cherry out of the hollow as a sacrifice, April couldn't do it. She was not that kind of elf.

"April," Peter tugged her closer. "April, the Giant only saw one of us." He was thinking along the same lines.

"Loug probably thinks it's me," April agreed.

"No, that's not what I meant."

"Peter, he's going to destroy the tree to get inside! And he can do it. He won't stop until he finds an elf." The finger disappeared and the eyeball returned. Everyone squeezed further back. Cherry didn't make a sound, she had wised up far too late.

The eyeball disappeared and the tree began to rock back and forth from the roots.

"That ... that was a Giant," Cherry babbled, as if they didn't already know.

April ignored her. "Listen," she said, over the distressing sound of cracking wood. "I have a plan."

Raina sobbed, "I don't like it."

"You haven't even heard it," April countered.

"You're going to be all heroic to save us and ... and go out there to face the Giant, aren't you?" Raina sounded mad. She always sounded mad when she was terrified.

"No. Not exactly. It's a better plan than that." Roots snapped below and the tree lurched left. They didn't have much time. "The Giant doesn't know about elves having wings because they don't in the Outer-world. I'll jump out and fly away – I'll make sure Loug sees me, then I'll fly too high for him to catch me. He'll follow and I'll lead him away. I'll meet you about a mile north of here, at the edge of the barren land. I'll find you. Okay?"

"No!" No one agreed with her plan.

Except Cherry. "Sounds good."

April ignored the majority response. "And Cherry – you owe me for this. It's your fault the Giant is attacking us. If you have any magic at all, use it to keep everyone safe until I get back. If anyone gets hurt, you'll be sorry."

"Like I'm scared." Cherry did sound scared, but it was because of the Giant, not April's vague threat. They glared at each other and the tree tilted right. Airron fell in the direction of the doorway.

"Airron, be careful," April shouted, clawing toward the exit. The tree felt like Gnash, when that tree had been truly alive with movement.

Peter blocked her path. "April, let's come up with a better plan."

"There's no time. I'll be safe with wings," she assured him.

"Airron! What are you doing? You're being all noble now too, aren't you," Raina accused hysterically. He was standing in the doorway, ripping off his robe.

"Same plan, but I'll do the flying. April falls down before she gets wings, I can fly straight up. I'll have a much better chance. See you a mile north of here." He tied his robe around his waist and launched out of the hollow with a huge leap.

Airron flitted straight up like a bat and Loug tore after him. It was torturous to watch. The Giant's hairy arms swung for Airron with unbelievable speed and the arms weren't stubby like the fingers, if anything, they were overlong, dangling to the knees. April wouldn't have been surprised if Loug touched the tips of Airron's toes. It was that close. Frustrated, Loug roared in rage and scooped up anything not rooted to the ground – stones and sticks and chunks of ice. He pelted all manner of debris at Airron.

One of the lumps of ice was as big as the Giant's fist, it sailed directly toward Airron. It was going to knock him out of the sky. April wanted to cover her eyes, but she couldn't look away.

Airron spotted the projectile at the last minute and tucked his wings. He dropped fast - he almost made it. The ice grazed his head and he spun out of control in dizzy loops before he opened his wings again, weakly. He needed help!

April tore off her top layers and took a running leap. She fell five feet before her wings appeared, then she flew up as fast as she had ever flown, screaming at Loug.

The Giant swiveled his massive head in her direction. The distraction of a second elf confused his dim brain. The precious seconds that the Giant stood dumbstruck granted Airron a chance to recover. And thankfully, Loug stayed focused on April. Airron was so dazed, he looked in danger of flying headfirst into the nearest tree.

"Airron, go up!" April flapped harder and angled towards him. She shoved him from below, using momentum to push him up.

"April?" he blinked.

"Can you fly? Try, we have to get a lot higher."

April swerved to his side and took his hand, trying to help. Airron made a valiant effort and April pulled, flapping beside him – up, up, up, out of the Giant's throwing range.

"Thanks, had a little trouble there. You weren't supposed to fly," Airron said regretfully. His head was dripping blood.

"Seemed like a good idea." April's voice shook badly. "Can you keep going? Or do you need to land?"

"I'm okay, I'm okay now. As long as the Giant follows, the others will be safe. I can fly," he vowed.

And the Giant did follow, far below he stomped through the trees, knocking the small ones viciously to the ground and even some of the not so small ones. Loug was clearing a path as he went.

After a frozen hour, Airron panted, "How long should we keep going?"

"Until the sun disappears, if we can." At least the sun set early on these short winter days. "That's when the Giant likes to stop for the night and we can disappear in the darkness. We're lucky it's not a really cold day." April only hoped that they could entice Loug far enough away so that he couldn't find his way back. At least he had stopped felling trees, he was no longer leaving himself a clear trail back toward New Haven.

"It's going to be a long day," Airron predicted.

It was. Hour after hour, they stayed tantalizingly out of the Giant's range. They meandered in all directions, trying to confuse him. Loug would not give up, he marched tirelessly, determined to capture elves. By the time the sun touched the horizon, April and Airron were both frozen and beyond exhausted.

"But why does he want us so badly?" Airron asked after a long silence. They were too tired to talk.

"It's the magic. Giants like to make elves do magic. Loug will think all elves have magic because they all do in the Outer-world. He will assume you have magic. And if it's not for magic, well ... they do like to eat elves. We're a delicacy." April had already mentioned this fact in the past.

"Thanks for reminding me," Airron gulped out. "I wish the sun would set and get it over with."

It did seem to be taking its time this day. The air grew even colder when the orange ball inched from sight; dusk transformed to darkness as if a candle had been snuffed out.

"Finally." April strained her pointed ears. She couldn't hear any stomping or crashing. The Giant had given up.

"Can we rest now?" Airron asked. "I don't think I can fly another inch."

"Sounds wonderful. We'll rest and watch Loug light his fire, make sure he's settled for the night, then we can ... go home."

The snow made it a lot easier to see the ground, contrasting whitely against the dark vegetation. They banked silently back toward Loug and landed in a dense evergreen treetop where they huddled together for warmth.

The Giant followed his usual routine but it was obvious he was in a towering temper. He had chased his prey all day only to lose it. Loug smashed branches into a pile with tremendous force, then kicked the pieces viciously for no reason except to vent his rage. That done, he heaved some dry orange pine boughs onto the top and sparked a fire with his flintstones. The flames flared high, they wouldn't have dared not cooperate.

The lovely warmth was too far out of reach. Airron pressed closer and wrapped his robe around both of them. April stopped shivering. "My thanks, Airron." They picked lumps of snow off the tree and melted them in their mouths for water.

It was at least an hour before Airron said, "Should we get out of here? I think I can fly. Can you?"

April was glad he had suggested leaving, she couldn't have done it. "I suppose. We can fly slowly, rest and warm up whenever we need."

"Lots of rests. Come on, April. Let's get home. Well – not home, but you know what I mean." Airron reclaimed his robe, inspiring them to move. April automatically tried to sense if the immediate area was safe, they were so close to the Giant that all she could sense was Loug.

Airron flew up out of the tree and April fell, as usual. She was struggling to reach his altitude when something hurtled out of the dark sky, Something large and feathery that could see in the dark.

"Airron, back in the tree!" April screamed, tucking her wings and tumbling toward the dense branches.

He plummeted back toward the tree even faster than April, but not fast enough. The huge white owl missed snapping Airron in its beak by inches, but it did knock him out of the air with a gigantic tail in passing. The owl turned to make another approach but thought better of it. Airron was spinning head over heels toward the Giant's smoky fire. The owl was too smart to go down there.

There was no way to stop it from happening. Airron fell and April could do nothing but watch with horror. At least he missed the fire, but he didn't miss the Giant. Loug blinked stupidly when Airron grazed his shoulder and slid down his fur clad stomach. The monster swung his lumpy head left and right before he peered down at what had landed in the snow beside his biggest toe.

Clearly, Airron didn't know where he was or what had happened. He lurched up and shook his head, unaware of the dark presence looming over him. When the Giant plucked Airron up by his wings and deposited him into the palm of his filthy hand, Airron lost his ability to stand. He collapsed onto the callused skin, mouth open in a silent scream. And April couldn't help him, she couldn't stop a Giant. If he ate Airron right now, she couldn't do a thing except offer herself as a second bite.

What the Giant did then was almost worse than that. April wished with all her heart that she had covered her eyes before it happened, but there was no warning. Loug simply reached out his stubby fingers and ripped off

Airron's lovely wings. He tossed the torn amber and black bits aside and they wafted down into the fire. Airron watched them spark and turn to ash, uncomprehending for long seconds before he crumpled into the Giant's palm.

April did close her eyes then, overcome with such sadness that it threatened to suffocate her. Airron's wings ... Airron's beautiful wings ... and Airron? She forced herself to look again, to know his fate. The Giant was moving, digging into his pack for the bone prison box. Airron was dropped inside, still unaware of what was happening to him.

"Airron," April whispered in a strangled voice, but he couldn't hear her. He couldn't hear anything.

A creature of habit, Loug placed the box on top of the pack. April stared at it, filling up with boiling rage. If she had been inside New Haven, a storm of unimagined proportions would have blown in around her. But it was the Outer-world, nothing happened, not even a rumble in the sky.

Loug settled down for the night. He retrieved the little box, shook it a couple of times, then fell asleep with it clutched in his fist. Airron wouldn't know he was supposed to sing or hum, if he was even conscious. April hoped he wasn't.

The fire slowly burned low and turned to orange coals. Hot tears were dripping down April's face when she fell into an exhausted sleep, filled with nothing but the worst nightmares where she ripped Airron's wings off with her own bloodied hands.

It took April three days of following and one crazy stunt before an opportunity to rescue Airron presented itself. The crazy stunt happened on the second day when the temperatures dipped sharply and April almost froze to death trying to keep pace with the Giant, and she didn't dare let Loug out of her sight in case she missed a precious chance to save Airron.

By the middle of that second awful day, April was simply too cold to fly. She couldn't feel her arms and had trouble moving them. Desperate, she eyed the Giant's pack sitting like a lump on his hunched back. It looked warm, and Airron's cage was sticking out of the top. Maybe she could even free Airron now! Right now!

Her brain must have been partially frozen at that point because it seemed like a good idea to fly on down there and crawl into the Giant's pack. And that's exactly what she did.

April landed lightly beside the prison box and slipped down into the gap formed between the bony wall and the lip of the sack. It was so much warmer than the air. Shivering violently, April tapped softly on the side of the cage and whispered, "Airron, Airron!" Nothing. "Airron! It's April. Answer me! But quietly." Still nothing.

Ever so stealthily, April wormed her way lower into the pack, squirming underneath the box. It was a tight fit, to say the least. When she was fully below the cube, April couldn't even move her arms to reach the latch and release the hook. Even if she could have managed it, the hatch wouldn't have opened. There was no room.

"Weasel whiskers," April hissed and fought to turn around. The Giant had impeccable timing, he shifted the pack higher on his shoulder with a strong jerk. Everything settled lower, including April. Her small gap disappeared entirely. She couldn't move even her baby finger. It was a battle to breathe. She was trapped as surely as Airron. But at least it was warm. "Bright side," she groaned, riding a wave of panic until it passed.

Immobilized that way for hours, April couldn't do anything but talk, and she did. Pressed against Airron's prison, she rambled quietly about anything, mostly nonsense. She told stories and even sang Peter's songs, all as soft as a whisper. She imagined that Airron was listening, even though there had been no sign that he was even alive.

Finally, the Giant stopped. The pack was dropped to the ground with a thump, almost crushing April inside. She still couldn't budge for the longest time and must have either fallen asleep or passed out from lack of air.

A rush of frigid wind brought her back to the real, awful world.

"April!"

She thought she heard Airron's voice in the distance. The box had been lifted out of the pack and the Giant was rooting around inside for something. With a squeak of terror, April lunged away from the hairy knuckles that were pushing her even deeper into a clump of matted fur. That fur was what the Giant sought, he hauled it out, taking April along for the ride. When it was free of the pack, Loug shook the folds open with a powerful flick. April was snapped high into the air, free as a bird and unseen by Loug.

Her wings were quick to appear. Disoriented, she flapped stiffly toward the nearest tree and landed. It had all happened so fast – and she was free! And she had heard Airron's voice, hadn't she? April rubbed her eyes and focused on the scene below. It was dusk.

The matted filthy fur was the Giant's blanket. Even he was feeling the more extreme cold spell. He did not set out to hunt dinner, but built a high fire and huddled close with the prison box in his fist. At least Airron would be warm for the night but April would not be able to free him.

When the Giant's habitual snoring disturbed the peace of the forest, April was desperately cold enough to fly down to the ground and cuddle closer to the coals, burrowing into a gap between two boulders at the edge of the campsite. The rocks were near enough to have absorbed some heat. The hidden cave was lovely and toasty, and worth the risk. If April froze to death, she wouldn't be able to help Airron.

She was perched back in her cold tree before the Giant roused.

The next day, the frigid temperatures eased. Loug filled the hours with walking and hunting for food, wandering randomly in all directions, often crossing his own path. And he didn't find a bite to eat. All the forest creatures had fled before him, April had seen the latest evacuation.

Late in the afternoon, the Giant stopped on the crest of a bare hill and raised his head to sniff the air in all directions. Something had caught his interest. April glided closer and could smell fresh blood. An injured animal was near, one that hadn't been able to flee. Loug dropped his pack and started running hard. The box tumbled right off the top, landing on its side.

"Oh, oh now," April gulped. She would not miss this lucky chance to free Airron, no matter what the risk. Like a hawk, she dove towards the pack, knowing every second counted. She landed right beside the box and banged a fist on the bones. "Airron, Airron." There was again no answer. She unlatched the metal closure and pulled the door open. Still nothing moved.

"Airron?" She forced herself to climb inside. He was huddled in the corner, unresponsive. "Airron! Come on, we have to get out of here before the Giant comes back!"

"April, that you?" he mumbled thickly. "Thought you left."

"It's me. I'm so so sorry … come on, climb out of the box. Quickly, Loug could return any minute." He didn't move. "Airron, do you understand? Can you get up?" April gripped his arm and tugged, his skin felt cold and lifeless.

"Go ahead. Go without me."

"What are you talking about? Airron, don't you understand? I'm trying to rescue you. The box is open and Loug is hunting, come on!" April pulled harder.

"You go," Airron mumbled almost incoherently, his tongue stumbled over the two simple words. He didn't care if he ever left the prison.

"No! Please come with me. I can't go without you, you must know that. If you don't come, I'll have to stay with you." April started to cry because she couldn't help it. Airron was in awful shape.

"Ah April, don't cry. Don't do that." Airron swiped a hand across his own eyes and fought to silence his grief.

"Please come with me," April begged. "Or we'll both be stuck here and it's not very comfortable or big and … and it smells really bad. Please, Airron." She hugged him hard and didn't let him ago. His back felt naked without his wings. April stroked it until he moved.

"Can't have you trapped." Airron rose stiffly and April linked their arms. She tried to tug him faster, terrified about how long this rescue was taking. They made the door and the earth shook slightly.

"Hurry, Airron. Hurry!" As soon as they fell outside, April reached behind to latch the door shut so that Loug would assume Airron was still inside. They scrambled away from the pack and April could both hear and feel Loug's approach.

There was nowhere to hide on the bare white hill. Even the surface of the snow was so icy hard that they could not burrow in and disappear. "Run Airron." April grabbed his hand and dragged him along. He tried to run but his legs must have been too stiff. He tripped and went down and the Giant was almost upon them.

There was nowhere to hide ... not unless you were really small. The wind had blown a scattering of leftover fall leaves across the snow. One was close enough, if she could reach it in time. April let go of Airron reluctantly and rushed for the leaf. It was thin and punctured with holes, but it might hide them. She dragged the large brown maple leaf over to where he lay curled up in the snow.

April dove down beside Airron and yanked the leaf on top like a blanket. And not a second too soon. The Giant's feet crunched across the crisp snow toward his pack. He dropped something heavy to the ground with a thud. The stench of death was overpowering.

Airron started to shake and it sounded like he was choking.

"Hush Airron, hush," April begged and embraced him. "No noise Airron. Please," she whispered in his ear. There was great comfort in a hug, she held him tighter. Airron stopped the noise but he couldn't stop shuddering.

She peeked out through a hole in the leaf. Loug was stomping around, rearranging the pack and draping his dinner over his arm. A poor deer hung limply, dead eyes staring at the ground and blood trailing from its snout to splat on the pristine white snow. Drip, drip, drip. There was one splat that shook the leaf before Loug moved on. He had not checked the box and his enormous feet didn't step on the leaf as he lumbered by.

When his passage faded to silence, April sat up and flung off the leaf. It was dripping red now. They needed to move, in case.

"Airron?" April turned to face him and had her first look at him in the light. She could have cried again. "Airron?" she said gently. "We have to leave. Come on." She took his hand, helped him to stand and didn't let go. He came willingly enough, but as lifeless now as the dead deer that Loug was carting around.

They walked into the shelter of the trees and put some distance between themselves and the Giant. April kept Airron walking until the sun set fully. He did not speak one word. As soon as it was dark and Loug was sure to be roasting his deer, April halted under a sheltering tree and started a small fire. She guided Airron to sit beside its warmth and left his side to find some seeds. She didn't dare go far and couldn't find a thing to eat.

When she hurried back, he was staring at nothing, eyes unfocused. Numb herself now, April heated some snow in the acorn cap that she had found the previous day. She had been wearing it on her head while she flew. Airron did share the hot water, but it was like he wasn't there at all, except for his body.

"Airron, do you want more water?" April asked helplessly. She didn't know what to do with him.

"No."

"Do you want me to find some seeds? I can look again."

"No."

"I'm so sorry ... about what happened. But it happened so fast,

Airron, I couldn't stop it. Your beautiful wings ..."

"Don't say it," he choked harshly.

"Okay. Okay, I won't. Are you up to walking?"

His face tightened in a spasm of pain. "Sure. Walking." It took April a minute to understand. Walking, not flying. He would never fly again. She bit her lip hard, took his hand and started them moving. She hiked west, towards where the elvan realm should be, wishing with all her heart that New Haven would be occupying its proper space when they got back.

It took seven days to walk back to New Haven, April counted. Airron remained as withdrawn as when she had found him. He followed where she led, answered if she asked a simple question, and ate and drank if she provided the sustenance. Only at night did he cry out in his sleep in the most heartbreaking way.

April really hoped Raina would know what to do when they were reunited, because April didn't and she was hesitant to bring up the subject of his lost wings again. Talking about it hurt him too much.

Finally one morning, they crossed a trail of broken trees and April knew they were close to home. The path of destruction had been left by Loug when he had torn after them. It seemed like years had passed since that day.

"Almost home," April told Airron, squeezing his arm.

He stopped walking and looked around. "Are we?"

"Yes. We'll see Raina and Peter and Salm soon." April had missed them dreadfully.

"Will we?" Airron didn't move.

"Yes. Airron?"

"April, don't tell anyone about ... about ..." He closed his eyes, his face looked like a white mask and his throat clenched. He couldn't even say the words. "Don't tell them." He left it at that.

"But Airron, they're going to find out about your wings. Wouldn't you feel better if you talked about it or something? I don't think it's good to keep it all inside. You can talk to me if you want, if it would make you feel better. I know I'm not as good as Raina at figuring things out or knowing what to say but - "

"April, shut up." Airron pulled her into a painful embrace and she cried all over his shoulder, soaking him. When he released her, her hair was wet where his head had rested upon it. "April, I will tell Raina and Peter and Salm, but when I'm ready. As long as I keep my robe done up, no one will know ... they're gone."

It was his decision. April nodded, tied his robe up to the top, turned him around and draped the cloth over his back, smoothing it down. No one would know unless he told them.

They turned down Loug's trail and followed it all the way to the hollow that had been their temporary home. The tree was leaning at an unnatural angle, propped up on another tree. It wouldn't sprout leaves when spring returned to fill the forest with life. The small clearing was too quiet and had a deeply tragic air about it.

"Onward," April declared, turning north. Airron nodded. He had been a little more responsive since they talked. Even though the words had been few, they seemed to have helped. April linked their fingers and let Airron set the pace. It was a slow one. April wanted to dash madly all the way and see that her friends were safe, but she curbed her impatience and strolled along with Airron as if they were in no hurry to get to school.

They reached their destination late in the afternoon. It was easy to find everyone, all kinds of discreet clues pointed the way, things only an elf would notice. There were branches pressed into the snow like arrows, and strips of birch bark tied onto bare shrubs. April could see Raina's hand everywhere. And she could sense the elves, the clues had really been unnecessary.

"We're home," April whispered to Airron when they stepped into a clearing filled with elf footprints in the snow.

Cherry was the first one to notice their arrival. "Oh, you're back." She turned a cold shoulder and flounced away.

Marigold was more welcoming and shrieked in excitement, alerting everyone.

"Oh. Oh! You made it!" Raina ran towards them, crying and smiling, her face all mixed up. She hugged them both at once, then separately. After a wonderful reunion, April and Airron were bombarded with questions.

"You've been gone forever. We were thinking the worst. What happened?" Peter asked.

April answered carefully, "We had a few problems with Loug."

"Oh, no! He didn't catch you again, did he?" Raina asked April.

"No." He had caught Airron, not her. Airron didn't say a word, it was not like him at all. Everyone noticed. They were going to start quizzing him. April spoke first. "Tell me, how did you manage while we were away? You were all okay?"

"Oh, we were fine. New Haven hasn't come back, but we found a new home, well, two homes. Cherry has her own, with Marigold." Raina pointed up at a tree with two black holes. "And we found food and stayed warm. Hardly any creatures have been around," she detailed proudly.

"That's because of the Giant, he's still nearby," April said. "You don't have any extra food, do you? Airron and I haven't eaten."

"We do. Peter's really good at finding squirrel stores. Most of the squirrels have run away now too, since the Giant came so close, so we might as well eat their food."

Peter added a couple of pinecones to the fire and Raina boiled tea and served them seeds. It felt like a homecoming because of their friends. Airron ate and drank silently. When the sky darkened, he left without a word, climbing up to the hollow that was their new home. No one spoke until he was inside the tree.

"April? What's wrong with Airron?" Raina asked first.

April simply shook her head and stared at the fire.

"What? What does that mean? You should see the expression on your face. What happened to Airron?"

"Raina, I really can't say. I'm sorry. He'll tell you when he's ready. I think he needs more time." Maybe forever.

"More time for what? What can be that bad?" Raina demanded.

It was worse that Raina could imagine. April closed her eyes against the memory that haunted her.

"There you go again, making that face. What's wrong?" Raina was getting distraught.

"He looks fine," Cherry scoffed from the far side of the fire. "Shut up about it."

"You keep your big nose out of this," Raina shot back. It looked like she and Cherry had built up a lot of resentment during their time together. But at least Cherry had distracted Raina.

Peter drifted away. He climbed up to the tree hollow. If Airron were able to open up to anyone about his tragedy, it would probably be Peter. They were best friends and Peter was very easy to talk too, since he was more of a listener. April hoped Airron would talk to Peter, it might help him to cope with his great loss.

Not long after, Cherry dragged Marigold away. April was pleased to see them go. It wasn't the same talking to Raina and Salm when Cherry was listening to every word with her sharp critical ears.

"Finally," Raina growled, of the same opinion. "April, what's wrong with Airron. Can you say now?"

"I can't. Please don't ask."

"But - "

"I can't."

"But - "

"I really can't."

Salm scooted closer and April leaned against him. Even through his layers, his shoulder felt thin and bony. April wanted to cry all over it, but she didn't break down. That would have caused too many questions.

"Drop it, Raina," Salm said wearily. April was surprised that Raina did.

They talked late into the night about everything but Airron, keeping the fire high and warm. Salm reported that there had been no sign of New Haven, not a shadow or a whisper.

Peter didn't come back and Raina didn't comment on his absence. She knew exactly where he was. She didn't ask April about Airron again, much to April's relief. It was really hard to keep things from her best friend, especially this.

11 – Home Away From Home

By unspoken agreement, they remained at the campsite near the circle of barren land. No one suggested moving on, there was nowhere to move on to. New Haven could be anywhere and they still didn't know how to find it. The Outer-world was stuck in deepest winter. Their survival depended on shelter.

The days amassed into one week and then a second, and it had not been an easy time. It was now the beginning of February, about one year since April had found New Haven. One year – her own special anniversary, and she wasn't in the wonderful world to celebrate the occasion.

Airron rarely came out of the hollow. He slept most of the time curled into a fetal position. When he did venture down to eat or stretch his legs, he was distant and withdrawn. Raina was growing more and more impatient with him, and she was becoming equally short with April because April knew what was wrong and wouldn't tell.

Peter knew the truth. He and April had been the last two elves sitting around the campfire one night and he had confirmed what she already suspected. Airron had told Peter what had happened. Peter was deeply sad for his friend, but didn't know how to help Airron deal with this.

And Cherry went out of her way to antagonize all of them. She seemed to enjoy it. The more short-tempered Raina grew, the more Cherry needled her. Only Peter seemed to have any influence over Cherry, often taking her off for walks when she was at her most maddening. April wasn't sure that Peter and Cherry being chummy was a good thing, but didn't question his role as peacekeeper, it was too appreciated, especially since Marigold was no help at all. She had developed a strong affection for Salm and always sat close beside him or followed him around. He did not return the sentiment and spent a lot of energy avoiding Marigold with a panicky look in his eye. It was rather funny, except to Salm and Marigold.

The animals did not return to the forest, which confirmed that Loug was still wandering around much too close.

Two weeks after April and Airron returned, Raina declared that she was calling a gathering. "An important meeting," she stressed. "Everyone has to attend, everyone except you, Cherry. You don't have to bother." Telling Cherry not to come was the best way to ensure that she did.

"I'll be there. Wouldn't miss the chance to see you making a fool of yourself trying to be the mayor of this stupid place," Cherry said in her most scathing tone. Raina lunged at her but Salm was quick enough to restrain his sister. She shoved him into the snow, Salm was almost buried.

The previous day, they had received several inches of sticky snow. They had spent much of the day building snow-elves and making a huge Keep. They had played like children, there was nothing else to do.

Raina had discovered icicles, she was fascinated by the frozen shapes. She collected as many as she could find and stuck them into the walls of the Keep, pointy end up. Even Airron had descended from the hollow and sculpted a small sad snow-elf before he kicked it to pieces and returned to the tree.

Raina scheduled her meeting for that very afternoon, before dinner. No one looked forward to the meal, they had eaten enough stale nuts and seeds to start scampering around like squirrels themselves.

As soon as it was time, Raina directed them into the snow fort, it was the best place to gather. She ordered Peter to get Airron, who hadn't turned up.

"I'll see if he wants to come," Peter said mildly and shared a helpless glance with April. Peter was successful, he came back with Airron.

"You're late," Raina snapped. Even Cherry and Marigold were seated on thick squares of moss on the snowy floor.

Peter handed Airron a moss cushion and they sat down.

Raina paced and didn't say a word.

"Raina, what's this about?" Salm prompted.

"It's about finding New Haven. It feels like we've given up. We aren't doing anything to find it and we have to find it. We need to do *something*. We need to find it."

"What would you recommend?" Salm asked.

"I don't know! That's why I want to talk about it," Raina cried impatiently.

Cherry stood up. "This is a boring meeting."

"Cherry, sit down," Salm ordered. "Raina's right. We do have to keep trying, even if it seems futile. We can't give up. And everyone's knowledge and ideas are important." He didn't add 'even yours' but he might as well have. It's not that Cherry wasn't smart, it was that she was so disagreeable.

"Fine. There's nothing else to do anyway." Cherry settled back down as if she was waiting to be entertained. "Might as well watch you all wrack your tiny brains trying to find New Haven."

"Well, at least we're trying," Raina snarled at her.

"You have as much chance of finding it as you do of - "

"Cherry, shut it," Salm bellowed.

Airron surprised them all by standing up and walking away.

"Airron, what are you doing?" Raina called. The meeting was out of control.

"Going back to bed. This is useless."

"That's not fair. We're only getting started. Stay Airron, we need your help," she pleaded.

"There's no point Raina." He turned around and faced her, defeat in every line of his body. "New Haven is gone. It's not coming back. I wouldn't be any help anyway."

"Of course you can help, of course New Haven is coming back. Why have you given up? It's not like you at all," Raina said.

Airron stepped closer again. "Maybe I'm not like me. Maybe I'm not me anymore."

"What are you talking about? Of course you are you," Raina cried in frustration.

"No I'm not," he said with finality.

"Why not, Airron? What are you talking about?"

"Do you really want to know?" he challenged. This was getting out of hand. Peter thought so too.

"Airron, not like this," he warned, shaking his head. "This is not the way."

"She wants to know, doesn't she," Airron said bitterly, yanking off his leafy poncho and untying the top closures of his robe.

"Airron, please don't," April stood up, wishing she could stop this. Raina didn't know what was going on. She wasn't prepared.

"Raina, do you want to know what the Giant did?" Airron asked.

"The Giant?" she whispered. "The Giant captured you?"

"Yup, spent a couple of days in that little box. Do you want to know what the Giant did?" Airron was so angry, and Raina was bearing the brunt of it. She met his gaze and changed her mind.

"No." She shook her head fearfully. "No, I don't."

"Well I do," Cherry interjected maliciously.

Airron kept undoing his robe.

April linked arms with Raina. "Don't look," she said softly. "I'll tell you. You shouldn't see …"

But Raina kept her eyes on Airron as though hypnotized. He held center stage. Then he looked into Raina's face and his hand stilled. The anger left him in one big whoosh. "I'm sorry," he apologized, closing his eyes. "I'm sorry. None of this is your fault. Forgive me."

"Of course, Airron. But I think you better tell me … I think I need to know."

He shrugged, dropped his robe to his waist and turned around. No one moved or made a sound. Even April, who had witnessed the horrible act, had seen it from a distance. Up close, a ragged tattered edge of amber was all that was left of his prized wings.

It was lucky April had a good grip on Raina. She swayed as if the ground was rocking beneath her feet. "No," Raina shook her head wildly. "No, no, no. Oh, Airron." She rushed up to him and yanked his robe back in place, tying it up with tears dripping down her face. Then she pressed her forehead against his shoulder. No words could convey her sadness more. "Come on, Airron." She led him away to privacy. The gathering was over.

Cherry kept her mouth shut for once and left with Marigold, proving she did have some good sense, on occasion.

Peter and Salm silently gathered wood and April lit it. They sat around the warmth, but April felt so chilled inside that the heat couldn't reach that place.

Salm broke the silence. "You knew?"

Both April and Peter nodded.

"April, did you see … how it happened?" Salm asked, aghast.

"Yes. An owl knocked Airron out of the air and the Giant … the Giant picked him up and … just like that … there was no warning. It happened so fast, I couldn't stop it." April hated to remember, but it was something she would never forget.

"Poor Airron. I can't imagine. No wonder you loath Giants." Salm hunched closer to the fire.

"They're cruel and awful," April said bitterly. "And without conscience, and big enough to do whatever they want." They had been the main reason that the elves in her world had failed to thrive.

They sat silently for the longest time, then discussed other things, giving Airron and Raina time alone. Peter talked thoughtfully about how to find New Haven and they all tried to guess where it could be, but they really didn't have a clue.

"Might as well look up and wish for it to float by in a bubble," Peter said, when they ran out of ideas.

Salm snorted in disbelief.

"Hey, Brag floated a Giant's hammer. Big things can float," April defended Peter.

"Yes, but there's a world of a difference between a Giant's hammer and a world, isn't there," Salm countered.

"There is," she agreed, too tired to argue. "Can we go to bed now?"

"Without dinner?" Salm asked. They had forgotten to eat.

"You two can eat all the seeds and nuts your hearts desire. I'm going to bed." April climbed up the tree, leaving the boys to eat seeds. Raina and Airron were sound asleep, curled up together. For once, Airron wasn't tossing and turning, fighting his battles in his dreams. April slept a little better herself that night and woke to bright sunshine. A new day.

Airron joined them at breakfast, it was wonderful to see him up and about. "Hey Airron," April smiled, handing him an acorn cap of tea.

"Hey." He looked a bit sheepish but ate a big breakfast and shared his tea with Raina when she turned up.

"The snow is pretty when the sun shines, isn't it?" Raina smiled sadly up at the sky. "Only one fluffy cloud up there. So, did anyone dream up an idea to find New Haven?" she asked. Cherry and Marigold were sleeping in, so the five of them could talk without all the disharmony.

"Peter said it might float by." April grinned at Peter. "That was his best idea."

"Thanks Peter," Raina said dryly. "We'll start watching the sky then."

"Hey, Brag can float hammers and elves. It is possible," Peter insisted stubbornly.

"Be that as it may, I think we will investigate other possibilities," Raina declared. "So you keep thinking Peter."

"Hey, I have been thinking. Straining my brain. Maybe we need to approach this from a different point of view." It really was turning into a meeting.

"What point of view? New Haven is gone. What other point of view is there?" Salm asked, stirring tea.

"Why is it gone," Peter said.

"Huh?" Salm looked confused. "I don't know."

"No, I'm not asking you. That's the different angle, or perspective. Instead of thinking about where it is, think about why it left."

"Okay. Why did New Haven leave?" Salm echoed. "It felt like a change? Went for a long walk? Got lost?"

"Salm, be serious." Raina furrowed her brow. "Why did New Haven leave? That's a really good question Peter. It could be important."

"Other things are gone," Airron pointed out. It was a good sign that he was participating.

"What other things?" Salm asked, puzzled.

"Is your brain still asleep Salm?" Raina shook her head at him. "Lots of other things are gone, aren't they? Alive things – animals, creatures, the squirrels that left all their nuts and seeds behind for us."

"Oh, right. Because of the Giant. They're scared so they ran away. But a world doesn't get scared and run away," Salm declared.

April jumped up. "That's it," she cried excitedly.

"That could be it," Peter agreed, thinking along the same lines.

"What's it?" Salm demanded. He was getting frustrated.

"New Haven isn't a regular world. The Echoes that protect it are alive. Maybe they got scared and ran away from the Giant, taking New Haven with them," April said.

"Or," Peter glanced at her apologetically, "Or the Echoes are supposed to move New Haven if a Giant approaches. Maybe that's how they protect the world from something so large and dangerous. They move it. They are supposed to move it. They protect New Haven by moving it." It was a better explanation than April's, it made more sense. And it explained the wasteland left behind, where New Haven used to be.

They had been talking for only a few minutes and already they had made some progress. It was heartening. And if the Echoes had magically relocated New Haven to protect it from the Giant, it wasn't really gone or gone forever. It would either come back when the Giant left, or settle somewhere else, far from the Giant. At least they knew to search where Loug wasn't. Everyone was cheered up by the logical explanation as to why New Haven was gone. But it meant that they had other decisions to make.

"So, do we stay here and wait for Loug to leave and New Haven to return, if it's going to? Or do we continue traveling west away from the Giant and try to find New Haven ourselves?" Raina proposed the direct question.

"What if the Giant never leaves?" Salm asked a different question. "What if he stays, then New Haven will never return to this spot. Maybe it has already settled elsewhere."

"April? Do Giants live in one place or travel around?" Peter asked.

"Live in one place for awhile. They knock down the trees and fence in animals so they have a steady supply of food. They'll move on once they have eaten all the food, trampled everything flat, and polluted the environment with their waste. But that's when there is a group of Giants. Loug is alone, he seems to be mostly wandering around." It was not a decisive answer.

"Group of Giants, good grief!" Raina looked horrified at the thought. One was a nightmare. A group of Giants was inconceivable.

They made more hot tea and stayed close to the fire. It was a frigid day, as so many lately. Winter was having a cold spell. They discussed their options until Cherry and Marigold turned up. Salm jumped to his feet as soon as Marigold sat so close to him that she almost sat on him.

No decision had been reached, and they discussed the subject again the next morning, but Cherry joined them almost right off so the conversation faded to silence.

"Hey, don't stop on my account," she drawled. "Pretend I'm not even here. I'll pretend you're not here."

It proved impossible because she kept belittling their ideas. When they discussed setting out to search for New Haven, she had her own announcement. "I'm not leaving so do what you want."

"Fine with me," Raina countered. "You sit here and wait for New Haven to float by while we go and find it. I'll be sleeping in my own bed while you're frozen up to your ears in snow."

Cherry gazed at Raina, a most peculiar expression on her face. "Why would you say that?"

"Why did I say you could freeze your lobes? Take a guess," Raina retorted.

For once Cherry didn't insult her back. "No – the other thing, about New Haven floating."

"I don't know why I said it. Peter said New Haven might be floating around, he was joking."

"What's up?" Peter asked, when Cherry bit her lip and stared off into space.

"I'm trying to remember something," she said.

Raina taunted, "Don't try too hard. You might hurt yourself."

Cherry didn't bother to answer. She really was thinking. "Ms. Larkin-LaBois," she finally muttered significantly. It was a strange thing to say.

"What about her?" April was truly intrigued. The old elf had unusual abilities for a New Haven elf – for any elf. April was one of only two elves that knew about her talent for seeing things before they happened. And not so long ago, Ms. Larkin-LaBois had made a point of telling April to come and speak with her if April needed advice. But April had not gone to see Ms. Larkin-LaBois. She had not even thought about consulting the elf before she left New Haven, starting this whole disastrous chain of events. "What about her?" April repeated when Cherry kept thinking with a wrinkled forehead.

"I'm trying to remember," Cherry snapped. "She came to my aunt's house the night before we left New Haven. She turned up out of the blue and my aunt offered her tea. The old elf was talking about stuff that didn't make a lot of sense. She insisted I stay for tea. My aunt thought she was really weird, crazy even." Cherry was getting sidetracked.

"Cherry, what did Ms. Larkin-LaBois talk about, when she made you stay for tea?" April pressed urgently.

"Oh, something about the sky, looking up, floating." Cherry motioned for Salm to serve her some seeds. "That's why I remembered it now, because Raina was babbling about New Haven floating around."

"I wasn't babbling," Raina declared hotly.

"Raina, quiet! Cherry, what else did Ms. Larkin-LaBois say. Think."

April could not explain how important the elf's words might be, not without breaking a confidence and revealing a secret that was not hers to share.

"I already told you. She rambled on about the sky and ... floating. That's all I remember. Marigold might remember more. She was there, too."

The sky and floating? Unless Ms. Larkin-LaBois was trying to warn April about Airron losing his wings? And using Cherry to pass the message because she foresaw that Cherry would travel outside New Haven and meet up with them. Maybe there had been a way to stop it all from happening. Was April supposed to watch the sky for the owl to save Airron? If that was the point of the message, April had missed the opportunity. Or Ms. Larkin-LaBois could have meant something else entirely. Floating had nothing to do with owls, but floating did have to do with Brag's bubbles.

April sighed with frustration. Cherry's information was too vague. If the old elf had been trying to send April a message via Cherry, the meaning had been lost. Unless Marigold remembered more. She was still sleeping in. April would speak to her as soon as she woke up. It didn't look like they would be traveling anywhere this day.

When April asked Marigold about Ms. Larkin-LaBois's words, Marigold claimed she didn't remember anymore than Cherry. It sounded like she remembered less. But her attention had been fixated on Salm, not April. April could have been standing on her head in the snow, chewing frozen worms, and Marigold wouldn't have noticed.

It snowed in the afternoon and they worked on their snow Keep, enlarging it and cleaning out the new fallen flakes. It gave them something to do. Airron helped and they ended up having a snowball fight over the walls of the fort.

Her friends were starting to get used to their new life in the Outerworld, April realized with a bit of a shock. And she was doing all right herself. Without the dangerous creatures and with the steady supply of food and the company of her friends, this world was not the nightmare she had known in the past - except for Loug. And he was still hanging around. The continuous lack of forest life verified that fact.

She was reminded of Loug in another way, quite by accident. April and Peter had traveled further than she deemed safe to harvest a small collection of frozen crab apples. It was a wonderful treat and therefore worth the risk. April borrowed Peter's pocket blade and cut loose the apples, letting them fall to the snow below. Peter piled them up on a bark sled.

When the tree was truly bare, April returned to the ground and wrapped up in her clothes and leaves. It was freezing, really too cold to fly. Having grown thin, April was easily chilled now.

The apples looked pathetic, all brown and shriveled, but they would taste delicious cooked over the fire.

Peter was eyeing the questionable fruit with distaste and April laughed at his expression. "They will be good, honest," she assured him, reaching into her pocket to return his blade. The chain holding the vial came out too, all tangled around it.

"You still have that?" Peter asked.

"Yes, I didn't lose it again." April grimaced. "Brag called it essence of Giant, it draws the wearer toward the Giant." It was one of the few bits of useful information that Brag had managed to remember. "I hate to think what he put inside." April dropped the chain over her head for safekeeping and tucked it out of sight. She would have to wash out the vial one day when she was feeling brave. She didn't want to lose the chain, it was a reminder of the elves from her world.

Peter pulled on the vine attached to the bark sled to get the apples moving. "This way," he called when April started walking in the wrong direction.

"No, this way. We have to go this way." She kept on going.

Peter abandoned the apples and took off after her. As soon as he caught up, he lifted the chain off over her head. "I don't think you should wear it," Peter said, dropping the vial into her hand.

"Oh. No, I guess not. It's still working, isn't it? I'm surprised the spell has potency after so long." April toyed with the chain.

"The magic seems very powerful." Peter tucked his blade away.

"When you wore the chain, I wonder why it didn't work on you," April said.

Peter flushed about taking the vial. "It just didn't," he said tersely, making it clear that the subject was still not open for discussion.

Curious, April said, "Try it again. Here." She stepped close and placed it over his neck. Peter allowed it. After the vial settled in place, he stood firm. His feet didn't move.

"Still doesn't work on me," he said almost angrily and yanked it off.

"Odd that it works on me and not you," April mused. And would it work on Cherry?

"Our magic is very different. Yours is much stronger." Peter started pulling the sled loaded with apples.

"I wonder how close Loug is." April said, at least she knew the direction to avoid.

"Too close. Let's get home."

Together, they pulled the apples back towards their temporary home. April checked the forest regularly and didn't sense one living creature, including the Giant, but with his huge steps, by the time she sensed him he could be upon them. It was a relief to reach the campsite. Raina and Cherry were coldly ignoring each other, Marigold was helping Salm tie up some swing seats and Airron was staring vacantly at nothing. He did that a lot now.

"Hey, Airron. Come unload the apples," Peter called. Airron looked like he needed distracting.

Airron took over the pulling, although he didn't look impressed with

169

the food.

"Beside the fire please," April instructed. "They'll be delicious cooked. I promise."

Airron muttered, "Ya, well, delicious isn't what it used to be, is it?"

"Not really. But they will be good and we won't be hungry," April said brightly. "If we're lucky, some might have worms. Worms are more filling than apples."

Airron leaned close and murmured, "Don't tell Raina about the worms."

"Has everything been okay here?" Peter asked, helping Airron unload the sled.

"I guess. Raina hasn't killed Cherry. And Salm, well … it is funny to watch him trying to escape from Marigold." Airron quirked his lips and motioned towards the pair. Marigold was determined, you had to give her that. Salm looked resigned to his fate now. He lifted Marigold onto the newly rigged swing when she made a feeble attempt to get on and appeared to need his help. Then he had to push her, since she didn't seem to know how to work a swing or maybe it was her legs.

Raina wandered up and kicked one of the apples. "Dinner?" She glared at the fruit.

"Dinner," April confirmed. No one seemed thrilled with the treat. She started poking at the fire to create an area of coals for cooking. She would enjoy the meal, even if no one else did. When Cherry joined them and curled her lip at the apples, April didn't care. Cherry didn't like anything and always kept everyone well informed of that fact.

"You're not very good at finding food, are you?" Cherry sniped at April.

"Hey, I don't see anyone starving and I don't see you finding food," April shot back.

"I could find rotten apples if I wanted too, but I don't! Why would I want to traipse around finding rotten apples?" Cherry challenged, her hands on her hips.

"The apples look great. We're lucky to have them so stop complaining." Raina had changed her tune in a heartbeat.

"There's nothing else to do. Marigold's stuck on Salm and the rest of you are no fun at all." Cherry's dissatisfied expression was a permanent fixture.

"You could try helping out around here if you're so bored," Raina suggested.

In answer, Cherry picked up an apple and tossed it in the fire. "There, I cooked dinner. That wasn't hard at all." Cherry dusted off her hands and crossed her arms, daring anyone to say a word.

"You don't cook them like that." April grabbed a stick and tried to rescue the apple from the flames. It was too late. "Well, I guess that's your dinner." Angrily, she flung the stick at Cherry.

"Hey, I'm helping out like you said. It's more than Airron does around here, isn't it? I don't see him helping, he sits around like a lump most of the time," Cherry said.

Raina gasped in outrage. They all did. "Shut up, Cherry. Airron's allowed, he has a reason. You don't!" she said furiously.

"So Airron doesn't have wings anymore. Big deal. The rest of us don't have wings and I don't see us crying in the snow. Now he's no better than the rest of us!" Cherry's voice was strident and hateful. But she had gone too far.

Raina lost her temper in a really big way. Before anyone could stop her, she tackled Cherry to the ground. It was lucky Raina didn't land them both in the fire. The pair rolled around in the snow like ferocious weasels. It was the first full-fledged fight since they had found Cherry.

Salm and Marigold dashed over but no one was sure what to do. Separating the fighting elves would be like jumping into the middle of a whirlwind. And Raina was holding her own. Only when the girls began to run out of steam did Salm leap into the fray and haul them apart. Peter latched onto Cherry and pulled her back, speaking intently into her ear.

"That's enough," Salm shouted, sounding exactly like his father. "Cherry, go to your hollow if all you can do is stir up trouble. Marigold, get her out of here."

Marigold urged Cherry away and she went, clutching a bloody nose. Salm breathed a double sigh of relief. He had gotten rid of both of them.

"And don't come back!" Raina shouted, waving her fists.

Airron laughed and put an arm around her shoulder. "You've gotten really tough living in the Outer-world. Thanks for defending me, but you didn't have to." He kissed her right on the lips and they sat down together, cozy by the fire's warmth.

April cooked the apples properly on the coal side of the fire.

Salm had small squares of birchbark ready to hold the steaming apples when April carefully lifted them off to cool. That didn't take long in the middle of winter. In minutes, they were peeling the skin back and digging in with sticks. The mushy fruit was the best meal in ages.

"Mmmm, not bad." Salm nodded in pleasure. "Not bad at all, April."

"Don't look so surprised. I told you they were good. Eat the skin too, you don't want to waste that part. It's the most filling. And if you find any worms, eat those," April added, forgetting to keep quiet about the worms. Everyone stopped eating as one. "You'll barely taste them. Worms don't have much flavor, they only taste like dirt."

Salm shrugged and devoured the rest of his apple, then a second before sheepishly lifting two apples from the snow. "Not Marigold's fault," he mumbled before heading for the smaller hollow.

"Good grief! Do you think Marigold is growing on him?" Raina hissed, aghast.

171

Salm was quick to return, without the food.

"Cherry calmed down at all?" Peter asked.

"Not even close. I was lucky to escape with my head."

Salm sat down beside April with a weary yawn. "Lovely and quiet now, isn't it? Beautiful stars." They stared silently up at the night sky, and it was beautiful, lit with so many stars that an elf could never count them all before the sun rose again.

They should have discussed how to find New Haven, but they didn't. The night was peaceful and they sat for the longest time before retreating into the warmer hollow. They needed rest to face another day and if they had known what was to come, no one would have slept so soundly that night. No one would have slept a wink.

12 – Very Fishy

"April, get up! Are you going to sleep all day?" It was Raina's voice.

"I could," April mumbled, burrowing deeper into the bedding.

"Well, breakfast is ready! More apples. You'll miss out if you stay in bed." Raina disappeared out of the tree. April groaned and followed.

Someone had revived the fire. Tea was steaming in acorn caps, the sun was shining and only one small cloud floated aimlessly overhead. Everyone was present, even Cherry and Marigold. Cherry was cheerful and April didn't like the elf's smarmy smile one bit.

"Great breakfast." Cherry was overdoing the good humour.

"Who cooked the apples? They're perfect," Raina asked, but not of Cherry.

"I did," Peter said. "I watched how April cooked them. They did turn out rather well if I do say so myself."

"They did," everyone agreed. Even Cherry.

When Raina reached out to toss a bit of core in the fire, April blinked to clear her eyes. There was something different about her friend this morning.

173

April couldn't quite put her finger on what it was. Maybe she was imagining things. April rubbed her eyes. No, it wasn't her imagination.

"Raina, are you feeling okay?" April asked.

"I'm feeling fine. Why? Why is everyone staring at me?" The others had noticed something amiss now, too. "April, what is it? And would everyone stop staring!"

"Raina, your skin is turning a little green – greenish," April tried to explain gently.

"Green? Greenish? What are you talking about?" Raina scowled and uncovered her arm. She scrunched up her face and uncovered her second arm. "Good grief, I am kind of green. How did that happen?" She looked at April blankly. "Does this happen to elves in the Outer-world? Do they turn green?"

"I've never seen a green elf, or an elf turn green. Not that I can remember."

"But you have some green streaks in your hair."

"I was born with those, my hair didn't turn green."

"Oh. Well, I wonder why I'm turning green. I don't think I like it." Raina stared at her arms and raised one to sip her tea. The fact that she was green didn't seem to have sunk in yet. And she did seem to be getting greener before their very eyes. April stepped closer, trying to sense anything amiss. There was nothing to sense, but Raina's tea looked off-colour.

"Raina, don't drink any more tea," April said. It was a hunch. She compared their tea. Raina's was greener.

Raina noticed it too. "My tea is kind of green."

"Who made the tea?" April asked.

"I did. But I didn't put anything different in Raina's, only bark like the rest," Peter said defensively.

"Of course you didn't put anything in my tea." Raina stared at her arms again in dismay. "Am I getting greener?"

"Only a little," Airron was lying. She definitely was.

Peter cleared his throat guiltily and said, "Umm ... I did go into the forest for a minute. I wasn't with the tea the whole time."

Everyone's gaze narrowed on Cherry. She was looking too innocent, as if maple sugar wouldn't melt in her mouth. In the past she had proven herself to be sneaky and willing to use poisons.

"Cherry? Did you do something to Raina's tea?" Salm asked pointblank.

"Me? No, of course not. Ask Marigold. We were together all morning, weren't we Marigold?" Cherry turned confidently to her friend. Marigold did not look nearly so sure.

"Marigold, were you and Cherry together since you woke up?" Salm pressed.

"Umm ... well ..." She glanced from Salm to Cherry and back again, several times. "Yes, yes, I think so."

"Are you telling the truth. You wouldn't lie to me would you?" Salm looked disappointed.

Marigold chewed her lip and shot a fearful glance at Cherry. "No, I wouldn't lie to you. Not if I didn't have too."

"What did you put in my tea, Cherry?" Raina interrupted sharply. "How did you turn me green?"

"Wasn't me," Cherry denied smugly. She continued eating as if the matter had been settled. April didn't believe a word that came out of Cherry's mouth but she knew a way to find out for sure. It was an anomalous magic that had connected April and Cherry's father, who had possessed the power of dark magic. It didn't work with other elves, but it might work with Cherry. She seemed to share much in common with her late father.

April tossed her tea aside and approached the elf with purpose.

Cherry edged backwards. "What are you doing?"

In answer, April lunged and grabbed Cherry's arm, concentrating hard. As had happened with Drake Pitt, Cherry's thoughts revealed themselves to her. Cherry had turned Raina green, using something Brag had given her when he was terrorizing New Haven.

"You turned Raina green!" April gasped in outrage. "On purpose!"

"Oh, big surprise! She deserved it," Cherry snarled, shoving April so hard that she fell backwards into the snow.

April's temper grabbed hold of her in a big way. As if they didn't have enough problems with the Giant roving close and New Haven missing - and now Cherry was poisoning them! April filled up with so much anger she couldn't contain it. But it didn't matter, she could lose her temper all she wanted in the Outer-world, nothing happened here.

She leapt up and launched herself at Cherry, too mad to think straight. Cherry tripped April's feet from under her and she went down again. Cherry was on her in a flash, shoving her face into the hard, icy snow. April was trapped, she squirmed wildly but couldn't dislodge Cherry's heavier weight. Raina had held her own against Cherry, April was getting beaten up. It was humiliating!

With a scream of pure fury, April strained to flip over. She managed, because Peter had hauled Cherry off her. He was holding the elf firmly by her elbows and trying to reason with her.

Sputtering and wiping snow off her face, April was fully prepared to renew her attack. Strangely, when April stood up and faced Cherry, the breeze was blowing harder, frigid from the winter temperatures. Thunder rumbled across the sky, in concert with the lightening flashing directly overhead. But it wasn't supposed to thunder or lightening in the winter, and the sky was perfectly blue.

April looked up in confusion. One cloud. Straight over her head, one cloud was floating. Lightening flared inside the fluffy white fog, illuminating a dense interior. The anger that gripped April vanished in a surge of elation. New

175

Haven! She knew where it was – she knew exactly where it was. She could see it! The world was hovering overhead, encased in a cloud.

"April? What is it?" Salm asked when she laughed out loud.

"New Haven," April pointed up, her smile too big for her face.

"Where?" Raina cried excitedly, turning in a circle.

Peter was looking up, so was Cherry. They had figured it out.

April laughed joyously. "New Haven's up there! Floating in that cloud. That's what Ms. Larkin-LaBois was trying to tell us. That was the message."

"New Haven is in that cloud? Wahoo!" Raina cheered, looking very green.

Salm whooped and bounded over to April, he picked her up off her feet and spun her around. "I am so very happy you got mad!" He grinned and kept spinning. They were all giddy with glee at having found their world, safe and sound – sort of. After more celebrating, they sat down to figure things out. But Raina had a question first.

"April, I really don't want to go home green. This is temporary, isn't it? You did find out from Cherry?" Her eyes begged for some good news. April had not learned if the condition was permanent when she shared Cherry's thoughts. She would have to ask.

"Cherry, how long does the green last?" April demanded.

"No idea, actually. Brag never said." She shrugged dismissively. "It might last forever. Time will tell, won't it?"

Raina surged to her feet furiously, Airron pulled her right down to sit in his lap. "I'm sure it's temporary, right April. Most spells are, aren't they?" His eyes told her to say yes.

She did. "Yes, of course." She avoided thinking about Brag's vial, which had held a potent magical charm for months now, or Blossom Tree Circle, which had retained its powerful love spell for over two thousand years.

"Anyway, we've found New Haven. So, how do we get up there? Or how do we get it to come back down here?" Airron asked, directing the subject to something much more heartening.

"I can fly up and tell everyone where we are," April said. Then their families could stop worrying.

Airron shook his head firmly. "April, an elf can't fly that high. I don't think even a bird can reach the clouds. It's a lot higher than it looks."

"Oh. Are you sure?"

"Positive." Airron did sound sure and Peter nodded in agreement. April was not so convinced, her wings were magical after all. They weren't like regular wings, maybe they could carry her that high. It was worth considering.

"So we have to get New Haven down," Salm declared. "How do we do that?"

Everyone gazed longingly up at the cloud.

"Cherry, did Ms. Larkin-LaBois say anything else? Have you

remembered anything at all?" April asked, even though she never wanted to speak to the elf again.

"No. I wish I had paid more attention. But how did she know about New Haven floating anyway?" Cherry's eyes were suspicious slits in her face.

April couldn't speak the truth and couldn't think fast enough to produce a plausible lie, she shrugged and left it at that. Cherry narrowed her eyes further, but didn't comment. Everyone's thoughts were fully focused on New Haven anyway. April turned the subject back in that direction. She knew one sure way to get New Haven to come down, but she hated to say it aloud. She said it anyway. "Getting rid of the Giant would bring New Haven back down to earth."

"New Haven will come down if Loug leaves the area," Raina repeated. "Well, that doesn't help us, unless he decides to leave for himself."

Salm was still looking up, the most yearning expression on his face. "How does an elf get rid of a Giant?"

"April? Any ideas?" Raina asked, gesturing with her hands. She blinked at them, the vivid green colour kept surprising her.

"I only know of one time when elves bested a Giant, and that was your Giant – Gnash, two thousand years ago. And striking a Giant with lightening would only work if he was inside New Haven, inside the forcefield. It won't work down here, neither do we have the thunderwands to perform the transformation." She could have simply said no.

"Well, there must be a way," Raina declared optimistically. "We'll figure it out, and maybe my skin will go back to normal in the meantime. I really don't want to go home green."

Over the next few days, they thought hard about how to scare Loug away. Sadly, no one came up with even one workable idea. The Giant was simply too big and they were too small. At least their situation didn't seem as hopeless as before, because they could look up and see New Haven. And Loug might decide to wander away on his own.

Every morning April awoke filled with hope that New Haven might have floated down while they slept. But each morning, the barren landscape greeted her. Each morning, Raina woke up hoping she wasn't green anymore, but each morning, she woke up a little greener. She had also developed a nagging cough, which seemed to be getting worse with each passing day.

On the fifth morning after discovering New Haven's location, it was still in the cloud and they were still freezing on the icy earth far below. April surveyed the circle of elves huddled around the fire; the boys were thin and worn out, Raina was coughing again, the wind was freezing and they had nothing to eat but more moldy seeds. All her friends were suffering because they had braved this world to save April from the Giant. Right then and there, April made a decision - it was time to try flying up to the cloud. It was not going to get warmer anytime soon, so she might as well try now. If they could let their families know that they were safe and alive, everyone would feel happier. Maybe she could even communicate with the Echoes and persuade them to come down to earth, at least long enough to pick up the lost elves.

April stood with purpose. "I'm going to try flying up to New Haven. Maybe I can get the Echoes to come back down. At the very least, I can tell everyone where we are," she said decisively.

"What? But you can't make it," Airron argued.

"Maybe I can," April countered, "My wings are different. They are magical. It won't hurt to try and if I can't reach the cloud, I'll fly back down." It sounded simple enough.

"You mean you're going now? Right now?" Raina asked.

"Yes." April checked the forest, it was perfectly safe. "Stay near the hollow, in case."

"Yes mother," Airron said. "Umm April, if you do make it, don't tell anyone about ... you know." He looked ashamed of not having wings.

"I won't, Airron."

"And April?" Raina touched her arm. "Don't say that I'm green, okay? And if the Echoes won't come down, bring some food back, okay? And be careful."

April had to hide a smile when she started climbing the nearest tree. She was getting used to Raina being green, not that she would ever tell her friend that, but Raina looked kind of cute – colourfully bright in a world of white. April removed her warm coat of leaves and extra layers, tied her overall straps around her neck and jumped.

Without her clothes and outside the shelter of the trees, the icy wind blew stronger and even her magical wings felt like they were coated in little bumps. Undeterred, April waved and started flapping, hoping the movement would warm her up. It didn't help. The higher she flew, the colder it became. But she stubbornly kept going, imagining herself delivering the good news to all their families, imagining the warm world overhead. A few minutes in New Haven would thaw her out in no time.

The cloud didn't look one inch nearer when April knew that she wasn't going to make it to New Haven, not without turning into a block of solid ice. Her teeth were chattering uncontrollably and she was shivering more than she was flapping when she began to descend.

The ground was so far below that it was a blur of light and shadow without detail. April plummeted through space, barely able to steer, growing colder by the second. When the ground rushed up to meet her, she fought to stop her freefall. A small wisp of smoke from the fire directed her at the last minute.

April wasn't in good shape when she tried to steer toward the campsite. And her tears kept freezing her eyes shut, blinding her. April dashed a hand across her face, trying to see. A dark shape loomed up, too close to avoid. And it was very solid, as April found out when she slammed into the tree trunk. Then she was falling, spinning out of control until everything went black with an explosive bang.

When she finally woke up, April didn't know where she was. For a lovely minute, she thought she was in New Haven, then she remembered everything. April struggled to move, as weak as a newly hatched bird. Fighting her way out of the pile of leaves felt a lot like escaping from a shell. The leaves almost won, especially since April only appeared to have one functioning arm.

She was sitting in a daze when the back door slid opened and a body climbed into the hollow with a steaming acorn cap of tea. Raina almost dropped it when she spotted April. "April, you're really awake! Oh, thank goodness. Here, drink this and get back under your leaves. You have to stay warm." Raina left the door cracked slightly for light and hurried over to place the fluid in April's hand.

"How long have I been sleeping?" She croaked like a bullfrog. Was that her voice?

"Much too long." Raina was greener than April remembered. "I didn't think you were ever going to wake up. I've missed you terribly. You do realize that I've only had Cherry, Marigold and boys for company. Here, drink the hot tea and I'll tell you what you've missed."

April relaxed back into her leafy nest and drank.

"You hit your head and you've been unconscious for days, if you can believe that. And you haven't missed a thing, except more snow," Raina reported. "The Giant still seems to be around and the New Haven cloud is still floating in the sky. I'm still green, in case you hadn't noticed. Of course you noticed. Peter and Cherry have been getting chummier, which is just plain weird. And Airron is still so sad." She sighed deeply. It sounded like everything was about the same.

"What's wrong with my arm?" April asked. It still wouldn't move. It seemed to be tied up.

"Oh, of course you don't know. Salm thinks it might be broken, but he's not sure. Anyway, he splinted it to be on the safe side, he did a good job, too. Lucky it was only swollen, not all bloody," Raina said lightly, then began to cough. Her cough was worse than April remembered.

Raina wouldn't let her out of the hollow for a couple of more days but April had lots of visits from everyone, except Cherry.

When she was allowed outside, it was an awkward climb down with only one arm. The air was crisp and fresh and the sky was beautifully blue. She smiled at New Haven cloud and sat down by the fire for breakfast. April didn't have to lift a finger except to eat and drink what was served.

It was wonderful to be outside again, and her friends had managed very well without her. They were experts at surviving the Outer-world by now. April felt deeply proud of them. She concentrated quickly and learned that no animals had returned to the immediate area. Loug must be stubbornly hanging around.

After April's afternoon nap (Raina insisted), Peter took her for a short walk. He had been thinking about how to get rid of Loug for days and wanted to discuss his ideas.

"Do you still have the vial with essence of Giant?" he asked straight off.

April pulled it out of her pocket. "I do."

"Does it still have power?"

April dropped the chain over her head. For no reason, she turned left and picked up the pace.

Peter lifted the chain off and nodded with satisfaction. "I think that's a yes, don't you?" He seemed pleased that the vial still worked.

"Yes," April agreed, not sure where he was headed with this. And she still hadn't tested the vial on Cherry.

"So we can always find Loug, if we want. Good to know. April, what can an elf do that a Giant can't do?" he asked pointedly.

"I don't know. What?" she asked.

Peter quirked his lips. "There's no right answer. What can an elf do that a Giant can't?" he repeated.

"Umm ... magic? Outer-world elves have magic and Giants don't."

"What else?"

"I thought you said there was no right answer," April reminded him.

"True, but there is more than one answer, isn't there. You know more about Giants and the Outer-world than the rest of us. What else? Think."

"I am thinking." April considered his question seriously. "Fly? And stay under water? But only if the elf is a fairy or a merrow from New Haven. Or me."

"Keep going."

"Okay. Umm ... elves are a lot smarter than Giants."

"Keep trying."

"I am trying. I hit my head really hard you know, I'm not sure it's back to normal yet," April reminded him.

"You don't have to tell me. I saw you hit the tree, you didn't even slow down."

"I don't think I remember that part."

"I wasn't sure you would recover. I'm really glad you got better." He got back to business. "What else can elves do that Giants can't do?"

"Be nice. Help each other and other creatures."

Peter arched an eyebrow. "I'm sure that's true, but it won't help us get rid of a Giant. I don't think being nice to him would scare him away."

"Umm ... elves can hide in very small places, like under leaves. Giants can't hide anywhere. Elves can travel through small holes and passages, Giants can't." April was saying things that Peter could figure out for himself.

"That's more like it. That could work to our advantage maybe. Somehow," he said thoughtfully.

"Too bad we don't have an eggstone mine to hide in. A Giant could never get inside and it would probably be warmer than here, so deep down into the earth ..." April trailed off when she remembered something about their mine tour.

"Do you have an idea?" Peter asked, studying her face hopefully.

"No, I was remembering the eggstone mine. Remember how I could sense unusual magic? Under all the tunnels?"

"Yes, that was weird."

"But it makes sense now. Do you think it's how the Echoes can make the whole world magically float away, even down to the deepest mine. The ancient scroll did say that the forcefield was created with combined magic of some sort. What if part of that magic is imp magic? Imps have incredible power, and Brag can float huge things."

"And imp magic doesn't work against Giants," Peter said her significantly.

"Oh! No, it doesn't!"

"So New Haven floats away if a Giant approaches." It made sense. "And Brag could work the forcefield," Peter added.

"He could." Elf and imp magic combined to create the forcefield? It was hard to imagine, then again, April and Brag could get along at times, and Cherry and Brag had reportedly combined their magic to make a bubble trap not so long ago. If April ever saw Brag again, she would have to ask him if he had ever heard any tales about imps being involved in the creation of the forcefield. "So, do you have a plan Peter?" she asked.

"No, not yet. I'm trying to come up with one. So elves are smaller, smarter and nicer than Giants. We should be able to outthink a Giant in our sleep," Peter decided. "It's the size that's a problem. What if it wasn't a problem? What if it could help us? When is being really big a disadvantage rather than an advantage? When is being very small good rather than bad?"

"I don't know. The size thing usually works in the Giant's favor. I'm sorry Peter, I'm not much help. My brain still feels as bruised as the rest of me," she apologized.

"It's okay. We'll all keep thinking. Getting rid of a Giant is no easy task but I'm sure there's a way and we'll find it." Peter turned them around and headed back towards the campsite. The walk hadn't been long, but it had been long enough for April.

"A bottomless pit would come in handy right now. A really big one," April muttered. "Do you think the Giant would follow me again? If I flew up high and led him away, like before? I think he could be tricked in the same way twice."

Peter stopped dead, scowling. "April, it's too cold. And what about your arm? You can't fly yet."

"Maybe I could. Salm said my arm might not be broken. I could wait for a warmer day and test it -"

"Give it some time, April. Your arm will heal and the weather will get warmer. What comes next out here? Spring?" Peter guessed.

"Yes, spring. Spring is not so far away, but it comes slowly, not fast. Each week is a little warmer than the week before. I think it's almost March, we've survived the worst of winter out here." But April didn't want to wait for spring, she wanted to go home now. She wanted to see her friends safely home.

"We'll think of something long before spring. Come on, let's get back to the fire." The sun was disappearing, the temperature was dipping accordingly. And Peter was right, April could not lead the Giant far away yet, she was far from recovered. And Airron no longer had wings to fly.

While she had the chance, April asked Peter about something that had been on her mind. "Peter, are you friends with Cherry now?" It did seem so.

"Uh ..." Peter floundered, not expecting the question. "Not friends exactly, but I thought she might confide in me if we weren't fighting. And there was some stuff I wanted to ask her about. I kind of hoped she could help us battle the Giant or get New Haven to come down, with her different kind of magic."

"Can her dark magic help?" April had never once considered that possibility.

"If it can, Cherry's not saying. She rations her information, even to me." With a self-depreciation smile, Peter picked up the pace. Darkness was falling fast.

In the coming days, April's arm stopped hurting. She wanted to take the splint off but Salm refused to allow that. She felt almost like her old self and started contributing again, exploring for food, traveling further in all directions when it became harder and harder to find enough to eat.

On one such trip, April, Peter and Salm came across a sizable lake. The surface was frozen solid, as smooth as a mirror. Every last flake of snow had been blown off by the wind. Ice was great fun.

"Try this!" April called, dashing towards the lake's edge. As soon as she hit the smooth ice, she pushed off and glided across the surface for the longest time, spinning in circles. Her slippers were very slippery.

Salm and Peter caught up. Searching for food was forgotten; they slid and pushed each other around, laughing like carefree children until they were quite worn out. It was lovely not to worry, even for a short time.

The trio finally collapsed together on the shore. Salm lay right down in the snow, warm from the exertion. "You know, there are a lot more dangerous things out here than in New Haven, but there are some fun things too. You can do stuff with snow and ice that you can't do with anything else. Hey, what happens to the fish in winter?" Salm sat up and eyed the frozen lake.

"The fish are still down there. They go to the bottom of the lake, only the very top of the water freezes. The fish get slow and sleepy down there until spring," April explained.

"So there is still lakeweed down there?" Salm sounded inspired.

"Yes."

"We could eat some lakeweed. That would be good right about now. Or a minnow fish, something different for dinner." He stepped onto the ice, peering down as if he could see through it. "Did you used to eat lakeweed?"

"Salm, I never had gills when I lived out here before," April reminded him.

"Oh right. No lakeweed. But I have gills, and you have gills now." Salm crouched down and tapped at the hard surface, testing it. "It's still watery down there, I could get some lakeweed."

"No Salm, the water is really cold. Colder than the air. You would freeze before you reached the bottom. And how would you get through the ice? It's inches thick," April said.

Looking thoughtful, Salm started sliding around again, trying to see under the ice. He kept going further and further from the shore.

"Salm, wait!" April called and went after him.

Peter followed, he slipped and went down hard. "Forgot how slippery it is." He winced and rubbed his bottom.

They caught up to Salm and followed him, he kept moving until he neared the middle of the lake. The longer they skated, the thinner the ice became until they could see right through the transparent layer.

Salm stopped and said, "Maybe we could cut through the ice where it is thinner, or break a hole." He banged with his foot, testing. "Why is it thinner here?"

April studied the nearest shore and pointed. "See the stream that flows into the lake? The continuous current stops ice from forming thickly, or forming at all sometimes."

He turned toward the creek and skated in that direction. The ice did get even thinner. He hopped up and down.

"Salm?" April twitched nervously, staring down. "Maybe you could go through the ice closer to the creek if we made a hole, but you would freeze. The water is too cold. Forget about the lakeweed. Come on, we have to go back anyway, the sun is going down."

Salm wasn't ready to give up on his idea yet. "But isn't the water warmer at the bottom, if it's not frozen?"

"Warmer than ice, Salm, but not warm," April stressed. "Not warm enough for an elf. We're not cold like fish, we're warm like ... like elves. And if you couldn't find the hole in the ice that you went down through, you'd be trapped under the ice and freeze for sure. And Salm, the fish are a lot bigger out here than in New Haven. Big fish eat elves."

"Oh." Salm gulped and backed up. "You could have said so sooner, April."

Gingerly, they edged off the thin skin of ice and headed home.

It was a relief to reach the campsite before full darkness. Airron and Raina had the fire burning, the flickering light was a welcoming beacon to guide them home. Since they hadn't found food, they each ate a small ration of seeds. It was not enough to stop hunger. Cherry choked down her meal, complained sourly and left, taking Marigold away with her. Raina glared resentfully at Cherry's back, Raina was still as green as ever and not at all happy about it.

Raina quizzed them about their day; she had been too tired to go exploring and her chronic cough often left her fighting for air. Once April had described the frozen lake, and Salm tried to sell his idea about seeking lakeweed under the ice, Raina came to her own conclusion. She shook her head at her brother impatiently. "It sounds too dangerous, Salm. It's a ridiculous idea to swim into a frozen lake filled with huge hungry elf-eating fish. I bet the snappy turtles are down there too, and those giant frogs," she cried. "We've all managed to survive so far and we have to keep it that way. We have to be smart, not stupid, if we're going to make it home. I would never be able to tell Mom and Dad if you got eaten by a giant fish, Salm."

"At least I'm not a fish!"

Raina gasped in indignation. "I am not a fish, I'm just a bit green - that doesn't make me a fish!"

"Uh … how deep would an Outer-world lake be, April?" Peter interjected, possibly to stop their bickering.

"I don't know. I never had gills when I lived out here before," she repeated. "But it must be really deep. Why?"

"Just wondering." Peter stared into the flames, lost in thought.

Salm rose impatiently. "I'm too hungry to stay awake, I'm going to bed." The rest of them soon followed. At least when you were asleep, your stomach didn't hurt and you didn't know how hungry you were.

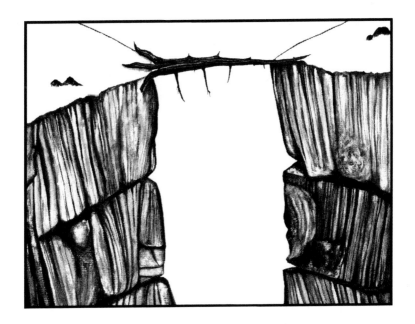

13 – Essence of Imp

The next day, Peter volunteered to try and find food again. "Who's going to help me?" he asked. April volunteered to go along before Cherry could say a word, April didn't like Peter hanging around with Cherry, for obvious reasons.

"I'll come too," Airron mentioned casually. It was the first time he had shown any interest in leaving the campsite and another sign that he was recovering.

"If I never have to think about food again, it will be too soon," Salm complained, staying by the fire. "Remember the good old days when we would go home and food would appear on the table like magic?" he reminisced.

"I remember," Raina looked nostalgic and sat down beside him, leaning toward the fire to warm her hands. "I'll never take another meal for granted again. Bring back something good for a change." She looked frail and had dark green circles under her eyes. Even sitting still, she was panting for air.

"We will, I promise," April said rashly, judging Raina needed a good meal and some cheering up.

"Have a rest while we're gone." Airron touched her cheek in parting. He looked worried about her, too.

Peter led them northwest along an unexplored route. A deep ravine

185

stopped them. The ground disappeared, only to pop up again about fifteen yards away. The area in-between looked like it had been sliced out by an enormous blade. Far far below, a foaming white torrent rushed by.

"I can barely see the bottom," Airron commented, leaning over to peer down.

April grabbed his robe and yanked him back. "Careful Airron."

"Right, no wings. Have to remember that in case I forgot." He jerked away from the drop off and her hand.

"I didn't mean it that way, Airron."

He stomped away without a word.

Peter touched her shoulder. "April? He'll be okay."

"Will he?"

"Sure, Airron is tough, smart. He'll come to terms with this."

"I hope you're right." Something across the ravine caught April's eye. "Hey, isn't that an apple tree, directly across."

Peter squinted. "Maybe."

It wasn't a far distance to fly. April had been wanting to test her arm for days, and Salm wasn't here to stop her taking off the splint. He had been overprotective since her collision with a tree, and inclined to fuss.

"I think I'll go see if there are some apples over there. Maybe you can cheer Airron up while I'm gone. Tell him I'm sorry."

"April, you didn't do anything wrong," Peter said. "And how are you going to check for apples? You can't fly, you can't get to the other side."

April didn't argue, she yanked off several layers and started to untie the bark splint, trying not to shiver. She seemed to feel the cold even more acutely since her near freezing.

"April, leave the splint on! Why are you taking it off?" Peter asked, even though he must have guessed.

"I have to test my arm sometime. Why not now, then maybe I can get some food." April eased the bark off and bent her arm. It felt okay. She lifted her arms into flying position. There was some discomfort, but nothing she couldn't handle. More confidently, she raised and lowered her arms, imitating flight. "See Peter, I'm fine. I can do this."

Peter wavered. "Well, do it quickly, before you freeze. And start from a tree, in case you need to land. You won't be able to do that in the ravine."

It was a wise precaution. April climbed the nearest tree and leaped. Both arms felt stiff and tight with disuse, and there was a sharp pulling sensation on the injured one, but it held up. April steered toward the ravine, glad it wasn't a great distance. A Giant probably could have spit from one side to the other.

The opposite side was a twin to the one she had left behind. April skimmed the tops of the trees until she located the one she had spotted. The fruit wasn't apples, but she was overjoyed to see one bough decorated with cherries. The fruit was shrunken and brown, but it was the most mouthwatering thing April had seen in weeks. She landed and picked a cherry for each hand, holding them by the stems. She even sucked on a frozen bite of fruit while she flew back across the ravine.

It took a couple of minutes to spot the boys, they had followed the edge of the drop-off and stopped beside a fallen tree trunk that bridged the expanse, joining the two sides. The wood was black with age and deeply cracked, but it looked sturdy enough to support a herd of moose. There had been no need for April to fly, she could have strolled across the ravine.

"Here! I'll be back with more," she called and dropped both cherries. Airron watched her soar overhead with the hungriest expression on his face and it wasn't to do with the food. April felt awful inside for having wings.

She made as many trips as she could until she grew too cold to continue, which was six. Peter rigged up another bark sled and the boys took turns pulling the food, they even pulled April some of the way. She had retied the splint on her newly throbbing arm and made the boys promise to keep her flying a secret from Salm.

For once, even Cherry didn't complain. The fruit was thawed beside the fire, then they stuffed themselves. April said there were more cherries in the tree if anyone wanted to cross the tree bridge, as if she had already done that.

Peter nodded. "The bridge is easy to cross, but the ravine is really deep, filled with rushing water. Makes Cayenne Creek look like a trickle."

"You don't see water like that in New Haven, it even made Fool's Falls look small," Airron added. April knew that waterfall personally, she had ridden down it in a hollow log to find New Haven at the bottom. It was not small.

"At least there's more food across this ravine." Salm helped himself to another cherry. His face was gaunt after months in the Other-World, but he never complained or took more than his share, unless there was extra, like now.

When it began to snow softly, they called it a night. Raina was the first to go to bed, she hadn't eaten much of the special meal and dragged her feet across the snow as if they were too heavy to lift. In spite of her day of rest, she looked sickly.

It was easier to sleep with a full stomach and April slept deeply after her active day. It felt like the middle of the night when Airron shouted in April's ear. "April, wake up. Something's wrong!"

April jerked upright. "What? What's wrong?" The hollow was impenetrable black and filled with a blood-chilling gurgling noise. It sent shivers of fear along her spine. "What is that?" It sounded like a monster.

"It's Raina. Can you light something so we can see?" Airron asked desperately. April felt around and grabbed one of their makeshift torches. She concentrated to make a flame while the wind howled through the edges of the ill-fitted door as if determined to rip it out of the hollow.

"Come on." Airron hurried April and the torch over to Raina. She was tossing and turning in her nest of leaves, it sounded like she was drowning.

187

"Is it a nightmare?" April asked in concern, shaking Raina's shoulder. Her friend felt cold and clammy.

"I don't think so. I've been trying to wake her, but she won't. Raina, wake up!" Airron said, very loudly, disturbing Salm and Peter. Raina, on the other hand, wouldn't wake up for the longest time, not until Salm cracked the door and brought back a handful of snow.

"Huge storm outside," he muttered and sprinkled the snow on Raina's flushed green face. Her eyes flew opened, but she continued to gasp and gurgle.

"Raina, what's wrong?" Salm demanded urgently.

"Can't breathe," Raina gasped, clutching her back. "No air."

"Yes there's air. Calm down, breathe slowly."

Raina made an obvious effort to relax. "Little better," she managed. "Not much, little."

Salm studied her with a tilted head, then sat her up and lifted the back of her shirt. "April, move the light closer. Peter, open the door a bit, it's getting smoky in here."

April held the light where Salm indicated and swallowed a gasp. Raina's gills were not almost invisible as they would normally be on land, they were pulsating as if she was under the water. And they were greener than the rest of her, and kind of scaled on the edges.

His expression grave, Salm lowered her shirt and rubbed her back soothingly. "Raina, you haven't been drinking any more of Cherry's tea, have you?" he asked casually.

She shook her head. "Make my own now. Always. What's wrong?" She sounded terrified.

"I don't know. It looks like your gills are trying to breathe underwater. But you're on land. You're awake aren't you? You're not dreaming about swimming?"

"Awake. Or having nightmare," Raina panted.

"Have you been feeling worse lately?"

"Not so good. Tired. Heavy. Trouble breathing, always coughing," she listed. "Thought it was the cold. Not the cold?" Tears welled up in her eyes.

Salm tried to smile reassuringly but didn't do a very good job. They had suffered too many trials, and now this. "I don't think it is the cold. Do you think this has anything to do with turning green?" He glanced at April questioningly, as if she might have the answers. April knew little of spells or potions, never having used them.

"I suppose it could be a reaction to Cherry's potion." April handed the torch to Salm and stood up. "I'll go and have a word with Cherry." She crossed the hollow with purpose and slid the door wider, surprised by the force of the storm. The snow was falling thickly and blowing every which way. The door was nearly yanked out of her hands.

Peter grabbed hold of the bark and held it in place while she climbed outside. "Hang on tight, don't blow away," he called, fighting with the door.

April almost did blow away, repeatedly, before she gained the lower hollow. She wrestled that door opened and fell into the smaller cave. The rush of snow and frigid wind disturbed both occupants.

"Who's there?" Cherry screeched.

"It's me, April." She fought to replace the bark door behind her. When it settled in place, she felt around for another torch to light. It was by the door.

As soon as they could see each other, Cherry snarled, "Why the heck are you waking me up?"

"Something is wrong with Raina," April began.

"Tough." Cherry cut her off.

"Cherry, shut up and listen. There's no time to waste. It looks like Raina might be having a reaction to being green – to whatever you put in her tea. What was Brag's spell? What exactly did you put in the tea?"

"And you couldn't wait until morning to ask that question?" Cherry retorted.

"No!" April shouted. How had Cherry reached almost sixteen without being strangled? "Raina can't breathe. Not properly. This is a ... a crisis. I need to know now!"

Cherry sighed as if greatly put upon. "Oh, it's some stupid fish spell, and fishy stuff. Turns things green. Maybe Raina is having more of a reaction because she's a merrow. I don't know."

"And you didn't think of that before you poisoned her?" April cried.

Cherry shrugged and lay down again.

April stepped closer. "What fishy stuff? Where did it come from?"

"Brag. Learned a lot of useful tricks from the stupid imp." Cherry was not being at all helpful.

"So, you don't know what it was? Do you know where he got it? New Haven or the Outer-world?" April pressed.

"Don't know." Cherry seemed wholly unconcerned. She either didn't realize the gravity of Raina's condition or she didn't care. Probably the latter. But maybe Cherry knew more than she realized.

"You are going to help me or I am going to toss you head first into the worst storm I've ever seen," April threatened, exaggerating for affect. "Think about when Brag showed you the spell and the potion, concentrate on it." She reached for Cherry's arm.

"No. No way." Cherry bolted up and shoved April against the wall of the tree.

"Cherry, Raina needs help. She can't breathe. You're the only elf who knows what you did and you are going to help or I swear you'll never see New Haven again, and if you don't think I mean that, you're not as smart as I thought."

"You're not going inside my head again. Forget it."

April wasn't about to wait for Cherry's consent. There was no time. She lunged forward and clamped onto the elf's arm as tightly as a crayfish. Marigold did not interfere.

"Think about Brag's spell," April ordered.

Cherry tried to shake her off but April was too determined, Raina's life might well depend on what she learned. And Cherry was thinking about the spell, because there was something else she was trying to hide. But one thought could not cover another. April heard Brag's incantation spoken in Cherry's voice, she saw the shiny flakes sprinkled in the tea and she learned that Cherry had a whole stash of such ill-gotten goods in this very hollow - substances that could be used to do all sorts of appalling things. But April didn't find out how to help Raina. Cherry didn't know and Brag had never spoken of a cure. Cherry had been honest about that.

And then April learned something so tragic, she cried aloud in pain and released Cherry.

One last random image passed between them before the contact was broken - Ms. Larkin-LaBois' wrinkled face talking about floating and bubbles. Magical bubbles? April already knew all about magical bubbles and she knew about New Haven floating. She dismissed it, too shocked by what she had just learned about Peter to think at all.

Before she could step away, Cherry pushed her to the ground. "Get out of my hollow. Now!" Cherry ordered. "Or I'll toss you headfirst into the snow."

"Is it true?" April gasped.

"Is what true? Which of my stolen thoughts are you inquiring about?"

April whispered, "Peter."

"Oh, that one. You'll have to find out for yourself."

April staggered up, yanked the vial out of her pocket and dropped in over Cherry's neck. Cherry allowed the action. She stood firm, gloating, not inclined to walk anywhere. Her dark magic was not affected by the magical spell.

Without a word, April reclaimed the vial and turned away. Raina's dire condition took precedence over everything.

"About time you left," Cherry snarled.

April wasn't quite ready to leave. She detoured by Cherry's leafy nest and rooted around for the elf's pack. It was exactly where Cherry had pictured it when she had been trying to hide the existence of her evil loot. "I'm taking this, there might be something to help Raina. You better hope she recovers, for your own sake."

"It's not like I meant to make her sick, she was only supposed to turn green," Cherry muttered belligerently. It might have been her version of an apology.

"Whether you meant it or not, you've made Raina dangerously sick. It's really stupid to use spells and potions, especially when you don't know what they'll do." April flung open the door and started climbing. Cherry could close her own door or freeze, April didn't care.

The storm had started to abate and the sun was rising. Snowflakes were drifting down, illuminated in the prettiest way. April banged once on the door and Peter slid it aside. Peter, her good friend, her trusted companion. Her heart cramped in pain and April bit her lip, fighting to act normal.

"Any improvement?" she asked tightly, as soon as the door slid shut.

"A little, she can breathe easier if she lies on her stomach and if I keep her gills wet." Salm didn't look reassured, but at least Raina was dozing more easily. "So?" he prompted.

"Cherry doesn't know much about what she did to turn Raina green, she only knows *how* to do it. But she did have a secret stock of ingredients for spells. Maybe something in here can help." April brushed a spot of floor clear of leaves. Settling cross-legged, she dumped out Cherry's pack. All kinds of weird bits and pieces fell to the ground.

"Do you know what any of this stuff is used for?" Salm asked.

"No." April shook her head regretfully.

They examined the dried herbs, and what might have been bits of skin and nails and insect legs and ... April picked up one hair. "This is Brag's hair." It was coarse and dark and smelled like the imp.

Salm grimaced. "I wonder why she has that souvenir."

"His magic is so strong, I bet everything about him has power, even his fur," April assumed.

Peter held up a shiny bit. "Is this a scale?"

"Yes, it looks like what Cherry put into Raina's tea." April had seen the memory through Cherry's own eyes. "But I don't know what creature it came from. Could be anything with scales." Without information, it wasn't going to help.

Salm stirred the pile and picked up a shriveled lumpy black thing. "What the heck is this?"

April peered closer ... surely it wasn't...? "Salm, maybe you should put that down and rinse your hands." He dropped it and headed for the door, where he rubbed his hands around in the wet snow that had blown into the hollow.

"Stuff is pretty useless if we don't know what to do with it," Peter concluded, quite rightly. They needed answers and Brag was the only one who had those answers.

April wished he would float himself over for a visit in one of his magical bubbles to answer their questions and help Raina. His bubbles could travel anywhere, even through a storm ... they could travel anywhere. Anywhere! April felt like she had been hit on the head with a Giant's hammer. She felt really stupid when the memory of Ms. Larkin-LaBois talking about bubbles became so real, it was as if the elf was standing before her. Brag's magic bubbles. They could float anywhere! They could float an elf safely up to

New Haven!

"Good grief," April gasped, "We need Brag. We have to find Brag."

"Why?" The question echoed around the hollow.

"Brag will know how to help Raina, and Brag can send us all home!" April could have cried for not thinking of it sooner.

"What are you talking about?" Salm asked.

"His magic bubbles can float us home. Up, up to the clouds."

"The magic bubbles? Yes, I bet they can," Peter agreed. "We do need Brag. We need him now."

"And he'll know how to help Raina?" Airron asked. He hadn't left her side.

"Yes, yes I think so. If anyone does, he does." April tried to sound positive.

"And if he doesn't, he can float Raina up to New Haven. I think she would breathe okay in a lake, and all the lakes around here are frozen and much too cold," Peter added. He was always thinking a step faster than the rest of them. April was surprised that Peter hadn't thought of Brag's bubbles on his own.

"So we do need Brag. I can't believe I'm saying that," Salm confessed. "Umm ... how do we find him?"

Finding Brag would be the key. April furrowed her brow, thinking. It would be impossible to track Brag on the ground. Too much snow had fallen since they had last seen him. And they never had discovered the exact location of the imp's garden. April couldn't sense him if he was standing right beside her. Finding Brag seemed an impossible task.

"April? Can spells and potions by altered?" Peter asked slowly.

"I know little of such magic," April confessed. "But ... I don't see why not. Do you have an idea?"

"Maybe." He hesitated, still thinking. "Maybe. It's a long shot but ... you still have the vial?"

"Yes." April pulled it out of her pocket.

"Is it still working?"

She slipped the chain over her head and felt an irrational desire to go outside. She yanked it off again. "Still working." Not on elves with dark magic, but on April.

"Good," Peter nodded. "What do you think would happen if we put a bit of Brag into that muck, would it change the essence? Draw you to Brag rather than the Giant?"

"I don't know. I suppose it is possible." She didn't say that it was a crazy idea but tampering with magic could have unpredictable results. Only minutes ago she had warned Cherry of the dangers of using spells and potions, and here she was considering that very thing. But April was willing to risk it, Raina needed help *now*.

April plucked the imp's hair from the pile in front of her, and twirled

192

it around before she handed it to Salm. "Don't lose it." Then she used a stem to poke at the shriveled black thing with a wrinkled nose. There was only one way to confirm that it was as gross an item as she believed and learn if it belonged to a particular magical creature of their acquaintance.

"I can't believe I'm doing this." April gritted her teeth and leaned forward to sniff the shriveled black thing. She swallowed hard and leaned away. "Yup, I think that belongs to Brag too," she choked. Salm returned to the door, he stuck his hands outside and washed them in the fresh snow for a second time.

"Is that important? Or just really gross?" Peter asked, glancing at April uncertainly.

"It could be important. I'm guessing we'll need lots of ... Brag, to change the essence of Giant into essence of Imp."

Salm rejoined them. "Should we try it now?"

"Depends. Is the storm over?" April asked him.

"Just about, but there's a ton of snow out there." The blizzard had come at the worst possible time – when they needed to help Raina and find Brag, when there was not a minute to waste. Raina was not breathing any easier. When April focused on her friend's gasping and gurgling, it felt like she was suffocating along with Raina. This crazy idea did have to work. It was time to tamper with the vial.

"Nothing we can do about the snow. Let's see if this will work. I guess I have to empty out some of the brown stuff, so Brag's ... essence will fit. I better do that outside," April said. When the vial was opened, the stench might kill them all if they were in an enclosed space.

"I'll bring the hair." Salm held it up. "Peter, you can bring the - "

"Thanks." Peter used a section of leaf to wrap up his object.

They carried everything to ground level. Salm handed Peter the imp's hair and kicked snow out of one corner of their snow Keep. He piled sticks together for a fire in the bare spot.

"April, could you give us a light," Salm said. She had been glaring at the vial, working up the courage to open it.

"Sure." April concentrated to ignite the fire, then turned her attention back to her own task. "Ready Peter? We might have to do this fast."

"The faster the better." Peter held up what was needed for the spell. April hauled in a deep breath before she yanked the stopper out and poured half the brown goop into the snow. It sizzled on contact. Peter forced the hair into the vial. The dung was too big so he pushed it against the glass edge and it crumbled, the fragments hissed when they hit the contents of the vial. April had run out of air and had to gasp in a small breath.

The fetid reek almost knocked her over. It was even worse than she remembered. She replaced the stopper with stinging eyes and walked towards fresher air, gasping in a full breath. "Oh, oh that was horrible," April choked. "Did you smell it?" she asked Peter.

"Unfortunately." His eyes were watering too.

April held the vial up and shook it. The contents foamed and bubbled, then got really hot! April could barely hold the glass. She didn't know if the reaction was bad or good. She approached the fire for a better look, dangling the vial by the chain.

Salm was waiting tensely. "Do you think it worked?"

"I hope so, but I don't know." She was afraid to put the chain around her neck and test the vial. If it didn't work, she didn't know how else to help Raina.

"April, try it on. Quit keeping us in suspense," Salm prompted grimly.

"Okay." But first April closed the vial in her hand and concentrated magically on Brag's image. When she opened her eyes, Salm took the chain out of her hand and placed it over her head, studying her face, waiting for something to happen.

Her feet didn't start walking but she did feel a pull – not a strong urge, but an inclination to walk east. She took several steps and they felt right. "Yes, yes, I think it's working, not as strong as before but I know where to go. Let's just hope the vial is taking me to Brag and not Loug." April had seen more than enough of that monster.

"Let's hope so."

"Well, I should leave right now. There's nothing to pack, is there? But I'll say good-bye first, to Raina, in case ..." April was getting all choked up again and not because of a horrible smell this time.

She climbed the tree and delivered the good news to Airron that the vial seemed to be working. But they both knew that April still had to find Brag and convince him to help them. If Brag didn't want to do that, he wouldn't and they couldn't make him.

"April, don't dawdle." Airron gripped both her hands hard. "I'll tell Raina where you went when she wakes up. I'll tell her you'll be back. I'll tell her ... she'll be fine." He was hurting her hands.

"Airron, I will come back with Brag, even if I have to hit him over the head and drag him here on a sled." She hugged Airron and left quickly.

The boys were waiting by the fire. "Bye Peter, bye Salm," April said in a rush. It was so hard to leave that she preferred to do it fast.

Salm stopped her parting words. "April, you're not going alone. It's too cold for you to fly, and your arm isn't strong enough yet."

It was still weak and aching from the previous day's flight, the one Salm didn't know about. But he was right, her arm would not yet sustain her for anything but a short flight. However, she had to be ready for every possibility.

April began to untie the splint. "I might need to fly Salm, I have to be prepared."

He nodded and took over untying it himself. "April, Peter will go with you. I would go except I have to stay here and look after Raina."

"I can go alone. You're both safer here."

"No, you shouldn't go alone."

And Peter's mind was made up. "I'm going with you, April. We'll do this together," he said firmly. He had such a noble and good heart, how could Cherry's information be right? It couldn't be right.

Salm tossed the splint into the fire and pulled April into a rough hug. "Come back safely," he whispered.

She nodded under his chin. "I will. You be safe too, Salm."

The vial urged her to get a move on. April turned towards the freshly risen sun and started walking.

"We'll be quick," Peter called to Salm. April hoped his words were filled with truth, and she hoped with all her heart that Raina could hang on that long. "East towards the Giant." Peter's words had a fatal ring.

"Yes, east towards the Giant. Hopefully east towards Brag." As long as the vial was guiding them to the imp and not Loug, April would have marched past a dozen Giants to help Raina.

They jogged without pause the whole day, and when they couldn't hold that pace, they walked and kept on walking, long past sunset. The new snow sparkled brilliantly under the moonlight like an endless field of crystals. It was almost as bright as daylight. Every time April checked the forest, she found it as strangely deserted as it had been for months, unless a parade of fleeing animals happened by.

"Do you want to rest for a bit?" Peter asked when the moon sat directly overhead.

"Do you? I can keep going. It's probably safer to travel at night when Loug is sleeping."

"Okay. We can nap in the morning, I'm sure we'll need to by then." They needed a rest now, but kept trudging along until the sun rose before their eyes once again. The world had turned a full circle and they were still walking.

They stopped around high noon and curled up in an evergreen tree. April didn't waken until Peter rose and an icy blast of air blew down her back. The sun was nearing the horizon. April hadn't meant to rest for more than an hour, they must have slept four.

"Awake?" Peter asked.

"Yes. I didn't mean to sleep so long." April struggled up and checked the forest before they left the shelter of the tree.

"We'll make up the time. Can you tell how close we are? From the vial?"

"No. It hasn't gotten any stronger. It feels exactly the same as when we left yesterday. I hope Raina is still okay. We shouldn't have slept at all," April moaned.

"April, we traveled more than a day. If we didn't get some sleep, we would collapse. We'll make it in time. Raina's tough, she'll hang on until we get back with Brag. Hey, are those his footsteps?" Peter stopped beside a shadowy trail in the snow. They were about to cross right over it.

April crouched down and studied the prints. One set of prints. She reached out a finger to trace the outline of a foot. "These don't belong to Brag, too small. He has big flat feet."

"They look like elf prints."

"They do. And recent, since the big snow." April could think of only one elf who might have made these marks and it was not an elf from New Haven. It was the elf who had escaped from the Giant, the elf who had left Brag behind, the elf who had written the note. It was the worst time to find the trail.

April automatically concentrated hard, to learn if the elf was within sensing range. Nothing. The elf was too far away. April stood up and started walking, leaving the tracks behind. Raina had to be saved, that was more important than anything.

"We can come back," Peter said. "Or they might find our trail and follow it. The elf might find us." He was trying to comfort her. Peter was ever thoughtful of others, and loyal to his friends.

It suddenly seemed the right moment to discuss what she had learned from Cherry. The knowledge was eating at her in the worst way. "Peter, I need to talk to you about something I picked up from Cherry, when I was sharing her thoughts," April began carefully.

His jaw clenched. He knew.

"About dark magic," April continued. "Peter, I know hardly anything about dark magic, but I do know that you are so good inside. Cherry knows more about dark magic than anyone else, but I think she's wrong about this."

Peter shook his head, his face a picture of torment. "I wish she was wrong, I've tried to believe that for the longest time, but ... I can find gold like her father."

"So? That doesn't mean anything."

"The vial doesn't work on me. If I had good magic like you, it would."

"That's not true! Maybe the vial's influence over the wearer depends on the strength of the magic, not whether it's good or bad." Another bit of information clicked into place. "That's why you took the vial, to test it on yourself?"

"And Cherry. I tested it on her, too."

No wonder Peter hadn't asked to see the vial. He couldn't have explained why he wanted it. "None of this is proof, Peter."

"But you and I could communicate in dreams, when I was stuck in forever sleep. You can only communicate with elves that have dark magic," Peter said, as if that was further proof.

"But when you were trapped in sleep, I could communicate with you through Brag," April stressed. "That had not a thing to do with dark magic. Hey, is that why you pull away every time I touch you lately?" Everything was falling into place.

"Yes. I didn't want you to know. I didn't want anyone to know about this." Peter dropped his head in shame. "Cherry was the only one I could talk to, and she approached me because I have the same magic as her late father."

Frightened and frustrated, April grabbed Peter's arm and pulled him to stop. "Peter, none of these things mean you have dark magic."

"Not by themselves," he agreed. "But put them all together and it starts to look like I'm evil."

April almost laughed. "You're not evil, Peter. You don't have an evil bone in your body."

"You don't know that, April," Peter said, almost angrily.

"Look, before he died, Drake Pitt said something to me about the elf determining the course of their magic. And you are one of the kindest, nicest elves in New Haven, so your magic can only be good. Cherry has probably been twisting facts to suit her own purpose, she would love you to believe that you're like her. She would love to mess up our friendship, to mess you up."

"I wish that were true, April. So much." But Peter wasn't convinced, he was too afraid to look at his situation logically.

"Let's try something Peter." Impetuously, April stripped off her mittens and motioned for him to do the same.

He removed his mittens with obvious trepidation. They faced each other and April took his hands firmly, concentrating. He closed his eyes and waited. Nothing happened. April could not read even one of his thoughts. She released him with a joyous smile.

"Anything?" Peter asked.

"Nope, not a thing!"

"And that's good?" he asked uncertainly.

"Very good. You don't have dark magic any more than I do. Cherry's just been messing with your head. You should have talked to *me* about this Peter," she chided.

"I was too scared that it was true. I guess I stopped thinking clearly. So, you're sure I don't have dark magic?" Peter still didn't look fully convinced.

"As sure as I can be, Peter." April hugged him hard. "Now, put your mittens on and let's find Brag. And next time you have magical questions, ask me! Not Cherry."

With lighter steps, they set off at a quick pace. They jogged again, through a second night and then a second morning. Finding Brag was taking more time than they had to spare. They didn't stop to sleep again and neither suggested it. Late afternoon found them stumbling along with heavy, burning eyes and singing to stay awake. Peter's lovely voice kept April moving, she could have listened to it forever.

"Don't stop," she kept telling him. He kept groaning, his voice was getting as tired as his feet.

Peter was singing and April was sleepwalking when they finally found Brag. More accurately, he found them. In one stride, April and Peter went from trudging on snow to hanging upside-down. The vial had worked!

14 – Gus

"Is this Brag's doing?" Peter asked.

"Yes. Brag!" April shouted very loudly. Something scuttled across the snow and April and Peter landed on their heads. The snow was surprisingly hard. "Brag?" April sat up and came face-to-face with his grizzled gray snout.

"April friend. Come visit Brag! And Brag visit April!" The imp thought the coincidence was very funny and giggled, hopping from one foot to the other.

"Yes, we were coming to find you." April smiled back, overjoyed to see him. He could save Raina and send them all home. He owed them that.

"Bad elf Peter!" Brag danced around and started a campfire right there in the snow. He didn't even need sticks to make it burn. Then again, he had burned a whole lake in the past.

As lovely and warm as the fire was, they didn't have time to waste visiting. "Brag, listen," April began. "This is really important. We need your help, that's why we came to find you."

"No picnic?" His ears drooped in disappointment.

"Well, yes. We can have a picnic, but after. After you help us. Cherry … you remember Cherry, don't you?" April checked.

"Very very bad elf." Brag displayed his teeth threateningly. She was not his friend anymore.

"Yes, that Cherry. She put some of the scales you gave her into Raina's tea. You remember my friend Raina? Well, the scales turned Raina green, and now she's sick and can't breathe. Do you know how to cure her, how to make her not green?" April asked in a desperate rush.

Brag squished his lips together and picked his nose, thinking. "Brag not know," he concluded.

"But Brag, there must be some way to stop it happening. To reverse the affects," Peter insisted.

"Brag not know. Brag sorry." The imp wrinkled his nose guiltily.

"Well, can your bubbles float really high up to the clouds?" April asked, sick with disappointment that Brag didn't know how to cure Raina.

"Bubbles float to clouds. Easy," Brag boasted. "Why clouds?"

"We found New Haven. It's floating in a cloud," Peter explained. "And we want to go home."

"You will help us, won't you Brag? I saved you from the Giant and the bottomless pit. You destroyed my room and left me with Loug," April reminded him in case he had forgotten.

"Brag help." It was said eagerly. "Brag coming to visit April. Brag need playtime," he added with a guttural growl, glancing over his shoulder.

"My thanks, Brag. I don't know if it will be much of a playtime, but we have to leave right away, Raina's really sick. If you float her to New Haven, she can breathe in the lake outside her house." And maybe her father could find a way to cure her in New Haven.

"Can you float us all back to the campsite in a bubble? We have to hurry," Peter pressed.

"Okey dokey. Brag say bye-bye." He hitched up his loincloth and stomped away.

"Brag? Where are you going? Come back!" April called in a panic. But another imp stepped out of the trees to meet Brag, a female. Her crabby black eyes surveyed them as if they were trouble. Was the female imp Brag's mate? He had never mentioned another imp.

"Brag help bad elfies," Brag told the new arrival. "Brag go."

The imp kicked him with her huge flat foot. "Brag go," she snarled crossly.

"Brag go," he warned.

"Brag go." She bit him on the arm.

"Brag go," he repeated. What was going on?

"Go." She bared her teeth. She had as many as Brag, and they looked pointier.

He patted the other elf on the head roughly, turned his back and marched away. Were they having an imp fight? He did not introduce them, but hustled April and Peter away without a backwards glance.

"Brag? What was that all about?" Peter asked.

He curled his lip. "Brag need time away."

"Why?" April asked.

Brag had to tell the whole story about how his mate nagged him nonstop to find food and make fires and clean the garden and say sweet things and find presents and, well the list was endless. "Brag need playtime," he concluded. It really did sound like he needed a break.

"Umm, Brag? Could we speed this trip up?" Peter reminded him.

He wiggled a finger and encased the three of them in one big bubble. April had pictured two or three bubbles, not one. But she wasn't going to complain, and it gave them an opportunity to talk.

"Brag make speedy bubble. Playtime." The imp scrunched up his face and wiggled one finger. The bubble floated up and began to race along at an incredible speed – for a bubble. At this rate, they would be home within the hour, not days.

"This is great Brag. I didn't know you could make bubbles go so fast," April said admiringly.

"Brag good at bubbles."

"Very impressive," Peter agreed, crouching down and studying the passing ground, his dark eyes darting back and forth.

"What are you looking for?" April asked.

"A couple of things. Brag, have you seen any other elves lately?" He was thinking of the trail they had crossed.

"No bad elfies," Brag replied.

"And? What else Peter? You said a couple of things." April nudged him with an elbow, the bubble was not roomy.

Peter hesitated to tell her. "Something a little larger," he mentioned vaguely.

"Oh. Do you mean - "

"No." Peter cut her off and arched an eyebrow in Brag's direction. He did not want her to say 'Giant' anywhere near Brag's droopy ears. Brag might disappear again if he realized the Giant was still close. They couldn't take that chance.

April nodded to Peter, kept her mouth shut and started watching the ground too. The bubble was warm and toasty. For the first time in months, April was comfortably able to shed her layers of leaves and outer clothes. It was also the perfect time to ask Brag a pressing question. "Brag, have you ever heard a myth about imps helping elves to create their forcefield?"

Brag was as informative as ever. "Don't know myths."

"Oh." April thought of asking him more questions. Exhausted, she fell asleep instead.

Peter woke her up. "We're almost at the campsite."

"Haven," Brag nodded and pointed ahead and down. He didn't mean the cloud, he meant where New Haven used to be. From so high above, the circular wasteland looked like a big white basin. The bubble started to descend smoothly, lower and lower.

"That was fast." April said.

As if her words were a curse, the bubble popped. There was no warning. It took a fraction of a second to notice and start falling.

Brag screeched, his arms flapped uselessly.

"Make another bubble," April screamed, adjusting her overall straps. Brag made a bubble – for one imp. Thank goodness her wings appeared and she managed to catch Peter by one arm before he plummeted out of reach. His added weight pulled her down almost as fast as falling. In spite of all her flying experience, she was not strong enough to keep them both aloft with an injured arm and only one free wing.

"Brag," Peter hollered, reminding the imp he was not the only one that needed help. The imp blinked as if surprised to see them, wiggled his fingers and made another bubble.

"Not very dependable, is he?" Peter gasped, collapsing inside the orb.

"No. What popped the bubble? Do you think the Giant is nearby, interfering with Brag's magic?" April asked, flipping over to search the ground.

"It's not the Giant. I've been watching the whole time and he's too big to miss. And Brag had no trouble making more bubbles. I don't know what happened."

Brag floated closer and the two bubbles pressed together, merging into one bigger sphere. "Brag, what made your bubble pop?" Peter asked.

"Pointy stick," he snarled. And then another arrow, of all things, whizzed through the air with force. The bubble popped, again.

At least April was prepared this time. "Grab my legs," she told Peter. It would leave her arms free. He caught one and April managed to slow their descent by spreading her wings wide and gliding. Brag screamed and fell until Peter bellowed at him to make another bubble. He did then, and floated himself towards them. They were a lot closer to the ground after two falls.

As soon as the imp reached them, a third arrow flew through the air and his new bubble burst. This time he didn't use magic to stop his fall, he grabbed Peter's leg. The imp's added weight was enough to pull all three of them out of the sky.

"Let go, Brag! Make a bubble," April cried, straining to stop the rushing fall while branches whipped by on all sides. Brag didn't let go but Peter did. April soared up, unprepared for the loss of both her passengers. She flipped around in the air and dove down to try and catch Peter again, but Peter and Brag had already landed in a groaning heap.

"Move!" Peter grunted, shoving Brag off of him. Brag kicked at Peter with his big feet. April laughed in relief to find them both alive and kicking, she had been fearing the worst.

She landed awkwardly and pulled Peter up. "Are you okay?"

"Ya, no thanks to him." Peter shook his head in disgust at the imp, dislodging clumps of snow. "You could have made a third bubble Brag, instead of knocking us out of the air."

It was not the time to offend the imp, who might stomp off in a temper. They needed Brag a lot more than he needed them right now.

"Well, we're all safe now," April interrupted. "No harm done, right Peter? So we should get going." She shot him a warning glance. He had every right to be upset, but it would have to wait. "Umm ... Brag, who was shooting arrows? Did your mate follow you? She seemed kind of mad." The other imp could have tailed them in her own bubble. Maybe she was trying to shoot Brag with an arrow.

"Brag not know," he huffed, pouting at Peter.

"Well, let's just get out of here. It's getting really chilly, isn't it? Can we start walking?" April didn't want to grant Brag time to think about leaving them. She scanned the small clearing until she spotted her clothes and leaves. Shivering, she started layering them on. Brag helped himself to a leaf and started chewing on the edge. He was eating it, rather than wearing it. With his thick skin and bristled hair, Brag gave no indication of feeling the cold at all.

When something flew through the air and thunked dully against the back of the imp's head, Brag got the blankest look on his face. He tipped face-first into the snow, dead to the world.

"Oh no! What was that?" April asked Peter.

In answer, he tackled her to the ground.

"Get behind a tree," he whispered, staying low and leading the way. They didn't make it in time. Something wild and hairy burst out of the forest and ran towards Brag. The creature was holding a fist-sized stone, raised high overhead. Brag was about to be pulverized as he lay unawares. And he hadn't done a thing to provoke this attack. He had actually been helping elves, willingly.

"No!" April screamed, leaping up and changing direction to intercept the attacker. It was lucky the creature was about her size or she wouldn't have had a chance to save Brag. April avoided the rock weapon and dove for the hairy legs; she managed to land them both on the ground. And then Peter was there, he took care of the flailing arms and the dangerous rock. The creature wrestled violently for a moment, then went limp and started speaking.

"What exactly do you think you're doing?" The precise voice sounded a lot like it belonged to an elf – but not an elf from April's world and not an elf from New Haven. The accent was different, it lay somewhere in-between.

April fell back and gawked. Peter released the arms, allowing the elf to sit up and dust off. It was done with exaggerated dignity. Dark blue eyes assessed April, then Peter, then April again.

"Why are you defending an evil imp? What kind of elf are you?" she asked April, in the snottiest tone imaginable.

April stared in fascination. "I'm just a regular elf. Who are you? Where did you come from?"

"I asked my question first, didn't I?" A mass of snowy blond hair was brushed back, fully revealing a pale face and the muddy blue eyes. April had never seen this elf before, of that she was certain.

"Uh, we need the imp, he's helping us." Peter kept his answer short, the situation was awfully complicated if an elf didn't know all that had come before.

The elf curled her lip at Peter. "What's wrong with your eyes? Why are they black like a bug?" It sounded like an accusation. "And you!" she turned back to April. "I thought you were an elf like me but then you sprouted wings like some sort of insect. You're not an elf at all, but you look like one."

"I am so an elf!" April snapped, insulted. "Did you pop the bubbles and almost kill us?"

"I was aiming for the imp, you happened to get in the way."

"If we'd fallen all the way to the ground, you would have killed us, too," Peter pointed out logically.

The elf crossed her arms. "Oh, my mistake." This introduction was not going well.

April tried to start fresh. "Uh … my name is April, this is Peter. We are elves. Who are you?"

"I'm Gus, if you must know. And I'm a real elf, not like you two." She stared down her nose at them. She didn't seem willing to start over. Had April been so rude when she first met elves after being lost forever? She didn't think so.

"We are real elves, from New Haven," Peter explained patiently. "Except for April, she comes from your world, hence the blue eyes. Now, we need the imp so you can't hurt him." Peter turned around to check on Brag's condition, he hadn't moved.

"Proper elves would never ally with an imp, they kill imps," Gus spat out in disgust. April had never met such a violent elf, except Drake Pitt, and maybe Cherry.

"Gus, you don't know everything," April said.

"I know enough. I know better than to hang around with imps." Gus straightened her mouse fur and brushed snow off with fur-covered hands.

"Gus, listen, we're going back to our campsite, with Brag, the imp. He's not so bad once you get to know him. There are other elves waiting … there's an emergency … " April trailed off, she didn't have a clue how to explain about New Haven floating around in a cloud and Raina turning into a fish. "Will you come with us? We can talk more when we get there," she added.

Peter was busy assembling a sled to pull Brag. It didn't look like the imp would be walking anytime soon, but he was groaning. It was a good sign.

"I don't know if I want to," Gus muttered. "I'm not sure you're real elves. I think you might be a bug."

April didn't have the time to convince her. "The campsite's not far, if you want to come, but we're leaving." She went to help Peter pull Brag along the snow. The imp was heavier than a load of berries.

Gus trailed behind, sometimes in sight, sometimes not.

"April?" Peter spoke quietly. "Is Gus from your world? Do you remember her?"

"I don't remember her, and she doesn't talk like me ... or you. And her eyes aren't bright blue like all the elves from my world. I don't know where she comes from. Gus is a weird name, and she's very ... hostile, isn't she? Maybe she'll tell us where she comes from when we get back to the campsite." As soon as Raina had been saved, April planned to find out.

"We're almost there. It's lucky the bubble burst so close." Peter strained to move Brag up an incline. April stepped to the back of the bark sled and pushed on Brag's feet. They crested the slope and a small campfire burned below. They had made it. But were they in time? They raced the rest of the way, gravity aiding their speed.

Cherry and Marigold were sitting by the fire. Marigold hopped to her feet shrieking for Salm as soon as she saw them.

"How's Raina?" April panted, her heart beating too hard with fear.

"Not good, but alive," Marigold answered. "And you found the imp?" She peered down at the sled. Cherry snorted, whatever that meant, and left quickly, probably before Brag opened his green eyes.

There was a shout and both Salm and Airron scrambled down the tree and almost flew across the clearing.

"Thank goodness," Salm gasped, skidding to a stop.

Airron gaped at the sled in disbelief. "April? Did you really hit him on the head and drag him here?" She had forgotten about saying that.

"No, that wasn't me. That was Gus."

"Gus?"

April glanced behind. The elf was lurking at the edge of trees. "That's Gus." As soon as they turned to look at her, she ducked back into the trees.

"Pretty hairy elf," Airron said, and didn't ask any questions. "Can you wake up Brag? I'll bring Raina down, we're almost out of time," he emphasized tightly.

"Airron, Brag doesn't know how to cure Raina. But he's going to send her home to her lake. We'll wake him up, get Raina."

Airron dashed for the tree and Salm went along to help. Raina mustn't be able to walk.

Peter grabbed a handful of snow and tossed it in Brag's face, April tickled his feet. Marigold screeched at the imp in her highest pitch. Marigold woke Brag.

The imp sat up and smacked his lips, then touched his head. "Ouch."

"Brag, how's the head?" April asked.

He sulked. "April friend hit Brag?"

"No, no. It wasn't me. I saved you, again. Three times now," she emphasized. Brag squinted one eye at her suspiciously. "It's true. Now you have to float Raina up to New Haven. She's really sick. Remember?"

"No. Head hurt. Brag sleep." He lay back down on his sled.

"No! You can sleep after you save Raina. Look, here she comes." Raina was being carried in Airron's arms, unconscious and gurgling horribly. She was greener than April remembered, and she had faint yellow stripes now. Those were new.

Brag leaped to his feet in fear and scuttled back. "Bad elfie not look so good."

"See, I told you. Raina needs to go home to her lake. Can you float the bubble right to her lake, the one outside her house? Now? Please Brag." April begged.

"Now?"

"Yes now!"

Brag rubbed his head and nodded grudgingly.

"I'll go with Raina, explain," Airron offered, "Make sure she's okay in the lake, make sure her family knows where she is, unless you want to go Salm."

"You go. We'll be right behind you."

"Can you float us both, Brag? Together?" Airron asked.

"Two same as one." Brag wiggled his knobby fingers and a bubble formed instantly around Airron and Raina. There was no chance to say farewell.

"Make it go fast," April said.

Brag pointed and the bubble soared into the sky, as fast as an eagle. They watched it until it disappeared towards the cloud in the last rays of light from the setting sun.

"Thank-you Brag. Can you send the rest of us home now?" Peter asked.

April had forgotten all about going home herself. She had forgotten all about something else. "Where did Gus go?"

Salm asked a different question entirely. "Who is this Gus?"

"An elf from the Outer-world, but not from April's home." Peter scanned the trees.

April concentrated her senses in that direction. An elf was standing amid those trees, unmoving.

"You're kidding," Salm said. "You found the lost elf?"

"We did, by accident. Gus, come and meet everyone," April shouted. Gus would come if she wanted, they couldn't force her. "Salm, is there any food?" April couldn't remember when she had last eaten.

"Cherries, I crossed the log over the ravine and found the tree. Climbed up and picked some." Salm pointed to a pile beside the fire.

"I helped," Marigold chirped up.

Salm kept watching the trees. "So, where did you find this elf?"

"Not far from here."

"Gus is the one that knocked Brag unconscious," Peter said and tossed April a cherry. He brought one over to Brag. Brag tore into the fruit, spraying juice on the snow to look like spattered blood.

The fur-coated elf stepped out of the trees and came striding over as if she ruled the campsite. Marigold shrieked and latched onto Salm's arm like a clinging vine. Marigold was over-reacting.

"Gus is a girl?" Salm asked, when she got closer.

Gus marched right up to the fire and grabbed a cherry.

"Greetings Gus. Help yourself," Salm said dryly, shooting a questioning glance at April. April shrugged, the elf did have an attitude.

"Gus, this is Salm and Marigold," April introduced.

Gus considered them with a superior tilt to her head. "They have black bug eyes, too. And that other one looked like an ugly fish," she complained. "And why did you let the imp send them up to the sky. I almost shot the bubble."

Brag leaped to his feet at that. "Very bad elf pop bubbles!" He pointed a finger and Gus flipped upside-down. Brag rubbed his head and snarled. "Bad elf hurt head!"

"Ya, hit it with a big rock! Surprised the rock didn't break. Now put me down." Gus swung back and forth furiously.

"Umm, Brag? Is this the elf that was trapped with you? In Loug's box?" April guessed.

The imp squinted. "Think so. Box dark. Elf annoying. Think so."

"Gus? Were you trapped by a Giant a little while back? With an imp?" April asked.

"I was. This is the same stinky imp? They all look the same. He told me that he knew some other elves and said he would send my message in a bubble. But I didn't need the help after all. Got away all by myself. Thought I left you behind to play with the Giant," Gus taunted Brag. The elf clearly lacked both commonsense and compassion.

"Brag," Peter stepped between them, trying to make peace, "Gus didn't know you were helping us. She didn't know we were friends. And I'm sure she is very sorry for leaving you with Loug, and shooting your bubbles, and hitting you on the head with a rock."

Brag latched onto one part of Peter's explanation. "Friends?" Brag's face turned into one big smile. "Peter Brag's friend?"

"Of course, sort of," Peter qualified. "Now I'm sure Gus will say sorry if you let her down."

"No."

"Please Brag."

"Maybe, for Peter friend." Brag picked his nose and waited for his apology.

"I'm not saying sorry! Not a chance. I should have hit him harder,"

Gus ground out and crossed her arms. The action didn't have the same effect upside-down.

April had barely slept in days. She was deeply worried about Raina and she wanted to go home to New Haven so badly that it hurt inside. She had no patience for this elf's stubborn display. "Brag, can you send the rest of us home now, home to New Haven?"

"Send April and Peter. Maybe shrieky one." Brag pointed a finger at Marigold.

"I'm Marigold, and Salm needs to come," Marigold said, still stuck to his arm like a burr.

"Send April and Peter and Salm and shrieky one," he agreed. "But no Gus." Brag also didn't know about Cherry.

"Brag, Cherry is in the tree. She needs to go home too, I guess." April hated to say it. "And Gus should come."

"No Gus, no Cherry very bad elf," Brag declared and attacked another cherry. It might have been a meaningful gesture, but he was probably just hungry.

"Well, I'm not going anywhere. Especially not up to the sky trapped in an evil imp's bubble," Gus countered. "I would probably end up on the moon."

April ached to go home, nothing more. Everyone wanted the same thing, except Gus. April had been trying to get home for months. She had starved and frozen and been injured and lonely and sick, along with her friends. It was past time to leave this icy world. April didn't see any reason to wait.

"Fine, Gus you can stay down here and keep Cherry company. You two seem to have a lot in common. When New Haven floats back down to earth there will be a whole world of elves, right over there, if you want to meet them, if the Giant doesn't eat you first and if Brag ever lets you down. I'm ready to go. Peter? Salm? Marigold? Ready?" April stood firm, dreaming of home.

Peter shared a concerned glance with Salm and hesitated. Why was he hesitating? "Maybe we should sleep on it and go in the morning, figure out Cherry and Gus in the morning," Peter said.

April couldn't believe her ears. Peter had suffered as much as the rest of them. He must want to go home as desperately as April. He was being too nice.

"How about we don't sleep on it and leave now. I want to go home." April's voice cracked embarrassingly as the longing gripped her. She didn't know why the emotion was suddenly so strong, it was probably because they really could return to New Haven right now.

"Oh boohoo." It was Gus. April ignored her.

"Brag tired. No more bubbles. More cherries." He was probably going to eat every last one. And April was going to let him, if he agreed to a different deal. She walked over to Brag and whispered in his droopiest ear.

"Okey-dokey." He chattered his teeth, pointed his fingers and trapped

Salm and Marigold together in one last bubble. They didn't notice until the shimmering sphere left the ground. The expression of outrage on Salm's face was comical. Then again, he was trapped with Marigold. April smiled and waved, happy to see two more elves safely away. "My thanks Brag, the rest of the cherries are for you, as promised. And here." April removed the crystal vial from around her neck and dropped it over his head. "A nice present for that other imp. But you might want to wash it out first, or she'll be able to track you wherever you go."

"Good present. Brag like cherries." He stuffed another one in his mouth.

"That was pretty sneaky," Peter said admiringly. "I'm glad you sent them home but don't think of trying it on me. I would pop the bubble before it left the ground."

"You would be gone too, if you had been standing next to Salm." April sighed and gazed longingly at the sky.

Peter put an arm around her shoulder and murmured, "Tomorrow. We'll sort it out tomorrow. We'll get Brag to send us all home, even Cherry and Gus. Somehow. Tomorrow."

April leaned against his shoulder weakly. Tomorrow had never seemed so far away. So much could go wrong between now and then, especially when their transport depended on the unpredictable imp. And Cherry had never been cooperative. Gus didn't seem any better, she might be worse. April was just too painfully aware of how many things could go wrong in the hours between now and when the sun rose.

"Haven't you heard, tomorrow never comes," she said to Peter.

"It will tomorrow," he promised.

15 – The Long Fall

April woke early, surprised that she had slept a wink. It must have been due to sheer exhaustion. Peter was still snoring softly against the opposite wall. The hollow seemed lonely and it was a lot colder without the body heat of four more elves.

"It's okay, we're going home today," April promised herself softly and her heart sang. It was time to have a chat with Brag.

As silently as possible, April shifted the bark door and slipped outside. Gus had spent the night upside-down, she was still hanging in mid-air, sound asleep. There was no sign of Brag and April's stomach clenched. Surely he hadn't left?

Before she could start searching for Brag, April found out exactly where the imp had spent the night. Cherry screamed. Brag flew out the door of the smaller hollow, and tumbled down the tree. Cherry was going to get Brag all upset at the worst possible moment.

"Cherry, quiet! It's only Brag," April shouted, cutting her off.

The elf smoothed her golden curls from the doorway of her hollow. "I know exactly who it is, that's why I'm screaming. He was sleeping in here, with me!" she cried in disgust. "Hey, where's Marigold?" It had taken her long enough to notice that her best friend was missing.

"Gone home," April was pleased to inform her.

They had disturbed Gus. "Ouch! My head." Gus clutched it with both hands. April knew exactly how the elf felt, having spent a night in the same position not so long ago.

Cherry's strident tone probably wasn't helping. "Gone home? What do you mean gone home? Did she go back to New Haven without me? I'll kill her. I want to go home – now!" Her last words were extra piercing as she climbed down the tree and approached the fire. "And who the heck is that." She pointed at Gus.

April had forgotten that Cherry had retired for the night before Gus turned up.

"That's Gus. And Cherry, you better be nice to Brag," April said. "He's the only one that can send us home. If you mess this up - "

"No Cherry, no Gus. Already said," the imp snarled from the other side of the snow fort. Unfortunately, he hadn't forgotten the previous night's decision.

"Where did Gus come from?" Cherry wanted to know, pointedly ignoring the imp. She approached the upside-down elf for a better look. "Crap! She has bluish eyes, she's a mutant elf like you."

"I'm not the mutant," Gus bit out. "You black-eyed elves are the mutants. You've got bug eyes. And you live in the sky! And she has wings, and that other one looked like a fish. And you hang out with imps. You're the weirdest bunch of elves I've ever had the misfortune to meet." Gus was a match for Cherry.

April edged away and left them to sort out their own introduction. April wanted to think about home. She would be home in time for breakfast. The Pooles must be expecting April, they were probably preparing a grand welcome up there in the sky. Maybe Raina was cured and sitting in the kitchen with her family. April smiled at the wonderful thought. It was time to convince Brag to send them home. But first they had to sort out what to do with Gus.

"Brag," April began delicately. "I would really like to talk to Gus. It's hard when she's upside-down. Will you remove the spell and let her down?"

Brag folded his arms. "Nope."

"What if Gus says she's sorry?" April was pretty sure Gus would, after a night spent dangling.

"Maybe. Maybe not."

"Gus? Say sorry and Brag might let you down," April prompted.

Gus was as stubborn as the imp. She swore first. Then she apologized, rudely.

"Brag, will you let her down now?" April asked.

"Nope." He was justified in his refusal.

"Well, I can't say I blame you. I guess I can talk to Gus even if she is hanging by her toes. Her mouth still works fine." April stepped closer.

"Thanks a lot," Gus snapped and clutched her head in pain.

211

"It wouldn't have hurt you to say sorry nicely. You did hit Brag on the head with a rock. Anyway, the rest of us are going home to New Haven. It's temporarily floating in that cloud." She pointed up. "Because there is a Giant roaming around. You can't see the cloud from your position, but there's only one cloud in the sky. There are thousands of elves up there living in the most perfect world you can imagine. It's always warm and there is lots of food and no dangerous animals. Are you going to come with us or do you want to stay here? It's your choice, but we're leaving."

"April, right? That's your name?" Gus asked.

"Yes."

"April, I don't believe one ridiculous word. I'll stay here." Gus had made her decision.

"Well, the world will float back down as soon as the Giant moves on, I think, so you can always find us if you want. But you better apologize properly or Brag will leave you hanging here without a second thought. He is an imp." April turned her back and returned to the fire and Brag.

"Brag go home now," the imp said.

"Can you make one more bubble first?" April sighed. "Send April, Peter and Cherry home. You don't want Cherry left alone down here, trampling in your garden, do you?"

Brag giggled and slapped his bony knee. April didn't know what he found so funny. "Brag take care of very bad elf. Cherry no trample in Brag's garden, never ever," he threatened with a show of teeth. "Brag send April and Peter home. No Cherry. No Gus." His mind was made up and April couldn't change it.

"Okay, no Cherry, no Gus. Send me and Peter." It wasn't such a bad deal.

And Peter had perfect timing. He came climbing down the tree, hair all tousled. "Hey." He blinked at them all owlishly.

"Peter, just in time. Brag is going to send us home," April called, jumping up. She was getting that urgent feeling again. They had to go while the going was good.

"All of us? In time for breakfast?" Peter frowned at Gus still hanging in the air.

"No, not all of us. Gus doesn't want to visit New Haven and Brag won't make a bubble for Cherry. She'll have to wait here until New Haven comes down." April wasn't overly concerned. Cherry had gone out of her way to harm all of them, and she had dark magic to protect her. She knew how to survive the Outer-world by now. And she would even have company – Gus. Cherry would be fine until New Haven came back.

She didn't think so. "No! You can't leave me here," Cherry cried. "I want to go home too. Living with my aunt is better than living here. Peter, talk to Brag. He'll listen to you."

Peter gave it a try. "Will you listen to me Brag, will you send Cherry home?"

"Nokey-dokey. Never ever."

"Well ... I feel bad leaving them behind. Will Gus be okay?" Peter was wavering.

"I'll tell Brag to make sure he lets her down. Gus and Cherry will be fine. And we're going home. We can't miss this opportunity. Brag wants to leave, he's not going to wait. It won't help either of them if we stay here, will it? I want to go see if Raina's better."

"I suppose," he agreed, but didn't sound wholly convinced.

April didn't care, as long as she got him in the bubble, everything would work out.

"Okay Brag, we're ready to leave. Don't forget to let Gus down before you go. Cherry, you'll be safe here. New Haven will be down soon, I'm sure. Brag, my thanks, I owe you this time." April walked over to Peter and linked arms, ready for a ride home. Cherry stared at them silently and for the first time ever, April felt sorry for the elf. Gus stared too, through a shimmering haze. Brag had made their magical bubble.

It launched up into the air as fast as a bat. "Peter, we're going home," April said, even though he already knew. She still had to say the words, she had to hear the words. Her voice was surprisingly hoarse. Her face wouldn't stop smiling.

"We are going home. Been a long time away." Peter rubbed her arm excitedly and the ground shrank until even the largest trees looked small. "Quite a ride, quite a view," Peter murmured in wonder. Yesterday's bubble ride had been much closer to the ground. The world looked different from up here, both smaller and much, much bigger – stretching for thousands of miles in all directions.

April couldn't stop beaming. They were almost home. She squeezed Peter's arm, too excited to stay still.

It was at that moment that they stopped going home.

It was lucky they were linked. When the bubble burst, April didn't lose Peter. They both swore and April worked to free her wings. It was fortunate that they were so high up because it took a while. The wind kept tangling her up in her layers. When she finally did succeed in tearing them off, Peter had the foresight to grab some of her makeshift clothing and stuff it inside his in mid-fall.

"Legs," April reminded Peter, when they kept plummeting. He rearranged his position. As soon as she had two flying arms, she fought to slow their descent and banked into a wide, spiraling circle.

"It's freezing up here. Do you think Brag changed his mind, popped the bubble?" Peter called over the rushing wind.

"I guess." April was going to ask Brag about that, as soon as she landed.

"April," Peter sounded strange, his voice flat. "It wasn't Brag."

"What wasn't Brag?"

"Bursting the bubble. It wasn't Brag."

It wasn't Brag that had burst the bubble? "It wasn't Brag," April whispered, devastated. They had almost gotten home. Almost. April didn't want to look down, but she did. And there was Loug – directly below and closing in on their landing position, fast. They were almost within reach of those long arms. If the Giant opened his great stinking mouth they could fly right in.

"April," Peter shouted, "You have to fly up. If you can't, I'll let go and you can get away, you can lead Loug away from the others." Peter was willing to sacrifice himself to save the rest of them, to save April.

"Don't you dare let go. I can fly up, I can do it." She had to. April strained her wings wide and fast, pushing every muscle to the limit and beyond. Her arm screamed in pain, she ignored it. And they did rise, first an inch and then another and another, slowly ascending to a marginally safer height. Loug roared furiously from below, inspiring April to fly even harder. But she couldn't keep this up for very long. Already the Giant was coming after them.

"What are we going to do?" April cried.

"Fly southeast," Peter shouted. April automatically turned in that direction. "A little more south, good. Can you keep going?"

April looked down and back. Loug was tearing after them, crushing everything in his path. If Loug caught them now, he would mash them flat. The Giant was that mad.

"I can keep going," April sobbed. "Do you have a plan?"

"An idea. I wouldn't call it a plan, but we have to land soon or we'll freeze. And you can't fly forever." April was faltering, her arms shaking visibly. "Try and make it to the lake. See it?"

April blinked through a haze of pain. She could see the frozen body of water in the distance, the one they had played on. It was not nearly close enough. They were supposed to be home now, eating a feast of a breakfast, not this - not flying over a frozen wasteland being chased by a monster. She bit her lip and flew. Her shoulders burned and cramped in the worst way, but she kept moving them up and down, up and down. Tears streamed across her cheeks and froze in place. If she had been alone, she might have given up. But it was Peter's life, too.

"There. We made it. Try and land near where the creek enters the lake. There, see!" Peter said.

April was in too much agony to think, she followed his instructions blindly and started descending towards the smooth ice. The Giant bellowed again, he wasn't as close as before. April chanced a peek over her shoulder and saw Loug at the edge of the lake, hesitating. And then they landed too hard, skidding across the glassy surface for the longest time.

As soon as she stopped sliding, April wanted nothing more than to curl into a ball and never move again. Peter didn't let her, he eased her up and she swung around on her knees to face the shore. The Giant was standing immobile, staring back.

The ice supporting her and Peter was thinner than the last time they had visited this lake to play on the ice. The high winds had kept it clear of snow.

"April, you're going to freeze. Here, put this on." Peter slipped her clothes around her shoulders but April couldn't lift her arms to help. They hung as useless as deadwood. Peter lifted them for her and it felt like he was ripping them off.

April didn't scream. She said, "I don't think I can fly again today, Peter."

"You shouldn't need to."

They both watched the Giant. He was pacing now, his temper building. It was terrifying to watch, but he did not step out on the lake.

"Is there a way to make him walk out here on the thinner ice? Maybe crack it? That was my idea. Giants can't swim can they? I forgot to ask."

"Giants can't swim. Too heavy." April's eyes were streaming and she couldn't raise her hands to rub them. The Giant was looking all blurry.

"Let's start walking towards the opposite shore. He might try to cross, if he thinks we're getting away."

"Okay." It wasn't easy to get up without arms and Peter helped. They started walking away from Loug, towards the far edge of solid land. If the Giant skirted the shore around the lake, they could retreat back to the middle. If he came after them directly across the ice - as long as it broke, they should be able to get away.

Loug didn't do either. He picked up boulders and heaved them through the air. The ice was thick enough that the rocks didn't smash through the surface, they landed and slid spinning across the glassy surface, coming closer and closer. The stupid rocks weren't even slowing down.

"Run!" Peter shouted and they took off, trying to outrace the boulders. One spun by on their left, another on their right. Peter tugged April aside when a third almost crushed them. They ran for their lives, until they were out of range.

Once the rocks stopped, so did they. Loug still wasn't coming after them. He still hadn't set foot on the ice.

"I'm glad Airron isn't here to face this," Peter gasped, bent double and fighting for breath.

"Yes, he's paid a high enough price for his time with Loug. I wish we weren't here either," April sobbed.

"Ya."

Too disappointed to say more, they resumed walking, closer and closer to the other shore. "If he's going to make a move, it's got to be soon," Peter predicted. "Get ready to run."

"Again?"

"Afraid so."

April hated this suspense, this waiting to be chased by a Giant. The day had started out filled with the promise of home and here they were, waiting to be chased by a Giant. April knew how that ended and it was never in the elf's favor.

And then Loug made his move.

With a roar that must have been heard for miles, tons of Giant stepped onto the ice. April could feel the vibration clear on the far side of the lake. And once he made up his tiny mind, Loug showed no hesitation. He pounded after them with great thundering steps, rocking the ice and the water below, probably scaring all the fish out of their winter lethargy.

"Now!" Peter cried.

Half-sliding and half-running, they sped towards the shore that suddenly looked a lot further away than it ought. And Loug was catching up, then he was almost upon them. It was always difficult to judge exactly how fast a Giant could move.

But Loug had his own problems. A sliding Giant traveled a lot further than a sliding elf. He made the middle of the lake where the ice was thinnest and lost control of his feet. He started skidding out of control and kept on going. Sharp crackling noises followed in his wake.

Peter grabbed April's hand and pulled, trying to go faster. That never worked on ice. They both went down. But so did the Giant, hard on his enormous behind. It was every bit as oversized as the rest of him. The impact shattered the thinner ice into countless jagged fragments and tipped large sheets of ice diagonally up into the air. As the Giant sank, April and Peter started to slide down their suddenly tilted section of ice, directly towards where Loug had disappeared under the water. The surface looked like it was boiling.

If the ice hadn't slammed back down to lay properly flat, April and Peter would have joined Loug in the icy bath. But it did. The sheet of ice danced wildly around before it settled to a gentle rocking motion. It felt like the world stopped, everything was too quiet and still. April held her breath and waited, lying as flat as the ice.

In a hushed tone, Peter said, "That was too close, let's get out of here."

They found their feet and began running as urgently as if Loug was still chasing them, leaping from one sheet of ice to another.

"Aren't we safe?" April gasped. "Isn't the Giant ... gone?"

"I'd rather not wait around to find out. Hurry." Something big and darker than the water surged beneath the ice, banging against the underside. The ice sheet vibrated and cracked. April looked down and screamed. The Giant's big face was directly below her, pressed against the frozen pane, gruesomely distorted by the translucent layer. A fist smashed up, trying to break through.

April shot forward with Peter, racing for their lives. The gap separating them from the next island of ice widened as they raced toward it.

"Jump!" Peter hollered. They really had no choice, there was nowhere else to go. They reached the edge and leapt over the open water. Peter landed with an inch to spare and skidded. April didn't make it, she splashed into the water in front of the ice. Before she could grab the edge and haul herself out, a strong surge of water washed her underneath the sheet.

She looked up and could see Peter's shape moving above, searching for her. April banged her fist on the ice and he crouched down, shouting something. His words were lost.

April fought the frigid water and swam back to the gap between ice sheets, only to find it gone. The ice had closed back up. April was trapped with a Giant in winter water that was so cold, her gills were having trouble breathing.

Loug was fighting his own battle, churning up mud and froth, battling to be free of the ice before he ran out of air. He had no idea that his prey was in the lake with him. One of his flailing arms created a strong swell that shot April through the water away from him. She kept kicking in that direction, searching for another way up through the ice.

April was almost frozen before she found it, a crack that was barely wide enough for her to squeeze between. She was fighting to haul herself through the gap before it closed when Peter's hands pulled her free.

"I thought you were gone." Peter hugged her hard, wrapping his poncho around her shoulders at the same time. "We have to get out of here."

April nodded and stood unsteadily. She could barely feel her legs. "I … I … I know," she chattered.

Peter linked their hands and got her moving. Soon, she could run. The exertion helped to warm her limbs and jar some feeling back into them. The water and ice continued to churn behind them.

As soon as they staggered onto the solid land, an explosion of water erupted offshore like a geyser.

Loug had broken through the ice; the lake was not deep enough to contain him after all. The Giant stood up to his chin in murky water and shattered ice. His bulging eyes didn't blink. A fish was flopping madly on top of his head. Loug plucked it off with his stubby fingers and stuck it between his bared teeth. He crunched it deliberately in half and held up the tail end. It was a gruesome message. They would suffer the same fate if he caught them.

"Let's get as far away as we can. He's going to have a hard time getting free of the lake," Peter cried.

April tore her eyes off the Giant and tried to keep up with Peter. They raced into the undergrowth. It was much sparser in the winter. There was nowhere to hide completely since their feet were leaving a clear trail in the unmarked snow.

"Are you sure you can't fly April? Can you fly yourself even, without me?" Peter must believe them doomed.

"Not even to save my life. I can't feel my arms, Peter." Even if she could have flown herself, she would never have abandoned Peter.

"Well, we can still run." He pointed south and they raced up the slope away from the lake. Behind them, Loug battled to free his weight from the sucking mud and thick ice. Every time he tried to pull himself free, more ice cracked beneath his massive chest. He was going to have to forage a trail all the way to the land, since the broken ice would no longer support him. It gave them a chance.

The sound of the Giant's struggle faded when they crested the top of the slope and the land angled down. They ran south, then Peter steered them a bit west, adjusting their heading as if he had a destination.

April felt a spark of hope. "Where are we going, Peter?"

"The ravine. All I can think of," he gasped. "We can escape across the log. Won't hold Giant." They didn't talk again. Every bit of energy was reserved for their legs. Loug would catch up with them as soon as he was free of the lake. His enormous strides would eat up the ground, and then the Giant would devour them. April kept picturing the decapitated fish and felt like throwing up. But she kept running.

"How far?" April groaned, her legs were starting to buckle.

"Almost there. We'll make it." Then the ground trembled. "Faster," Peter shouted. Did he really think she could run faster? She tried. "There," Peter exclaimed.

Directly ahead, the ground disappeared into the ravine. It looked like the edge of world. They skidded to a stop, there was nowhere to go but down.

"How does this help?" April wailed.

"The log! Like the ice, I think this is another time that being small is better than being big." Peter clasped April's hand and turned right, running along the ragged edge of earth with empty space on one side and a rampaging Giant closing in on the other. The ground didn't just tremble now, it shook. Heavy clumps of snow fell out of the branches around them, creating a new danger. A flash of darkness flickered between the trees – Loug was almost upon them, following the trail left by their small footprints.

"How far is the tree bridge?" April sobbed.

Peter shook his head. "Not sure, might be more than one tree across the ravine. Faster." He was dreaming. April kept moving, but not any faster.

Loug smashed through the bare trees behind them, roaring. He knew he was close, he could probably smell their fear.

"There," Peter gasped. It was the fallen tree. But they still had to reach it and cross the ancient wood.

A foot as big as a house stomped down and blocked their path. They changed course, rolling under the low branches of a scraggily pine tree. Loug had almost stepped on them, but he hadn't spotted them yet. His own footprint had obliterated their trail.

"What now?" April whispered, wondering if Peter had an alternate plan. He had already thought of the lake and the ravine. He might have another brilliant idea up his leafy sleeve. "What now, Peter?"

"Don't know. It won't take long for him to figure out where we are. We need to cross the ravine. Sure you can't fly?"

April shook her head sadly. She couldn't fly if she couldn't lift her arms, could she? Unfortunately, there was a complete lack of anything but open ground between their hiding spot and the bridge that would carry them to safety. "I suppose I could try flying if there's no other way to escape. What are you thinking?" she whispered.

"I'm thinking you could climb this tree, jump and fly across the ravine. You would be safe." Peter turned her to face him and looked so sadly into her eyes. "It's the best idea I have, April. There's no point in both of us - "

"No," April said adamantly. She wasn't leaving him behind.

"April," he whispered, his face tightening with pain. "I would rather know you were safe. Please climb the tree, get out of here. Go."

"How could you have ever believed you were evil, Peter?" April leaned against him, her arms couldn't lift to hug him.

The Giant was pacing back towards them, shaking trees, searching. If April coasted over the ravine, Peter would be trapped, unless … April suddenly had an idea. It was similar to Peter's idea, but with a twist. She didn't think Peter would like her new plan, so she didn't fill him in.

"I might be able to glide across the ravine, at least, even if I can't really fly. Get ready to run, Peter," April hinted, since he had to be prepared. She started climbing as fast as she could. It wasn't very fast with her useless arms.

"What does that mean? April? April? " Peter called urgently, his voice so quiet it barely reached her ears. She didn't answer, she kept climbing awkwardly. The tree was not terribly tall, maybe twenty feet, not quite as tall as Loug.

As soon as she reached the tip, she peeked out. Loug was still between them and freedom. Stupid Giant. But his back was turned; he was scanning the ground, swinging his great lump of a head back and forth. It gave her a chance, if she could glide. The plan hinged on April being able to lift her arms at least once.

"Now or never," she whispered. She shrugged off Peter's poncho and launched away from the trunk as forcefully as she could. When her wings appeared, she was almost halfway down the tree but at least the wind blew her arms upward and the air current from the ravine buffeted her higher. There was no denying that it hurt worse than she had expected and she couldn't fly, but she could glide!

April coasted silently toward the gorge, tilted a wing and steered in the direction of the log bridge. As soon as she was on course, April shouted as loudly as she could. It was time for Loug to know exactly where she was. With a bellow, he swung around and spotted April almost over the chasm. One earth-shaking step was all it took for him to reach her. She kept underestimating his pace.

With a scream of terror, April swooped towards the yawning crevasse in the earth, aiming for the tree trunk that spanned it. She would be in big trouble if she missed the natural bridge, since she couldn't fly up and the rushing torrent of water at the bottom would be completely unforgiving. She wasn't in New Haven anymore.

Loug swung his ridiculously long arms towards her and April felt a rush of air. His fingertip actually brushed her toes, catapulting her forward over empty space and out of his reach. But the tree trunk wasn't in the right place anymore, Loug had knocked her off course.

The trunk was too high and April was too low. She was going to pass underneath the tree on her way down, unless – her heart surged with hope. Several broken boughs jutted off the tree bridge, poking down into the ravine. If she could catch one and climb up, she would have a chance. A good chance.

April aimed directly at one broken branch and slammed into the thing. She hadn't wanted to risk missing it. The stick of wood saved her life. April clung to the limb and pressed her cheek against it, imprinting the bark into her skin, trying to recover her wits. She might not have moved again, ever, if Loug hadn't kicked the end of the tree.

April looked way, way up at the Giant, looming over the edge of the ravine, blocking the sun. He was determined to capture her at any cost, she could see it in his evil black eyes. Loug kicked the trunk again and April clung tighter.

The tree seemed solid enough for the moment. Loug must have decided the same thing. He growled and placed one foot on the bridge, testing it. The tree held.

He was reacting exactly as April had hoped, unfortunately her present position was not part of her plan. She was supposed to be standing on top of the tree, taunting the Giant to come and catch her. She was supposed to be ready to run to safety as soon as he was over the ravine.

There was no doubt in her mind that the tree would break under the Giant's bulk. It was old and weak, and Loug weighed a ton or two. When the Giant trusted his full weight to the tree bridge, that would be the end of it. He would fall into the chasm. New Haven would return to earth. Everyone would live happily ever after, except April.

"I want to live happily ever after, too," she whispered.

Loug cautiously placed his second foot on the tree, then edged forward until he was over empty space. April closed her eyes. She didn't see Loug's next step, she felt it. The tree bowed slightly and cracked. April was having trouble breathing. She opened her eyes to see how close he was. Much too close. Another step. The next crack was so much louder and the tree buckled.

"April, let go. Glide over to the edge of the ravine and grab onto something," Peter shouted. He had left the safety of his hiding spot. "I'll find a way to pull you up."

Loug heard Peter too and howled like the beast that he was. He took an angry step back towards land, towards Peter. It was too much for the weakened tree. And April hadn't let go yet.

Everything fell at once - April, the tree and Loug. And she was on the bottom of the pile. There were too many things coming down on top of her. The Giant was directly overhead and he was everywhere.

Loug screamed all the way down. It felt like the falling was happening in slow motion and a hundred images flashed through April's head. She saw all her friends at their happiest, and her new family. Even Brag's face flashed briefly through her thoughts as she fell slowly and the powerful roar of water transformed to sound like thunder.

The wind coming up off the violent water had tremendous force, gusting wildly in all directions. April was light enough to be buffeted around when she neared bottom. Without thinking about it, she opened her arms as wide as she could manage and let the air fill her wings. At the last second, she was tossed sideways, out from under the Giant before he smashed into the water and sank under the white foam. Loug did not reappear, he was finally gone.

The broken sections of tree trunk came down as well, miraculously missing April as she tumbled willy-nilly in all directions. This was another time that being small was better than being big, April realized giddily. She would have to tell Peter, if she ever saw him again.

And then a draft of wind shot straight down, taking April along. She finally hit the water and discovered it wasn't really water, it was liquid ice and felt strong enough to tear her limbs off. April was dragged under so many times that if she hadn't had gills, she wouldn't have survived more than a minute. As it turned out, the cold proved more dangerous than the current.

April began to feel so sleepy that even the sound of an approaching waterfall didn't inspire alarm. It was the enormous gush of water that tumbled into the barren basin of land that used to be New Haven. April was falling asleep in the fierce rapids that raced her toward that waterfall, and she had lived in the Outer-world long enough to know what that meant – she was dangerously cold. But she couldn't stay awake so it didn't matter. Nothing mattered. She was asleep before she went over the edge of the waterfall.

16 – Long Live August

When April woke up, and she certainly hadn't expected to wake up, the world was wonderfully warm. The sun was directly overhead, it was high noon. April hadn't been asleep very long.

The sky was as blue as a dream. Everything else was green, not white. Insects buzzed and chirped softly from all sides, like a welcoming chorus. This time, April knew exactly where she was and smiled euphorically up at the sky. New Haven had come down around her, and just in time it seemed.

"Home." April loved saying the word. She drew a slow deep breath into her lungs. The scent of leaves and flowers and green filled her, the soft air was full of life. The sun beat down, warming into her bones. After months of freezing, it was paradise.

Aside from being home, April didn't know where she was but decided it was time to find out. She sat up and looked around. She was lying on the bank of a small, gentle stream. Interesting - in the Outer-world it was a raging river. Maybe in New Haven this was the slow end of Cayenne Creek.

April struggled to her feet and started walking, not flying. Her arms and shoulders were as tight as a bow string. She randomly walked north and found berries to eat along the way. She stuffed herself.

The first distinct landmark that she spotted was Gnash, the Giant transformed into a tree. It seemed significant somehow. And it meant that home was a long enough walk. April set off with an energetic spirit; sadly, her body lagged behind. It was slow and sore, stiff and bruised - it felt rather like it had been crushed under a Giant and tossed over a waterfall. Regardless, April was determined to arrive home in time for dinner. The pace she managed was slow but steady. She smiled all the way home.

From a distance, April's house looked exactly the same as she remembered. On closer inspection, the Giant's hammer was still a monument on the front lawn and her tower room had been rebuilt. April stopped and gazed up, filled with warm joy. The Pooles hadn't given up hope that she would return!

Unable to wait another second to see everyone and find out about Raina's condition, April stumbled inside only to find the house vacant. She searched the interior from top to bottom and took a look at her new room. The walls were a soft blue-green now, the colour of water. April turned in a slow circle and admired her room, she had a new bed with four legs and a matching box dresser. She couldn't wait to try out her bed, but first she had to find everyone.

April walked the shore of the lake, but there was no sign of Raina or anyone. The most likely place to look for elves was the town square. But it meant more walking.

Disappointed at the delay, April set off for town. When she reached it, the square seemed as deserted as the Pooles' house. This was not normal. Where were all the elves? Had the magical world come back to earth without its population?

No, there was noise coming from Seelie Court. Maybe an important gathering was underway. It was peculiar that no elves were attending the entrance but April dismissed it with a shrug. Excited to reunite with everyone, she hurried down the corridor and slipped inside the door a bit shyly, expecting a huge fuss over her triumphant return. With the help of her friends, she had survived a Giant, and they had stopped his rampage.

The room was packed with elves. There were so many elves that it was standing room only. Head-Elder Falcon was installed beside the King at the front of the room. They were deep in conversation with an elf that looked like Gus.

April squinted - it was Gus. The elf had cleaned up beautifully. She was wearing a silken red gown with golden embroidery, and her white-gold hair hung shiny to her waist. Her face was quite beautiful and animated as she spoke with authority to the two important elves. August looked older all dressed up, maybe as old as O'Wing who was twenty. All the elves in the room were watching her avidly. The elves nearest to April frowned at her for disturbing them. One elf shooed her aside as if she was a pesky fly.

April shrank back against the wall, filled with a dark, foreign emotion. It didn't look like anyone cared that April had disappeared beneath the wild water with the Giant. Now that New Haven had Gus with her strong Outer-world magic to keep them safe, April had been forgotten. No one was mourning her disappearance. One magic elf was enough, it appeared.

She was filthy and unkempt (her usual mess) while Gus looked like a princess sitting at the King's side wearing the royal colours. April slumped lower, wishing she had at least cleaned up before rushing here. She was about to slip out of the room unnoticed when Head-Elder Falcon rose to speak, raising a hand for silence.

"I have consulted with August about how best to deal with the Giant that is threatening New Haven. She assures me that she is knowledgeable in the use of the thunderwands and eager to transform this Giant into a tree and save our world. August, we are deeply in your gratitude. You have come to our world when our need is great and your help is appreciated more than you will ever know. We thank you and honor you for your courageous heart and heroic spirit." Head-Elder Falcon bowed his head to August in respect, in front of every last important elf in New Haven. He had never done that to April, had he?

Gus had become August, the name on the vial. It was hers, after all. And it was a much prettier name, April didn't like it one bit. She felt like she had been tossed away like rotten turnip. The Head-Elder hadn't even mentioned April's name! And April had already taken care of Loug, sort of. He'd fallen and she had almost been killed, but he was gone now and New Haven was safe. The whole elvan realm needed to know that Loug was no longer a threat. And it wouldn't hurt if elves knew that April and Peter had gotten rid of the monster, not August.

Scowling, April shoved her muddy hair off her face and moved forward. As soon as she started weaving through the congregation of elves, she was noticed. "April! Where the heck did you come from? Thought you were … gone." Elder Scarab looked happy to see her, at least. If she had been in a better mood, she would have hugged him.

"I'm not gone, I'm back," she muttered, giving him a tight hug anyway.

"Something fishy going on around here," he mumbled in her ear, before accompanying her to the front of the room.

Head-Elder Falcon rose from his cushion more casually. "April, you are returned to us safely. We thought otherwise." It was not the most effusive greeting after months away.

April bowed before the King. He forgot to tell her to rise, his eyes were fixed on August. April stood up anyway. He didn't notice that either. "It's great to be back, and I have some good news. What you were saying about the Giant is wrong. Loug is dead. He's gone."

Head-Elder Falcon frowned at her in annoyance. "The Giant is not dead or gone. He has come into our world somehow. We are indeed fortunate that he has not yet discovered us and that August is here to guard us. Fairies are watching him from hidden locations at all times, ready to inform us if he starts moving toward the populated areas of our world."

"But … no, that's wrong. Loug is dead, gone," April insisted.

August rose to her feet and smiled patronizingly at April. "You don't know what you're talking about. Did you think that *you* had bested the Giant?" she asked in a belittling tone, in front of everyone.

"Yes, and Peter, mostly Peter," April said weakly.

"Certainly not! The Giant is here and I'm going to defeat him," August declared. The elves in the room applauded enthusiastically for the longest time. But they were being misled. Loug was gone forever, April had seen it with her own eyes. Elves would find out soon enough.

April scowled at August and said, "Oh, well, good-luck with that. Rather you than me." It wasn't the most gracious thing to say to the elf that had very publicly volunteered to save the world but April didn't care. August would not be battling Loug and April had other things to worry about. She turned around, ready to reunite with her friends (if she could find them) and find out what was going on around here.

"April!" Head-Elder Falcon said sharply.

She turned back around. "Yes?"

"August is a guest in our world, she is here to save us from the Giant. I would like you to apologize to her for your rudeness."

"Huh?" April could not believe he was saying that.

"Apologize," he ordered.

As tempted as she was to refuse, April took the easy way out. She was simply too drained to argue. "Sorry," she said insincerely and started walking, scanning the room for her friends or family. She didn't spot them anywhere. But she did see Prince Skylar, he had given up his special cushion to August. He was standing at the front of the crowd of elves.

April veered toward him, relieved to find one friend. "Skylar, it's wonderful to see you."

"Yes. Isn't August amazing?" Skylar didn't take his starry eyes off the elf to glance at April or ask how she was after her long absence. Skylar was as captivated by Gus as the other elves.

April yanked on his sleeve for attention. "Skylar, where is Raina, or Peter, or Airron? Have you seen them?"

"Raina is sick, her family is with her. I think Airron and Peter are as well," Skylar answered absently, showing no concern.

"Where are they, Skylar?" April was beginning to believe that she had entered the wrong New Haven.

"Try the laboratory. Mr. Stone's office perhaps." Skylar didn't even know Raina's location. April bit her lip before she said something she shouldn't and escaped the room.

She almost ran over Ms. Larkin-LaBois, who was about to enter the

225

gathering. The old elf stumbled back and gawked at April in obvious shock, as if she was seeing a forest spirit. She reached out a shaking hand to touch April's cheek. "April, you are alive? Are you really here?"

"Yes and yes." April gripped her elbow and moved her over to the wall, the aged elf needed the support.

"But I saw you fall into the ravine. The Giant crushed you. I saw it so clearly in my vision, it was heartbreaking." Her reedy voice trailed into a whisper and she pressed trembling hands together.

"Well, I did fall, like you said. But the Giant didn't crush me, he missed. Are you okay?" April asked in concern.

"It is a shock, that is all. I believed you gone forever and our world would have been doomed if such a tragedy had occurred. I believed us all doomed," Ms. Larkin-LaBois said.

"What are you talking about? New Haven doesn't need me." The hurt and jealousy flooded into her voice. "August is here. She says that she's going to defeat the Giant and fix everything, not that there is a Giant. Loug is dead. But elves seem to believe her about the Giant, they believe her about everything. And I'm not needed or wanted."

"But you are, April, more than you know. Everything will be fine now." Ms. Larkin-LaBois smiled with sunny relief and touched April's cheek. "Did you ever receive the message I attempted to send you, through Cherry?"

"Sort of, she couldn't remember most of it. And she only remembered after weeks out there," April said ruefully.

"I did wonder. Well, everything seems to have sorted itself out regardless, but I do wish you had come to speak with me before you left this world. Ah well, it is wonderful to see you again, April. We must talk further, but at the moment I need to attend the rest of the gathering, I need to see how August is affecting our world."

April had been about to ask Ms. Larkin-LaBois about that very thing but the elf pushed off the wall and strode urgently into Seelie Court. And April had a pressing errand of her own.

The laboratory was a couple of buildings over. April remembered where Mr. Stone's office was from when she had tried to revive the ant trapped in forever sleep. The door was ajar and the room was lit. April peeked nervously inside, unsure of what to expect since the rest of this world was skewed somehow. But everyone she wanted to see was in the laboratory, she had found her friends and family! They were standing around a vat, looking gloomy and subdued.

"April?" Peter spotted her first and gaped like he too was seeing a spirit. "April, are you really here?"

"Oh my goodness." Mr. and Mrs. Poole rushed over and made a great fuss. "We feared the worst. Peter said you fell under the Giant. He was not sure if you had survived." Mrs. Poole got all choked up and Mr. Poole took over.

"And when you didn't return, it did not look good." He swallowed hard. "You've all been through so much." He glanced sadly at Airron, who was standing beside the wooden enclosure.

"But where's Raina?" April didn't see her anywhere.

Mr. Poole motioned helplessly towards the tub.

"Oh." April didn't want to look inside. She had hoped with all her heart to find Raina cured by her return to New Haven. If she was in that basin, she was not cured, she was worse.

Salm moved forward from the other side of the tub. Without a word, he enfolded April in his arms and murmured, "I can't believe you're here, that you're alive. It's the first good news we've had." He closed his eyes tightly, looking overcome. A cool splash of water doused them.

"What was that?" April asked.

"Raina - she'll want to know you're okay."

April stepped up to the edge of the basin and looked inside. The enclosure was filled with water and Raina was floating face up, staring at the ceiling. She was very green, with distinct yellow stripes now. Her skin had gotten scalier. She made an 'O' shape with her mouth and did look happy to see April.

April reached a hand into the water and Raina took it. Her fingers were webbed and scaly. "We'll figure this out," April promised. "You'll be back on your feet in no time." Raina kicked a finny foot. "You know what I mean." Raina nodded and rolled her eyes.

"Has there been any progress, curing Raina?" April asked Mr. Poole.

"No. I have never seen a condition like this. Well, it is a magic spell or potion, isn't it? And with everything else going on ..." Mr. Poole trailed off, as despondent as April had ever seen him.

"What else is going on? Do you mean August?"

"August? No, we haven't met her yet. I mean the Giant." Even Mr. Poole believed that a Giant was in New Haven.

"There's no Giant. Loug is dead," April declared.

"No, he's not," Peter said. But Peter had seen the Giant fall into the rapids and sink. Peter should certainly know better.

"Is there really a Giant in New Haven?" she asked, feeling sick.

"Yes." Everyone in the room confirmed it. Peter included.

"Is it Loug?"

"Ya," Airron said bitterly. "He's here."

"But how? He didn't survive the fall and if he had, New Haven would not have come down from the cloud." It didn't make sense.

Mr. Poole cleared his throat roughly. "Peter's father has a theory. Mr. Stone proposes that the Giant was so near death in the cold water that he was more dead than alive. New Haven – well, the Echoes - were no longer able to sense his presence and returned our world to earth. Mr. Stone believes the warmth revived the monster, brought him back from the brink of death inside New Haven."

"Is that possible?"

"It must be, and it is the best explanation we have. It is the only explanation that makes sense because the Giant is here in our world, and very much alive," Mr. Poole affirmed.

It was devastating news, April still didn't want to believe it. "Gus said she was going to take care of the Giant using the thunderwands, she announced it at the gathering at Seelie Court. I stopped there first," she said.

"August?" Mr. Poole nodded. "I heard that she had volunteered to save New Haven from the Giant."

"I'm here, too. I could save New Haven, I have more experience using the wands," April pointed out.

"Yes, but you've been through enough, April. More than enough." Mrs. Poole stroked April's muddy hair. "August is here. Let her have a turn at him," she said reasonably. "I'm sure you wouldn't mind some time to recover."

"No, I wouldn't mind, I guess." Why did April want to take on the Giant again anyway? That was stupid. Let August stop Loug. Let her have the glory, April would have a good sleep and a hot dinner.

Raina splashed more water at April, wanting to tell her something. Salm wanted to talk too, but not with his parents in the room. "Mom, Dad, maybe you should attend the end of the gathering, find out what's going on. We'll watch Raina." He urged them out the door.

As soon as April was alone with her friends, she asked. "What's going on around here? Everyone was almost worshipping August at the gathering. No one cared that I was even alive. Is this the right New Haven?"

Raina nodded under the water.

"It's Gus," Peter explained, which was no explanation at all.

"Ya, once they've met her, everyone in New Haven gets weird around her, like she's the most important elf in this world. Like she's some sort of super-elf to be worshipped," Airron snapped.

"But why don't you worship her?" She looked at each of them in turn. "And I don't worship her, I don't even like her." Raina splashed her again and wiggled her fingers. April didn't understand.

"I think she means magic," Salm guessed, wiggling his fingers like Brag.

"Oh."

"Yes, I was thinking about that," Peter said.

"What?" April pressed.

"You know how your magic is a lot stronger inside New Haven?" Peter began. April nodded. "Well, Gus must have magic. She is from the Outer-world, she has blue eyes. They're a lot darker than yours, but they are blue. What if her magic is stronger inside New Haven too? And more like Drake Pitt's magic," Peter said significantly. "Darker magic."

"And everyone thinks she is so wonderful because she's using her magic to charm them?" April concluded. "And that's why no one cares that I survived the Giant and made it home? And no one cares about anything but her?" she asked indignantly.

"We care that you survived." Salm smiled, tugging on her braid.

"We do," Peter agreed. Airron nodded and Raina splashed.

"Well, I'm glad someone cares," she sniffed. "But why doesn't August's magic do the same thing for you, or me? I don't like her at all, I don't think she's special. Elder Scarab seemed normal too, when I ran into him. He was happy to see me, he didn't look through me as if I was almost invisible. And Ms. Larkin LaBois was glad to see me, really glad."

"We've been trying to figure that out since yesterday." Peter leaned against the vat.

"Yesterday? You got back yesterday?"

"Yes. You took a lot longer. A whole day longer."

"I must have slept for a day," April realized. "And August has been here since yesterday too?"

"Yes. Anyway, we think that maybe elves with their own magic aren't affected in the same way. You, Elder Scarab, Ms. Larkin-LaBois, me," Peter listed.

"But Salm and Airron don't have magic."

"No, but they met August first outside New Haven. They saw her without the strong magic – the way she really is, so maybe they still see her that way. It's a guess, but it would explain why they haven't fallen under her spell like the rest of New Haven." Peter's reasoning did seem logical.

"What about Cherry and Marigold?"

"Haven't seen them since we got back, so I don't know. I imagine they see August as she really is, as we do."

"Oh." The last thing April had expected to find upon her return to New Haven was a Giant threatening the world and almost everyone in love with August.

Peter described how New Haven had reappeared around him when he followed the rushing river into the barren land, trying to find April. The world's return made him believe that Loug was dead. He had searched for April in vain, then returned to the town square. Gus had arrived ahead of him. "She had already made herself right at home. Elves were practically eating out of her hand and bowing as if she was some sort of princess. She stayed in the King's Keep last night," he reported.

"Well, at least she's going to get rid of Loug. I've had enough encounters with him to last a lifetime." April was determined to find as many bright sides as she could. And that was a whole sun.

When the Pooles returned, gushing about August's endless wonderful qualities, April had to bite her tongue - hard. They were under her spell now that they had met her. Mr. Poole said he was staying with Raina overnight, he and the Stones were going to continue working on antidotes. Then he said maybe he would consult with August, who was sure to know a cure. Mrs. Poole said if August didn't know of a cure, she could surely cure Raina herself.

It was their cue to leave.

Raina waved good-bye from under the water, pantomimed going to sleep and closed her eyes. She did look tired in a fishy kind of way. Mrs. Poole accompanied them into the town square, it was very crowded now that the gathering was over. Elves were milling around and talking about August and nothing but August. It was peculiar that they didn't seem overly concerned about the Giant but perhaps that was due to August's strange influence as well.

From the other side of the square, Airron's parents motioned for him to join them. They must have been told about his wings, but they looked as relaxed as all the surrounding elves. It had to be the August influence; at least she was keeping elves happy in the middle of a Giant crisis.

"See you later," Airron said, and turned towards his parents.

"Bye Airron," everyone called.

He wove through the crowd, his carriage proud, his shoulders straight. He was going to be okay, April realized out of the blue. He was going to be okay without his wings. She felt her eyes mist over emotionally. But he might not be okay without Raina. He had lost enough, he couldn't lose Raina, too.

Peter stayed with them. "Salm, is it okay if I sleepover in your room? My parents will be working at the laboratory all night and with the monster in New Haven, I'd rather not be alone," he admitted frankly.

"Of course it's okay. We've spent the last few months together in a tree hollow, haven't we. I've gotten used to having you around. I'd miss you if you weren't there," Salm joked.

April couldn't wait to get home and shower for the first time in months, and eat real food and sleep in her new room. She started walking until Mrs. Poole called her back. "We have to wait for dearest August. I am sure she will be out directly."

April hoped her ears had misheard. "August?"

"Yes, she asked to stay with us. And I am simply thrilled, we are so honored! Did I not mention that August wants to stay with us?" Mrs. Poole looked foggy for a moment.

"No, you didn't." April would have remembered.

August took her time turning up. When she did, Skylar was escorting her by the arm, his eyes fixed on her face. He wasn't even blinking. He accompanied her all the way to Mrs. Poole, as if August couldn't manage a single step without him.

"Good grief," April muttered, since Raina wasn't there to say it. This was getting ridiculous. April started marching out of the town square. She didn't have to wait for August. Peter and Salm were of the same opinion. They all hurried ahead until Mrs. Poole called them back again.

"We will all walk together. New Haven won't be safe until August has transformed the Giant." Mrs. Poole beamed at August.

"August, why don't you transform the Giant now, while he's sleeping?" April asked. It would be safer, for August as well as New Haven.

"Umm ... no. I'm really tired. I'll do it in the morning, it's not like it's hard or anything." August waved an airy hand, supremely confident. Her magic must be much stronger than April's if she felt no fear or doubt about taking on Loug.

They walked together with one small torch. The less light the better with the Giant nearby, although he was unlikely to move around before midmorning if he followed his usual routine.

"Where's DewDrop?" April hadn't seen the little elf anywhere.

"Sleeping at a friend's house, I can't recall which one." Mrs. Poole looked hazy again. April couldn't believe her ears, Mrs. Poole was acting completely out of character now that she had met August. There was a Giant in New Haven and she couldn't even remember where DewDrop was staying. Was August's magical influence powerful enough to make a mother forget about her child? It did seem so.

Salm leaned close and said softly, "Don't worry. I know where DewDrop is staying."

"Glad someone does," April growled. August was making her grumpy. April's homecoming was not nearly as welcoming as she had imagined. Not even close.

"So, I am going to take care of the Giant tomorrow, in the morning," August mentioned, as if she still had an admiring audience. "What do you think April? Tomorrow morning a good time?"

"Whenever you like. The sooner the better, as I already said," April snapped.

"Skylar showed me the very pretty thunderwands. I'm going to need someone to help me carry them. April, would you like to carry the rods for me tomorrow?" August asked, speaking to April as if she was two years old.

"I already have plans." April planned to sleep late in her lovely new room.

"April, that's not very nice," Mrs. Poole chided. "August would like you to carry the thunderwands for her. It is the least you can do to help take care of the Giant. I am sure your plans can wait."

"I couldn't carry the rods even if I wanted to," April said. "I hurt my arms escaping from the Giant, before he fell down the ravine on top of me, and I broke one of them not so long ago," she emphasized pointedly. "Someone else will have to carry the wands."

"Oh." August actually sounded disappointed

When they arrived home, it was automatic to enter the kitchen. April was starving, in spite of all the berries she had wolfed down. That had been a long time ago.

"August, are you hungry?" Mrs. Poole asked, pulling out a cushion for the elf.

"Yes, I am a little peckish. The King's feast was delicious, but I could eat a little more." August perched on the cushion, arranging her skirts and waiting to be served. April's jaw dropped. The rest of them hadn't eaten a decent meal in months, and Mrs. Poole was ignoring them to wait on August, who had already feasted with the King.

"We'll get our own, Mom. Don't worry about us," Salm said in disgust and started rummaging in cupboards. He pulled out some peas and a crab apple, flat bread and yam chips. April's mouth started to water, she poured carrot juice for the three of them.

"Don't forget to pour some for dearest August," Mrs. Poole reminded her. April was tempted to pour it on August's head, she poured it in a cup instead.

They sat down and stuffed their faces. After months of hunger, April felt like she would never be full again.

By the end of the meal, April was losing the fight to keep her eyelids up. She needed one night of sleep before she worried about Raina and the Giant. "I'm going to bed," she yawned, struggling to rise from her cushion. Her body had stiffened up in the worst way. "It's great to be home. I can't wait to sleep in my new room. Night." She would thank the parents for her room when they were more themselves.

"April, August has been given the new room," Mrs. Poole stated breezily.

"What? You gave my room to August? But it's *my* room," April insisted hotly. It was the last blade of grass.

"Well, they didn't think you were coming back," August said. "They thought you were dead, didn't they? The Giant fell on you, who would have expected you to come back? Not anyone in this world. So stop making a fuss, I'm sure you can find somewhere else to sleep."

"Yes April. Raina's room is empty, you can sleep there. Surely it is an improvement over the Outer-world accommodations." It was no surprise that Mrs. Poole sided with August, and it probably wasn't Mrs. Poole's fault, but it still hurt.

April limped out of the kitchen, fuming. In spite of the bone-deep fatigue, she detoured outside and showered in the waterfall. As desperately as she needed to get clean, she also needed to cool her anger. She was back in New Haven, she didn't have the luxury of losing her temper anymore. April used almost all the flower soap trying to calm down and scrub off layers of grime. Once clean, she went to Raina's room and borrowed a nightshirt. After months in the same clothes, the cloth felt soft and fresh. She was tucking herself into bed when Salm knocked on the door.

"Come in," April called.

He did, followed by Peter. The boys pulled up cushions and Salm displayed a small vial. "Let me look at your arm, since my Dad isn't around."

April extended her nicely clean arm. Salm examined it thoroughly.

"It's a little swollen again, you've been using it too much."

"No choice."

"Guess not. Here." He handed over the vial and motioned to her arms and shoulders. "That should ease the stiffness. Apply it liberally before you go to sleep."

"Yes Salm." April couldn't help but grin. "You sound just like a Healer." She tested the medicine on her arms, using a generous amount. They started to feel better instantly. "Wonderful I think you would make a good Healer, if you could stand the sight of blood."

"That's not going to happen. I found the cream in my Dad's medical sack. Is it really helping?" Salm asked.

"Yes, a lot. Hopefully I can use my arms tomorrow."

"All ready for bed, then?"

April yawned on cue. "Yes."

"You look clean. I almost don't recognize you," Salm said teasingly.

"It's been awhile."

Both boys had cleaned up as well, at some point.

"Sorry about your room. Mom's not herself," Salm apologized, for his mother.

Peter looked worried when he said, "August has quite a powerful influence, doesn't she?"

"Yes, she really does." April yawned again, too sleepy to worry about August.

She must have fallen asleep without realizing, because the next thing she knew, it was morning. The sun was lighting the sky, August must have already left to transform the Giant. Maybe Loug was nothing but a tree now. April hadn't heard any thunder, but she might have slept through it. She snuggled into her covers and almost went back to sleep, except she had visitors – loud visitors. August hadn't left to take on the Giant after all. She sailed into Raina's room with Salm and Peter on her heels. All three were in the middle of a heated argument.

April jerked upright. "August, what are you doing here? Did you already transform Loug?"

"She hasn't even left yet!" Salm raged, as angry as April had ever seen him. "She's looking for you, searching the whole house, woke me up – and she hasn't even left yet!" He was so livid, he was repeating himself.

"August, you have to stop the Giant before he starts moving around." April kicked to be free of her covers.

August shot Salm and Peter a dismissing glance. "I want to talk to April, in private."

April didn't want to be alone with August. She didn't trust her even slightly. "Forget it. You can talk in front of Salm and Peter, if you want to talk. Or you can leave, go see Loug." April knew which choice she preferred.

August didn't leave. "Okay. Listen, here's the thing. I need you to come with me," she said frankly.

"Me?" April checked.

"Yes, you. You can work those wand things, can't you?"

"So? It only takes one elf to work them, and that's you, and you better get a move on." There was nothing to discuss as far as April was concerned.

"Uh ... bit of a problem," August began.

April thrust to her feet. Of course there was a bit of a problem. When wasn't there a bit of a problem? "What's the problem?" she asked suspiciously.

"I can't work those rod things," August stated very clearly, no beating around the bush.

"What?" April hoped her ears were playing nasty tricks on her.

"The wands - I don't have the type of magic needed to make them work. You'll have to come with me and work the wands. I have a particular kind of magic, and not much else." August plucked at the embroidery on her dress and didn't look up. "Even I know that working the rods takes very powerful magic. My strongest magic has to do with influencing elves." They had already figured that out for themselves.

April closed her eyes in pain. Ms. Larkin-LaBois had said this world would be lost without April and she was right. April was still the only elf who could power the thunderwands and challenge the Giant. She would have to face Loug one more time to save New Haven. Her stomach suddenly felt queasy.

"Am I supposed to take on the Giant? And you'll say it was you? And everyone will believe you saved New Haven?" April asked.

"Yes," August said with satisfaction. "Now you understand."

"Why would April do that?" Salm demanded angrily.

"She'll take on the Giant and save the world because it needs saving. If she doesn't, most elves are goners. And everyone will believe I saved the world because I'll say I saved the world. That's the kind of magic I have," August said baldly. "You know, I really like this weird place. Elves believe everything I say and I barely have to concentrate. It happens almost all by itself here. Isn't it great? I usually have to work so hard at it, but not here!" she boasted. "I think I'd like to be Queen of New Haven, Skylar's kind of cute, isn't he? A bit young for me, but I can live with that - "

April cut off her ramblings. "August, the Giant should have been transformed last night, while he was asleep. You should have told me this yesterday! Now it will be so much harder." Maybe impossible. If April had known the truth last night, she would have already done the deed. Heartsick, she pointed everyone out of the room. She had to get ready.

Salm yanked August away, he looked about to strangle her.

With shaking hands, April donned a pair of Raina's overalls, knowing exactly what she was about to face - Loug.

"This is one time too many," April murmured hollowly, winding her hair into a messy braid in front of the mirror. A stranger gazed back. April's face was thinner now, and older looking. Her skin was pale, colourless. "Loug," she whispered, and her heart started pounding with fear. She wished the day was already over, but it wasn't. It had to be endured, and hopefully she would live through it.

17 – Against All Odds

Salm and Peter were waiting in the kitchen. The three friends shared a bleak glance.

"Where's August?" April asked. Her wooden voice sounded like a stranger's.

"Said she'd be right back." Salm handed her a cup of bark tea that was so strong, it was black. She drained it, knowing she would need all her energy. At least her strained arms had eased, and she had no doubt that she would need her arms to fly on this day. The tea did not sit well, her stomach was churning with nerves.

Mrs. Poole bustled into the kitchen humming as if there was no Giant in New Haven and Raina was not a fish. "Lovely morning," she said brightly and cracked a hummingbird egg onto the grill. "August will need a hearty breakfast before battling the Giant." No one corrected her about who was truly going to face Loug, there really was no point.

Salm simply said, "August won't have time for breakfast."

"Of course she will," his mother insisted.

August waltzed in at that moment, wearing one of Raina's best dresses as if it were her own. April wanted to rip it off the bold elf, but she didn't want to ruin it. Raina would want to wear it again when she wasn't a fish.

"You don't have time for breakfast August. We have to get to Loug before he starts roaming around," April said tersely, standing to leave.

Mrs. Poole disagreed. "Stop rushing August. She has plenty of time for a relaxing breakfast. We're so lucky that you are staying with us, August," she gushed and kept cooking.

April arched an eyebrow at the door. "I'm leaving now, August. You can come or not. Your choice."

With a dramatic sigh, August rose from the cushion she had just settled on. "No breakfast, how sad. But since April has decided to carry the wands for me and do her little part to help, I shouldn't keep her waiting." August smiled sweetly at Mrs. Poole.

Mrs. Poole looked misty. "Oh August, you are always so thoughtful of others. I think April could learn a lot from you - "

"Mom," Salm interrupted curtly, "Peter and I are going along too, to help with the other wands. There are three of them."

"Nice of you to help August with the Giant, dear." Mrs. Poole blinked vacuously. "We don't want August tired out from carrying the wands, now do we?"

"No we don't," Salm said, the sarcastic tone clear to everyone but his mother. He had just informed her that he was going to confront a Giant and she hadn't batted so much as an eyelash or tried to talk him out of it. She hadn't even said 'be careful'.

"Well, got a date with a Giant," August said and sauntered for the door. "I'm sure he will be a tree by lunchtime. Come on April, hurry up."

April swallowed the foul words welling up in her throat and choked out a good-bye instead, in case she never saw Mrs. Poole again.

Salm hugged his mother close. "See you at lunch, Mom," he said, looking strangely vulnerable.

"Yes. Look after August now!" She waved to them from the front door as they walked away, looking weepy – for August.

Preferring to think about anything but Loug, April started discussing something that she had grown extremely curious about. "August, where did you come from? Where did your parents come from? What happened to them?" August had very different magic, and it was proving to be more evil than good. Not as evil as Drake Pitt's, but maybe that was because August herself was less evil, but she was definitely self-serving.

"I don't come from anywhere. I've always traveled through the forest, moving around with my family, we were part of a small caravan of elves. But my parents have been dead for a couple of years now." August skirted around a boulder. "My father used to talk about some weird make-believe place, a lot like here. Said his great-great-great grandfather had been tossed out of that world for some reason."

"Haven't you been alone for six years?" April asked in confusion.

"No. Why would you think that? I've only been alone since we ran into that Giant and the caravan scattered, and I was unlucky enough to get caught. Six years? Are you nuts? I'd have gone insane." August strolled gracefully along, looking like she didn't have a care in the world.

"August, the elves you were traveling with, were those elves like you?"

"Of course. They certainly don't have black bug eyes, or insect wings or fish gills. They were normal elves, like me. Why do you ask?"

"Once upon a time, elves with magic were banished from New Haven, banished to my world, the Outer-world," April said.

August was smart enough to guess the rest. "So, you think my ancestors are a mixture of elves from New Haven and elves from outside? Half and half?"

"Makes sense," Peter commented.

August simply snorted. "Imagine that." She didn't sound the slightest bit interested in the past.

Salm had his own question. "How do you stand elves falling all over themselves to please you? Agreeing with every word you speak? How do you stand it?"

"Are you kidding? Everyone hanging on my every word, waiting on me hand and foot - I could stand it forever. I'm going to like living in this world, being Queen will be a blast, too. That palace is really something," August danced a few steps down the path. "King Skylar already told me that he is interested in a match between Prince Skylar and myself. He said he had already approached the parents of some other elf about an arranged match, but luckily it hadn't been officially accepted yet, so Prince Skylar is available. Once April gets rid of the Giant, it will be perfect here." August brushed back her shining hair with a dreamy smile.

It was interesting news, and it gave them something to think about other than Loug. "I wonder who the King planned for Skylar to marry. I bet Skylar doesn't know a thing about it," April said, feeling bad for him. But if he was stuck with August, that would be worse.

August was the one that answered. "The King said it was some elf with spectacular wings. But now that he has met me, he prefers me. Well, that goes without saying, doesn't it," she assumed arrogantly.

"Spectacular wings?" April said faintly. Surely it couldn't be?

"Not you?" August sneered.

"Oh no" April shook her head automatically. "No! Salm? Your parents never said. They would have said."

"Maybe they didn't have a chance. Remember the night the Giant's hammer landed on the house? They had been summoned to meet with King Skylar."

"I do remember. And I left the next night," April recalled. It seemed so long ago. Had the King planned on a match between Skylar and April? Had he discussed it with her adopted parents? "But I thought such ... arrangements," she could barely say it, "Were a thing of the past."

"Normally they are, but it has always been different for the royal family." Salm looked as stunned by the news as April felt. "They tend to follow more archaic traditions. But I can't believe it – you and Skylar?"

"Hey, not anymore," August reminded them all. "I'm here now and I will be Queen. April will have to forget it."

"Be happy to," April said. She really liked Skylar, but not in a special way. And she was too young to think about that stuff. She had much bigger things to worry about anyway. "We should figure out how best to transform Loug," April said, changing the subject.

"Right. So what's the plan?" Salm asked April.

August looked annoyed that she hadn't been consulted, and answered anyway. "We're going to get the wands, take them to Loug, turn him into a tree, go home for lunch. Or maybe I'll have the King prepare a special celebration feast. Oh, he's probably thought of it already, I bet he has." Her plan had some gaping holes in it.

April stopped walking and turned to face the boys. "Salm, Peter, please don't come. August and I can manage the wands. Please stay here, where it's safe," she pleaded. She wanted to keep them as far away from the Giant as possible. They had been through enough.

"We're going with you April, you're stuck with us," Salm said adamantly.

"Can't let you take on a Giant alone," Peter added.

"With no help whatsoever," Salm emphasized, looking at August as if she was a loathsome Outer-world cockroach.

April hadn't expected them to cooperate. She considered tying them to a tree, but that would have involved a messy struggle and precious time lost.

"Come on." Peter started walking with a determined stride.

When they reached the town square, it was packed with elves. The air filled with cheering as soon as August appeared, as if she was the greatest hero this world had ever known. The King and Prince Skylar were waiting in front of Seelie Court, flanked by a contingent of smartly uniformed guards all standing in a ruler straight line. And the three thunderwands were polished and waiting. The fine base had even been dragged over from the museum to hold them. It was quite a display.

"Well, this is more like it." August shoved Peter aside and took the lead. She marched right up to the King and Prince Skylar. She didn't bow and no one seemed to expect it. Silence fell over the crowd when the King addressed her.

"August, this world is in your debt for what you are about to do. As you embark on this battle against the largest and most formidable of foes, know that we are with you in spirit. Our hopes for your safe return are boundless. I have handpicked twenty of my most able archers to accompany you and aid you in any way you ask." The twenty archers stood taller. "The thunderwands are awaiting your magical touch, dear, valiant, fearless August."

Thank goodness the King ran out of adjectives, April's ears were suffering. The crowd applauded and cheered so loudly that she hoped the Giant hadn't wandered any closer since the sun rose. Some elves even tossed flower petals into the air around August.

It was a lovely sendoff but August clearly wasn't pleased about one part of the arrangement. She likely didn't want twenty guards to witness April battling the Giant. But it was not a problem, given her talents. "Thank-you for your concern, King Skylar, but I am going to do this alone. I have some helpers to carry the wands." She flicked a hand vaguely behind her. "That will be all the help I need."

King Skylar acquiesced. "As you wish. The Giant is in the same location as last night."

"August, may I have the honor of accompanying you?" Prince Skylar asked, stepping forward eagerly. He hadn't acknowledged his three friends. They were invisible to him.

"No, but we can spend some time together when I return from destroying the Giant. A feast would be nice." She smiled into his eyes and plucked at the ties on his robe. Skylar swallowed hard and looked wholly besotted. Enough was enough, April stomped over to the wands and hauled one into her arms. The rod was heavier than she remembered, or her arms were weaker.

August led the way out of the square, waving to the cheering crowd. They parted before her. April, Peter and Salm followed in her wake with the wands. No one cheered for them, they might as well have been pack-mice. April wished there was enough time to visit Raina before they faced Loug, but there really wasn't. They were already hours later than they should be.

At least they had the wands and the knowledge of how to turn Loug into a tree. April knew exactly how to do it, she had witnessed Gnash's memory of when he had been turned into a tree. And the brain-toad had shown her the same thing. Loug would have to be inside the triangle of thunderwands and April would have to get really mad to draw the firebolts needed to power them. She didn't think getting mad would be a problem when facing Loug. And August's annoying presence certainly helped there. April was already feeling kind of mad.

It was a relief to leave the adulation behind. April had never had a send off like that, and it galled.

Salm echoed her thoughts. "Glad we're away from that racket."

"Oh, I don't know. I kind of miss it," August said regretfully. "Too bad Skylar couldn't come along. I would have enjoyed his company." Obviously she did not enjoy her present companions, they didn't scrape and bow before her.

"Why didn't you let him come?" April asked curiously. "Even if

Skylar saw me using the wands rather than you, you could have simply told him to forget what he saw." Skylar would do whatever August told him, she could have ordered him to fly to the stars and he would have died trying.

"It doesn't work quite that way," August revealed.

April shifted the wand to her other arm. "What doesn't?"

"If elves see me as I really am, they always will. The magic loses power. If Skylar caught me in a lie, my magic is nullified. It's always been that way and I can't control it. I have to be careful not to get caught out, that's all." August shrugged as if it was no big deal.

It was interesting information. It didn't sound like true magic though, it sounded more like August herself was under some sort of spell if she couldn't control it.

"Where is Loug?" April asked. No one had told her.

"Southwest. Why don't you fly ahead and scout his location," August said.

It was a good idea, if April could fly. "Here." April shoved the wand at August and lifted her arms to test their recovery. They were still stiff and the injured one hurt, but she could lift them and bend them. April might as well test her wings now in case she needed to fly against Loug. "Maybe I will scout ahead," she said. "Take care of the wand."

"April, don't go too close to Loug," Salm cautioned.

"I won't. I won't be long, keep walking straight and I'll find you." April started climbing a tree and August looked at her like she was nuts. She didn't know that April couldn't get her wings unless she was falling.

April adjusted her overall straps and jumped. The flying hurt, but it was not unbearable. And it was so much nicer to fly in warm air, it felt soft and easy instead of harsh and stinging.

She swooped overhead and waved to Salm and Peter, then she soared southwest. April stayed above the woods since there was no sign of Loug, no uprooted trees or paths of destruction. When something breezed by overhead, she gasped in fear until she saw that it was only O'Wing.

"O'Wing!" April cried.

He pointed urgently to a tree. "Land."

April coasted into the top branches and O'Wing floated in after her. It was great to see him. They shared a quick hug. "Welcome back April. No time to talk. The Giant is on the move."

"What? No!" April cried. "We have the wands. We're going to turn him into a tree."

"I know. I've been kept informed. The monster is meandering around, seems hungry. Nothing big for him to eat here. He's heading this way. If we can get him to slow down, August can use the rods. Haven't met her yet but I heard she's going to tackle the Giant instead of you." O'Wing started when the tree trembled.

"Keep watching the Giant, O'Wing. We'll intercept him, we'll stop

241

Loug, somehow." There was no time to say more.

O'Wing nodded tightly and flew toward the Giant's noisy approach, April jumped and banked back the way she had come, towards the wands. Nothing else in this world could stop Loug, only the thunderwands.

April spotted a glint of metal and landed so fast, she almost crashed into August. August poked April in the back when her wings disappeared into thin air. "You are so weird," August said.

April brushed her off. "Loug's on the move, headed this way," she gasped in a panic.

"Now?" Salm moaned.

The ground trembled, confirming it.

"Yes, now," April cried. "We have to slow him down long enough to plant the rods and … and I have to make a storm. A hilltop would be best, for the firebolts – the lightening." April couldn't think clearly, her head was filled with fear. Loug was approaching the populated section of New Haven. If he wasn't stopped, the realm was doomed. He had to be stopped.

"April, there's a hill a little way back. We walked over it, it's not big but it's higher than the surrounding land. We'll take the wands there," Peter said. "Then we have to get Loug onto the hill somehow."

August shoved her wand into April's arms and stepped away. "Well, I'll let you take care of the Giant. I'll be hiding far away. Make me look good." She turned to leave.

"No," April shouted furiously, filling up with the emotion. "You have to carry the wand up the hill. I have to get the Giant to the hilltop."

"Forget it. I'm already too close to the monster. Salm can carry more than one wand, so can Peter. Don't mess up." She walked off, just like that. April honestly couldn't believe her eyes or her ears. August didn't care about anyone but herself.

"Forget her, she's no help." Salm lifted the rod out of April's arms, and leaned his forehead against hers. "You're going to lead the Giant to the hilltop, aren't you," he said sadly, eyes closed.

April nodded against his head. They all knew that there was no other way. "Try and place the wands somewhere he won't step on them, in a big triangle. Switches set in the middle. As soon as he's inside, I'll make the storm."

"I think you already are," Peter said. Thunder was rumbling around on the distant horizon, building in intensity. Peter stepped closer and April hugged him tight.

"Be careful, Peter. Place the wands and get away from the hill. Loug will arrive faster than you can believe." April didn't say good-bye, she climbed the nearest tree and jumped. The wind was already picking up. She flapped hard to gain altitude and tried to calm her ragged emotions. The storm could not arrive before Loug was in place. It had to arrive at the precise moment that he stepped into the center of the wands.

She flew southwest, but didn't get far. Loug's angry tirade broadcast exactly where he was – dead ahead and stomping towards her. April held her position, waiting. She glided in circles, absently counting how many times she flew around and around.

In the middle of her nineteenth circle, she caught sight of Loug. He was limping, that's why he had taken so long to arrive. Her wings faltered and she dropped several inches.

The fall into the ravine had been rough on the Giant. Aside from the dragging limp, he was black and blue and scraped. His temper had not improved either. He looked enraged enough to stomp the town and its entire population into dust.

He didn't notice April circling ahead of him for the longest time.

April kept flying and working on her temper. Terror fueled a storm as well as anger, so she should be fine because she was terrified. Her body felt as chilled as if she was flying in the Outer-world; cold sweat trickled down her face. Thunder echoed across the sky, rumbling closer.

"Soon," April whispered, attention fixed on Loug. "Soon."

Then he looked up – their eyes met. Suddenly, April was glad that she was the elf to stop this monster. She was the elf to do it, not August. Loug had pulled Airron's wings off and he had terrorized them for months. Who knew how many elves he had murdered in his lifetime. If he wasn't stopped, he would destroy this whole world with his stomping feet, grinding teeth and rabid temper. And April was going to stop him. She couldn't wait to stop him! April glided closer.

With a guttural growl, Loug lurched forward, picking up the pace.

"Come and get me," April shouted angrily, looping away.

The Giant followed, exactly as she had hoped. April stayed enticingly out of his reach while he tried his utmost to catch her, growing more enraged with every step. Losing control, he filled the air with obscene roars and stamped his good leg hard enough to shake the trees.

Then she spotted the hill, it was higher than she had dared hope. The Giant swung an arm towards her and she felt the rush of air. April flapped a little faster and let her anger grow. To lose her temper, all she had to do was remember Loug ripping Airron's wings off and the storm would be upon them. "But not yet. Not yet." She glided faster, trying to spot the thunderwands on the top of the hill.

Loug started up the slope, grabbing rocks to pelt at April. Her only defense was to fly erratically, diving and swooping in all directions to avoid the weapons. The Giant was halfway up the hill when she spotted the wands, widely spaced and … lying on the ground. The boys had not been able to push them into the earth without the proper magic. She had forgotten that detail, it could be a very costly oversight.

April hurtled for the first rod, landed and shoved it into the rocky hill. Unable to fly off the ground, she ran for the second wand and thrust it in while the earth shook around her. One more. Only one more. The Giant crested the hill as April was dashing across open space aiming for the third and final wand.

She reached it and jammed the device into hard rock, then swung around to face the monster, finally granting her anger free reign. The storm surged overhead, blowing and rumbling and spitting hard rain. Loug didn't like storms. He slowed and flung his arms over his head, ducking low. He hadn't noticed her on the ground and he was going to run. Lightening struck nearby. Loug turned around and took one big step to flee. If he left this hilltop, they were all doomed. And his toe had dislodged one of the rods, it lay sideways – useless.

"No!" April cried, running wildly for the uprooted rod, and she had to stop Loug from leaving the hilltop. April screamed as loudly as she could and waved her arms. He didn't see her or hear her. Desperate, April did the stupidest thing she could think of - she grabbed up the wand and scrambled on top of Loug's foot when it almost stepped on her. April stabbed the wand through the Giant's thick skin, without a clue if it would work in this location. It sank into his foot as easily as it did into the earth. Best of all, it ensured that Loug would stay within the triangle of the rods because this one now moved with him.

Loug felt the rod pierce his foot, it probably felt like no more than a thorn to him but he looked down, and stilled. He forgot all about the storm. His bruised face pulled into a vicious snarl, he had lost a front tooth since April had last seen him. It was probably in the ravine. Loug wouldn't even have to open his mouth to devour her, the black gap was like an open doorway into his mouth.

Loug plucked her up off his foot between his thumb and finger, ignoring the wand. He left it stuck in his foot. That was the important thing.

"Elf," he lisped thickly, and then Loug opened his cracked lips and raised her slowly towards his bared teeth. The Giant was going to eat her here and now - just like that. She had caused him no end of trouble and he was going to bite her in half like the fish. April closed her eyes so she could concentrate on the storm before it was too late, she closed her eyes because the sight of the Giant's gaping maw was unbearable.

There was a strange little *thunk* and Loug cried out in pain. His hand stopped moving. April opened her eyes when another *thunk* was followed by a third and a fourth. Small stones were hitting the Giant in the nose and eyes with tremendous force, rather like rockput stones. *Thunk.* Loug rubbed his eye and snorted, flinging his head left and right. *Thunk.* He shook his head wildly and almost fell over, rocking the hilltop.

"April!" O'Wing came out of nowhere. He dove towards her. "I'll distract him. We need a firebolt, fast."

Loug was distracted, he swung his free arm up and snapped O'Wing right out of the air, hissing with satisfaction.

"O'Wing," April screamed and wriggled like mad. Loug ignored her and raised his other hand towards his mouth. The Giant was going to eat O'Wing first, Loug wanted her to watch. April felt the Giants fingers pinch her tighter in anticipation when O'Wing neared the cave of a mouth, the enormous bared teeth, the disgusting fat tongue. April's eyes met O'Wing's, his were filled with resolution and fear and heartbreak. He knew he was giving up his life, he was willing to pay that price to save New Haven. He was the bravest elf she had ever seen. And then he was gone.

"No," April whispered, overflowing with rage. Her head tipped back and she screamed at the sky. Finally, one great firebolt arced straight down through the boiling clouds, almost blinding her. It was going to strike them all. April didn't care. It was far better to be struck by a firebolt than eaten by a Giant!

April ducked her head and felt the electrical surge crackle through the Giant's body. He shook violently and his skin hissed like a thousand angry snakes. The air turned to steam and the Giant's hand stiffened, transforming to wood around April, snapping and cracking all the while. Then nothing.

The storm faded away as fast as it had arrived, leaving the hilltop tragically still. April slumped into the clawed branches, too sad to move. New Haven was saved, but O'Wing ...

"April?"

April looked around. Where had that voice come from? It had sounded like O'Wing. "O'Wing?" She didn't dare to believe he had survived.

"Yes, it's me." His hoarse voice was the most wonderful thing she had ever heard.

"O'Wing, where are you?"

"In here and I can't say I like it." A flap of bark pushed outward from between Loug's wooden snarling lips and O'Wing hauled himself out. He was wide-eyed and coated in gray ash, but otherwise unharmed. The lightening must have struck before the Giant's teeth closed on him.

"O'Wing! You're alive!" April cried out joyously. She couldn't believe that O'Wing was right in front of her eyes, but he was! Not many elves got eaten by a Giant and lived to tell about it – none. Only O'Wing.

"Yes, I'm alive." O'Wing laughed outright and leaped across open space to land in the branches beside April. She touched his arm as soon as he was within reach. His skin was warm flesh, not rough bark. And the Giant was a tree. They had done it!

"Are you okay? You look okay! You look great!" April beamed into his eyes, overwhelmed.

He beamed back. "Yes, I'm okay. Not eaten, but it was a close call, wasn't it?"

"It was." It couldn't have been any closer. April released a trembling breath, still absorbing the fact that New Haven was safe and O'Wing was safe and she was safe.

O'Wing moved first again, he began breaking off the branches that were trapping April. She hadn't realized that she was trapped. He kicked others aside as if he greatly enjoyed ripping the Giant's branch fingers to pieces.

April laughed with him. "O'Wing, you're the bravest elf I ever saw. You saved my life again. And you saved New Haven."

"We all did," he said, modest even now. "Hey, whatever happened to August? I thought she was supposed to do this."

"Long story." April didn't want to think about August or talk about August.

"Come on. Let's get out of here. You can tell me this long story somewhere else, anywhere else." O'Wing pulled her free of the last of the tightly tangled branches. They flew down to the ground in a daze.

Peter and Salm and Airron were just cresting the hill. It was the happiest reunion imaginable. The three boys had makeshift rockput vines hung over their shoulders. They had stopped the Giant from eating her. And Airron had turned up.

"Airron?" April acknowledged, as soon as they stopped celebrating the fact that they had all survived the Giant. "What are you doing here?" It was the last place he should be.

"When I heard that you had come to stop Loug ... well, I figured I better help. Got in a few good shots before he became a piece of wood. I like him better as a tree, looks good on him," Airron said with satisfaction.

"It does," April agreed and hugged him. She stroked his wingless back, wishing some things had turned out differently.

"It's okay," Airron murmured.

"No, it's not. It's not okay ... what happened to your wings."

"April, it is okay," Airron said, and she could tell he meant it. He had come to terms with his loss. "Now, have a good look at New Haven's newest resident," he ordered gently.

April turned and stared way up at the new tree. It wore Loug's face. The eyes bulged outward and not one leaf sprouted from the skeletal branches. It looked a lot like Gnash, except for the face.

"It's over. It didn't look like we were going to win this battle, not until the end," Peter declared, gazing up too.

"And O'Wing, you actually got eaten by a Giant. What was that like?" Salm asked.

O'Wing shuddered. "About as disgusting as you'd expect, let's not talk about that."

"Well, now we've got two Giant trees," Salm remarked.

"Two are better than one," Airron said.

"Two are much better," everyone agreed since a tree was infinitely preferable to a Giant. Their sentences were disjointed but they were all still a little shocked. Together, the five elves had beaten the Giant and saved New Haven, against impossible odds.

246

As one, they started walking away from the long shadow of Loug without a backward glance, going home. The whole world felt newly welcoming.

The boys recounted the tale of the battle all the way back to New Haven. The longer they talked, the greater the conquest sounded. April couldn't help but smile until her face hurt. How did Mrs. Merry-Helen do it?

August was waiting for them at the fork in the path outside the town square, not a hair out of place. "There you are, took you long enough. I take it I've turned Loug into a tree," she assumed, and started walking with them. "Who are you?" she asked O'Wing, leaning over to look into his face.

"O'Wing, and you are August?" he guessed. It wasn't much of a guess, given the colour of her eyes.

"I'm August. I turned the Giant into a tree," she stated clearly.

"No you didn't. April did and we helped. You weren't even there." O'Wing looked at August suspiciously. "What are you trying to pull?"

August shrugged. "I wasn't sure if you had seen ... I had to try. You might as well know that I'm going to tell everyone that I beat the Giant and they will all believe me. So don't waste your breath saying otherwise, no one will credit your words over mine."

O'Wing was truly bewildered. "What is she talking about?"

"It's true." Salm snorted in disgust. "August has weird magic from the Outer-world, elves believe everything she says and they all adore her," he informed O'Wing shortly.

"And why don't I adore her?" O'Wing asked

"She lied to you and you knew it was a lie, so you see her the way she really is without the magic, without the love," Salm explained.

"Oh." O'Wing squinted his eyes and tilted his head at August, as if trying to see her differently.

"Elves won't believe our words over August's," April verified. "But we'll have our own victory celebration. I can't wait to tell Raina the good news."

At that moment, April didn't even care if August stole the glory of saving New Haven. The world was safe and not one elf had been injured. And their small group knew the truth. April knew of Airron's bravery, to come and help them face Loug. And she knew that Peter had thought of the rockput, stopping the Giant from eating her. And Salm had come to face the Giant willingly and had hit him with stones. And O'Wing ... O'Wing had flown right up to the Giant's face and been eaten alive, trying to buy April enough time to draw the lightening needed to save New Haven. And Raina would have been in the thick of the battle if she hadn't been transformed into a fish. A braver group of elves did not exist. April was proud enough to burst when she looked at her friends.

They turned towards town to visit Raina, and O'Wing volunteered to report the Giant's defeat to the Elders and the King. August said that he didn't have to concern himself, she would do it. O'Wing said that he would go along anyway. August informed him that she would be reporting her version of how the Giant had been beaten, with herself in the starring role. O'Wing said he would stuff a leaf in her mouth if she tried. They marched ahead, still arguing. O'Wing could hold his own against August, he had survived a Giant after all.

The center of town was packed to overflowing with elves waiting to welcome August home as their heroine. April, Peter and Salm had to fight their way through the celebrating throng to reach Mr. Stone's laboratory door. When they arrived at his office, the vat was empty. The whole room was vacant.

"But where's Raina?" April asked. She wanted to see her best friend quite desperately after the morning's events.

"Maybe my father took her back to our lake, if they thought the Giant was heading this way. Loug did get pretty close," Salm said. "Don't look so worried. We'll find her." They recrossed the square in time to see August being helped into the King's royal mouse cart.

"Figures," Salm grumbled. "She's probably going to her celebration feast now." And they hadn't been invited. They stood and watched while August was applauded out of sight.

"Let's go home," Salm said. "Let's go have our own celebration."

The square was emptying around them and they joined the exodus. They didn't get far.

"There you are. Been looking everywhere." Elder Scarab scowled before he crinkled his wrinkled face into a lopsided grin. "You lot. Should have expected it."

"Should have expected what?" Airron asked blankly.

"Never mind. Come with me. King wants to see you."

"Now?" Salm asked.

"Best time. Don't want to miss the feast, do you? I sure don't."

"I don't think we're invited, and I do want to miss it," April countered. It was in August's honor, after all. And they were not dressed for a feast. Every last one of them was dirty, disheveled, scratched and bruised. They did look like they had been wrestling a Giant. And April was wearing overlarge drooping overalls tied around her neck.

Elder Scarab motioned them forward. "Come on, we'll have to walk. Carriage left without you."

"The carriage wasn't for us," Salm pointed out dryly.

"Do we have to go?" April asked.

"Stop whining. I said so, now move it." Elder Scarab jostled them forward. They went, they could fill their bellies and leave early. April had worked up quite an appetite. Peter leaned closer and picked some sticks out of her hair.

"Pieces of Loug," he grinned, offering her one. "A souvenir of your victory."

"Our victory." April accepted the stick, not sure if she wanted to keep such a memento. She twirled it around and looked at her battered, treasured friends. She stuck the stick in her pocket, deciding she did want to remember this day.

They all brushed off and tidied up as best they could, they didn't look any neater when they arrived at the Keep. Elder Scarab looked better than all of them, and that didn't happen often.

"This way, this way." Elder Scarab took them to the largest gathering room, which meant that lots of elves would be in attendance. Only the best for August.

And there she was! Seated at the head of a ridiculously long table, between the King and Prince Skylar. She was talking and smiling, not a hair out of place. She had managed to stay awfully neat while battling the Giant, if an elf was to believe her story. There were five empty cushions at the opposite end of the table, Elder Scarab chivied them that way and joined them. O'Wing was waiting.

"Haven't had a chance to talk to anyone yet," O'Wing told them right off.

"It's okay, O'Wing. It really wouldn't do any good." April looked down the table filled with elves and spotted all the Elders, many of the High Court, Airron's parents, Peter's parents, and some of her teachers. Even the Pooles were in attendance, but not Raina.

As soon as they were settled, the King rose and the occupants of the room fell silent. "Welcome, welcome! We have gathered to celebrate the defeat of a Giant, and the saving of our whole world," he began. It sounded like the start of a long speech. April snuck a parsnip chip from a nearby platter and tried to crunch quietly.

The King continued without pause. "It is almost impossible to believe that a great monster could be defeated by one of our size, but it has been done. And it has been done with the greatest bravery imaginable. I cannot express how proud I am, there are not words … " The King trailed off a bit vaguely and looked like he couldn't recall what he wanted to say. August stood up without any prompting.

April grabbed a handful of chips and munched loudly. She didn't want to hear August's lies. She had heard enough of them already.

"It took all my skills and magical powers to defeat the Giant. It was a great battle, and I feared for my life more than once. But all I had to do was think about saving this world, and I kept on fighting the Giant," August declared dramatically, placing a hand over her heart. She hadn't offered any details, she had simply spouted vague nonsense knowing that the rest didn't matter. Elves would believe and accept whatever she said.

Salm cursed under his breath. April offered him a handful of chips. "Eat Salm, you're so thin." He helped himself.

August droned on, "Yes, I used the thunderwands to transform the Giant into a harmless tree - "

"Wait ... but no -" The King blinked as if waking up. "No, that is not right. That is not how it happened."

"Of course it is, I stood alone against the Giant," August broadcast, but she looked worried now.

"Enough!" King Skylar interrupted her. He didn't usually speak to August that way. No one did, unless they saw her as she truly was.

August gaped at him. "What do you mean 'enough'? I haven't finished telling my tale about defeating the Giant."

The King thundered, "It is not your tale!"

"It's not?" August asked, a resigned look on her face. She knew.

"No. This conflict you describe was not so far from town. It took place on a hill that can be seen from the tallest towers of this Keep. Many elves witnessed the fight to save our world. The elves at this table assembled to watch the battle, while awaiting your return. I watched the Giant as he was transformed into a tree. I watched as five elves ... five elves, not one... but I couldn't recall the events until this very moment, until you spoke of the battle with nothing but lies! It was not you, it was five elves ..." The King was getting all choked up.

"You five," Elder Scarab winked.

"You knew?" April hissed at him. He could have told them.

"I knew, that's why I invited you, made sure you came. Lied about the King inviting you." He grinned wickedly, enjoying his subterfuge.

King Skylar cleared his throat and struggled to continue, he raised a hand towards the far end of the table. But all heads were already turned that way. "Five elves took on this Giant, two nearly eaten alive. April, O'Wing, Airron, Peter, Salm – rise."

They shared a glance and stood. It looked like it was their feast after all!

With flushed cheeks, they were honored and toasted for the longest time. Mr. and Mrs. Poole rushed over, Mrs. Poole was overcome with emotion now that she could remember what she had witnessed from the tower of the Keep. "My own son, standing against a Giant. And April ... the monster almost ate you. And ... and I didn't even try and stop you from going." She sobbed openly. It was great to have her back to normal, but April wished Mrs. Poole wasn't so upset. None of it was her fault.

They finally got to eat when they were almost fainted with hunger. Skylar joined them for dessert, flushed deeply with shame. "I can't believe I treated you as I did when you returned to New Haven after months of hardship, trapped in the Outer-world. I barely spoke to any of you. All I could see was August, she filled my eyes and my mind and my heart. Do you know, I think she intended to be Queen to my King," he lamented. Only then did April recall the disturbing news that August had let slip. "You must all forgive me. And Airron, my condolences, I heard of your tragedy. I cannot imagine the pain of losing your wings so young."

"Thanks Skylar, but I'll survive," Airron told him.

"And I have not yet visited Raina or inquired about her progress. Tell me her condition is improving." Skylar looked heartbroken for forsaking his friends.

"No improvement, as far as we know," Salm answered.

"Skylar, don't be so hard on yourself. It's not your fault," April said firmly. "August's magic is very strong, it affected everyone!"

"April's right." Salm leaned closer. "My own mother couldn't remember where DewDrop was staying, and didn't even care that I was going to battle a Giant. Told me to look after August."

"Imagine that." Skylar arched a brow and did look slightly unburdened.

August was nowhere to be seen. She had slipped away as soon as her lies had nullified her magic. April didn't care where she had gone, as long as it was far, far away. Their end of the table had endless visitors and it was almost dinnertime before Salm leaned over to say, "I think we can leave now. Ready to go home?"

"I've been ready for an hour." April was longing to visit Raina. The Pooles had confirmed that she was in the lake in front of their house. Salm nudged Airron and Peter, they rose together. Any hope of slipping away quietly was dashed when they were cheered out of the room until their ears rang. It was embarrassing.

18 – Tickled Pink

They found Raina at home in the lake. DewDrop was playing in the sand on the shore, the little elf had been found.

"April!" DewDrop rushed up and clamped her arms around April's middle. They had not seen each other in months. She had grown, she didn't seem so little anymore.

"You're going to be as tall as me soon, Dewy," April smiled, hugging her back and fighting tears. Today felt more like a true homecoming.

Mr. and Mrs. Poole arrived on their heels, not yet ready to let them out of sight. Mrs. Poole started sniffing and apologizing again. She fussed over Salm in particular, as if she would never stop. It was understandable, she had just gotten him back from the Outer-world only to almost lose him to a Giant.

"And how is Raina?" April asked a little desperately, looking toward the water. A splash confirmed her friend's location near the shore.

"The same. But she is happier in the lake than in the laboratory." Mr. Poole sighed sadly. He placed an arm around April's shoulder and hugged Salm with his other arm. He was more emotional than usual. "So, you battled the Giant? And won?" He puffed up proudly and kept them pressed against his side.

"Yup," Salm agreed. "You saw the whole thing?"

"From a distance, although I couldn't remember any of it until August spoke her lies. It is a strange magic that she possesses," Mr. Poole said.

"I'm not so sure it is real magic, the way elves react to her," April mentioned, watching for Raina.

"What else could it be?" Salm asked.

"It seems more like someone has placed an enchanted spell or curse upon her," April said slowly.

"Some curse," Salm said shortly, and changed the subject. He wanted to talk about battling Loug. "Did you see O'Wing get eaten by the Giant, Dad?"

"Unfortunately," Mr. Poole confirmed. "And I never want to see such a sight again. He is a very lucky elf." Salm and his father continued to discuss the details of the dramatic encounter.

April waded into the water in her clothes. She had never been happier to have gills and dove underwater to swim with her friend.

They couldn't talk but April tried to act out the battle with the Giant. It was hard to make some parts clear, but she flapped her arms like wings and made a vicious Giant's expression as she pretended to eat elves then stiffened up as if she was turning into a tree. Raina laughed at her attempts and tried to communicate her own questions.

Raina asked about Airron by shouting his name in April's ear, it sounded bubbly but April understood. She nodded, he was doing okay. She pointed to the shore, Airron was here. Raina sighed and touched her heart, motioning towards land. She missed Airron. April nodded, she would tell him. When April waved good-bye, Raina started to cry in earnest. April tried to stay then, but Raina shoved her away. April had never felt sorrier for her friend. If there was no cure for Raina's affliction, it was going to be heartbreaking for all of them.

As it turned out, April did not have to search for a cure. It came to her. Ms. Larkin-LaBois turned up after dinner and joined them for tea. She spoke of nothing of consequence and no one was sure why she was there, but April suspected the elf had a purpose. She always seemed too.

After the refreshments, Ms. Larkin-LaBois thanked the Pooles for their hospitality and had some news to share. "August will be staying with me for the time being. She has much to learn about New Haven and a great deal of knowledge to share about the Outer-world."

"Oh." Mrs. Poole was transparently relieved. "Well, that's good then. April, I guess you have your new room back. Sorry about giving it to August. So sorry."

"It's okay." April wished Mrs. Poole would stop apologizing for everything.

"April, would you escort me home please?" Ms. Larkin-LaBois asked, rising.

"Oh, okay."

253

"April might be awhile," Ms. Larkin-LaBois mentioned in parting. April grabbed a torch, filled with curiosity.

She didn't know where the elf lived, and was surprised when Ms. Larkin-LaBois stopped not far along the first path and sat down on a rock. "We will stop here and talk. It is private." Ms. Larkin-LaBois motioned for April to join her. April sat on the moss near her feet and held the torch between them.

"Talk about what?"

"Something very important. You already know about my visions, but there is something you do not know. Something of greater importance. It is time to share this knowledge with you, and it must go no further," the elderly elf warned.

April nodded, her curiosity growing like a weed. "I won't tell anyone."

"I fulfill another role in this world," she stated.

"You do?" April exclaimed. "But what?"

"I perform a rather important role at the birthday ceremony when elves transform to gain gills or wings or occasionally a touch of magic." Ms. Larkin-LaBois did not have to say more. She was the mysterious robed elf – the Seer! April should have guessed. The elf fit all the criteria – she was small and old and had the strongest magic in New Haven, except for April.

"But … how do you make the wings and gills appear? How do you do that?" It was an amazing feat.

"It is not me so much as this world. You will see for yourself very soon, you will experience it with me and then you will know. Words cannot explain, you must feel it," Ms. Larkin-LaBois stressed.

"But … how will I see soon? The birthday ceremony isn't for a long time." April didn't know why Ms. Larkin-LaBois was telling her this secret now.

"Three weeks, April. The ceremony is in little more than three weeks," Ms. Larkin-LaBois supplied. "It is already March. You will turn sixteen in three weeks, on April 1st. That is not so long."

"No, it isn't so long. Not really." April was shocked. She knew she had been in the Outer-world for a long time, but she hadn't realized quite how long. School was almost over for another year.

"April, listen well. There is a reason I am revealing this to you. I believe that together we can help your friends. I am going to attempt to restore Raina and Airron to their proper states, and you are going to help me. I will need the strength of your magic since this will not a normal transformation. However, I am hopeful it can be done or I would not have approached you." Ms. Larkin-LaBois' penetrating gaze cut across the torchlight. "You are willing?"

"Yes. Of course." April was more than willing. She was thrilled and afraid and hopeful all at the same time. And impatient. "Now? Can we fix Raina now? What do I have to do?"

Ms. Larkin-LaBois smiled slightly, turning her face into a collection of soft folds and deeply carved lines. "I wish it were so, but it cannot be attempted until the transformation ceremony. That is the only night it will be possible, if it is going to work."

All of the sudden, three weeks did not seem like a short period of time. It stretched before April like an eon. Three more weeks before Raina could be cured. And Airron? "Will Airron get new wings?"

"I believe it is possible."

"But not for three weeks?"

"April, the time will pass quickly. You will see."

"But what will I do at the transformation ceremony." April pressed her for details. She wanted it to feel more real.

"Your part is not complicated. I need your power and strength, I will draw on that. I do not have the resilience of my youth. You will feel the process as it happens, then you will know. Words really cannot explain."

It seemed simple enough. "Oh. So I just have to be there?"

"Yes, more or less. And you will wear a robe as I do, to hide your identity. You will stand with me during the ceremony."

"Okay." That wasn't a big deal.

"And … there is one other task that you must accomplish. It might be the hardest part," Ms. Larkin-LaBois tacked on.

"What is it?"

"You must convince both of your friends to attend the ceremony, without revealing the reason. Airron should wear his robe and Raina will have to be placed in the fountain. I see no other way. Can you arrange that?"

It did sound hard. "I will, somehow. But why can't I tell them?" April asked. "They won't tell anyone, they can keep a secret."

"April, it is for their own good. Airron has accepted the loss of his wings. If he anticipated their return and we did not succeed, it would be horribly cruel. He would feel like he had lost them all over again," the elf explained slowly. There was too much truth in the words she spoke.

"And Raina?" April asked.

"Raina will be harder to transform than Airron. Much harder. Let us not raise her hopes, the disappointment might be too much for her to accept, and for her family. It is better if you do not mention this to anyone."

April wasn't sure that she agreed about not telling Raina or her family. They were already so sad. Hope might be exactly what they needed. April said tentatively, "I think it could help if Raina knew she might be cured, and if her family knew too."

"April, you would not be able to explain without mentioning my name. I require separation – complete anonymity to orchestrate this magic, to draw it to me. That is why I must wear the robe, I must be … invisible to accomplish the magic. Do you understand?"

Sometimes April could not use magic if she was too close to other elves, especially if there were a lot of them. Maybe it was like that. "But couldn't I tell them without mentioning your name?"

"I would rather you didn't, April. Let's leave it at that, shall we. It is three weeks, no more. And I have every faith that you will be able to convince your friends to attend the changing ceremony." Ms. Larkin-LaBois' mind was made up.

"Three weeks." April sighed. It was going to feel like forever.

Ms. Larkin-LaBois started walking and April escorted her all the way home. She lived very near the town square in a small pixie's home, nestled into the split base of a tree trunk.

"Thank you for the company. Come and see me before April 1st, we will need to discuss this further. And you can visit with August." Ms. Larkin-LaBois disappeared through her door before April could tell the elf exactly what she thought of spending any more time with August.

Over the next few days, New Haven slowly returned to normal. Columns of elves journeyed up the hill to gawk at the new Giant-tree. It was widely agreed that it was a lot scarier than the old Giant-tree. It also had a more convenient location, being so close to town. At one point, a line of elves stretched almost to the town square, all waiting to climb up the trunk and have a closer look at the face and step inside the mouth.

The first Saturday back in New Haven was Changeling Night. April had no interest in attending. She stayed with Raina in the lake. Salm went to the gathering for a little while but he didn't dress up and he came home early. He reported that all too many elves had dressed up as Giant-trees.

April learned from Elder Scarab that the forcefield had altered all by itself to stop elves from leaving New Haven when the world floated up to the sky, otherwise elves might have walked off the end of the world and fallen to their death. When New Haven returned to earth, the forcefield had remained that way. It was good news, elves couldn't leave and they were safe again.

April kept waiting for the Pooles to mention the King's request of an arrangement between her and Skylar, but they never did. Perhaps the whole ludicrous idea had been forgotten when April was away so long.

School reopened on Monday. It had been closed due to the Giant, but classes had run as normal the rest of the time that the world was floating. Elves hadn't even known they were in a cloud, all they had seen was a mysterious wall of fog in the distance. The waterfall had disappeared and the rivers had stood still. The scientists hadn't been able to explain that phenomena.

And seven young elves had been inexplicably missing.

When April and Salm walked into the meadow on Monday morning with Airron and Peter, they were welcomed as if they were returning from the moon, not merely the Outer-world. The tale of their conquest over the Giant had spread to every ear in New Haven, but students still wanted to hear their version of the heroic encounter. Conquering a Giant to save the world was a very big deal.

When Cherry and Marigold turned up, they were fussed over as well. Cherry smirked at April and turned her nose up, they were back to that it seemed. It was fine with April, especially since Cherry had turned Raina into a fish. Marigold made a beeline for Salm and latched onto his arm like a leech. He was trapped.

The best news April received on her first day back at school was that not one of her teachers expected her to catch up on the months of missed schoolwork. Even Mr. Parsley was agreeable in a grouchy way. Airron said Ms. Hawthorn must have insisted he let them off so easily. Airron was probably right.

In sports, Mrs. Myrrh was tremendously proud that her students had used the rockput skills she had taught them in their fight against the Giant. She was so pleased that she said all of them would receive full marks for the whole year, even April, who hadn't actually rockputted.

It was wonderful to be back in New Haven and back at school, but April missed Raina terribly. She rushed home each day to spend time with Raina in the lake. They would swim around and communicate as best they could. Airron would often sit on the shore and send birchbark notes to Raina. She had to read them really fast before the water washed away the charcoal, and she couldn't send any messages back to him, wet charcoal didn't write.

Airron had tried swimming underwater to visit, but Raina was so embarrassed by her increasingly fishy appearance that she had refused to swim up to the surface or let Airron see her at all. April kept assuring Raina that everything would be okay. She would pantomime the message and count days on her fingers. Raina stopped believing her when one week slipped into a second. The ends of her legs slowly began to look more like fins than feet, and she grew deeply depressed. She wouldn't play underwater or communicate at all by the end of the second week, instead she hid in the weeds and refused to come out.

Airron didn't believe April either when she attempted to reassure him that everything would be fine if they gave it a little more time.

On Saturday morning, with less than a week left before the changing ceremony, April walked over to Peter's house so that they could talk privately, so she could enlist his help. Peter seemed very surprised to see her. It was true that she had never come alone to call on him at his house before.

"Do you want to come in?" he asked hesitantly.

"Are you alone?" April asked.

"Yes, my parents are at work."

"Good." April slipped inside and closed the door.

"What's up?" Peter asked after she had refused snacks and they were settled on the squishy cushions in the sitting room.

"It's about Airron," April began.

"What about Airron?"

"He needs to attend the birthday celebration. You have to convince him to go with you."

"But why should he? He won't want to see other elves getting wings, believe me. Why would he want to go? Why should he go?" Peter asked.

"Umm … I can't say why he has to attend," April answered, biting her lip. "But he does. It's important, very important."

"Why can't you say?" Peter tried a different question. He was tricky that way.

"Umm, because I can't. I'm not allowed. I promised." April clamped her mouth shut.

Peter smiled mischievously. "Promised who?" He was so much happier now that he wasn't worried about having dark magic.

"Peter! I can't say. Trust me that Airron needs to go. He has to be at the ceremony. That's all I can say. Will you help?"

"I'll help. But I don't know how I'll get him there. He's really withdrawn lately, because of Raina."

"Oh, Raina will be at the ceremony too. He'll go to see her," April realized.

Peter looked at her oddly. "April, Raina can't be at the ceremony, not unless she's in the fountain." He meant it as a joke.

"Yes, she'll have to be in the fountain."

"What's going on?"

"I can't say but it might be very good news," she hinted, and hoped Peter would leave it at that.

He didn't. "Does Raina know she's going to swim around in the fountain at the birthday celebration?"

"Not yet," April said reluctantly.

"That will be a challenge, getting Raina to agree and transporting her to the town square. She'll be a bit of a spectacle, won't she? She won't like that." Peter was trying to guess what April was up to. She could tell his brain was working hard.

"I know she won't like it. Getting Raina to the ceremony is going to be a lot harder than getting Airron to go. I'm still figuring the Raina part out, I'm going to get Salm to help. And you'll help with Airron, right?" April double-checked. She couldn't do this alone.

"I'll help. I know you must have a good reason for wanting him to go, even if you can't tell me why."

April knew she could always count on Peter. "Peter, I would tell you more if it was up to me. You know that, don't you? But this isn't up to me, it's up to someone else. I'm sorry."

"Don't worry about it. I'll make sure Airron gets to the ceremony."

"My thanks, Peter." April left soon after, to discuss the issue with Salm.

She brought it up while they were sitting on the shore of the lake watching for Raina, who was hiding again. Salm was as bewildered by April's request as Peter had been. "You want Raina to attend the transformation ceremony? In the fountain? Are you sure?" he verified.

"Yes.".

"Why exactly?"

"Can't say."

"Interesting. Well, you convince Raina and I'll arrange transport. Or maybe …" Salm trailed off.

"What?" April prompted.

Salm arched an eyebrow. "We could be sneaky about this."

April leaned forward eagerly. "Sneaky might be good. What are you thinking?"

"If we told Raina that my Dad needed to run more tests at the laboratory, she might cooperate. We could take her to town in the same vessel that we carried her home in, pulled in Mr. Tilly's cart."

It was a great idea. "Perfect."

"We'll need my father's co-operation, though. He might not agree without understanding why you want Raina to attend the ceremony," Salm hinted. Clearly he wouldn't mind knowing himself.

"I'm not supposed to say, and … and I don't want to get anyone's hopes up." April feared she had said too much.

"Well, let me talk to my Dad." Salm would be better at arranging that end of things. "Do you want to find Raina now? Start preparing her for this?"

"We should."

April and Salm ran into the lake in their shorts and began the search for Raina. They found her in the deepest part of the lake, submerged in the thickest patch of lakeweed. She refused to come out. April tried to explain about the trip to town on April 1st. It was impossible to communicate the information since Raina couldn't see April's sign language in the dark weeds. And April's arms kept getting tangled in the rubbery strands.

April gave up and swam ashore with Salm. Peter was waiting in the sand, napping. "Hey Peter!" April dripped water all over him and he jerked up.

"Hey. How did it go? Did you talk Raina into attending the ceremony?" Peter glanced toward the lake.

Salm tossed April a sunwarmed towel and pulled a face. "It's useless. Raina wouldn't come out of the weeds. I hate to say this but we might have to catch her in a net and haul her to town. If that's the case, I don't think we should involve my father. We should simply trap her like a fish."

"Raina won't like being caught in a net, not at all." April sighed. Raina might never speak to them again, even if she was restored to her proper physical state. April lay down in the soft sand and let the sun dry her off. It had been chilly in the bottom of the lake, and they had been underwater a long time.

One week to go, it stretched like an eternity. Ms. Larkin-LaBois had been wrong about time passing quickly. It was passing the opposite of quickly.

And April still had to visit Ms. Larkin-LaBois before the ceremony. She had been so busy with schoolwork and Raina that she hadn't made the trip. And to be honest, she was in no hurry to see August again.

On Thursday, April decided it was time, she had procrastinated long enough. She slipped away after school and hurried to Ms. Larkin-LaBois' house, hoping to find her alone.

Ms. Larkin-LaBois was waiting with snacks, as if April was expected. "Greetings. Come in, April." They sat down in a small bare kitchen at a table with only two thin cushions.

April glanced nervously around. "Umm … is August here?"

"Not at the moment. O'Wing has taken her out for the afternoon. Dinner as well, if I am not mistaken. It gives us the opportunity to talk alone." The elderly elf pushed a shell of cookies closer.

"O'Wing?" April was surprised.

"Yes, he is helping August adjust to our world. They get on well, at times." It was said with a twinkle in her eye. April hoped O'Wing knew what he was getting into. "Have you convinced your friends to attend the ceremony?"

"I'm working on it. Raina and Airron will be there." They would be in the town square if April had to tie them up and drag them by their heels.

"Good. I would like to explain how we will proceed at the ceremony. You will participate in the transformation of all the elves, not merely your two friends. It is time that another elf knew how to do this. I am not getting any younger." It was said without regret. "You will stand by my side, you will keep one hand on my back at all times to maintain a physical contact. I think this will be necessary. You will open your mind and senses to what is happening. And you will offer me your magical power and energy, it will be channeled through me. At least I believe it will unfold in this way. It has never been done with two elves, and it has certainly never been done with an elf from outside of New Haven or to transform sixteen year old elves." Ms. Larkin-LaBois was very matter-of-fact.

"So that's it?" It sounded too easy, at least April's role.

"That's it," Ms. Larkin-LaBois confirmed.

"Are you sure?"

"As sure as I can be. Have a cookie."

They ate the snacks and talked. April had a lot of questions and the elf was willing to answer all of them. Apparently, there was always one elf born in New Haven with the unique magic necessary to perform the transformation. The knowledge was passed from one Seer to the next.

"Who is the elf that will replace you?" April asked.

"I don't know yet. They have not approached me. But I admit that I am curious myself."

When April rose to leave, Ms. Larkin-LaBois issued one last instruction. "Meet me here before the ceremony. We shall dress in our robes, then travel unseen to the town square. Don't be late."

"I won't, I'll be here," April promised and hurried away, glad to have missed August and very tense about the coming event. If the ceremony did not restore Raina to health, the future would be bleak for her friend. This year, April 1st fell on a Sunday - three more days to wait.

The last day of school was filled with fun and no work. Under different circumstances, April would have enjoyed it. As it was, she felt distanced from the revelry. It seemed inappropriate when Raina was suffering in the lake and unable to join in. April slipped away from school at lunch since there were no real classes anyway. She had planned to spend time with Raina, but Raina refused to come out of the weeds.

Saturday felt as long as a week and April was too antsy to sleep at all that night. She was in her new room and comfy new bed and she couldn't fall asleep. When she finally did drift off, the sun was starting to rise. Salm came to wake her up at high noon, for lunch.

"April, time to get up. Come and eat, then we have to get to work," Salm said, shaking her.

"Work? School work? Am I late for school?" April mumbled dozily. Her brain wasn't functioning yet.

"Not school. Raina. We have to catch Raina and transport her to town. Remember?"

April struggled to sit up. "Yes. I remember. Of course I remember. Is that today?"

"Yes – today. Meet me downstairs. Oh, and happy birthday." With a fleeting kiss on her cheek, Salm fled.

"Oh. Uh … happy birthday," April called after him. "Today." After three weeks of waiting, the transformation ceremony was today. "Owl pellets."

April rushed to get ready. Lunch didn't take long, her stomach was filled with butterflies, leaving little room for food. As soon as Salm stood up, April leapt to her feet and knocked over her juice. "Oh, sorry." She grabbed a cloth and mopped up, knocking over DewDrop's juice in the process. "Sorry Dewy." She cleaned that up too.

"April, is everything all right?" Mrs. Poole was watching her keenly.

"Oh. Yes. Yes, everything is fine, good. My thanks for lunch." April hurried out of the room before she spilled everything.

Salm followed, trying not to laugh. He led her to where a cart was hidden by the shore, away from the house. It held a container, already filled to the brim with water. All it needed was Raina. "When did you get this ready, Salm?"

"Borrowed Mr. Tilly's handcart yesterday. Filled the container with water this morning, while you were snoring." he teased. "But that was the easy part. Convincing Raina to come with us is going to be tough. Ready?"

April nodded and stripped down to her shorts and halter top, eager to get this part over with. Salm pulled off his shirt and waded in. April paused by his side, not looking forward to trapping Raina like a fish. Raina was going to be very upset.

"Poor Raina," April murmured.

Salm dropped an arm over her shoulders and pulled her against his side. She didn't mind, she hugged him in return and could feel all his ribs. She ran her fingers over the undulating bones and sighed sadly. Her head rested against his shoulder and she could feel nothing but bone, no warm padded pillow. Three weeks had not been enough time for Salm to regain his strength. And Raina was still a fish. And Airron didn't have wings. It had been hard times for all of them.

"Ready?" Salm nudged her.

April hated to cause Raina further distress, but it was unavoidable. "Ready." She stood straighter, gathering her resolve.

"Okay, let's do it." Salm grabbed a woven net off the cart, it was as big as two blankets. They slipped silently into the water together.

Raina proved elusive. She was hiding again, and very well this time. She was not in the thickest patch of weeds at the very bottom of the lake. She didn't seem to be anywhere.

April and Salm split up; Salm searched one half of the lake bottom and April searched the other half. If she could have sensed things underwater, she would have found Raina easily. But she couldn't, she had to search inch by inch. April finally discovered a sort of piled rock cave near the far shore, away from the house. It was a new addition to the lake. Was it Raina's lake home? April went to find Salm, and pointed him to the surface to talk.

"You found her?" he guessed.

"I think so."

"Lead the way. We're running out of time." Salm motioned to the sky. The sun was lowering, almost brushing the tops of the tallest trees. April hadn't realized it was so late. It was hard to judge time underwater.

She dove down and swam directly to the rock cave. Salm nodded and they peered into the dark mouth. April knocked on the rock and Raina appeared, she did not look happy to see them.

April waved and smiled, Raina scowled back. Salm waved too. Raina raised both webbed hands questioningly. Salm pointed up. Raina shook her head. April pointed up more emphatically and motioned for Raina to follow her. Raina started retreating into her cave. April grabbed her arm and tugged, Raina kicked her in the stomach. She was not going to cooperate. April held on anyway.

While Raina was wrestling to free herself from April, Salm seized the opportunity to trap Raina in the net. He tossed it over her head and grabbed her from behind. April let go of Raina's arm and wriggled free before she got tangled up too. She caught the trailing ends of the net, pulling them tight, tying Raina's arms against her sides. But Raina still had her finny legs, she rolled and kicked furiously.

The longer they wrestled, the tighter the net pulled until Raina could barely wiggle. Suddenly, all the fight went out of her and she started to cry. April felt like the most traitorous of friends and tried to apologize. It was impossible underwater.

Salm motioned up and they towed Raina along between them, toward the far side of the lake. They had to kick hard and it took too long. When they waded ashore dragging Raina underwater, the sun was hidden behind the trees.

"Cat's claws," April swore.

"April, wheel the cart into the water. I'll lift Raina inside. Quick!" Salm was having a tough time, Raina was squirming with abandon again.

"Right." April shoved the cart into the shallows. Salm had Raina hoisted into the container before she realized what was happening. Together, they hauled hard to get the cart back out; the wheels kept sinking into the soft sludgy bottom.

When they finally reached solid land, April asked, "Should we untie the net?"

"No. Better wait until she settles down." Raina was thrashing and splashing like a wild eel in the small enclosure. "Pull," Salm said wearily.

April pulled as hard as she could and Salm pushed, it was slow going through the underbrush. It got a lot easier once they gained the path towards town, but the sun was almost sitting on the horizon by then. They were too far behind schedule. When Peter appeared on the path up ahead, his strength and fresh muscles were a gift.

"Pull, Peter," Salm ordered without any greeting.

Peter did. The cart sped up at once. "I wondered what was taking you so long. The ceremony has started."

"Raina was not very cooperative." Salm left it at that.

"Well, there's bad news," Peter said.

April groaned. "Bad news?"

"I got Airron to the town square, but he left when Raina wasn't there. I couldn't stop him. Sorry," Peter apologized.

"Oh no! Where did he go, Peter?" April cried.

"Home, I guess. He didn't say."

"Slug slime." April was not going to panic. Yes she was. No she wasn't. The situation wasn't hopeless yet. "Okay, can you pull Raina to the town square and put her in the fountain? I'm going to try and find Airron. I'll meet you there."

"Go April. We'll meet you in town. Go fast." Salm said.

"I'll fly." April climbed the nearest tree, glad she was wearing the proper haltered fairy clothing for flying. Mrs. Poole had gifted her the special outfit, sort of an apology for giving August her new room.

She jumped and soared directly towards Airron's house. It was not too far from town. April hoped she might still make it, although Ms. Larkin-LaBois must be wondering what had happened to her by now. And where would April find her robe? "One obstacle at a time," she muttered.

April spotted Airron's treehouse and dove down. There was no time to knock on the door, she glided right through his window and almost hit the wall.

"Ahh!" Airron hollered, startled. He had been lying morosely on his bed, but he leaped to his feet in a single bound. "April, what are you doing here?"

"What do you think I'm doing here?" she fumed. "You are supposed to be at the town square. Raina is there now! And you left. Now I'm late and everything is messed up," she ranted, wasting too much time talking. "Now put on a robe and get to the town square as fast as you can run," she ordered.

Airron stood frozen, his face filled with painful longing. "A robe?"

She had said too much. "A robe, Airron. Wear a robe. But I can't promise," April warned. If this didn't work, he would be devastated. "Hurry. Please." He did, he grabbed a robe and ran out the door.

April jumped out the window but she wasn't sure where to go. Town square or Ms. Larkin-LaBois's house? The house was close to town. April tilted a wing and aimed for it. She landed by the front door and banged hard.

August opened it and shoved an armful of silky black cloth at April. "You're late," August snapped. "The old elf's already left. Didn't think you were going to show."

"Am I supposed to meet her at the ceremony?" April gasped.

"Duh!" August slammed the door in her face.

"I better hurry." April started running; she pulled the robe over her head while dodging branches and leaping over weeds. She was completely hidden under the black veil when she reached the square and slipped around to the back of the platform.

Ms. Larkin-LaBois was already transforming the latest group of elves that had turned fifteen this day. She was almost finished, the last student was kneeling before her. He rose and walked away as April scrambled awkwardly onto the platform. The crowd started whispering, two Seers was unheard of.

"You are late." Ms. Larkin-LaBois' voice was barely audible.

April was still trying to catch her breath. "I know. Sorry," she panted. "Is Airron here?"

"He should be." April scanned the crowd. Yes, Airron was standing beside the fountain with Salm and Peter. He was winded and flushed, but he had made it. "Yes, he's here, by the fountain. Raina's in the fountain."

Ms. Larkin-LaBois raised one hand and motioned Airron forward. There was a buzz through the crowd. Sixteen year old elves were never transformed.

Airron climbed the stairs to the platform, his eyes huge in his pale face.

He glanced at April before he knelt before Ms. Larkin-LaBois. She thought he recognized her under the robe. Even if he didn't recognize her, he could probably guess that she was involved in this.

"Let us begin. Touch my back," Ms. Larkin-LaBois murmured to April. April closed her eyes and tried to do everything she had been told, even though she didn't know how exactly. As soon as her fingers made contact with Ms. Larkin-LaBois, she could feel a tingle in the air all around them. It was part of this whole magical world. April tried to relax against the strange pull of magic being drawn out of her from deep inside. She could feel Airron too. Airron was supposed to have wings. The pull grew stronger and April tried not to fight it. In some indescribable way, the strange sensation reminded her of what she had felt in the mine when the eggstone was cracked.

Time seemed to hiccup in the strangest way, and then Airron had wings. April knew he did and hot tears flowed down her cheeks, she couldn't stop them. And Airron knew he had wings, but he touched his back as if to make sure. April had never seen a happier elf than Airron, but he merely walked calmly off the platform. He was not nearly so calm when he rejoined Peter and Salm. Their shared joy and celebration was a delight to watch.

"Now we will attend to Raina. This will be more difficult. Come." Ms. Larkin-LaBois moved slowly across the platform and down the stairs. The crowd buzzed again, the Seer never left the platform.

When she reached the fountain, Ms. Larkin-LaBois hesitated. Raina was under the water and she couldn't come out. April had no idea how they would proceed. Then Ms. Larkin-LaBois hitched up her robe and faced the fountain wall. Salm dashed over and lifted her into the water as if she weighed no more than a child. April scrambled in after her and they both stood unmoving, wet up to their waists. The crowd quieted, waiting as well.

A shadowy figure surged by April's legs. Raina! And she must have recognized April's feet, her unusually knobby toes were not her most attractive feature. Raina pinched April's big toe in passing and stopped in front of her. Raina was finally ready to cooperate and trust her.

Ms. Larkin-LaBois reached both hands into the water. "April," she prompted. "Now."

April stepped closer and laid a hand on the frail back. The electrical tingle returned to surround them and the water began to dance and sparkle as if it was alive. As before, April felt the magic tugging at her from all sides. She could sense Raina, but faintly. Airron's aura had been strong, Raina's was so very weak. Maybe too weak.

Nothing happened for the longest time and April was gripped by fear. This had to work! She bit her lip and squeezed her eyes closed, wondering if she could help the process along. The tingle seemed to be fading around them and Raina remained unchanged, still much too fishy. They were losing their window of opportunity.

It was a gamble but April hauled in a shuddering breath and pictured Raina as she should be. She concentrated every bit of her magic on the mental image of her friend walking and smiling. April focused on the image as if she could grow Raina from a seed into an elf. The tingle grew stronger again, then a strong wave of it surged through April as if it had physical weight, knocking her to her knees. Ms. Larkin-LaBois gasped and stiffened. April grabbed her when she would have collapsed into the water and the connection with Raina was broken.

"No," April whispered. The magic was gone. And Raina ...? There was a surge of waves and Raina stood right up, looking like her beautiful self again! April almost dropped Ms. Larkin-LaBois and leaned towards her friend.

"No." Ms. Larkin-LaBois spoke quietly but sharply. "Later. You must remain unseen, unknown, or the magic will not come to you."

"I forgot." April stayed where she was and it was the hardest thing in the world to not rejoice with her friends. Airron leapt into the fountain, followed by Salm and Peter. Raina ordered them all out of the fountain, saying she never wanted to be wet again.

"April, assist me." Ms. Larkin-LaBois wanted out of the water too. April helped her climb over the fountain wall. "Now, come with me."

They walked through the undergrowth in the direction of her house, two dark shadows moving slowly and quietly. April was longing to return to her friends but matched the snail's pace all the way. At her front door, Ms. Larkin-LaBois removed the dark veil and hood, motioning for April to do the same.

"Thank you April. I am so pleased that both your friends are restored. Do you understand now?" she queried.

"I think so. The magic comes from inside this world, doesn't it? Through you?"

"Yes, in a way. The magic is born in this world, and channels through me to transform elves, and through you this night. But it will only happen on April 1st. I was not prepared for the concentrated magic needed to transform Raina. It was tremendous. In all my years, I have never felt such intensity." She did look aged by her efforts. "Now, I will take the robe and you may return to your friends. I expect to see you over the summer holidays. We have much to discuss." The elf nodded precisely at April, dismissing her.

"I'll visit," April promised. She yanked the wet robe off, handed it over, hugged Ms. Larkin-LaBois and took off running. When she reached the square, elves were milling about, all dressed up and eating fancy food. April was a disaster as usual, but she didn't care.

She spotted her friends looking just as unkempt, clustered around one table of snacks. Raina was smiling euphorically and crunching a chip. April rushed over and finally got to hug Raina. Raina almost crushed her in return. Her time as a fish had not weakened her arms any.

"April! Look, I'm eating dry food! Crunchy food! And I'm pink, pinkish, tickled pink, and not green at all!" Raina exclaimed, quite giddy. "I never thought I would eat dry food again. Thank-you," she whispered in April's ear, respecting her secret identity. Or not so secret identity.

Salm said softly, "You could have said something."

"You really should have told us," Peter backed him up.

"I would have, if I could have, but I couldn't. And it's still a secret. Hey, where's Airron?" He was missing.

"Guess?"

April guessed, it wasn't hard. "Flying?"

Raina bobbed her head "Yes, a little flutter. He'll be right back. Happy birthday by the way."

"Oh. Happy birthday." Automatically, April checked her tag. Yup – sixteen. Her fifteenth year was officially over, and fifteen had been a most interesting year. She pressed the tag into her hand and made a wish; she wished that her sixteenth year would not be nearly as interesting as the one that had come before.

About the Author

PATRICIA SRIGLEY lives in the West Island of Montreal. She is a graduate of both Concordia University and McGill University. A high school teacher and visual artist, the transition from painting to writing has been an exciting and fulfilling experience. Her love of the natural world is strongly reflected in her imaginative stories.

ABOUT THE ILLUSTRATIONS

Each illlustration is rendered on a clayboard.
A white clay panel coated with black india ink,
The ink is scratched off with fine pointed tools,
Revealing the white surface beneath.

Illustrations for Chapters 7 & 16 created by Nathan Srigley.

Book Four in the April-May June series

out soon!